The Master of Shearhaven

Jon Wesley Huff

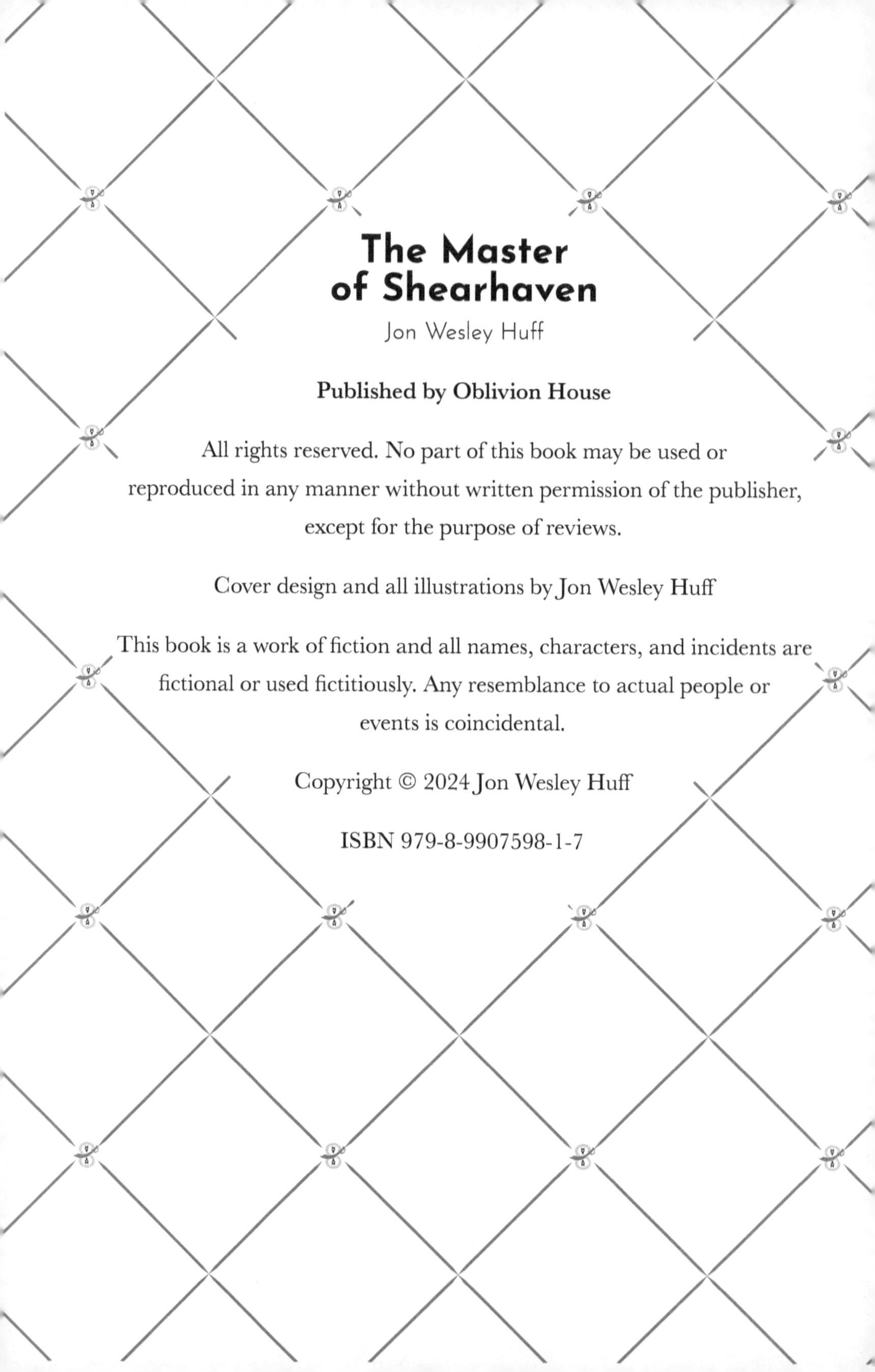

The Master of Shearhaven

Jon Wesley Huff

Published by Oblivion House

ISBN 979-8-9907598-1-7

To everyone still picking up the pieces.
Sometimes the path to joy is twisty and strange.

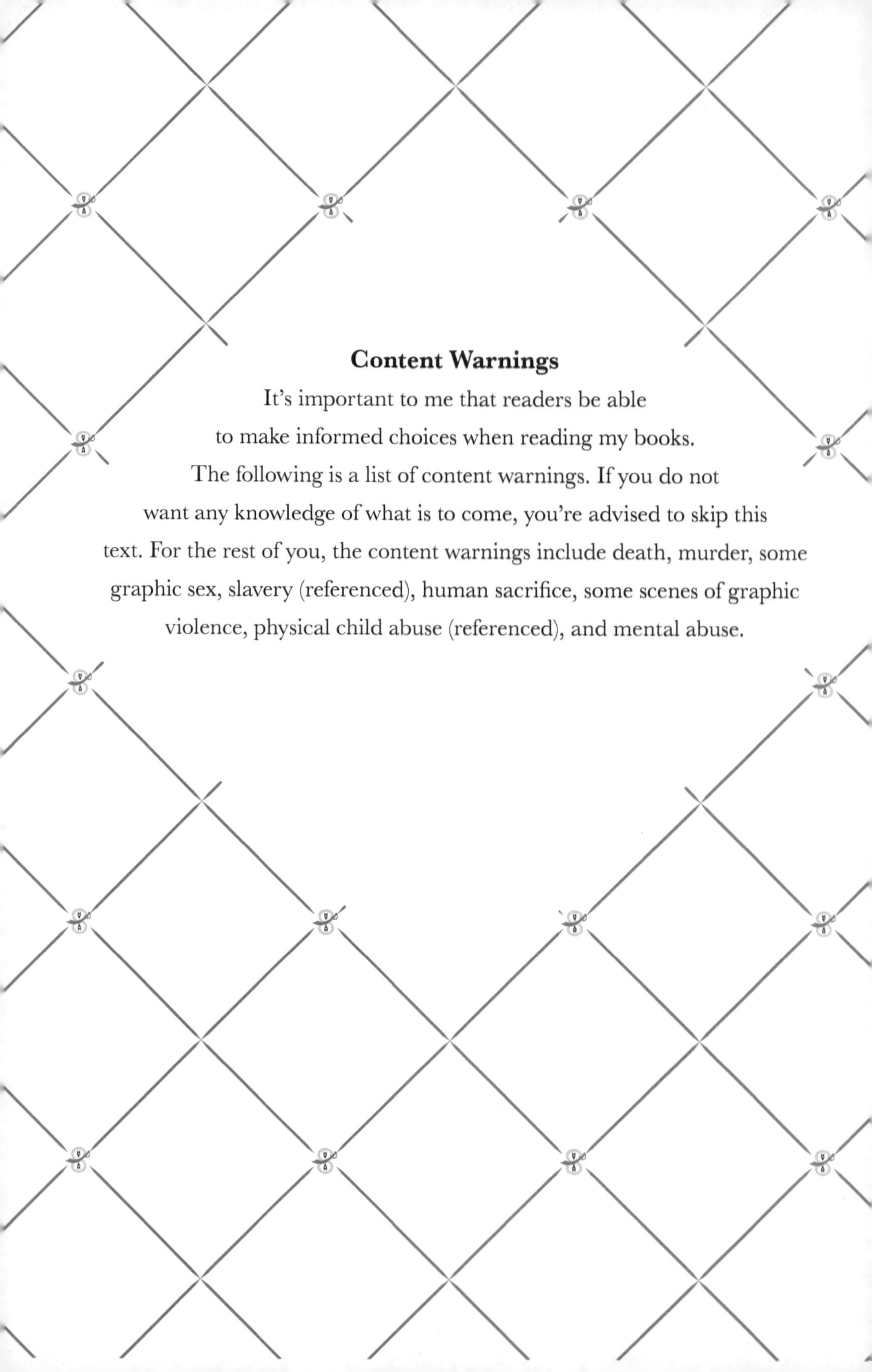

Content Warnings

It's important to me that readers be able
to make informed choices when reading my books.
The following is a list of content warnings. If you do not
want any knowledge of what is to come, you're advised to skip this
text. For the rest of you, the content warnings include death, murder, some
graphic sex, slavery (referenced), human sacrifice, some scenes of graphic
violence, physical child abuse (referenced), and mental abuse.

Part One

Tomas

1

When I was a very young child I'd catch fireflies with the neighbor boy. I don't remember his name. I might have never known it. It seems, at that age, that details like names really didn't matter. We'd scoop them up in jars, of course, and watch as they swirled around—their glow filling the glass vessel. What a thing of wonder they were. I remember thinking of how strange it was, the night-cooled jar in my hands as light shone from within. But it was a sort of cold light. Like the light of the stars. And then we'd watch as they became sluggish, their light slowly faded, then extinguished, and we'd shake their bodies into the dirt. Or we'd tear the little luminescent ember off their backsides and wear them as glowing rings. We'd try to squish them into paint and decorate rocks. Which was all to say that some things are meant to be admired from afar.

Shearhaven lived in my dreams before I ever stepped foot in it. When I was eight my mom took me to the banks of the Mississippi, not far from Alton. That'd been a strange day. It was a day trip to see the finish of a steamboat race between the *Robert E. Lee* and the *Natchez*. Turns out Mom had gotten the info turned around. The race was ending in St. Louis. But we made a good day of it, despite my sullen mood. She spent that trip staring at me, probably wondering who'd taken her loving son and replaced him with the angry-eyed monster sitting by her. She knew the root of the problem, but not the cause. The year before, a young man with deep brown skin wearing Union blues knocked on our door. I can't remember what he said. The news he brought flooded my mind, erasing most everything else. I just remember how kind his eyes seemed. My father had been run through with a bayonet by one of Lee's boys.

I wasted what would end up being precious time with my mom because I was angry at her. Not for anything she'd done. She simply had the misfortune to be the only one left to be angry with. I had no idea she'd end up leaving me an orphan not too much later. But that day, she got through to me with that most potent weapon—the promise of an ice cream soda.

"Tomas," she whispered to me, crouching low, as if she were about to impart a grave secret. "The secret to a great ice cream soda is ice. Plenty of ice. Sometimes they'll try to skimp. Never be afraid to ask for more." She grinned at me wolfishly as my eyes went wide. I'd never thought about asking for more. My mom never had a problem with that. It's all she'd ever wanted. Her and Dad had planned to move out west once the war was over. Get some work on a ranch, maybe, with an eye toward starting one of their own eventually. I eyed the apothecarist carefully as he scooped the ice in, about three-fourths of the way up. I turned to my mom, who looked pleased. Therefore, I was pleased as he added the raspberry syrup, cream, and soda water.

Mom wanted to watch the sunset over the Mississippi, so

we returned to river, a mile or two further up than we'd been and watched as the steamboats chugged their vapor into the air as they broke the golden surface of the water. As we turned from the river to head back to town, I saw Shearhaven for the first time. I remembered it as a castle. In my dreams, I imagined who would live in such a place. Perhaps a gray-haired king with kind eyes, crinkled at the edges. He'd returned from his war campaign triumphant—a warrior king worth serving. A patient queen with her long brown hair in an intricate braid, plucking at a lyre. She was happy and healthy and never disappeared to her bedchamber to shed tears of grief. And, yes, there was a young prince there too. His name was Tomas, of course. Now, all these years later I have walked the halls of Shearhaven. Well, one hall exactly. The king and queen were gone. And the prince had grown up into a slight young man whose hair grew too long, whose thin limbs and full lips made him the soft target of all the other boys' slings and arrows. And, of course, this "prince" was, for the night, a member of the waitstaff.

Shearhaven—as ominously impressive as it was jutting up from the tree-capped bluffs lining the Mississippi—was no castle. Here, a mile north of Alton, the bluffs still rose to great heights, but I'd found them less appealing all these years later. They were broken and sporadic—like teeth in a diseased mouth. Shearhaven was situated on the edge of one of these jagged outcroppings, nestled between dense thickets of oak and hickory. It's strange, how innocent my perception of Shearhaven had been as a child. Now, with ten wearying years of experience under my belt, I wondered how I could have ever imagined this house—with its walls of strangely black stone—as a place fit for a kindly king. Tonight, as I'd approached the house, it looked like a great black bird of prey, clinging to the bluff and waiting to strike.

"All right, all right, let's settle down, *les jeunes hommes*," Mr. Chaput, the butler said, clapping his hands together twice in quick succession and pulling my wandering mind back to the moment at hand. This had the desired effect, as all of us in the room quieted. Chaput began his introduction—emphasizing the importance of our training—but I couldn't help looking around. None of the men looked older than twenty-five. Some had softer features like mine, but others were thickly built, and lantern jawed-like Henry, who greeted me when I first arrived like I was an old friend. Others were more angular and lither like Ian. The two of them had already settled into good-natured ribbing and I had enjoyed their banter. Most were clean-shaven, although one man had a short moustache. The one factor that they all had in common, however, was that they were attractive. In different ways, perhaps, but I couldn't help but notice the unusual beauty of them all. I'd already felt out of place in this elaborate house, and this wasn't helping. I don't want to appear falsely modest. I had a certain sort of beauty, I knew that. But it was the kind that mostly older women appreciated—as if I were a doll they wanted to secret away in a glass case.

"One more note, and this is critical." Chaput straightened and stamped a foot in punctuation. His eyes gleamed from behind heavily wrinkled lids, which made him look like he was perpetually squinting. He was nearly bald, except a wispy ring of gray that defied gravity and arced upward. He stood board-straight, his shoulders back and both his hands resting lightly on the head of a cane.

"In an hour, the master will be down to inspect you. We will run a short demonstration of your skills, and he'll judge whether you're fit to serve at Shearhaven. If not, you will be given a small percentage of the pay you were offered and sent on your way home." A murmur of surprise rose from the assembled men.

"I rode three hours for this," said one of the thickly built men, who had broad shoulders and a mean look to him.

"Many of you have come from far away. Which is why I offer my word of warning to pay close attention to my teachings today. Master Vanguard is what is called an aesthete. Do you know what that is, Mr. Galloway?" Chaput tilted his head back and at an angle and peered out at the man.

"Beats me. All I know is I'm expecting to get paid my full wages," said Galloway. Chaput smiled thinly at him.

"It means he is a great lover of beauty. In all its forms. It's something he inherited from his father, and his father's father, as you can see all around you." Chaput walked across the library and ran his hand along one of the bookshelves. "You'll notice the wood of the shelves matches the wood of the molding which, in turn, matches the wood used in all the furniture. The dark color and luxuriously reflective appearance are achieved by a costly and time-consuming method perfected in a small village in Irkutsk Oblast at the turn of the previous century."

"I don't understand how that makes a difference to me getting paid. Something you promised me personally, Chaput." The big man crossed his arms. The butler seemed unfazed by the display of machismo.

"My point is that the Vanguards have a long history of surrounding themselves with beauty. The current Master Vanguard has carried that to new heights. The select few who attend his parties have come to expect nothing less than perfection in every detail. That includes the appearance and manner of the staff who wait on them." Galloway had no response, but the exchange had made things clear to me.

For the next hour, I watched and tried to remember every

detail Chaput attempted to teach us. I never thought there could be so much complexity to carrying around a platter with food or drinks on it. But for every aspect there was something to remember. Towels were draped over the right arm, trays were carried with the left arm, matches were carried in the right suit pocket, drinks were poured with a particular hand, and so on. Just as I was sure I couldn't stuff another detail into my brain, Chaput took out his pocket watch, noted the time, and sighed.

"Nearly time for Mr. Vanguard to come for the inspection. Get in a line, please."

All of us tried to stay as straight and still as possible. The butler stood in front of us, his hands behind his back. A minute passed. Then two. I let my shoulders relax a fraction, suddenly aware of how tense I was. We all were, I could feel it in the air. Henry's eyes darted to the door of the library and then back to the front. Chaput simply stared forward, relaxed and almost glassy-eyed as he looked beyond the line of men. Clearly he'd grown accustomed to waiting for Vanguard over his years of service.

After ten minutes in this awkward stillness, I saw a man next to me—younger by a few years—ball up his fists and scowl. I wasn't the only one getting tired of waiting, but the man next to me seemed ready to walk. The young man's lips parted. I never found out what he intended to say, as at that moment the door opened with the soft scrape of wood on wood.

2

"Thank you, gentlemen. I am Jackson Vanguard. Welcome to Shearhaven." The man walked through the library door. His voice resonated at the back of his throat in a way that made it feel as though you were hearing his words and a deeper echo of his words in unison. He was barely older than the oldest server in the room. At a guess, I'd say he was in his late twenties. "My great-grandfather built this house before Illinois was even a state. I, like my father, do my best to continue his legacy. I appreciate you taking the time to come to Shearhaven and submit yourself to Chaput's stern and thorough training." This comment drew a chuckle out of a few members of the crowd, and Vanguard smiled slightly and lowered his shoulders a fraction.

"I know, to some of you, this might all seem—well, a bit 'butter upon bacon,' as they say." Vanguard smiled broadly this time, and the whole of the room relaxed. This was the owner of this great estate? Every wealthy person I'd encountered (granted it wasn't many) wielded their status and privilege like a cudgel in both subtle and overt ways. Despite Chaput's warning, the man seemed to want to put us at ease. Even his dress was disarming. He wore simple breeches and a loose white shirt. I, for my part, did not relax. Not fully. I relaxed my face, and tried to match Vanguard's tone, but I didn't let myself get too comfortable. What if this was some form of test?

"But every man lives or dies in this world on his reputation. I find myself, by nature and by happenstance, to be a man for whom this is truer than most. That's why the details mean everything to me. I can't put it any plainer than that." Vanguard walked down the line of men, looking them up and down. The precision with which he did this belied his easy, good-natured presence. I could tell he was taking in every detail. Vanguard stopped in front of the man with the moustache and stared at him with his gray-green eyes set between long, dark lashes that matched the jet black of his hair. I watched the warmth drain from them.

"Sir, your moustache is certainly fetching. But untidy."

"Apologies, Sir," the man said, looking like he wanted to run for the nearest exist and expel his supper.

"No apologies necessary. When you dress, just see you give it a good trim. As symmetrical as possible and be sure to wrangle the stray hair with some oil. Chaput can assist you if needed, I experimented with a moustache for a while, and he kept mine well groomed." Chaput nodded in confirmation, and a relieved smile spread across the other man's face.

Vanguard continued down the line, until he got to me. I was sandwiched between Henry and Ian at the very end of the line. I both liked and hated the intensity of the man's gaze as he took me in. I hadn't been sure if the man would prefer me to maintain eye contact or not, as the men who underwent inspection before me had chosen a variety of tactics. Vanguard was so stony it was hard to tell what pleased or displeased him. I chose to look the man in the eye. Something about his manner made me think he'd appreciate this, and it had the added benefit of giving me a chance to get a better look at him.

Vanguard was four inches taller than I was, with hair that was short on the side but longer on top and swept backward from a side part. He had a strong, dimpled chin and smelled of lavender, spices, and wood. His lips—full and symmetrical—parted and I thought he was going to speak. Instead, he raised his hand, cupped my cheek, and gently turned my head to the side. The pressure of his hand on my face—strangely intimate and clinical at the same time—sent my groin tingling. Another dash of emotion in a brew that was heady enough for me as it was.

"You have a small, very flat mole just below and to the right of the lower lid of your left eye," he said. Of all the things I'd expected the man to say, this was not one of them. The surprise of it, the feel of his hand—so warm—on my face, and the intensity of his stare caused a giddiness within me that I could not prevent escaping in a small, choked laugh.

"I amuse you?"

"No, Sir, sorry. I'm just not used to—" I wasn't sure how to finish the sentence. I wasn't used to being touched? Being touched by a man? Being touched by a man in this particular way? All of it was true, and none of it felt appropriate to say. Thankfully, Vanguard cut me off before I had to sputter through the end of the sentence.

"I suppose it must seem silly for me to point out something on your own face."

"No. I'm just—" *Stop babbling*, I screamed at myself. "What I meant to say is that I'm sorry. For the mole." I raised my hand reflexively to cover the offending mark, but Vanguard stopped me with his elbow as he extended the pointer finger of the hand that gripped my chin and touched the mole.

"Perfection," Vanguard said, letting the word sit for a while, "is not about symmetry." Vanguard let go of me and stepped back, now addressing all the men again. "Perfection isn't the meeting of one ideal. That way would lie folly, for in truth we all hold slightly different concepts of what the 'ideal form' might be. For me, perfection is about the ordering of disparate elements into one, beautiful balance. Even the guest lists to my parties are carefully considered. The different aspects of the different personalities at play. The gentle way they will collide and swirl in some, and the tantalizing frisson of the way they'll interact in others. Or, to put it more succinctly—a certain number of loudmouths to a certain number of shrinking violets." A few of the men laughed, me included, even if we weren't sure why we were laughing. It wasn't as though Vanguard had made some joke. But what he was saying, the manner in which he was saying it, and the context of it all struck me as strange and hilarious. Vanguard was too serious and not serious enough.

"You are all here, to be blunt, because you are beautiful young men. My last party had a staff of only beautiful young women, there were complaints, so I vowed to correct my supposed wrong," Vanguard said, raising his hands to his heart as if his guilt were an arrow. "So it isn't about perfection, my selection. This is round one of two. The next time I see you, you'll be clothed in the provided attire for the evening, and each of you will serve me as you would serve any of my guests tonight. This, initial walkthrough is all about finding the balance in what Chaput has presented to me. It's about finding the beauty in the disparate parts."

"So do keep that in mind." Vanguard's voice was drained of good-natured camaraderie now. I straightened up reflexively. Just as I did, Vanguard strode past the front of the line once more. "No, yes, yes, no, no, no, yes…" and on down the line he went. Once he'd gotten to the last man he kept walking right out the library door, turned left, and disappeared from view. I'd been chosen. I was a yes. I'd made it through, somehow. After a few seconds of stunned silence, Chaput cleared his throat.

"Very well, then. Anyone who received a yes, please go to the right two doors down. We'll have some last-minute fittings for your attire tonight. All who received a no, follow me and I'll give you the twenty percent promised for your time," Chaput said. There was a second pause as everyone processed his words before they scattered.

"Sorry, brother," Henry said to Ian, who'd been in the chopped group and the only one who Vanguard hadn't given a thorough once-over.

"Twenty percent? Still the easiest money I've ever made," Ian said, shrugging. He lowered his voice before continuing. "Besides this Vanguard is a little much, right?" Mindful that Chaput could be watching, Henry and I gave him weak nods.

"You ever get down to Paducah, just look for my pa's shop. We'll get a beer." Henry shook the other man's hand. Chaput was glaring at Ian now, so the three of us exited quickly and went our separate ways, with Henry and Ian exchanging one more quick glance before they went on their separate journeys. It was a glance I recognized. A tension underlying the gaze. I thought of the way Vanguard had gazed down on me from his window just days before.

I'd come here to deliver supplies to Shearhaven. A request that had mystified all of us at Blake's Mercantile and Sundries. We were based in Gillsborough, a two-hour ride away. Mr. Blake took me in when I was eight, after my mom died, and raised me up right beside his own daughter, Dottie. She and I joke that he took me in for the free labor, as I began working in the shop shortly thereafter. But the truth was Blake was an exceptionally kind man. A rare thing, in my experience, sadly. I'd just finished dropping off the supplies via the servants entrance, and turned back toward the door, when I noticed movement in one of the windows above. My eyes shot upward and saw the faint impression of a man standing in the window. He was mostly obscured by the reflections of the trees that surrounded the house, but there was an intense amber light near his face, and where it shone, I could make out his features.

He was handsome, a finely chiseled statue come to life. The amber light cast his eyes into shadow, where they glimmered with intensity. I expected the man to look away—it's what I would have done if I'd been caught staring at someone. He did not look away. If anything, his gaze intensified. I wanted to look away, but I stayed locked in a voyeuristic stalemate. Inexplicably, I felt myself harden and scrape against the wool of my undergarments.

"Here you go." Chaput emerged from the servant's entrance, tearing away my attention. I was equally grateful and sad to have my concentration broken. I glanced back up to the window as he handed over the bills. The man was gone. "My compliments to you and your employer. Cook is most pleased. We've had some pest problems with the most recent shipments from Alton." I nodded, excited to take so much cash back to Mr. Blake and Dottie along with an answer to the mystery of why they'd ordered supplies from so far away. That's when a young, serious-faced maid with light blonde hair ran out and whispered in Chaput's ear. The butler smiled, nodded, and turned to me.

"Mr. Doyle. I have an opportunity you might find enticing. You see, we have a party coming up this weekend, and we could use an extra pair of hands on our wait staff."

I couldn't turn that kind of offer down. Now here I was inside Shearhaven, the queer house on the cliff that had sent tongues wagging in Alton and nearby for decades. I thought of the way Henry and Ian had looked at each other. And then Vanguard's face in the window, watching me. What was it in the set of those eyes—Henry's, Ian's, and Vanguard's—that stirred some instinct in me? Some knowledge deep within that these looks were not fraternal admiration or some intense, but platonic curiosity? Windows of possibility appeared before me. Windows I didn't have the nerve to allow myself to open just yet.

3

It was hard to describe why Shearhaven felt wrong, even early on. I supposed I had a set idea of what a home was. The only homes I'd ever known were filled with small rooms. To get from one room to the other, you had to pass through them. Mr. Blake's house had a hallway so short you could see yourself in the mirror on the other end of it. I'd catch a glimpse of us, coming in out of the cold through the front door, in that mirror. Mr. Blake, Dottie, and their strange visitor—out of place in this family scene. The cuckoo in the nest. By contrast, Shearhaven was a house of hallways, with rooms so huge they could have fit both of my childhood homes within them. I didn't see much of the house, but the scale of it was evident in every room and hallway. I couldn't imagine how anyone would feel at home here. Everything was too perfect and too orderly, as if the house only truly needed itself—its occupants reduced to an irritating, but necessary flaw.

We had our fittings, and the seven of us who'd survived

the cull sat around in various stages of undress waiting for our suits to be altered. They were a friendly group, and we enjoyed each other's company—even Galloway, who I'd taken for a big tough—was relaxed and joking with the rest of us now that his payday was more assured. Henry was, by far, the one I chatted with the most.

"How long am I s'posed to be standing around in nothing but a shirt and undergarments," Henry said, his hand errantly coming up to scratch the soft trail of fuzz on his belly. I only caught a glimpse as the sides of the man's shirt parted to allow his hand entry. I was in no hurry for Henry to get dressed.

Another inspection followed, but this one was almost cursory. Chaput lined us up in the ballroom, having to snap his fingers twice to keep us from goggling at the grandeur of the room. It'd been fully decked for the party, of course, but would have been staggeringly impressive to us just on its own. High above a chandelier spiraled, its hanging crystal facets catching and scattering the light. The same lacquered black wood that accented the rest of the house was here as well, but the walls were dramatically covered in red fabric so shiny it almost looked wet. Sconces jutted from the wall, each capped with a faceted teardrop. On top of this were yards and yards of ribbon fashioned into bows. There were so many flowers I wondered, should one take every flower in every garden in Gillsborough, if they'd even come close to the number that decorated the walls and tables.

Vanguard was busy talking over some last-minute preparations with the head housekeeper, Ms. Coghlan, so we'd had to come to him. Once we were settled, Vanguard lifted his head, scanned the line-up once, had each of us approach with a serving tray, and waved his approval. No one was sent home.

"Very well. The guests are due to arrive in a half hour. You have exactly fifteen minutes. You may relax or use the facilities next to the changing room you were escorted to earlier. But all of you should return here, lined-up, ready for one final inspection and your instructions. Understood?" The butler crooked his head to the right and waited for our acknowledgment. We all wordlessly nodded our heads. Satisfied, Chaput turned toward the door. He stopped and turned back toward us.

"You are not to venture further into the house. You may go back through the kitchen and out the servant's entrance you arrived through if you wish to take in some fresh air. Otherwise, confine yourself only to the rooms and halls you've traversed." This time, Chaput did not wait for an acknowledgment before disappearing from the ballroom through a door on the opposite side we'd entered. I knew exactly where I needed to spend the short time I had before the party began.

I turned into the hall and saw the maid I'd seen on my previous trip, sweeping underneath the window at the end of the hallway. She was very small and thin with long blonde hair gathered back into a very loose ponytail, so that much of her face was hidden by the bunched-up hair on the sides. There was something childlike about her, but as she peered at me with large blue-gray eyes, the dark circles underneath them made her look much older.

"Hi there," I said as she continued to stare. She nodded her head, and quickly looked away. Do you ever get that feeling, somewhere deep inside, when you see a creature or person that's suffering in some fashion, even if it's unclear how? That feeling that maybe just a kind word or a smile might help, in some way? It overcame me now. I did not know what was wrong with her, but something about her hunch and the quick strokes of her broom gave her a haunted aspect.

"My name's Tomas. I'm one of the waitstaff." The woman continued to sweep for a few moments. Then she closed her eyes, as if stopping pained her, and looked at me. Her mouth curled into an unconvincing smile.

"Gladys. Now. Please, I need to finish quickly. No one's supposed to see me tonight." With that, the young maid practically ran from the spot to a nearby doorway and closed the door behind her. I was caught somewhere between worrying about why she was so frightened to be seen, and half-understanding why Vanguard might have wanted her out of sight, as she did strike me as slightly bizarre.

A wall of heat pressed against me as I entered the kitchen. All three ovens were blazing, a pot simmered—lid rattling in uneven titters—on the stovetop. Ten loaves of bread sat to one side cooling, smelling of yeast and crisped edges. There was a bowl full of carrots and greenery near the central table. In a far corner, seated at a small table, was a familiar face. A face that was, currently, glaring at me.

"Potatoes, Tomas," Dottie said, the bangs of her light brown hair pasted against a face beaded with sweat. She held a small knife in one hand, and a half-peeled spud in the other.

"Oh, Dot, I'm sorry," I said as I made my way toward her.

"It just had to be potatoes." There were few things Dottie hated as much as peeling things. She was terrible at it, for one thing, to the point that Mr. Blake would look at the scraps and loudly complain that half the potato or carrot hadn't made it to into the dish. *Well, the pigs at Ma Howard's will sure be happy. Sometimes I think you're in league with them*, Mr. Blake would say. As soon as he was out of the room, Dottie would put her pipe in her mouth and chew at it in annoyance. I tried my best to give Dottie a sympathetic look. But I was too amused, so it ended up more like a smirk.

"Where's Cook?" I asked.

"Asking Ms. Coghlan to get him a bottle of wine so he can—I don't know, exactly. Something to do with the dish he's making. Right now, it's just me, this knife, and three pounds of potatoes that need peeling."

"Don't look at me like that. This is all your own doing. We're lucky Coghlan didn't have a conniption fit when I showed up here with you in tow. I can't believe I let you come with me." I shivered a little inside. The head housekeeper was hard to figure out. Outwardly she was nice enough. She was squat and wide, with a black dress that emphasized this fact by bulging out in a grand waterfall of material from her waist. She had reddened, freckled cheeks and black hair that shone with streaks of silver. There was a stiffness to her that undercut the warmth of her face.

"If it makes you feel better, Tomas, it's not like I'd have given you a choice," Dottie said with mock sweetness. Dottie. My best friend. Practically a sister. "This is for your own good."

"I'm just glad Vanguard didn't send me home like he did with some of the others."

"So, you did meet him?" Dottie asked, lowering her voice to a whisper, and giving up any pretense that she was still trying to peel the potatoes. I snuggled in next to her at the table.

"I did." I tried looking interested in a potato with too many eyes, the beige protuberances bursting through the skin.

"Uh-huh. So… was he the one? The mysterious and handsome stranger in the window?"

"Yes. Definitely." My face flushed with a potent brew of emotions. Dottie was just being Dottie. If she weren't ribbing me on this, that, or the other, I'd get worried. But hearing her summarize what I'd told her about my previous trip this way made me feel foolish. Did I really imagine the master of so grand a house saw me standing there and was the one who insisted I come back? I must have misinterpreted something. The thing was, Dottie was completely convinced, which is why she'd insisted on coming along.

"Do you think all this is sort of weird?" Dottie removed a pipe from a satchel wedged between us and started packing it with her favorite tobacco.

"Of course, it is," I said, taking the small knife and going at the potato with too many eyes, peeling it and carving them out as I went. "Are you sure smoking in here is smart?"

"Eh. Cook already said I could. He seemed amused by it." Dottie lit the pipe and gave it a few good puffs before releasing the smoke from her nostrils and mouth with a contented sigh. "I suppose that's what's fun. It's an adventure." I waved away the cloud of smoke before it could waft toward me.

"You look like a fish when you do that." It was a joke. It was also a small way of venting my general annoyance.

"I always thought smoking a pipe made one look rather studious and respectable."

"For a guy, maybe. *Maybe.* It just makes you look like a woman of ill repute."

"Excellent. The intended effect. I'm not sure you're the best arbiter of what makes a *girl* look any particular way, Tomas Doyle." Dottie eyes bored into me while she drew in another puff, exaggerating the pucker of her lips, and crossing her eyes. "I think I look quite handsome." I laughed despite myself, feeling my sourness abate. I was trying to think of a suitably witty response, but I saw the mood shift on Dottie's face. Her eyes narrowed, and the wry turn of her lips flattened.

"I'm not trying to play mother hen. No feathers need plucking here." Dottie threw the last sentence away, so that it had the vague substance of a joke without any of the mirth. The mirth had been swallowed down and transmuted into something else that hung in the air between us. "But I've had gooseflesh the moment you told me the story of your last visit. I'm not really going to feel better until we both get home."

"The money they're offering—it might be just the nest egg I need to get my own place." There was a too-long pause.

"Right. Fine. I mean, it seems normal enough. As normal as the rich get, I guess." Dottie got this way whenever I started talking about getting my own place. We both knew neither one of us could stay at her dad's house forever. I was a grown man, and I had no plans to stay in Gillsborough forever. I'd always be grateful for Mr. Blake taking me in. We'd woven a little family together with strands of mutual understanding, hard-won experience, and a little desperate need. But it was never going to last. Her father still expected her to marry. There was no way she was ever going to do that, and neither of us had any idea how he'd react once he knew the truth. Life at the Blakes' always felt like it was one truth too many from falling apart at any moment. I'd already been through that once. I was eager to figure out my own path before that happened.

4

A half-hour later, it was all hands on deck as the party guests started to arrive. We helped take and store guest's belongings, helped in the kitchen—anywhere we could assist before the party began. I was assigned to be one of the early servers, making sure there was plenty of wine to go around immediately. Vanguard's friends, Chaput explained, would expect no less. I was sad not to get assigned to the kitchen and have the chance to confer with Dottie. On the plus side, this meant I had an excellent viewpoint as the guests were brought in and announced one by one. I tried to remember everyone's names, thinking I might impress Vanguard by addressing his guests personally. And I did want to impress Vanguard. I only missed a few names toward the end when, my tray empty, I had to quickly refill it in the small staging room nearby.

One by one they entered, dressed in their best finery—elaborate dresses with jewels and cut-outs and linings of vibrant colors. Or handsomely tailored suits with ornamental brooches, top hats with brightly patterned ribbon, and canes of metal that flashed in the light. I understood, now, that the extravagance of the decorations, and of the ballroom itself had to compete with such vibrant attire.

"Ladies and gentlemen," Chaput announced, "I am pleased to present to you the master of Shearhaven, Jackson Vanguard."

The host for the night entered through the ballroom's double doors, and a woman in the back actually gasped. This sent a wave of laughter through the room, and Vanguard smiled at the commotion, very much enjoying his entrance. He wore a tightly tailored three-piece suit of a dazzling white that reflected the lighting of the ballroom so that it had an almost spectral glow. Around his shoulders hung a white cape with golden clasps. As he strode forward, the lining of the cape, a patterned azure silk, was revealed. He wore a white top hat. Vanguard strode past me—grabbing a glass of rosé as he went—allowing me to take in more detail. The suit was adorned with gold buttons, a gold pocket watch chain, and small golden studs that shone from the center of each divot in his quilted white vest. The guests surrounded and swallowed him into the crowd seconds later.

"The man knows how to make an entrance, I'll give him that," Henry said, sidling up next to me. I was about to reply when I saw Chaput glaring at us. We'd been told not to talk to one another. My cheeks reddened, Henry noticed and followed my gaze, and immediately took off away from me and into the party. Neither one of us wanted to go through all this trouble just to get sent home now. I only saw fleeting glimpses of Henry the rest of the night, as we were both kept busy serving guests who got louder and more demanding the more alcohol they consumed. For the first hour, I never caught sight of Vanguard again. I was surprised by how disappointed I was about that.

"Ladies and gentlemen," the throaty voice of Lady Bridget Acton rang out across the ballroom. "Ladies and gentlemen, if I might have your attention? We're due a toast, aren't we?"

"Well past due. I need an excuse to drink more!" answered a bald, German man with glasses by the last name of Schreiber. Lady Acton laughed jauntily at this and nodded her head.

"Well, the first toast of the night must be to our generous host. Love you, Jax," the woman said, giving Vanguard a wink. Lady Acton, like everyone gathered here, was what Mr. Blake would have referred to as "a character." A designation that could be good or bad, depending on how he said it. Acton was dressed in a sparkling black gown. Her hair was back in a severe bun, and her lips were coated blood red to match her long gloves. The ensemble would have been overly dramatic on most but seemed natural on her. Her eyebrows were naturally arched, and smile lines had been etched into her still-young face. "My dear friend has brought us all here from far and wide for what is sure to be another boisterously entertaining evening. It's good to see you all. Even those of you who thought this party was fancy dress."

"I'll have you know," said a large man decked out as a turn-of-the-century foppish dandy, complete with powdered face and painted features, "Everywhere I go is *automatically* a fancy dress party, my dear. Never more so than when I try to blend in with the rabble." This elicited hearty laughter from the crowd. The man was Lester Cosgrove of Maine, and I could tell he was used to being the life of the party. My impression was that applied to a lot of the guests here.

"Of course, my dear Mr. Cosgrove—your utter lack of self-censorship is one of the charming reasons we keep you around," Lady Acton purred. Vanguard watched from the sidelines, amused and willing to see this little tête-à-tête play out.

"I thought that was because he was a minor royal," Schreiber chimed in.

"Even a *minor* royal is a *major* royal in the colonies." Cosgrove emphasized his point by slapping the sides of his enormous white wig, sending powder floating out in a cloud.

"A major royal pain in the derriere, perhaps." Lady Acton delivered the barb with an abrupt curtsy.

"We're quite independent now, I can assure you," Vanguard said, finally compelled to jump in.

"For now, perhaps." Cosgrove took a deep drink of his wine as he said this, never taking his eyes off of Vanguard.

"Oh, I doubt our friends over the pond would want to poke this particular bear. We've only gotten better at war."

"Indeed. We've even been practicing on ourselves!" Cosgrove swiped another glass of wine from Henry's tray, nearly sending the others toppling over. Peals of laughter rang out from all around me, but all I could focus on was the rush of blood in my ears. I tried to remain calm, but couldn't stop my cheeks from reddening. They'd be burning scarlet already, and there was nothing I could do about it. This man—this pompous blowhard who isn't nearly as funny as he thinks he is—had trivialized the conflict that had ravaged our entire nation into a joke. A quick laugh at the expense of a mountain of sacrifice. A mountain my own father called his grave.

"Enough of your coarse 'entertainments' Cosgrove," Vanguard said with a slight edge. I saw then that Vanguard was staring directly at me. Perhaps he had been the whole time. The lightness returned to his voice. "Bridget, would you play us a piece on the piano?"

"Very well, but only as a tease for later." Lady Acton nearly bounced to the large piano in the corner and began to play. The music had a mournful quality to it, which seemed at odds with the general mood of the party. But all in attendance listened. There was no clinking of wine glasses or murmur of voices. It's as though the music had cast a spell on them all. Even the servers, me included, seemed to intuit that we should stop moving around. I assumed it was an instrumental piece as it lulled me with its rich tones and minor keys, so was surprised when Lady Acton began to sing. Her singing voice was as husky as her speaking voice, although it brightened on the higher notes. She was certainly better than the warbling churchwomen back in Gillsborough, who praised the Lord like choking birds.

> *Line them all up, in one single line*
> *Moments like dominos, fall in time*
> *Sweeter than nectar, and no less sublime*
> *Ashes on the tongue as the bells chime*

I would have liked to have heard the rest but felt a tug on my arm. I startled, as if woken from a dream, to find Chaput was next to me. He nodded his head to the nearest exit, and I followed swiftly behind. I turned one more time, and watched the crowd of guests and servers—transfixed as Acton's strange and sad song continued.

> *So, I'll raise my cup, to what I gave*
> *Set it down and mer-ri-ly say*
> *Take me, take me, take me to*
> *To that shining—*

The heavy door swung shut and muffled the delicate song into oblivion.

"I'm sorry I wasn't doing my job," I said. Chaput shook his head and smiled.

"Do not worry, *mon garçon*," the butler said. "The lady has a remarkable gift. She sings from the soul, no? I did not bring you here to scold you, but because I require your help."

"Of course." My relief was immeasurable.

"Excellent. This way, please." Chaput briskly walked away from me, and I scrambled to keep up. We walked the long hallway to the stairs, up to the second floor, and then up a small set of stairs that led to the attic. As we walked, I tried to take in as much as I could of the house. Most of the central rooms had the same color, design, and décor as the first hallway I'd seen. But as I passed by interior rooms, I noticed that some rooms had the same wallpaper pattern, but with the colors rearranged. Some rooms had dramatically red walls with cream detail and—most dramatically—some rooms had black wallpaper with red detailing. It was all striking, although I wasn't sure how long I'd want to stay in such rooms.

"What exactly am I helping with? If I may ask?" We climbed the stairs to the attic. I'd kept hoping Chaput would offer an explanation, and my patience was wearing thin. Chaput surprised me by chuckling.

"Sorry, I do not mean to be mysterious. I'm just a hair frazzled if I'm honest," Chaput said. I enjoyed that the butler had let his guard down, a little. His manner seemed much changed toward me. "Master Vanguard wanted to gift Lady Acton one of the souvenirs he'd picked up in his travels, and I completely forgot about it until she started performing."

"What sort of souvenir?"

"A statue, made of jade, I believe. It's been stored up here for quite some time," Chaput said. The "attic" was more of a third floor. The ceiling was shorter, but still very comfortable to walk under. The small staircase led to another hallway. This lacked the detail and ornament of the rooms downstairs, however. The walls were painted in cream, and there was no wooden molding. There were three doors on either side of the hallway, and one at the end, which is where Chaput seemed to be heading. As I passed by the second door on the left, I was struck by a strange vibration in the floor, accompanied by some sort of mechanical noise coming from behind it. There was a sign, as well, that simply read Danger: Keep Out.

"Mr. Doyle?" It was Chaput, standing in front of the open door at the end of the hallway. He stared at me, and I was embarrassed I was being so nosey. In fact, I'd expected some sort of admonishment. None came. "It should be in here." I nodded and followed the man in. The storage space was dusty and full of a couple lifetimes of cloth-covered accumulations, but it was organized. It didn't take long until Chaput found the statue. It was roughly hewn and made of mottled, dull green stone. It was a feminine figure, with large bosoms and hips and one stylized wing on the right side. I tried, unsuccessfully, to keep my face neutral as the butler handed me the statue.

"I know. There's no accounting for taste. But Master Vanguard assures me Lady Acton will be excited," Chaput said. The statue was heavier than I expected. I turned it around, and where I expected to see a fractured blemish where the left wing should have been there was none. The figure had apparently always been one-winged. "Now, for the reason I brought you up here. I must get back to the party and make sure things are running smoothly. I would like you to clean and polish this and package it up for gifting. It needn't be ostentatiously presented. But you'll find cleaning supplies and various wooden boxes suitable for gifting in the room directly out the door and to the right. Use whatever you like there." Before I could say anything in response, Chaput was out of the attic door and heading to the hall, the wisps of his hair shaking as he sped away. Probably fretting about all the things that could be going wrong downstairs.

I cleaned the object with a few shavings of soap and water. There was some grime and dust on it, but it came off easily enough. I tried to be gentle, unsure of how old or precious the statue might be. I found a beautiful birch box, lined with red silk, that was closest to the size of the statuette. Satisfied with my work, I headed back downstairs. I couldn't help but stop at the door with the warning sign on it. I checked to make sure no one was around, and then held my ear up to the door. I heard a rhythmic thrumming that gently shook the door and fluttered against my ear. Maybe a house this size had its own coal burner to supply the lighting in the house with gas? It was certainly far enough outside of Alton to make that necessary. But it seemed odd to have it in the attic.

I heard a door close on the floor below me, jostling me out of my thoughts, and I continued downstairs. Lady Acton was most appreciative of the gift as Vanguard had expected.

"Oh, Jax, you found a *Corithe da Lumyera*? And in such excellent condition," the woman marveled. Her upper-class British accent emphasized syllables strangely, to my ears at least, so I didn't quite catch what she'd called it. It was in a language I didn't recognize, at least. I stood dutifully to the side after handing Vanguard the box and felt more out of place than ever. The men and women in the room, as a group, were intimidating. Not because of their physical presence—in fact most seemed too slight or too large or too pale—but because of what they talked about, and the lives they led. They might as well have been from another planet.

It was with great relief, then, that at half past ten Chaput excused the waiting staff for a half hour break. Lady Acton's performance was to begin, and Vanguard wanted all attention focused on her. The cool autumn air pleasantly prickled my skin as I walked out into the night air with the other young men. I hadn't realized how hot and stuffy it had gotten inside, with all the guests and activity. I closed my eyes, and took in the earthy damp of the trees, the intense brimstone spikiness of matches being struck, and the sweet scent of tobacco smoke as the men around me indulged.

"Well, they are quite a group," Henry said, sidling up next to me. His eyes sparkled in the dim light coming from the windows, the only illumination in the vast darkness atop the bluff. Henry wasn't unattractive to start with, but I liked him better the more he talked. There was kindness in his eyes that contrasted with his bluntness. Plus, he had a way of pulling you in and making you feel as if you'd been best friends for years.

"And this house," I said.

"House? Hardly seems the word. One man and a few staff in a place like this. Seems almost criminal." Anger or resentment hardened the man's eyes. I understood it. You could probably house the entire population of Gillsborough in this place. Except, Henry had an air about him, as though he'd be happy to collect his pay and never see the place again. I admired that. Because seeing Shearhaven up close only made the fierce need and desire for it burn hotter. If there was a proverbial top of the heap, this was it.

"Want to walk?" Henry asked. The last thing I wanted to do was walk more. But there was a glint in his eyes I could not say no to. And, once we'd begun, I had to admit taking in the cool air had an energizing effect. We walked around the gigantic house, through an archway, and out the front. I'd been too nervous on the drive up to really take it in.

Atop the bluff was a circular clearing with a well-manicured lawn of vibrant, deep green grass. The long gravel drive—smoothed stones of black, brown, and white—stretched from the edge of the clearing, past ornamental hedges, and then finally to the house itself.

Shearhaven was a marvel up close, and not quite like anything I'd seen before—although my experience was admittedly limited. It was made of brick so dark that it was nearly black, marbled with coppery-brown rock. The house was shaped like a bracket, with wings projecting forward from both sides like arms waiting to draw you in. Tall, thin windows lined up like soldiers along the bottom two floors. The windows on the upper floor were squatter. Three arches were centered on the ground floor, all leading to a large vestibule where the doors to the house were located. Ornate bouquets of wild roses and candytuft above each window of the house were cheerful additions for the party.

"The stone was a queer choice, wasn't it?" Henry asked. "And that wallpaper. So strange."

"Someone recently told me that the rich can afford to be strange." I hadn't looked at the wallpaper that closely, other than to note its strangeness. But I wanted to impress Henry.

"Still, can't complain too much. A week's pay for a few hours work. And we even got a break. Although did you see that 'gift' Vanguard gave the lady singer? That'd be going in the garbage at my place."

"See it? I had to clean it and wrap it up." I enjoyed the

sensation of sharing "inside secrets" with this man. The pressure of my groin against my pants when I was near him made that evident. I shifted to angle myself away from him slightly. "Even Chaput seemed to think it was hideous. Still, Lady Acton seemed to like the thing."

"Lady Acton. That was her name. I wish I were better at names, like you are," Henry said. I was about to protest the compliment, but Henry cut me off before I could start. "You knew everyone's name. It was impressive."

I smiled widely, sensed that I was being uncouth, and immediately toned it down. When had it gotten so hot out here?

"Well, not everyone's—"

"There you are!" Dottie ran up to me. She wore a wet, dirty apron. Her hair was stringy with sweat, and she was stalking toward me with wide eyes. "Nice of you to find me."

"I didn't know if they'd let the kitchen staff have a break." Truthfully, I had been too caught up in conversation with Henry to remember that Dottie was still here.

"I think Cook wants to chain me up and keep me, so I'm surprised they did." Dottie wiped her hands on her apron, which I thought might have made things worse, and turned toward Henry. "My name's Dottie."

"Pleasure to meet you," Henry's eyes weren't exactly communicating the sentiment.

"Dottie's my best friend," I said quickly. "Really more like a sister. Her dad took me in when I was eight."

"That's great! I mean, it's great that he took you in."

"Yes, yes. He's practically a saint. Henry, would you mind if I steal back my brother-friend for a moment?"

"Of course. I'll talk to you later, Tomas," Henry said, taking a hesitant step before quickly making his way toward the spot at the side of the house the other servers had gathered.

"Well, I see why you forgot all about me, your loyal friend performing excruciatingly tedious physical labor because she tried to help you." Dottie took off her apron and started flapping it in the air to cool herself off and dry it out.

"It's not like that. I mean, a little. Mostly I'm just still trying to wrap my head around this place."

"Well, tell me! All I've seen is the kitchen and that endless vat of potatoes." Dottie and I sat in the grass away from the rest of the group. I took a moment to revel in the brisk night wind coursing over the bluff and through the trees. I quickly brought Dottie up to speed with everything I'd seen and done—she managed to only interrupt me twice to ask questions. She sat back, propping herself up with her arms.

"Huh. While you've been rubbing noses with the fancy people, I've been peeling potatoes, stirring roux, searing meat, and more besides. Cook ordering me around like a dog."

"I really am sorry. I wish you could see that ballroom. And it's *elbows*, not noses."

"It's fine. I probably wouldn't know what to do with myself anyway." Dottie wiped the sweat from her brow. "Oh, had a real fun moment with the head housekeeper."

"Ms. Coghlan?"

"That's the one."

"What happened?" I asked.

"Well, I was halfway through bag number two of the potatoes when she comes to the kitchen and has a few words with the Cook. Then as she's about to take off, she starts eyeing me. She walks up to me, stares at me like she's a sailor eyeing up a Christmas ham, and says 'You know, you'd be quite pretty with some effort.'" My eyes widened. Before I could respond, three loud claps resounded through the night air. Chaput was at the kitchen entrance door.

"Ms. Acton's concert will be finishing soon. Please begin returning inside. Check to make sure you and your attire are properly composed to finish the rest of the service," he said.

"Back to the kitchen," Dottie said with a crooked smile. "You're going to owe me."

"Again, I did not ask you to come." We walked back into the house, though of course I knew I did owe her. A lot. For everything. "But I'm glad you did. Having you here makes this all slightly less disorienting." Dottie smiled, but she turned her head to try to hide it.

"I'm glad you came to your senses."

5

By midnight, the novelty of the experience was beginning
to wear off. My eyelids felt too heavy. I was an early riser—had
to be, really—since I was the one that helped Mr. Blake open
the store every day. Dottie only ever worked noon to close, as she
was a night owl and useless in the mornings. The good news is
that I was used to being on my feet most of the day. That being
said, depending on the day and time, Dottie and I did usually
get a little time to sit in the back and talk when there were no
customers. Tonight, however, I had to be constantly alert to
everyone's needs, talk with the occasional chatty guest, and run
back and forth to get new trays of drinks and food. This was
a different sort of exhaustion from the fairly mindless tasks of
working at the shop.

I'd hoped the party might get more intimate or settle
down after Acton's performance, but the opposite happened.
These friends of Vanguard's were fond of drink and got louder
and more boisterous as the night went on. At one point I saw

Schreiber pour his drink down a woman's bosoms, which she'd helpfully squeezed together, and greedily lap at the liquid pooled there. Henry had just served him the wine, and I saw his eyes go wide. This made me feel better, as I got the sense that Henry was a more worldly man than I was. If even he was shocked by the display, I didn't feel like such a hapless small-town waif. Men and women danced in pairings that disregarded gender. Cosgrove pinched bottoms and made lewd jokes toward the servers, toward Vanguard—toward anything with a pulse, really.

It all became too much. My underarms were soaked. I could feel the beads of cold sweat on my forehead. Then I saw the wine flutes on the tray in my hand trembling. My hands were trembling. I nearly ran into the small room next to the ballroom where we kept the extra matches, handkerchiefs, and other supplies. I leaned against the wall next to the door, taking deep breaths and letting them out slowly.

"What do you think?" Lady Acton said into my ear, startling me and causing the wine-filled flutes on my tray to clatter slightly. I was grateful none spilled. "My apologies."

"None necessary," I said with too much cheer, overcompensating for my tiredness and the expanding anxiousness buzzing within. "What do I think about what, exactly, Ma'am?"

"Please, call me Bridget" The woman relieved my tray of a glass and downed it in one go. "I mean about all of this. The house. The party. Vanguard." There was a wolfish gleam in the woman's eyes that made me nervous.

"It's a beautiful home." I judged my words carefully. "It certainly isn't like any party I've ever seen. But it seems like everyone is having a good time."

"Oh yes, that's always assured." Lady Acton moved so that

she was directly in front of me now. "And Vanguard?"

"He seems like a very generous host." The woman waved this off, tired of my generic answers.

"Yes, yes. And he has a head and two arms and two legs," she said impatiently. "Do you have a handkerchief?" Thankful for the distraction, I retrieved the one I'd been given—embroidered with Vanguard's initials in case one of the guests took it as a souvenir—and handed it to Lady Acton. I replaced it with a new one from the box of them on the table nearby, thankful to get a few feet away from the woman. But when I turned, she was right there again, her eyes boring into me.

"I mean, as a man. One grows accustomed to their dear friends. It's refreshing getting an outsider's perspective." Lady Acton dabbed the sweat from her head. "It is hot in there. All that body heat. It's electric but can be somewhat taxing." She wiped the back of her neck, and then slowly ran the handkerchief past the side of her neck, and then down to the graceful well between her breasts. Her dress only allowed the faintest hint of it, but it was enough. She watched me intently as she did this. I noted what she was doing in my periphery, but I never broke eye contact. What was all of this? Was it a game the wealthy played, to get the staff to do something inappropriate?

"I think Mr. Vanguard is very impressive, from what I've seen of him. Thoughtful, too, seeing how much you enjoyed your present." I kept my tone as cheerful as I could. Lady Acton's expression was inscrutable. There was a softening of her features at the edges, but whether that was because she was pleased at my answer or disappointed and losing interest, I couldn't say.

"Yes. Well. Thank you. Illuminating chat." She dropped the handkerchief on the tray and exited the room. I exhaled a blast of air in relief, straightened my shoulders, and headed back to the ballroom.

An hour later, I was nearly dead on my feet. Slowly, all the young men who had served as waiters emptied out of the ballroom. The party settled into cozy enclaves of people drunkenly chatting about what businesses they were in, where they'd recently traveled, who was stepping out on who, and the relative merits of adopting a metric system for measurement. I didn't relish the ride home, so I was slower than the rest to get changed out of the clothes I'd been given and back into my own. It didn't hurt that Henry and a few of the other men were still in there. I stole a few quick glances of muscular calf, a chiseled groove of collar bone, and—with Henry, a flash of fur-covered abdominals. Chaput came in very briefly and handed each man a small, slim envelope containing their earnings. I thought it would be uncouth to open the envelope, but the thickness of it made the reality of the wealth I'd earned from one night's work all the more real and I couldn't help a wide grin from spreading across my face.

"Remember, if you ever get down my way, you should stop by. We'll grab a pint at my pa's tavern. Only one in town, so it's easy to find," Henry said as he headed out of the storage room that had been turned into a makeshift changing area for us.

"I'll do that," I lied. It wasn't that I wouldn't like to. But something told me it would never happen. It was just a polite thing one said.

After I finished dressing and was relishing being back in the relative comfort of my own clothes, I went to the kitchen and was surprised to see Dottie seated at the table across from Cook, playing chess. I resolutely hated chess, but Dottie loved it. Her eyes were focused on a rook that was too close for comfort to her queen. Her pipe was in her mouth, and she chewed on the end of it in concentration. No one else in Gillsborough had much interest in it either, so this was a real treat for her. I stood in the doorway for a moment, just watching my friend. She'd spent all these hours here for me. Just so she could be near me if something was wrong. If it hadn't been for the late hour, I would have felt too guilty to interrupt the game.

"Party's over, Dot," I said. "We'd better get on the road." Dottie and Cook exchanged a strange glance—some shared secret—that I didn't understand. Dottie got up and brushed her hands together.

"That's okay, I had him in checkmate in three moves anyway," she said. Cook let out a short, skeptical laugh, then a barely audible *Mmhmm*, and then waved them off. As we stepped out of the kitchen and into the hallway that led to the kitchen entrance, I chanced a whispered comment.

"Talkative fellow, eh?" he asked. Dottie's eyes went wide.

"Oh, you'd be surprised. Once you get to know him." Before I could press further, a familiar French-accented voice rang out behind us.

"Excuse me, *Monsieur* Doyle," Chaput said. "I have one last request of you." I looked over at Dottie. Neither one of us was hiding our exhaustion and desire to leave very well.

"I'll get Caroline ready for the trip home," Dottie said. "I could use some cool air anyway. I'll walk slow, and meet you out there?" I nodded reluctantly. The butler turned on his heels and started back down the hallway that led further into the house. I noted that the floors were immaculate and shining once more. The work of the tiny maid Gladys, I supposed.

"This shouldn't take long," Chaput said apologetically, taking on the air of a comrade-in-arms. "Mr. Vanguard requested to speak to you before you go." I felt a twist at the pit of my stomach. There seemed to be no *good* reason Vanguard might want to see me. Perhaps it was just my own innate worry, but I started to replay the events of the night. Had the statuette been improperly cleaned or presented? Had I been rude to Lady Acton by not playing along with her flirtations? Or had I not followed one of the myriad rules from Chaput's training, and ruined the "aesthetic" of the night? This coursed through my head as I followed the butler to the end of the hall, around a twist to the right, up a small staircase, and then a few more turns until finally we stopped at a partially open door.

"Please wait inside. Master Vanguard will join you shortly." Chaput walked on, and I couldn't help but be envious of the butler's unflappable energy. Surely his day had started long before mine. I was about to push the door open when I remembered Henry's remark about the wallpaper. I decided to give it a look. In truth, the entire interior of Shearhaven was much like the exterior, which is to say it was startling. It had the basic form of the familiar, but the colors and textures were unusual. The floor was polished black stone. The walls were framed by richly black wood molding. Only the whirls of deep brown lightened it some. It was covered in a finish that was so reflective it looked wet to the touch. I willed myself not to reach out and double-check. It'd be just my luck if it had just been resealed and was, in fact, wet. Instead, I watched my reflection, a faint outline surrounded in inky blackness.

The cream wallpaper had a diamond pattern on it made of thin black lines that came to sharp points on either end. Sometimes the lines connected. But on alternating rows, in the space they would have connected, there was a small ornamental detail. I leaned in and took a better look, mindful not to take too long as Vanguard was due to arrive at any moment. That's when I realized that what I'd first taken for some meaningless decoration was much more specific and far stranger. It was a symbol, composed of a red figure eight, crossed by an old-fashioned cutlass. In both loops was another symbol that looked vaguely familiar, but I didn't immediately recognize.

As I looked, the intersecting lines seemed to vibrate. Then the symbol. I turned away and wiped at my eyes. I really was overtired, and I still had a long ride home.

I decided I had pressed my luck long enough and entered Vanguard's study. It was bathed in orange light from a large fireplace made of uneven gray stones. The only other light was an oil lantern set upon a large desk of dark oak. This meant that much of the room was bathed in shadows, and until my eyes adjusted, I could only make out the general contours of it. There were bookshelves on one wall, filled with books, certainly, but other objects too. I thought I could see a small globe, and a glass dome that held something that sparkled in the light. The desk was spartan in its decoration, especially considering its massive size. A green cloth pad, framed by wood, sat in its center flanked by a bottle of ink, a pen, and a matching holder. There was a leather portfolio sitting on the desk that contained a bundle of loose pages. The rough strap of leather that closed the portfolio was undone, with one page tantalizingly peeking out. I resisted the urge to look inside, and instead focused my attention on the three paintings above the desk.

All were done in richly textured oil paints. The first one had a grandly intricate frame and felt most at home with the

rest of the study. It depicted a wizened man with dark eyes—as
shiny and black as the chitin of a beetle—peering out from the
twin wells of his eye sockets. He had a regal, European look to
him, with pale skin that let the reds and blues and purple of his
internals through too plainly. I found the painting disturbing
and fascinating in equal measure. I was hardly an art critic, but
the heavy brushwork lent the painting a grotesque texture. The
second painting was in a less ornate frame, and its colors were
less muddied than the first, lacking as thick a film of dust and
soot. The man in this painting had a stronger jaw than the first.
His hair was jet black—only frosted silver at the temples—and he
had brilliantly blue eyes. This one reminded me of my old pastor,
a similarly handsome man in his fifties that I'd had a confused
infatuation with when I was much younger. I'd even thought
about going into the clergy, wrongly thinking my interest might
have been in the church or the man's vocation. Finally, the third
painting was in a very simple, slightly smaller frame. It depicted
a young boy with long brown hair, nearly blonde in places, and
with warm brown eyes. I knew immediately it was a younger
version of the current Master Vanguard. Though this boy had
none of the danger in his eyes the man had. None of the dark
allure. Those things must have been earned with experience.

The entire study felt like it belonged to another house. The
wood was not the ubiquitous dark Russian-lacquered wood of
the rest of the house and furniture. The only constant was the
strange wallpaper pattern and symbol, except here the walls were
dark green, with lines so dark that you could barely see them. An
enormous bear pelt had found its eternal rest on the study floor.
Most of the house clearly communicated something—even if
I wasn't sure what that message might be. This room, however,
seemed a discordant note in that symphony. Of course, I had

seen precious little of the less public rooms. Perhaps they were all this way.

"Sorry to keep you waiting," Vanguard said as he strode into the study. I startled out of my reverie.

"No need to apolo—" I began, but Vanguard cut me off as he sat in the wide leather chair behind the desk.

"Perhaps not, but even so." Vanguard motioned for me to sit in one of the smaller wooden chairs in front of the desk. I settled in, trying to calm nerves that had been jangled for the last few hours. I desperately wanted to apologize again—for whatever issue I'd caused—but since Vanguard had cut me off the first time, I thought better of it. The master of Shearhaven slumped backward in his chair and regarded me with hazy eyes. Vanguard had partaken of plenty of alcohol that night. The precision of his earlier demeanor was gone, replaced with something more relaxed and inviting.

"I am the master of this house," Vanguard began after another moment. "So, perhaps I needn't apologize to you—the hired servant. But I wanted to because I have something else to apologize for. Not as an employer speaking to an employee, but as one man speaking to another."

"I see." Truthfully, I wasn't following any of this.

"I doubt you do," Vanguard said, a playful smile breaking through his apologetic tone. "Which is my point. You see, Mr. Doyle, all of this has been something of a ruse. And I think it's time I came clean."

6

My heart seemed to beat with the furious pace of Caroline's hooves as we raced away from Shearhaven. Moonlight shattered across the Mississippi to my left. Dottie, wrapped in her father's borrowed cloak next to me, tried to share but it wasn't working well. Which was fine by me. An early winter chill was in the air, and I welcomed it. The cold air was helping to provide some measure of reality to an unreal night. I'd been too terse with Dottie, when she complained that I didn't want to talk about it. She looked momentarily stung, but she shrugged it off almost immediately. She had a way of forgiving me for my spikier moments, which I both appreciated and always worried over later. I needed some time to process my conversation with Vanguard. Fear and excitement pulsed through me, manifesting as a tingle at the back of my head and a tightness in my chest. It was exquisitely painful, and the wind prevented any chance of conversation.

The ride home was a blur, and when we arrived in

Gillsborough, we were chilled and weary. We returned Caroline to the stall Mr. Blake rented in Ma Howard's stable, Dottie promising to give her a proper brushing in the morning. I'd expected Dottie to start interrogating me as soon as we dismounted, but it wasn't until we crept into the small, ramshackle home we grew up in and boiled some water for tea that she retrieved her pipe and looked at me expectantly.

"First, sorry I was short earlier," I said, fumbling around an empty cup, wishing the water to boil faster. To this, Dottie removed the unlit pipe from her mouth and twirled it dismissively at me.

"If there's any advantage to knowing someone most of your life, it's being able to be short with them without them holding onto it. But I do want the full story. The *full* story, Tomas Eugene Doyle." Dottie began to pack tobacco into her pipe just as the kettle hissed. I got up to retrieve it.

"Well, he said he had something to confess. That this had all been a—"

"Ruse?" I asked, hating how it sounded coming out of my mouth. As if I didn't understand the meaning of the word itself.

"Yes. I should—" Vanguard began, before stopping himself. The man got up out of the tall leather chair that nearly dwarfed him and turned toward the painting of his younger self. I wasn't sure what caused it—the alcohol or what the man had to say— but the shyness that had overcome Vanguard appealed to me. As with Chaput earlier in the evening, I suppose there was a certain sense of satisfaction in seeing one of these high society types being vulnerable. Especially as I barely knew the man. I wondered, then, if that meant that neither Chaput nor Vanguard were particularly exemplary members of high society. I'd just seen how easily he could command the attention of a party full of men and women that intimidated the hell out of me. Now here he was, alone with me, being hesitant. I'd be lying if I said it wasn't a thrill—whatever the cause—to imagine that small measure of power I held over him.

"I was very lonely as a child," Vanguard finally continued. He stared up at the painting, and I wished I could see his face, as his voice betrayed little feeling. "Sometimes I'm not sure what came first. Did I isolate myself from the other children at the orphanage because I felt different, or did they isolate me because they sensed I was different? Perhaps it doesn't matter. The end result was the same." Vanguard turned around then, and must have read the surprise on my face, because his thoughtful expression turned into a hint of a smile once again.

"I was adopted by Gabriel Vanguard—the man in the middle painting with the startlingly blue eyes. Like his father before him, he was unable to conceive an heir with his wife. It's one of the many ridiculous 'curses' the people around here like to mutter about under their breath."

"Your father was adopted too?" I asked, too intrigued to worry about the propriety of the question.

"Yes. Cyril Vanguard—the man in the first painting— adopted him. The Vanguards of Shearhaven have had less of a family tree and more a small grove of saplings since stepping foot on these shores. But I digress. Your companion is waiting for you. I don't mean to avoid my point but give you context." Vanguard, unable to stay still, walked over the moonlight-filled window. "My father adopted me shortly after losing his wife. When he brought me to Shearhaven, I thought all my desperate prayers had been answered. I had more money than I'd ever imagined. Every toy or sweet I could desire. One wing of this house was larger than the entirety of the Alton Children's Protectory."

"It's a beautiful home," I offered weakly when Vanguard did not immediately continue. I saw the man's chest rise and fall slowly as he stared out of the window. A sliver of silver light rimmed his strong jaw and handsomely sharp features as if the moon was reaching out to caress him. And who could blame the moon the indulgence? Its light scattered like jewels in the wells of his eyes. Here, bathed in the glory of starlight is where Jackson Vanguard belonged. That's what I thought to myself. I immediately felt ridiculous, of course. I wanted to hate him. It wasn't fair for a man this handsome to be this wealthy and have such a forlorn backstory. Care sprouted where bitterness and jealousy had been keeping me safe and distant.

"Yes. Very beautiful. And very lonely, as it turns out. A different, larger sort of lonely." Vanguard turned to me once more, steeled himself, and sat back down in the large leather chair. "That 'difference' I felt as a child has never left me. A difference I believe you understand." I was too gripped by fear and expectation to respond. I thought I knew what Vanguard spoke of but didn't dare to confirm it. Not yet. Perhaps sensing this, Vanguard continued.

"Wealth and status are grand things. Having been on either end of the spectrum, I can tell you where I'd rather be that's for certain. However, they do bring about certain expectations. And watchful eyes. Which makes ones—*differences*—harder to act on. These parties sprung out of the deep pit in my heart that was carved by that loneliness. I was inspired by Lady Acton after visiting one of her extravagances at her home in London. They help, for a while, yet once they are done, I find my return to real life quite numbing and the loneliness more acute.

"So, during the last party Lady Acton had an idea. She thought that I should send my loyal butler, Chaput, out into the world on a little tour. From Chicago to Indianapolis to St. Louis and back. He would seek out candidates. Men like us, who might make a suitable companion for me." Vanguard stared at me intently. My face reddened. I hadn't dared dream it, but here it was as real as anything. Vanguard had meant exactly what I'd thought he'd meant. My shock left me mute.

"Chaput was at the end of his journey." Vanguard looked away from me, and toward the study window. "He belatedly remembered Cook had requested he order supplies outside of Alton for the upcoming party because the town was suffering an infestation, when he came upon the small shop in Gillsborough where you work."

"So, you see, it all has an air of destiny about it, doesn't it? I have many shortcomings, which I hope you'll discover in due course. One of them is a deep well of romanticism. But when I saw you down there, looking up at that very window," Vanguard said, nodding to the place he'd just stood. "There was something in your eyes—look, I've taken too much of your time already. But I want you to think about it."

"If I've misinterpreted things, or if you're simply not interested, then we shall part now as friends and no more need be said." Vanguard's face darkened, and his tone grew more somber. "I only ask that you keep my confidence. I'm risking a great deal even having this conversation."

With that, Vanguard got up from his chair, clasped his hands together, and let the moment hang awkwardly between us for only a moment before striding toward the study door. I felt bad. I thought I should rush to him. I thought I should embrace him. I feel like he'd made space for a moment like that, and I'd let the moment slip by. But you must understand. I was just trying to get my head around it all. When he spoke again, his voice was all business. The cool and aloof lord of the manor.

"If you do wish to see me further and explore what this—what *we* could be—I'll have a carriage waiting near your workplace next Friday at five in the evening. Simply enter it, and it will bring you back here. Otherwise. Well. In any case, Chaput is just outside, and will see you out. Good evening, Tomas."

Dottie leaned back in the kitchen chair and placed her pipe in her mouth. She was swept up enough in story that she'd forgotten to light it.

"What did Chaput say? On the way out?" she asked.

"Nothing. I suppose he could tell I was shocked. The way Vanguard talked about it was so coded, and yet so forthright at the same time. Far more forthright talking about it than anyone I've ever known, except you and I."

"I honestly can't decide if it's disturbing or romantic. I understand the need for secrecy, but I'm not sure I understand all the—what's the word I'm looking for? *Machinations*. That's it. I'm not sure I approve of or understand all the machinations. You know?"

"I know," I agreed. "Not sure I care for all the theatricalities. But he is handsome."

"And wealthy."

"And lonely. You should have seen the look in his eyes."

"There is one other thing. Something Cook let slip. The party wasn't over. Not by a long shot. In fact, the way Cook talked about it, the party was just about to get started when we left. They sent the servers home, but he said they were usually up until dawn. Slept until the afternoon. All those potatoes I peeled? They were for some sort of huge breakfast Vanguard served the next day." Dottie finally lit her pipe and puffed until it smoked properly. "You have to wonder what sort of person would want to go to that kind of party. Consider whether they're worth getting involved with."

"You'd love to go to that sort of party," I narrowed my eyes and smiled crookedly at her.

"My point exactly. You already have one bad influence in your life," Dottie said. She'd said it lightheartedly, but I saw a twinge of sadness in her eyes as well. She always got that way, whenever circumstances seemed poised to carry me away from her. Our souls were intertwined. I knew that a short while into our friendship. I wanted to tell her nothing would change. But I knew too much about saying goodbye to people I loved to lie.

"I don't know what I'll do," I said with a sigh. I meant it, but Dottie knew exactly what I'd do.

7

I stared out the window of Blake's Mercantile & Sundry, fidgeting with the dark blue jacket that was just a little too small for me, pulling on the sleeves and willing them to be longer. I experimented with only moving my arms up a little way so the sleeves wouldn't ride up so much.

"You look like you're made of clockwork," Dottie clucked as she watched my movements. She was sitting hunched over on the counter—a habit her father had never successfully broken her out of—and swung the buckled shoes on her feet.

"Dottie, be nice," warned Mr. Blake, shaking his head (as he often did) at his daughter's bluntness—hard enough to send the fine white strands of his bushy head of hair trembling. "But she's not wrong. Just leave the sleeves be. Forget them. Show you're confident in yourself and what you're wearing. Most people don't notice the details."

When Mr. Blake learned I'd been invited to Shearhaven as a guest, he'd talked to a friend of a friend who still had his late son's jacket. It was out of style and a little worn at a few seams, but it was better than going in a button-up shirt and pants. Still, Mr. Blake didn't know Jackson Vanguard. If anyone were to notice the details, it'd be him.

"Now, Tomas, a word." Mr. Blake wedged himself between my face and the window I'd been staring out of the last fifteen minutes. "I want you to mind yourself tonight."

"I'm not going to make a fool of myself." It came out sharper than I'd intended. "Or the shop." Mr. Blake closed his eyes beneath the twin white caterpillars of his eyebrows and sighed heavily.

"Of course, I trust you, Tomas. I meant, be aware of where you are and how you're moving about the world. It's the world I don't trust. And believe you me when I say it's given me plenty of reason not to trust it." I loved the man like a father, but he'd say things like this from time to time that made me wonder how much he held back from us. Every once in a while, he'd give us a peek into the world before Dottie was born and before I'd stumbled into being a permanent part of their lives. Dottie and I'd compared notes about it before, as she'd not had any more luck getting him to open up about it. Unlike me, she wasn't afraid to ask him directly about his life before we came along. He still gave vague answers. Or, on a particularly chatty day, would simply say, "old world, old problems," and wave his hands dismissively. It was a sentiment I'd heard Ma Howard and a few of the other people in town who were more recent transplants to this country express, though not in the same words.

"Don't worry. It's not a big party this time. And Mr. Vanguard seemed nice." I glanced over at Dottie; afraid she might snicker. But there was something else there. Uncertainty or worry, I couldn't be certain. I'm sure Mr. Blake wondered why a rich young man had asked me to spend more time with him after I'd served as a waiter at one of his parties. It was, well, a strange request from the outside. But I suspected whatever ulterior motive Blake suspected wasn't close to the truth.

I looked away and out to the street, and startled when I saw the elegant carriage outside, pulled by two brilliantly white horses. The carriage was as shiny and dark as the wood that adorned the interior of Shearhaven. A driver sat stiffly on his seat, face half-hidden between his long brown hair, his high collar, and tall hat.

"There's my carriage," I said, trying not to let my nerves creep into my voice too much.

"Very good. Be back home at a decent hour, and—" Mr. Blake looked at me, as if there was more he wanted to say. Instead, he pulled me into a short hug. I gave him a pat on the back and we separated. I looked over at Dottie. She'd been outwardly supportive of all of this but wouldn't stop looking contemplative or sad since I'd told her about Vanguard. I knew her concern was a complex brew of protectiveness of her friend, fear she'd lose me, and perhaps even a dash of judgment that I was so eager. Was Vanguard's wealth part of the draw? I couldn't deny it. There was a great deal of appeal in the buffer from society's judgment that sort of money could provide someone like me. I pushed all these thoughts away as far too premature.

"Don't make me come looking for you," Dottie said as she slid off the counter and started toward the back of the store. An exasperated chuckle escaped my mouth.

"Don't worry, you two. I'll be back before you know it." I set my sights on the carriage as I opened the door, worried now that if I dawdled too long it'd leave and give Vanguard the wrong impression about my interest. That's why I gasped in shock when a cold hand clamped around my wrist.

"Don't go in the black carriage," Ma Howard said, her skeletal hand gripping me with more power than I'd imagined it capable of. Which was probably silly of me. It's not like the woman didn't spend all day on her feet working with her hands.

"Ma, I don't think—"

"Back in my village, young people listened to their elders. It was cold and dark and too many people disappeared in the forest, sure, but at least the children were smart enough to listen."

"I've just been—"

"That place—the place that thing is going to whisk you off to—" the woman began, her Eastern European accent—I'd never heard which country she'd come from—getting thicker, as if she were drawing upon some ancient well of wisdom that required it. "Is no good. I used to work in Alton when I first came to this country. The whispers about that house on the bluffs would chill the marrow in your thin little bones."

I wasn't sure what to say to that.

"But I didn't need to hear the rumors. I knew by the wood. The black wood, young Tomas. The forest dwellers made the black wood. Black as night but swirled. In some lights it's brown swirls. In some lights it's copper. But if you look closely, at the right angle you'll see it's red, young Tomas. Dark, flowing red." I glanced over at the carriage, the stoic driver shifted in his seat, perhaps from restlessness. I wrenched my wrist from the old woman's grip.

"Ma. I appreciate it. I do. But I'll be fine. Really," I said it with all the cheer I could muster through my annoyance. I put my hand gently on her shoulder. I could feel muscle, bone, and ligament shift slightly under the pressure.

"Bah!" She brushed my hand away and spun away from

me, muttering in a language I didn't recognize. I watched her
go for a moment, wishing there was more I could say. It's not
that I didn't appreciate the concern. She'd always been good to
me, Mr. Blake, and Dottie. She'd lost her husband a long time
ago, just as Mr. Blake had lost his wife. Without ever consciously
acknowledging it, she'd tried to step in when she could when
Dottie or I needed a "motherly" touch. But the people of this
town needed to see me as I was. I was a man, more than capable
of making my own decisions. I strode over to the carriage. The
driver—an eagle-faced man with a nose as sharp as a beak and
watery gray eyes—gave me a simple nod of acknowledgment,
hopped down from his perch, and opened the door for me. I
stooped down and entered the richly appointed vehicle. The
carriage lurched slightly as it began the journey to Shearhaven.

This ride to Shearhaven was far more comfortable, although
the weather was being uncooperative. We ran into a gray sheet of
rain halfway through the trip, my third time on this road in less
than two weeks. The speed at which things had progressed made
my breaths short and caused sparks of doubt to flare in my chest.
Experience taught me three remedies for when I felt this way. I
closed my eyes. I took in a slow breath. And I started noticing
details around me. Sometimes enormous, uncontrollable feelings
were best battled by focusing on the minutiae. The handles on
the carriage were silver and decorated with the same intriguing
crest or symbol that adorned the walls of the house. I rubbed my
thumb over the debossed crest, tracing the figure eight broken by
the sword. I settled back into the upholstered seat, and wondered
what it was stuffed with. I stroked the smooth, red cloth below
me, luxuriating in its softness. What would it be like to live this
way all the time? The blandly pleasant carriage driver taking
me wherever I might like? I pushed the thought away. It was too

early to have thoughts like that. Too many fragile support beams
in the house of dreams I was building despite myself. For now, I'd
just try to enjoy the experience.

The carriage had just begun to climb the narrow road up
the bluff when it stopped and pulled to the side. Another carriage
was coming down, and the space was tight. I was grateful we'd
just started the journey up, as the road only grew narrower. I
looked out the window and saw an elegant white carriage pass.
The lone passenger was a grave looking man with small round
spectacles and a riotous tangle of black hair that erupted from
an otherwise bald head like a unicorn horn. The man's gaze
was fixed forward, so he didn't see me watch him as he passed.
He held a small doctor's bag on his lap, which he gripped with
both white-knuckled hands. The lights of the carriage helped
the ghostly white of it stand out in the inky well of dark that
surrounded Shearhaven, until it turned onto the main road and
blinked out of view.

As the carriage climbed the crest of the bluff, I was
surprised to see numerous pools of warm light poking through
the trees beyond. The trees thinned enough that I could see all
Shearhaven was alight, warm orange firelight pouring forth into
the dark. Was there another party? Had the guests simply stayed
all week? As the carriage neared the front of the house, the front
doors swung open, and Chaput and Ms. Coghlan stepped out
into the vestibule. The warm glow behind them rendered them
half in shadow, but their distinctive shapes were easy enough to
recognize. The carriage stopped in front of the great house, and I
clambered out quickly into the dryness of the house's vestibule.

"Welcome, my dear," Ms. Coghlan said, waving
enthusiastically at me. Her cheeks were reddened with heat or
exertion. Chaput was more reserved, but he gave me a polite nod

and smile.

"It's good to be back, and to see you both," I said.

"Right this way, *Monsieur* Doyle." Chaput turned and walked toward the front doors. I suddenly realized how drastically things had shifted from my last visit. The butler addressed me much more formally, and I was entering through the front doors. I suppressed my smile. Delight mixed with fear at my change of circumstances. I wasn't sure how to operate in this world. I wanted to tell Chaput to call me Tomas, but thought that might be impolite or, at least, uncouth.

"How was your journey, dear?" Ms. Coghlan took my coat.

"Very comfortable. That carriage rides like it floats on the air." I was about to compliment the carriage more—I certainly had plenty to say about it. But I was caught short as I entered Shearhaven. I'd seen the kitchen, the hallways, Vanguard's study, and the ballroom on my previous visit. All intriguing and awe-inspiring in their own way, but nothing had prepared me for the grand front hall.

The dark wood and cream walls with their decorative grids and symbols were still present. A massive staircase was centered in the hall, leading to a railed landing that mimicked the bracket shape of the house itself. On the landing were three doors right, left, and center, made of the same ubiquitous black wood. The back wall of the hall was composed entirely of bookshelves—laden with leatherbound books of all sizes and colors—that extended all the way up to the base of the landing. Twin fireplaces faced each other on the right and left walls, both with two chairs and a settee arranged in half circles before them. Their symmetry was pleasing, if slightly curious. Roaring fires flicked and danced within them. Immediately to the right of the front door was a coat rack stuffed with wool coats, cloaks, and men's hats—top hats, bowlers, and a wide brimmed straw hat. To the left an elegant silver card receiver, its basin decorated with etched concentric circles, sat on a small table. Paintings were carefully arranged on the walls, their subject matter a motley mix of landscapes, narrative scenes, and portraiture.

"Ah, yes, I'd forgotten you didn't get to see this bit," Ms. Coghlan said. "It can be overwhelming the first time." I thought the woman a master of understatement.

"It's especially beautiful in the mornings," Chaput chimed in. "The two windows in the upper floor let in golden shafts of light and it is—the English word is too harsh. It is *réconfortante*."

"Our dear Mr. Chaput likes to take his morning tea in here." The housekeeper pointed to a small chair next to the central door in the far wall of the upper landing. "Master Vanguard has allowed him this one special allowance. Which is no small thing, let me tell you." The house's spell on me broke with the mention of Vanguard's name.

"Where is Mr. Vanguard?" I asked. The two servants exchanged a quick look. Coghlan opened her mouth, as though she were about to speak, but Chaput beat her to it.

"I'm afraid Master Vanguard has been delayed. He has been in New York on business. He shouldn't be more than an hour or so, according to his telegraph."

"You have a telegraph here? In the building?" Though incredulous at the thought at first, I remembered the strange room in the attic with its warning sign. Chaput shook his head.

"No. I'm afraid Mr. Vanguard has not indulged in that yet. Although now that you say it, I'm surprised he didn't try to make it happen."

"He already has his hands full with too many of his 'experiments.'" Ms. Coghlan sighed. "You'll be doing us a favor not to mention it to him. He's already nearly burned the place down as it is." Chaput narrowed his eyes and shot the housekeeper a fierce look. Her eyes went wide.

"We've been tasked with making you comfortable until Mr. Vanguard arrives," Chaput said, eager to change the subject. "Please feel free to browse the library and find a comfortable place to sit at one of the fires. Ms. Coghlan will bring you some tea shortly."

"And if you need anything," the housekeeper added quickly, "there are ropes to the right of either fireplace. Pull on one of those and I'll hear the chime and come straight away."

"Thank you. Thank you, both," I said. "I really don't want to be any trouble. But a warm fire and some tea sounds wonderful." The two servants nodded and exited by unusual means. They walked to the corner of the room and opened a section of the wall. A secret door. I desperately wanted to investigate the other fireplace and see if it had a matching door. I felt like I was in an adventure novel. There were no obvious means into the rest of the house otherwise on the ground floor, as all the visible doors were on the landing upstairs. I walked over to the bookshelves, thinking of how much Dottie would love the place, and wishing she was there with me. In time she could be, of course. If things worked out. We'd insist Cook make that breakfast dish for us. She'd get to eat the potatoes instead of peeling them. Now, however, with nothing but the crackling of the fire and a distant whistle of wind through trees, I understood why Vanguard would have found the place lonely as a boy. I was surprised a place could be so full of things and feel so empty.

8

I was groggy as my eyes fluttered open, an unpleasant film on my tongue. I took in the warmth of the fire. The many books on the walls. A throw placed over me. Then the pieces fell into place. I'd selected an intriguing book, bound in green leather, called *Three Feathers* by a writer named William Black that featured an illustration of a forlorn man walking along a beach with the sun behind him. I drank the tea Ms. Coghlan gave me and read a good chunk of it before succumbing to the warmth of the fire. Someone must have placed the throw on me.

"Chaput! Chaput, is he—oh," said Vanguard, somewhere behind me. I heard the patter of heavy rain, and the quick and determined clap of boot on stone.

"Mr. Vanguard?" I asked, turning to face the man coming toward me. Vanguard's face was creased with worry.

"Tomas, I'm so sorry to have kept you waiting this whole time." Vanguard knelt beside the settee so that he was eye to eye with me. "Though you really must stop calling me Mr. Vanguard.

Call me Jackson, please." I nodded and, realizing I was still lounging, straightened up and willed myself more awake and more collected. How tired had I been?

"No need to apologize, Jackson. As you can see, I've made myself comfortable," I said. Vanguard smiled.

"Ah yes. I was intrigued by that one." Vanguard picked up the book splayed out in my lap, letting his thumb drag over my leg and linger just a moment. "I've been meaning to read it. For, well, a couple years now I suspect. My plan for retirement is to start at the highest shelf of this library and work through them all until that final bottom shelf."

"That sounds wonderful. What exactly is your business? If it's okay to ask?" Vanguard let out a snort.

"Why would it not be okay to ask that? Unless you thought my business might be something untoward?"

"Not at all!" My cheeks burned. "I'm just not sure if things are different in, uh, polite society."

"Another thing you must realize about me, Tomas. I am many things, but I am most definitely not a member of polite society. My society can be very impolite. But only to those who deserve it." Vanguard winked at me, and then stood up abruptly. "I had such a lovely dinner planned too. I selected the menu myself—all my favorites of Cook's recipes. It seems too late to bother with all of that. But you must be starving. I know I am. Let's see what we can find to eat, and we'll talk more about my impolite business."

Vanguard reached out his hand. I took it, and found my hand immediately enveloped in Vanguard's strong, precise grip. I was almost embarrassed how much I thrilled at the other man's touch. But it was exquisite. His hands weren't cold which surprised me as he'd just come in from outside. His hands were

neither bony nor overly padded. The grip squeezed just enough
so that I could feel the pressure, but nowhere near painful.

"Sounds wonderful," I said, realizing I'd taken too long
to reply. Chaput, who was standing sentry in the corner, took
Vanguard's coat and hat. It was then that I realized that neither
of the man's outer garments were wet. The rainfall had been so
powerful, my own had become half-sodden in the quick sprint
from the carriage to the vestibule. I was distracted from my
thoughts as I followed Vanguard as he walked through the secret
door and into a short hallway beyond. "Secret doors?"

"My great-grandfather had a flair for the dramatic. Plus,
it helps direct guests to the more public rooms up the stairs."
Vanguard slowed his stride, perhaps realizing I was going slower
so I could take in the surroundings. I was trying to orient myself
as I went, but the house still felt maze-like. It was not long,
however, until Vanguard and I stepped into the familiar kitchen.
Cook was gone for the night as, unlike Chaput and Coghlan, he
didn't live on the premises. I never thought to ask why.

"Let me see." Vanguard rummaged through the pantry.
"Perhaps we can have a more informal feast."

"I'm happy to fix something for you, if you like," Ms.
Coghlan said, emerging into the kitchen.

"No thank you." Vanguard pulled out a small wedge of
cheese and a sealed jar made of dark glass. "Get some rest.
That's an order." The housekeeper smiled. She looked exhausted.

"All right then. You boys have a good night." Coghlan
headed down the hall and toward the back staircase. Vanguard
found a few plates, half a crust of bread Cook had made that
morning, and a couple apples.

"This is more like a midnight picnic than dinner," Vanguard
lamented as he placed slices of cheese and apples on my plate.

"Looks good to me." I hadn't felt that hungry until some food had been placed in front of me. Now I felt ravenous. "What's in the jar?" I'd been eyeing the ovoid shapes jammed into the jar since the moment Vanguard retrieved them. But the glass was such a dark amber I couldn't make out its contents.

"A treat. Direct from Greece." Vanguard opened the lid of the jar with a satisfying pop of released air. "Stuffed grape leaves. I became obsessed on a trip there, and have a shipment sent over now and again."

"That must be incredibly expensive," Tomas said, eyeing the gloopy things Vanguard retrieved from the jar. They were brownish green in color, resembling a worm with veins running along them. They were not exactly what I'd call appetizing.

"Not really, I'm on good terms with the man who owns the shipping company."

"Who's that?" I took an experimental bite.

"Me." Vanguard winked. "And now you know what I do. Well, what every Vanguard has done for the last couple hundred years or so."

"Do you get to travel to all these places?"

"Sadly, not all of them. But I have been to quite a few. What do you think? Of the grape leaves, I mean."

"It's definitely not like anything I've had before," I said diplomatically, which only made Vanguard laugh.

"I appreciate your tact. But please don't finish it if you don't like it." Grateful for the reprieve and enjoying the curve of Vanguard's mouth as he grinned at me, I put the stuffed grape leaf down. "But this cheese is amazing."

"Also imported. That book you were reading was, as well. They produced some editions here, but without the author getting a dime. I imported a case of them for myself and a few collector friends." All of this could have sounded boastful, but Vanguard had a way of tossing his words away, as if he were talking about sweeping a floor. It felt like he was enjoying sharing it all with me. He poured me more wine, and we both drank deeply of it—it was by far the best I had ever tasted—and chatted about the books that we'd read. There were some overlaps, but not many, and I was boggled by how many books were on Vanguard's list. It seemed like he had to travel a lot for his work, so maybe that provided ample reading time. We talked in non-particulars about other subjects. Our favorite classes and studies. What sports we enjoyed playing or watching. It was intimate in its way, as we sank together into the warmth of the wine. But we both avoided anything too personal.

It was hours later—I couldn't recall the next morning how many—before we both felt groggy and floaty enough to suggest it was time to call it a night.

"You must stay," Vanguard said, his head lolled to the right.

"Oh, is the carriage driver gone?" I asked. Vanguard laughed a high, unguarded laugh.

"I meant you must stay because I am having too much fun. If I had money to bet with—I mean, I do, but I'm being metaphysical. I mean metaph—I'm not being literal. What I am attempting—quite poorly—to say is that I'm sure Ms. Coghlan has already prepared you a room. Just in case."

"Dottie and Mr. Blake, though—they'll be worried sick if I don't go back." I turned my head and stared at the house's kitchen entrance, just a short walk away from me past the pantry. The thought sobered me. But just a little.

"Nonsense, we can have word sent first thing tomorrow."

"Oh. Yes, I suppose that'd be okay. Makes sense." The wine made me surer of myself than I should have been. I did not think about how sending word first thing in the morning would be difficult if neither I nor Vanguard were awake to instruct anyone that it should be done.

"Where are you taking me?" Vanguard took my hand into his and guided me out of the kitchen. That exquisite, careful, and forceful pressure.

"To your quarters for the night."

"I am very sleepy." The upper lids of my eyes felt like two wet pieces of loose dough, forever glopping downward. We went down the hall and up the backstairs, and then past the study.

"Your study is so different than the rest of the house. What I've seen anyway."

"You noticed, did you?" Vanguard stopped moving forward. He walked the few steps back to the study and pushed its door open. He propped himself up on one arm against the doorframe. "I like to think of this as my little hideaway. The little part that's just me." I looked at the man, not really understanding, and saw a shadow fall over Vanguard's eyes like a curtain being lowered.

"Well, onward," Vanguard said, striding forth with new purpose. He didn't hold my hand anymore, and I hated how much I missed it. A vague thought shuffled through my mind, unable to stick on the alcohol-lubricated surface of my thoughts. This was all too quick. A few more doors down, and he opened the door to a gorgeous and spacious bedroom.

"This seems very large for a guest room, even for this house," I said, my drunkenness loosening my tongue. I slumped down onto the bed, amazed at how bouncy and fluffy it was. I started undoing and sliding off my boots. Even if it was too extravagant, I'd sleep in it. I fell backward, with only one boot off. On the bed now, it seemed like far too much effort.

"Well, there's a good reason for that," Vanguard said in the distance. Through the fog of the wine, I could sense his motion, but was laying back too far to see what he was doing and felt too good to bother getting up. "This is my room."

"Ah," I said, as I felt Vanguard take my foot in his hands and start removing my second boot. I liked the feel of the man's hand on my heel as he untied the boot's laces in a motion so quick and easy it felt like magic. It was then that the meaning of the words really hit me. "Oh." I sat up quickly, only to discover Vanguard standing before me, stepping out of his pants and kicking them to the side. *He's divested himself of all his clothes so quickly,* I thought, enjoying the word "divested" too much in my stupor. I giggled. Vanguard kissed my forehead, tender and soft. Time was passing strangely. Vanguard was next to me now, the heat of his body burning so near to me. Had I nodded off for a second? My nose and lips tingled, the taste of the wine still on my tongue. I took in the sight of the man. His arms were tightly muscled. What I could see of his torso, half hidden by his white button-up shirt, was less so but in a thoroughly pleasing way. There was just the barest suggestion of abdominals showing as he breathed in. Lines curved in his hips, traceable to his hardening member. It was thicker than any I'd ever seen, with one strong vein—so straight and purposeful it looked like some kind of supportive strut— jutting toward his proud and full head. Already, a glistening drop perched perilously at its tip. I felt my own strain against the front of my pants.

"Don't be scared, Tomas. It's only us here." Vanguard shifted forward so that our knees touched. He reached out his left hand and caressed my cheek and chin. My skin seemed to dance and spark under the pressure of the man's fingers on his skin. Was I scared? Why?

"I'm not new to this. I just thought—are there protocols for this?" I stumbled through the haze of my thoughts. They floated around me, disconnected, and jumbled, and I found it difficult to make them behave. Vanguard cupped my chin and raised my eyes toward his. His voice was thick and breathy.

"Like what? Courtship, Tomas? Whose approval should we curry? Both our parents are gone. We have no brothers or sisters. Should I worry about what Chaput, Ms. Coghlan, Gladys, or Cook think? They work for me." He let out an amused snort. Somewhere, in the back of my mind, I thought about how I had been just another servant days before. That I should be irritated by his bemusement. But I felt my hips buck instead, my need growing more persistent.

"Who's left? *Society*? They can't see in the windows up here on the bluff, can they? God? We're already damned in his sight, and I say damn him right back!" Vanguard's face reddened, and his muscles tightened as he spoke in a mixture of purpose and belief. He blazed with passion, and it only made me throb harder. He caught himself then, looked chagrined, and shook off his mood with a wry smile. When he continued, it was much quieter. "Here in Shearhaven *I* make the rules. Now you can, too. We can make the rules together."

"I would—" I began, but Vanguard smothered my words with an insistent kiss. I returned it eagerly craning my head upward so that we could be closer. This was the reaction he'd wanted, clearly, as his soft full lips parted mine and he was fully upon me. He grabbed my pants by the waist and tugged. I bucked my hips upward, and he pulled harder, freeing me from my pants and undergarment at the same time, dragging my dick with it at first before it was freed and slapped backward and smacked my stomach. Our hands searched frantically for the motion and grip that felt right. Vanguard's was too hungry and almost painful at first as he gripped my shaft. Mine was too weak. My hands felt like slabs of ice on the man's molten tool which was now slick with his leaking.

We found the pressure and rhythm before too long, and upon finding it, we squeezed into each other, sending exquisite pulses of pleasure where skin met skin. The man's eager lips were insistent, and his tongue was exploratory, which surprised me. I'd never kissed anyone like that. The salesmen and the other brief fumblings I'd experienced had never been like this. With him, kisses, if they came at all, were perfunctory. With Vanguard, our tongues caressed and sucked each other, our movements small echoes of what our bodies were doing. I was frightened by the greediness of it. The way Vanguard would pull on my tongue in a way that almost hurt. His weight on me. The hardness of his muscles as they flexed and writhed. But the fear and pain only seemed to fuel my excitement.

Something slipped and then clicked in my mind. Fear turned to need. A realization or an urge I still can't make sense of seized me. I pushed Vanguard off to my left and then rolled myself on top of the man. Now I was the insistent one. I ran my hand over his stomach, felt the tightness there. I wanted to see more. I ran my hand up to the buttoned seam of his shirt, and with one forceful movement upward ripped his shirt open to the sound of snapping thread and scattering buttons. Spasms of delight ran through Vanguard. I felt them in the subtle movements of Vanguard's hardness sliding between my ass cheeks. I looked into the man's eyes as I guided myself down onto it. Vanguard's eyes were wolfish and locked onto mine. He watched me as though he were seeing me for the first time. We didn't break the gaze as I lifted myself up and then guided myself downward.

I saw myself in Vanguard's eyes—sweaty and red, blonde

hair already stuck to my forehead—an animal lost to the primal instinct to rut. This thought pushed me past some unseen and heretofore unknown edge. I became more violent in my need. It wasn't just the sensation—in truth, it was a little painful as it was the thickest I'd ever taken. But the look in Vanguard's eyes was only half the motivation for this newfound fervor. He wanted me, and he wanted all of this from me. But it wasn't the one-sided hunger that Lee, the salesman, had. Vanguard was eager to give, as well. And I relished in the receiving.

9

I would have stayed there, in folds of Vanguard's bed, if weren't for my stomach. Our dinner was hardly filling, and I'd been too nervous to eat much. I found the heat of the blankets stifling. I wasn't used to such luxurious and thick bedding. But the cool air, as much as a relief as it was, only served to awaken me more, making the grumbling in my stomach harder to ignore. With grit teeth and a whispered grumble at my own hunger, I slipped from the covers and crept to the door. As old as the house was, I was happy with how hearty the wood underfoot seemed to be. I'd been in houses far newer that creaked with every step. I cracked open the door and stopped, looking at Vanguard's beautiful face, half lit from the faint light seeping through. I thought of the way he felt in me, the soreness of where he'd entered me was painfully pleasurable. Like pressing on a bruise.

I tried to remember the path back to the kitchen, fearful of what would happen if I got lost. I thought the house could easily become a maze. Thankfully, even in my lust-filled stupor on the way up to Vanguard's room, I'd taken in enough details to find my way. I was surprised to find the kitchen occupied, a soft glow emanating from the stove.

"Hello," I said softly. The woman in the kitchen still jumped.

"Oh! Sir!" Gladys said over the rattle of a spoon in the bowl before her. She'd knocked her knees on the underside of the table trying to get up.

"I'm so sorry. No need to get up." Gladys watched me with careful eyes, the left one betraying the slightest wince of pain, before settling back down in her seat. "I just got hungry. I was hoping to find something."

"Oh, I've got just the thing," she said, pointing down to her bowl. She smiled toothily, revealing straight little teeth yellowed on the edges. Her smile was sweet and disarming, and before I could protest, she was up and ladling something steamy and warm from a pot on the stove. She sat it before me along with a spoon and got back to her own bowl.

"Thank you. This smells wonderful," I said. It did. It smelled like roast vegetables, beef, and rosemary.

"Cook stores a bit of leftovers for me in a little hidden cubby outside near the stables when it's cold."

"Just what I needed." I savored the warmth of it and had to stop myself from gulping it down.

"Me too. I was about to drop, to be honest. Ms. Coghlan doesn't like when I don't eat all day. Says I need my strength for the work. But she doesn't like when things aren't done just so and on time. So's it's a choice I gotta make." Gladys's eyes widened, perhaps feeling she'd been too open, hastily adding: "Ms. Coghlan is very good to me. So is Master Vanguard. I'm learning a lot."

"How long have you worked here?" I was genuinely

interested. But I also thought it might be an opportunity to get some information on the man upstairs.

"Just a few months. I was surprised when I heard there was a posting. I was looking for work without much success. Most take a look at me and think I'm gonna snap in two I suppose. But I'm tougher than I look." She winked at me. I was trying to reconcile this smiling chatterbox with the haunted, mute waif I'd seen sweeping earlier.

"I saw flyers posted. It caused a little stir. The lady what rents our apartment to me and my mom said it was queer as could be, the great manse on the bluff hiring. She said I should go for it, what was the harm? Of course, she has an interest in making sure her rent is paid. But I figured it was worth a try. No one was as surprised as I when I was hired on."

"Long hours?" I asked. The woman studied me again as she worked on her last spoonful of stew.

"They hiring you on too?"

"No. That's not—I'm here as a guest."

"I see." Gladys's smile didn't falter, but there was a hardness in her eyes. I could feel the wall go up. "Well, the hours are long. But I wouldn't complain. The pay is very good. And I don't mind hard work." There was a defensiveness to her now that confused me, at first. Then I realized that she felt a little betrayed. She must have thought I'd been working somewhere else in the house. I was wearing the clothes I came here with, as I had no bedclothes and certainly hadn't planned to sleep over. I was certain I wasn't going to hear the truth now.

"Thanks for the soup," I ventured, hoping I might get us back to our amiable chatter. Instead, Gladys got up.

"Well, you'll excuse me, Sir. I've got a long walk home. Take more if you like and don't worry about cleaning up. Cook'll do that first thing in the morning."

"Thank you, but I think I've had enough." I looked down at my empty bowl. I could probably have three more bowlfuls, honestly. But it felt like Gladys was keeping something from me. I had no clue what and why, but it intrigued me. I didn't know if we'd have a chance to chat like this again. Then inspiration struck. "Why don't you wait a moment? I can retrieve my jacket. I was thinking of going for a walk. Just to clear my head. I could walk you to the edge of the woods."

Gladys sat her bowl on the counter near the wash basin, and there was fear in her wet saucer eyes.

"Don't do that. Go for a walk, I mean. Not with a night as thick as this. And no need to be a gentleman and escort me. I know my way well. No problem for me getting home. But you're liable to walk straight off the bluff. The edge can come quick in some places. And Mr. De Artte might be out there. He's known to do that in the wee hours of the morning."

"Mr. De Artte?"

"Yeah, he hunts the woods. Ain't no one told you? Warned you about him?"

"I guess there wasn't any reason to."

"Keeps to himself. I haven't even seen him, to be honest. But I was warned first thing by Ms. Coghlan. Don't wander the woods, because De Artte hunts out there," Gladys nearly whispered it, as if saying Coghlan's name might summon the head housekeeper.

"He hunts game for Vanguard?" I took my bowl over and stacked it on top of the other.

"I suppose. Though I can't say I've seen anything other than meat from the butcher's in the larder. Chaput once said De Artte came on before the current Mr. Vanguard took over the estate. In any case, you don't want to get yourself killed by an errant arrow or bullet."

"Well, thanks for the advice. Maybe I should just get back to bed and see if I can't sleep some," I said. I'd probably imposed more on Vanguard's hospitality than I should already, creeping into the kitchen like I did. I wondered at my own boldness, and Gladys's warning was a good reminder that I was in unfamiliar territory. The maid nodded, and watched as I left the kitchen.

I crept back into Vanguard's bedroom and was pleased to see he hadn't shifted an inch. His robustly muscled chest rose and fell softly with his breathing. I slipped in as delicately as I could into bed and under the covers. I thought about what it would be like to sleep in a bed like this, and in a house like this, every night. And I thought of Gladys, walking home alone. How long would she have to sleep before it was time to come right back here? Then I thought of Mr. De Artte, out in the woods before the sun had come up. Sleep took me much quicker than I thought it would, but it was still turbulent and troubled.

10

I awoke to dazzling light. Every detail of our rented carriage was rendered in full detail now. The chipped wood and the torn upholstery had been hidden in darkness at the port, but now I could see all its imperfections.

"Good timing," Vanguard said. I could feel the rumble of his voice, as I lay with my head nuzzled against his chest. The place I'd settled when I'd fallen asleep. I wiped the sleep from my eyes, looked out the window, and found myself staring at a dream ablaze with orange fire.

"This is Paris?" I asked. Not because I had any doubts as to where we were. It's just that no descriptions or illustrations had prepared me for the sight in person. We were in a great square, surrounded on all sides by elegant buildings that were six or seven stories high, all made of cream-colored stone, and capped by gray-green roofs. The buildings had a uniform appearance and seemed to stretch as far as the eye could see. On the corners were clusters of gas streetlamps whose ornate casings sparkled in lustrous bronze.

"The Place de l'Opéra to be exact," Vanguard said. His voice was warm and light, obviously taking pleasure in sharing the sight with me. "My apartment is nearby. In fact, why don't I have the driver drop us off here and we can walk the rest of the way? I could stretch my legs and you could use some air to wake you." I nodded. I could use the air and hoped it might crystalize the reality of it all. Vanguard surprised me with the trip, and I was grateful for it. Was I running away from Mr. Blake and Dottie's annoyance and suspicion? Yes. Although both had lessened a great deal since the fateful night I'd sent them into a frenzy by not coming home from Shearhaven. My announcement, a month later, that Vanguard had asked me to move in with him set off a new round, however. They meant well. Their fears came from a place of caring. I knew that. It doesn't mean I chafed at it any less.

Soon the two of us were walking together down the golden-lit streets. I was always nervous when we were in public, let alone in a completely different country with different laws and ways of thinking. Maddeningly, Vanguard always seemed at ease no matter where he was. A benefit of growing up with wealth, I suppose. One I hoped I'd learn eventually. Because a wave of joy was building inside me as we walked the street, taking in the city. It held a strange bouquet of smells—baking bread, coal smoke, coffee, an undercurrent of sewage, and a thousand other things my mind couldn't place. The elements mixed and balanced each other until it wasn't pleasant or unpleasant. Simply different. And that difference was enough to excite me. Still, I made sure to keep some distance from Vanguard, and tried to stifle any movement that might make it obvious we were a couple. As the men and women passed by us, nodding, giving us a friendly smile, or simply ignoring us altogether, I knew that I was being paranoid. But it didn't stop me worrying.

"Everything looks so new. Even the lampposts look clean enough to eat off," I whispered, as though the city itself might hear me.

"Some of it is. New, I mean. That building there, for instance, on the corner of rue du Quatre-Septembre was finished just last year. The French, like us, have been healing their wounds," said Vanguard. He stopped short and put a hand on my shoulder. "In fact, let me show you something." He grabbed my hand—causing me some alarm—and pulled me into a small alley. It only took a few steps for the bright sodium-orange lighting to feel very far away, as we plunged into darkness. Rats skittered away as we walked, and a mélange of unpleasant odors hit my nostrils, the delicate balance of that earlier bouquet broken. I wished we'd stayed on the main street, but Vanguard strode forward with purpose. We crossed another main road and then ducked back into another alley, until finally Vanguard stopped walking, and urged me to stand next to him.

"Here we go," Vanguard said. "What I wanted you to see." The sight held a different sort of awe than the glittering Paris I'd awoken to. A terrible awe. It seemed incomprehensible, but we were just blocks away from where the carriage let us out, and I was staring into a gaping pit surrounded by rubble. The surrounding blocks looked restored and cleaned. But this one building was an utter ruin.

"The war?" I asked.

"Yes. Well, war and revolt. And then, a neglectful landowner."

"That's terrible. The rest of the city seems to have tried so hard to rebuild, and then someone just lets this hole sit here."

"That's certainly the viewpoint of the Parisian and French governments." Vanguard smiled wryly, and I winced as I made a terrible realization.

"You're the landowner?"

"Guilty as charged, I'm afraid," Vanguard said, raising his hands in surrender.

"But why?"

"I've been trying to figure out what to rebuild here. Should I recreate it in the image of what came before? It was an elegant building. A hotel, in fact. My father purchased it after an exceptionally fantastic stay here twenty years ago. He said he'd never had such amazing service and wanted to make sure it stayed that way. Thus, he bought it." There was something in the man's tone that struck me as strange. It was wistful—almost regretful—but also full of pride.

"That seems like a worthy thing to rebuild, then," I offered.

"Perhaps. But Paris has so many hotels. I don't know, it seemed sort of boring. The government has been badgering me for years about it. And I do feel guilty. But if I was going to go through all the effort and expense of building something new here, I wanted it to be special. I suppose that put my wishes and the government's wishes at cross purposes." Vanguard stepped out of the alley and into the street, the bright streetlamps making deep shadowed pools of his eyes. "Plus, the manager—*Monsieur* Fournier was his name—was the real secret to the hotel's success. And he died in the shelling, along with four other staff members and ten guests."

"I'm sorry," I said, coming up close behind Vanguard, and resisting the urge to hug the man. Vanguard blinked, as if from some secret reverie.

"Worrying over the past isn't why I brought you here. I was

going to save it for later, but it felt right to show you this now."

"Why?"

"Well, you were dazzled by the Parisian lights. As you should be. But I wanted you to see some of the grit, too. Some of the old wounds. All things you should take into careful consideration for your decision."

"Decision? Maybe I'm groggy from the nap, still, but this is all going over my head," I said, letting some frustration creep into my voice. Vanguard just smiled at me mischievously.

"Because I want you to figure out what should go here. Work with the architects. Bring it to life."

"What? I-I don't—" I couldn't believe what I was hearing. It made no sense.

"You don't have to know anything about architecture or business or whatever you're about to bring up. You'll have a team to help you make decisions and guide you. But you'll be in charge. If you'd like to, that is? I want this to be a fun project, not a chore."

"No, I mean—I can't say I've ever even considered this as something *anyone* did. Let alone wanted to do it myself."

"The world is a big place. Full of strange and wonderous things, Tomas. Possibilities you never imagined. Opportunities beyond whatever dreams you might have conjured drifting to sleep at night in Gillsborough, Illinois. The only question that faces any of us who have the privilege to travel it is this—will we seize the opportunity when it's right before us?"

"I will." I was surprised at the certainty in my own voice. I wanted this. I thrilled at this. It was ludicrous and amazing. I would have it. A pleased smile turned Vanguard's lips.

"I knew you would."

"But I still don't understand why."

"Because I love you," Vanguard whispered, before resuming his normal volume. "And because I want you to start thinking bigger. You've spent your whole life in a tiny town, Tomas. That doesn't matter in the end, but it can tend to limit the boundaries of the imagination. I want to expand those boundaries within you." Vanguard looked from side to side, and seeing no one, pulled me back into the shadows of the alley. He pushed my back against the alley wall, so that I could still see the ruin.

"I do have dreams," I whispered as Vanguard pressed against me and kissed my neck. He traced my neck, then my jawline, with his kisses. Until he reached my ear, flicked out his tongue, and sent a wave of desire through me that nearly brought me to my knees. As he tongued and gently bit, I goggled over the fact that no one had mentioned how intimate and amazing this might feel.

"I know, that's what I love when I look in your eyes. I see something of myself in them. That hungry look." Vanguard slid his hand down the front of my pants until he found the fleshy root he was looking for. My cock was half-hard anyway, and it sprung to fullness in moments as Vanguard rhythmically stroked it. He already knew the pressure and motion that most thrilled me. I pressed the back of my head against the rough brick of the alley. Even the odor seemed a little sweeter as Vanguard pleasured me. More of the baking bread. The coffee. The crisp air. The scent of sweat. The musk of sex. The thrill of being here, just barely out of view of the passersby sent waves of fear and excitement through me that comingled with Vanguard's physical efforts and sent my eyes rolling backward.

"Jackson— not sure—we should—" I stammered as best I could through waves of pleasure, my thoughts dashed upon the rocks as I felt the familiar pull. The stretching ache of desire that wanted nothing but release.

"I think we should do anything we want, Tomas," Vanguard hissed throatily. "That's exactly my point. A gendarme could see us, arrest us, and I'd have us out in an hour. There's a reason no one has done more than pester me about the building." The words seemed far away from me now as I shifted my efforts to trying to keep my moans bottled. "I saw the hunger in your eyes, Tomas. The need. The belief that you were destined for more than sweeping up flour."

"Ngggh," was all I managed to get out as my precum coated the inside of Vanguard's hands and the man began working faster and more fervently on me, the rough feel of my pants adding to the pleasure as my dick was manipulated in their confines. Vanguard's forehead was pressed against the stone wall, and he whispered into my ear as though he were reciting a prayer.

"You're like me. You want to leave your mark, Tomas. You want to mean something. Anything. To prove to everyone that you're more than where you started. This is your first chance. A new building in the middle of one of the world's greatest cities. My gift, Tomas. And, perhaps, my lesson." Vanguard's words burned into me even though my conscious mind was lost elsewhere. I don't know if I responded. All I remember was needing him to squeeze just a little harder. To bite my earlobe just a little harder. I wanted everything just the way it was, but just a little more. My need felt colossal. I shuddered as I released—Vanguard's steady, forceful strokes unrelenting until I could take no more, utterly spent of every drop, and pushed him away. I heaved great breathes of air, my legs feeling shaky, and watched Vanguard lean against the other side of the alley. He licked the wetness from one of his fingers, like a cat savoring its cream. There was a look in his eyes that I couldn't quite read.

Satisfaction would have made sense. But it almost looked like triumph? Or something even stranger that Vanguard expertly hid behind the intensity of his gaze. There was darkness in that gaze. A darkness that I knew called out to the same darkness within me. It scared, repulsed, and excited me all in the same measure.

11

I sat back on the chaise, and rested my head against the back of it, listening to the rain fall in heavy pelts against the roof of Shearhaven. I'd taken over this attic room a few months after moving in. The same room Chaput had retrieved the ugly green statue for me to clean and wrap for Lady Acton. Over half a year or half a lifetime ago, I was surprised that both could feel much the same. My studied existence, measured by a routine of getting up, working at the shop, cleaning up after dinner, whispering with Dottie into the late hours of the night, sleeping, and then waking to do it all over again had been replaced. It'd been replaced by a life without routine, without the need for me to do anything at all.

The window looked out toward the Mississippi, and I liked the view when I was up here painting. That was something new I'd taken up now that I had the means and the time to pick up a hobby. I wasn't very good at it, but I enjoyed it. And Vanguard seemed to enjoy them a great deal, even hanging a couple of them up in his study. He'd purchased me an expensive set of oils from overseas. I spent several days with the oils, trying to capture the way the light sparkled on the vast expanse of the river. The results had been blocky and unconvincing. I couldn't capture the transparency of the water and reflection of the sun the way they mixed in real life. A knock on the door woke me from my reverie.

"Dottie's here, love," Vanguard called through the door.

"Thank you!" I flung the door open, and found Vanguard waiting for me, standing at an angle with one hand on his hip, the other supporting the side of his head with his elbow propped against the door frame.

"Getting a little painting in before the visit?"

"No, I tried listening to the rain to try to calm my nerves." I stopped at the mirror in the hallway, an ancient thing that was warped at the edges and had faint amber lines scored through it. I adjusted my ascot, trying to achieve the right balance of jaunty and carefree but also ordered. Vanguard came up behind me, pulled the ascot out a bit to give it more volume, and looked at me in the mirror.

"It'll be fine. It'll be more than fine. It'll be fun. Dottie's always fun." Vanguard gave me a peck on the cheek. I suppressed a giggle, both at the contact itself and the casual ease of it all. Here, atop this bluff above Alton, above the river—above everything—we were ensconced in the walls of Shearhaven. Walls that held our love just for us, away from the judgments of the world. This gift, more precious than I could have ever realized, still made me giddy. Even more so since those same walls had felt so strange and forbidding before. I kissed him back, on the lips. We held there a moment, before I pulled myself away. Dottie was here.

"It's been so long since I've seen her. We've barely exchanged a word." I walked side by side with Vanguard down the back stairs. Vanguard didn't say anything else, perhaps thinking it best to let me sit with my own thoughts. Which was for the best. It'd been nine months since I'd moved into Shearhaven. A lot had changed. For me, it'd been a dream. For the people that mattered the most to me, though, it'd been a far different story.

Halfway down the stairs, Vanguard let out a small grunt.

"What's wrong?" I asked.

"Nothing much. Just this pain in my lower back. I must have strained it again. It'll be fine." I nodded, knowing Vanguard hated talking about it, as if ignoring the pain lessened it. But the man was waking up with this pain more and more frequently.

As we came to the bottom of the stairs, Chaput approached us. Directly behind him was Dottie, dressed in a simple, but beautiful, emerald dress embellished lightly in gold. Her hair was shinier and straighter than I had ever seen it, and she was wearing a light dusting of powder and makeup. It was disorienting. Almost as disorienting as seeing the man by her side. He was shorter that she was by at least four inches, with wavy auburn hair, golden-brown eyes, and a thick beard.

"Mr. and Mrs. Bellwether are here, Sirs," Chaput said, nodding toward Dottie and the man.

"It's great to finally meet you," Grant Bellwether said, shaking our hands in turn with great fervor. "Feels like I can finally put some of the puzzle pieces in place when it comes to my blushing bride." Grant grabbed Dottie around the waist and looked into her eyes with a mixture of admiration, pride, and love. *The poor fool*, I thought. Dottie put her hand up to her heart, tilted her head, and returned the man's gaze. She was doing a fantastic job of it, but I knew her too well to not see right through it.

"We're so sorry we couldn't be there for the wedding," I

blurted out, wanting to shoo the elephant from the room as quickly as possible. Dottie's eyes crinkled slightly, although she maintained her mask of a smile.

"My fault, I'm afraid," Vanguard said. "I was so excited to show Tomas some of my favorite places. I should have known we were cutting it too close getting back." Dottie opened her mouth to speak, but Bellwether got there faster.

"Nonsense, we'd all be so lucky to have a mentor like you, Mr. Vanguard. I mean that. My father and I are huge admirers."

"And we enjoyed your present," Dottie said, finally getting the chance to speak. She practically bored holes into me. "Although really, it was too much." Bellwether laughed a quick, too-loud laugh, as if the statement was nonsense.

"The new carriage is splendid. We're thinking of painting the new name of the store on the side. Just to help spread the word," he said.

"New name?" My eyes darted between Dottie and Grant.

"Yes, my husband has all sorts of ideas—"

"Yes. You're going to love them. My dad was so excited he's going to be our first investor."

"Well, that sounds like a fine tale for dinner," Vanguard said quickly, no doubt reading the worry on my face.

Dottie and I sat across from each other at the large dining table, as did Vanguard and Bellwether. Those two seemed to be instant friends, Vanguard nodding with interest as Bellwether told them all about the plans to rename Blake's Mercantile & Sundry to Blake's Grocers.

"We're going to carry fresh food—meat, vegetables, and some fruits. They'll be right in the same store with everything else. And instead of ordering everything at a counter for someone to fetch, it'll be more self-serve," the man said. Dottie, for her part, worked silently at her soup in dainty sips, only occasionally nodding her head slightly when Bellwether looked to her for confirmation he'd gotten some small fact correct.

"Fascinating," Vanguard said. "I've only been the once, but it hardly seemed like there was room for all of that."

"Grant is going to use the funds from his father to expand it," Dottie said, finally jumping into the conversation. Now she seemed dead set on avoiding eye contact with me. "Out toward Pike Street to the south."

"But that's—" I couldn't finish the sentence. The only thing behind the shop was Mr. Blake's house. His former house, at least. The house Dottie and I had grown up in. Our house.

"Oh yes, the plan is to tear down the old house," Bellwether said excitedly, oblivious to the dangerous waters he was entering. "With you living here at Shearhaven, and Dottie living with me there's no reason not to use the property for something more useful. We could have sold it, but who knows who the store would get as neighbors. And I doubt anyone would want to buy the house anyway. It was so old-fashioned."

Neither Dottie nor I said anything, but our eyes locked together—a flickering of shared grief.

"Yes, well, here's to your exciting new venture. Both of you." Vanguard raised his glass. We all followed suit, although only Bellwether's had any enthusiasm behind it.

Vanguard, unlike Bellwether, was aware of the souring mood. "Ah, it seems the second course has come." Ms. Coghlan and Gladys entered the dining room. The housekeeper carried a large silver tray, covered with a matching cloche. Gladys had a white gravy boat, filled to the brim with a thick brown gravy. Coghlan said the name of the dish as she presented it to them, but I didn't hear her. I was too busy holding back tears and wishing Dottie and I could just get away and have a good talk. But that opportunity didn't happen until after two more hours of meaningless blather and strained facades of cheer.

"I'm going to show Dottie my studio," I said as the four of us sat in front of the fire and drank brandy.

"That sounds fantastic," Dottie said, practically shooting out of her seat.

"Of course, m'dear," Bellwether slurred, starting to make an effort to get up off the settee. He'd taken a liking to the wine being served with dinner and overindulged. Vanguard didn't seem to mind and kept looking at the man as one might look at a precocious pet. I pushed that thought away. I didn't like to think of Vanguard that way. Grant Bellwether was from one of the richest families in St. Louis, but that wealth was dwarfed by the Vanguard family fortune. There was always a bigger fish.

"I'm sure Grant and I can entertain each other while you two do that," Vanguard said. I gave him an appreciative nod. Bellwether seemed relieved he didn't have to move, settled back into the settee, and took an appreciative gulp of the golden liquid in his tumbler. Dottie and I walked wordlessly down the hall, up the back stairs, and to my studio.

"Well, here it—" I began once I closed the door.

"Oh, stow it, Tomas," Dottie said, shoving her way past me to the padded bench by the open window. She looked out toward the sheets of gray rain that obscured most of what lay beyond, except the gentle amber glows of the boats as they passed. "You know what really pisses me off about all of this?"

"Well, I—"

"That was a rhetorical question, Tomas, not an invitation to speak." Dottie sighed and seemed to deflate as she did so. Her shoulders sagged into her usual slouch. It might have been the strange lighting from the window, but she seemed older. "I just hate being the harpy. I hate being the woman you left behind. I hate that I have to come here and be annoyed and sad and angry inside but act like everything's all right because that's what my husband expects. And it's what you hope for, too."

"Now that's not true." I rushed over to the bench and sat on it, back to the window, and looked my friend in the eyes. "You think I didn't see all of that? You think it didn't break my heart to see it?"

"Oh, is that why you haven't seen me? Afraid of the heartbreak of sad, orphaned Dottie? Is that why you've barely exchanged two words with me since Dad's funeral? Why you didn't come to our wedding?"

"Dottie—" I wasn't very good at lying to Dottie, and I'd learned after so many years to not even try. But, not saying anything was basically an admission too. I just wasn't sure what I was supposed to say. The truth hurt too much, and I didn't like how I looked in it. "I know I've been a bad friend."

"Friend? You've been a poor acquaintance, never mind a friend." Dottie's voice cracked. She pushed off the bench, crossed her arms, and regarded the pile of canvases and loose sheets of paper that represented my total artistic output so far. "I hate this. I hate being all weepy in this ugly green dress."

"Well, quit crying and come over here," I patted the bench. Dottie looked at me, defiant, but only for a moment. A second later she was curled up next to me, feet folded under her, resting her head on my chest.

"You left. Dad left. I know neither of you did it to hurt me. You found someone. Someone I like, and he's rich too. And Dad… well, Dad didn't have any choice in the matter, did he? No more than most of us will. But it still all felt like it's happened to me. That I got the raw end of the deal."

"I should have been at the wedding. I really did plan to," I said, squeezing the arm around her in tighter.

"Then why the lie about being stuck in Europe?" Dottie asked, catching me off guard.

"We were a couple days late. I was exhausted. It's strange how exhausting travel can be." I stroked Dottie's hair. I was so used to my fingers catching in its tangles, I was surprised when they flowed right through the soft strands.

"But you were back in time," Dottie pressed.

"Yes. I was. The day before. But to be honest, Dot—I just couldn't do it. I couldn't sit there in a church and pretend you were off to be happy with him. Not when I knew it was a—well, it's a—"

"Marriage of convenience is the term they used to use, I believe," Dottie sat up, sloughing my arm from her shoulder. "Grant's not a bad guy. A little too caught up in himself and his ideas, sure. But as far as guys go, he's not bad."

"I just don't get why you married him. You could have sold the store. Gotten out of Gillsborough. Paris is as beautiful as we always imagined." I was going to say more, but Dottie turned toward me, and her eyes spat daggers.

"I'm sure it was lovely." She bolted up off the bench and toward an easel with my latest attempt at a landscape balanced upon it. She looked at it thoughtfully for a moment as I stayed silent. I decided I should wait for her to speak first.

"Dad spent most of his life getting that store up, running, and thriving," Dottie said quietly as she studied the painting. "I wasn't just going to hand it over to the Bellwether family. The first thing they'd have done was take the Blake name off it."

"So, you married him?"

"Two birds. One stone. People always talked about me, even when I was little. I've always been an odd duck. You know that better than most. With Dad gone, it was like the whole town sensed blood in the water and started circling. I can play their game if I must, Tomas."

"And your husband? Does he know it's a game?" Dottie lowered her eyes.

"No, he's completely in love," she said. "You know, the other day he said he liked how mannish I was." I laughed.

"Well, that's certainly... something."

"And he's not—well, like you. I did wonder. But he seems completely into women."

"Well, that's good for you both. It's good to have things in common," I said, sidling up next to Dottie to look at my latest work. She gave me a playful shove.

"Apparently Illinois is all out of attractive, wealthy women in power so I couldn't follow in your footsteps," Dottie said. An awkward moment passed between us. "This painting isn't very good." At this, we both started to laugh. Our old, easy laugh.

"I've really missed you," I said.

"Me too." Dottie moved back to the bench and settled in, some of the tension released between us. "I know my wedding would have been hard on you. But did you think how hard it was on *me*? I really could have used your help. Just being there would have been enough." I walked over and joined her on the bench once again. She settled back into the crook of my arm and laid her head back on my chest.

"I know. It's easy to lose your sense of reality here in this house. It's like a little world unto itself. And then when you're traveling, most of the time it's easy to leave everything you left behind in the background. Until the moments when it isn't, and it all hits you at once."

"Well, enough of my whining for the moment. How are you? How are you and Vanguard? He looked sort of gaunt. And almost like he had some powder on his face?" asked Dottie.

"He's not doing well," I whispered. I hadn't had the courage to discuss this with anyone else. Gladys was always friendly but kept me at a professional distance. Coghlan and Chaput would have been aghast at the impropriety of it. And, miserably, there was no one else to talk to. "There's a doctor who comes in the middle of the night when Vanguard thinks I'm asleep. I saw him one of the first few times I visited Shearhaven."

"The middle of the night?"

"If you have enough money, you can buy all sorts of discretion, I suppose. Do you remember that first night I came up here. Not for the delivery or to work as a server, but the first time for real?"

"Of course. It's hard to forget. You never came home, and I nearly pulled out all my hair with worry." Dottie poked me in the chest to make her point. I winced at the memory but decided to just keep going.

"Well, Coghlan and Chaput said he was away. But I saw the doctor leaving. When he finally came 'home' he was dry as could be despite the torrential downpour outside."

"So, he wasn't away?"

"I think he might have been upstairs recuperating. He'd begun to feel bad, but I was already on my way. He faked 'being away' until he was ready to come downstairs."

"Well, he certainly seemed to regain his strength, if I remember your account of that night correctly," Dottie said. I blushed.

"Well, yes."

"Call me old fashioned, but I think elaborate ruses should be saved for later in a relationship."

"I don't disagree. But, don't you see? It means he's been feeling poorly from the start. I found papers in his study, too. I didn't go digging for them. Though they weren't exactly in the open, either. They were his doctor's notes, left behind by accident. I couldn't make out most of the chicken scratches he calls writing and I don't think the notes were all there. But I saw enough words like 'mysterious' and 'resists treatments' to know it's something bad."

"That's horrible." Dottie sat up again and looked me in the eyes. "But, Tomas, why don't you just ask him?"

"Well, I don't want to appear too interested."

"Too interested in the health of the person you love?" Dottie was confused, and I didn't blame her. But that last word made me flinch, and she saw it. Did I love Vanguard? That was a hard question to answer. I cared for him very deeply and liked our life together. But the specter of money hung over everything. To the point that I wasn't sure if I could trust my own mind. Did I love Vanguard for who he was, or because of what he offered me? And did it really matter? Was what I was doing all that different from what Dottie was doing?

It wasn't just about the money. There were trust issues, too. Once I realized that the doctor had been there to visit Vanguard the night we met, I put the puzzle pieces together. If I'd known he'd been in poor health, I'd have understood. The elaborate performance for my benefit disturbed me. I couldn't be too critical of Vanguard wanting to make a good first impression—and it worked—but the whole deception left a bad taste in my mouth. The apparent ease of it, especially.

"It's not that simple. He's asked to adopt me."

"To what now?" If Dottie had started off confused, she was completely baffled at this point.

"Apparently, it's common with couples like us. It's the only way to legally secure the other person financially. As his heir, Shearhaven and all his assets would come to me." The words still sounded unreal, even though Vanguard had asked me days ago about it.

"That's incredible."

"That's why I haven't brought up his illness with him. I don't want to come off as too eager. I know it's nearly been a year since we first met, but the speed of things has felt sort of…"

"Aggressive? I thought so. But I was never sure if that was me being protective or possessive. So, I never said anything," Dottie said. I let out a quick snort of laughter.

"Oh, believe me, you made your doubts known."

"Well, be thankful I didn't say everything I *wanted* to say."

"Moving me in, suggesting this adoption—I'm just worried he's planning for the worst. I might not be sure I love him. But I'd miss him." I caught the look in Dottie's eyes, and we both went silent. The words had taken us both back, to someone else we both missed.

"He'd be proud of you," I said. "For continuing the business with the family name."

"Would he be? I keep telling myself that. I never got to tell him that I—well, I always thought when I met someone, I'd cross that bridge. Now I just feel like I cheated him of ever really knowing me. And I can only *guess* how he would have felt about it. What he would have said. Somehow that's worse than if I had told him and he reacted badly. Maybe. Of course, maybe I only think that because I didn't have to experience him being whatever way he would have been had he known."

"He always loved you just the way you were. I can't believe this would have been any different," I said, after a few moments of thought.

"That's the problem, though, isn't it? Would he have liked me doing all this pretending? Just for a name on a building? Or would he be disgusted with it? Because I am."

"There you two are," Bellwether said as he burst into the room, reeking of alcohol and sweet tobacco.

"Sorry, our friend Grant here was very insistent on seeing the studio," Vanguard said apologetically. He was looking very tired. Late nights used to be nothing to him. But I could see the strain in his face.

"I'd be jealous if you liked girls," Bellwether said as he tottered over toward the easel. I looked at Dottie in alarm. Had she told him? "Oh, don't look that way, Tommy my boy! I'm not an idiot. Even though my wife thinks I am. No, don't try to deny it, dear. You're very smart. I know that."

"Perhaps we could get Ms. Coghlan to make us a fresh pot of tea—" Vanguard started to say, once again trying to wrangle Bellwether in.

"No, no, let me get to the point. This is very impotent." Bellwether's eyes drifted as he tried to form words, even if some of them were the wrong ones. "I like being around people smarter than I am. It makes me feel safe. But I'm not stupid. Two men jaunting around the world together. Living together. Sure, the whole 'ward' thing is a decent cover, even if there's not more than a few years between you. But it wasn't difficult to deda.. duda...deduce."

"Right," Dottie said icily, her patience ended. "I think we'd better get you home, dear. Tomas and Vanguard have had a long day, I'm sure they'd like to get to bed soon anyway."

"I start speaking the truth and everyone wants to leave. Story of my life," Bellwether said as he swayed from side by side, looking at the painting I was currently working on. "This is actually very nice, Tommy. We should buy one of these."

"I'm sure that could be arranged." Vanguard gripped Bellwether's shoulders lightly and turned him toward the door. "Now, let's see what Ms. Coghlan can get for us. Maybe some coffee?" As they exited, Vanguard flashed me an amused look.

"Your fella is very nice," Dottie said after they were gone, although the way she said it almost made it into a question.

"He is. I'm glad they went away, though, as I did have a nefarious reason for bringing you up here." Dottie's eyebrow arched in interest. I walked over to the corner of the studio that housed my completed canvases, reached behind one, and produced a handsome wooden box.

"It's gorgeous," Dottie said as I handed it over.

"I hope you like the actual gift as much." I watched expectantly as Dottie lifted the lid. Dottie's eyes grew wider as she reached for what was inside. She picked it up and admired its beauty. It was an elegantly shaped tobacco pipe, with a large, oversized bowl that tapered upward and then into a curve at the lip. It was made of a light wood, stained, and varnished so that the finish was that of cinnamon clouds in a cocoa sky. Etched into the side in fanciful letters, and then inlaid in gold, were the initials D.B.

"I've never seen anything so beautiful," Dottie said, squeezing the object to her heart. "It's stunning."

"I bought you some intriguing tobacco, as well. I'll ship it all to you later, I just wanted to see your reaction."

"Thank you. I mean it. I'll treasure it forever. And, as you probably guessed, I haven't shared my hobby with my husband yet. So, the shipping is appreciated." Dottie looked down at the pipe in her hand and rubbed her finger against the etched initials, enjoying the contrast of the smooth wood and their edge.

"Glad your initials didn't change. I ordered this before I knew about you and Bellwether," I said. Dottie ignored this, and instead inspected the pipe's bit.

"This is so nice, I'm not even going to chew on it," Dottie said, the light air of her demeanor feeling increasingly forced. I placed my hand on hers. She looked up from the pipe in her hands, and my hand on hers.

"I didn't get you this so you'd stop chewing on the end of a pipe. I got it so you could chew it in style," I said. Dottie's eyes welled with tears. She flung her arms around me and pulled me in for a hug.

I stood beside Vanguard at the door of Shearhaven, waving goodbye to Dottie and her husband as their carriage disappeared into the dark of the woods.

"That went better than expected," I said finally. I'd shared my worries about seeing Dottie again, of course. And Vanguard had been a great support. Now he was strangely silent. I looked over and saw the man's eyes were unfocused. "Jackson?" Vanguard stumbled slightly, but I was there to support him and keep him standing. I yelled his name. My worry was quickly turning into pure fright. This brought both Chaput and Ms. Coghlan running toward the door to assist. We got him to one of the chairs in front of the nearest fireplace and Ms. Coghlan made him drink some peppermint tea.

"Please, this isn't necessary," Vanguard said, trying to wave the three of us away from hovering over him. "I've just been

pushing too hard. I've got a whole week to rest up. I'll be fine."
Chaput and Coghlan exchanged a look, and I dug my fingernails
into my palms. I was annoyed that they were keeping Vanguard's
obvious sickness from me. But I didn't want to admit that I knew
something was wrong, since it'd required a small amount of
snooping on my part.

"Of course, Sir," Chaput said finally. "Should I prepare the
guest room for you?"

"As long as Tomas doesn't mind," Vanguard said. "I know
it's not ideal. But I'd hate to keep you awake with all my tossing
and turning."

"That's never a problem." I lowered down on one knee and
grasped the man's hand. "I do miss you when you're not beside
me. But I understand. But let me sleep in the guest bedroom. You
take the bed in ours." Vanguard was about to protest, but I shut it
down with a look.

"Well, you heard the man." Vanguard smiled weakly.
"Prepare one of the guest bedrooms for him." I patted his hand,
grateful he hadn't put up more of a fight, but worrying about
how weak he seemed.

"Good. I'm going to get Dottie's presents ready for the post,
and then I'll be up to say goodnight after you've settled in." I got
up and exited the front hall through one of the hidden doors. Just
as the door was about to shut, I heard the murmur of whispers.
I stopped the door from closing all the way with my heel and
leaned over to see if I could hear things more clearly. I hated
being reduced to eavesdropping, but it's not as if Vanguard had
left me much choice, if I was going to get any truth about the
man's health.

"You're cutting it close, Sir. Too close," Coghlan said in a
whisper. Thankfully the acoustics were in my favor and I could

hear them now with relative ease.

"I don't want to rush things. I feel like I've already pushed things too fast," Vanguard said. He wasn't whispering, but his voice was so weak he might as well have been.

"Well, I think he's ready. You have the future of this place to think about. Your legacy," Chaput said.

"Do you think anyone understands that more than I do?" Vanguard said, with more venom than I would have expected him to be able to muster.

"Of… of course not, Sir. My apologies," Chaput said. I heard the butler's footsteps as they started away from Vanguard and thought I shouldn't push my luck. I walked briskly down the hall. I would accept Vanguard's generous offer of adoption. I still felt strange about it, but what choice did we have, legally? And obviously it was important to Vanguard. He wanted me to have Shearhaven. And the thought of going back to my old life terrified me more than anything.

12

I couldn't sleep. I was in the most comfortable bed I'd ever been in, but no amount of tossing and turning—blanket off, blanket on, blanket off again—would help. I was still thinking about how unwell Vanguard was looking. I'd been able to tell myself the man wasn't that bad. His decline was slow, and he went for long stretches without showing any outward signs of illness. And, truthfully, I didn't want to think about Vanguard being sick. The man had picked me—literally from a roomful of handsome men—to be his… mate? That was another complication. I wasn't sure I could say what exactly we were to each other.

Lover, certainly. Beau felt strangely childish for what we had. Most other words seemed too serious. Or, when the darkest thoughts took over, I pushed ugly words like "consort" away. Whatever we were to each other, I cared for him. And I liked being cared for. The thought the universe would take that away from me so soon after finding it seemed cruel. Sometimes,

I wondered if this wasn't God's way of punishing me. My parents weren't particularly religious. But I attended church with Mr. Blake and Dottie like good citizens were expected to in Gillsborough. Could this be some payback for the terrible sin Vanguard and I committed? I pushed that away, too. Dottie and I made a pact, long ago when we revealed our truths to each other, that we weren't going to let the world bog us down with their often-hypocritical ideals. Still, no amount of reasoning kept the question—a whisper from some hateful space within myself— from slipping in time to time.

Dottie was the one that broke through the illusion that I'd crafted. The illusion that, perhaps, Vanguard was just having a bad spell and it would get better. She'd seen how awful he looked. And, as if on cue, he nearly fainted after she left. A physical weakness I hadn't seen before. I was broken out of this tortured reverie by the sound of voices in the hall. This was a strange occurrence, indeed, as Shearhaven tended to be unnaturally quiet at night—to the point that I'd found it unnerving my first week there. There were the usual shifting and settling sounds any old house experiences, and the whistle of the wind through the trees on occasion. Still, there were so few permanent residents in such a big house, that at times it felt like the only presence in the house was the house itself. When Vanguard was off busy with work, I had begun to assign its various groans, rattles, and creaks with emotions. Tonight, the house seemed positively indifferent.

I threw off my covers and got up slowly, feet searching for my slippers. I put my housecoat on, tied it off, and then crept to the door. I'd been doing a lot of creeping about lately. A bad habit, to be sure, but I felt a little justified considering the secrets Vanguard was keeping, even if the man's intentions were noble.

"Sir, I must really insist you return to bed." The voice

belonged to Chaput. He was speaking in whispers but sounded almost frantic.

"I think you might be forgetting who is employing whom," Vanguard retorted harshly.

"I would not forget, Sir. And I know I may be out of line. But the treatments aren't working. If you—"

"That is why I am up!" Vanguard hissed. "If the doctor's science is going to let me down, then I must rely on my own." I took a careful step forward, trying to adjust my ear closer to the gap between my bedroom door and its frame, which sent a loud creak reverberating into the silent hall. I stared at the floorboard, annoyed at the house's betrayal. Thankfully neither man seemed to have noticed.

"Now enough of this," Vanguard said, more controlled and quieter. "You'll wake Tomas. I'll be okay, old friend. I'm close. I know I am." I didn't hear the butler reply, but I heard the footfalls as both men walked on. I waited a few moments, took the unlit oil lamp near my bedside, and walked as silently as I could past Vanguard's empty bedroom and its ajar door. Our bedroom—not Vanguard's, I reminded myself. I felt a sudden surge of guilt. Was there a part of me, a vile part, that was excited about being able to put my own stamp on Shearhaven? I'd miss Vanguard, of course, but in some ways I barely knew the man too. It'd been hard to think of this bedroom as ours anyway. We stayed in it together most nights when we were at Shearhaven, except when Vanguard's old back injury started acting up. But most of the last nine months had been a blur of travel. I'd not done much of anything to make the bedroom my own. Maybe, one day soon, that'd change drastically.

My slippers provided an advantage over the other men's shoes. Those made a steady clap against the smooth floors whereas mine barely made a sound. Most of the lamps in the halls were off, but there were enough still lit that I was able to make my way. Which was fortunate, as I didn't want to light the one I'd brought with me unless absolutely necessary. I was about to turn a corner when I realized the footfalls had stopped. I skidded to a halt, cursing myself to be more careful.

"Well, I'll be off to bed then, Sir, if there's nothing else you need. And if you're certain I can't convince you to go to sleep yourself," Chaput said.

"Thank you, old friend. Sincerely. I know you mean well. But you know what this means for me. The chance I have," Vanguard said. His voice sounded ragged and distant, which scared me. It was like the youth and vitality were utterly drained from it.

"And if it doesn't work?"

"Then I'm dead. But I choose—no, I must believe it will work. I must."

I chanced a quick look around the corner. Vanguard had one hand on his butler's shoulder. Chaput had been Gabriel Vanguard's butler before his death and Jackson's ascension to master of the house. I'd sensed a bond between the two men, although it was never expressed as plainly as this in front of me before. Vanguard was hunched, almost as if he was using Chaput to keep himself upright. I wanted to run to him, to carry him to wherever he was going. To help him with whatever secret project he had going on. The tantalizing prospect of being the new master of Shearhaven dissolved as I watched the man. His intense eyes, his full lips, and his hair—premature streaks of silver just starting to emerge within it—reminded me that I *did* know this man. Just as Vanguard knew me in ways that not even Dottie would understand.

13

I followed Vanguard up the stairs to the attic, the pace of my heartbeat quickening with each step. I felt the thrum and vibration through the wood and wasn't surprised when I saw him slip into the room with the mysterious warning sign on the door. Somehow, I'd known whatever was in that room was a part of it all. I had no idea how, but it made sense the two mysteries of Shearhaven that had occupied my thoughts were connected. Now I wanted to find out the answers with a desperation verging on need. If there was a chance to save Vanguard I wanted to be a part of it. I wanted to help. Except, he kept shutting me out with little white lies and elaborate ruses. I still felt like a guest in the house—a bad guest who was constantly snooping around—and I can't say Vanguard's deception helped allay that feeling.

I walked softly across the hall, past the crackling and buzzing behind the door, to my studio. I kept the door open just a crack and watched and waited. I had no plan. Standing in this room I thought about all the time I'd spent in here, dipping brushes into watercolors and oils and imagining I might be good at something just because I wanted to be. And Vanguard, all this time he'd been—what? Wasting away? Fighting some mystery illness?

After an hour, Vanguard finally emerged from the room. Strange light—cold and erratic—spilled from behind him, casting his form as a parade of shifting shadows onto the other side of the hall. And the sound! It was as if a swarm of bees had filled a cathedral, their drone multiplied a thousand-fold. The master of Shearhaven was slumped over, looking as though he could barely stand. My first instinct was to run to him and assist, but I held myself back. That course of action would mean too many explanations. I could say I couldn't sleep and decided to get some painting done, I suppose. Except, I didn't trust I could lie that well. And if he bothered to come into the room, he'd see my paints were all tightly lidded and no canvas sat on my easel.

And what exactly was I accomplishing here? From this vantage point, all I could see was flickering white light coming from the cracked open door. Why hadn't I been more direct? I should have just walked right into the room and demanded answers from Vanguard. What sort of relationship was built on secrets? I was pondering this as I watched, when I got extremely lucky. Vanguard, apparently too exhausted to think clearly, barely closed the door and stumbled down the hallway without locking it. A frantic, buzzing excitement filled me as Vanguard continued down the hallway. The man might realize his mistake and double back. I knew I should wait and see if that happened—hell, if I were a decent human being, I'd run to him and help him—but I feared missing this chance to understand what was going on here. Wouldn't that, in the end, be even more helpful? I clung to this notion, however morally flimsy, while I watched him turn the corner. As I heard his steps descending the stairs, I bolted toward the door.

As I opened the door, a waft of metallic-tasting air overwhelmed my senses. I felt as though I could taste and smell it simultaneously. I looked inside, shuddered, and walked a few fearful steps backward and into the hall. Inside was a machine. A machine unlike any I'd ever dreamt of, let alone seen. Two seats, fashioned out of metal, sat across from one another. Large metal rods were attached to the back of each chair. And between these rods, a great white arc of electricity blazed back and forth. The only thing I'd seen like it was the wild electric snap of the telegraph. But comparing this mammoth bolt to that was like comparing the Mississippi to a drainage ditch.

Beyond the wild thrashing of the electricity, I could only capture brief, kaleidoscopic impressions of the rest of the room. There was a large metal drum—taller than me and three times as wide, in one corner. Thick cables snaked along the floor. Mechanical drawings were nailed to the far wall, though I couldn't see them clearly in the painful brilliance. My eyes darted from one thing to the next, willing my brain to make sense of it all, when a stern voice called out from behind me.

"Master Doyle," Chaput said with equal parts incredulousness and anger. My head snapped around. I couldn't keep the look of guilt off my face.

"Chaput. Sorry, I was just up and—"

"And nosing around in Master Vanguard's private efforts," Chaput said as he swiftly crossed the distance between us, closed the door, and locked it tight. I glanced down at Chaput's key. It was silver, and on a ring with a skeleton key that matched the one I'd been given. A "skeleton key" that opened every door in the house except this one.

"I was going to get some painting done," I said, adding some force and indignity to my voice. I thought back to that evening in Paris. The sense of power Vanguard had tried to instill in me. Chaput was, after all, nearly as much my employee as Vanguard's at this point. "And I saw this door was ajar. I was about to close it—and to seek out why it hadn't been properly secured—when you came along."

"I see, *monsieur,*" Chaput said with a wide smile that was reflected nowhere else on his face or in his manner. He had even peppered in a French word, which I was starting to think was a tell. That what the butler was saying or how he was acting wasn't entirely truthful. "Never fear, then. I always make sure this door is secure. Even when the master cannot."

"Well. Very good. That sort of dangerous equipment. I'd hate for Gladys to end up in there," I said. I definitely wasn't a very good liar. I didn't think Chaput believed me. But this game we were playing—I thought I could be good at this game. The game where Chaput had to go along with whatever I said because Vanguard paid the bills. Yes, I could play the game if it might help me get some answers. "I've heard terrible stories about people getting electrocuted by telegraph machines."

"Likely just stories," Chaput countered. "But just as well we don't have any on the premises."

"Of course," I said, wondering how far I could push this little dance. "But it seems electricity in any form is such a wild and dangerous thing to have in a home." Chaput looked at me for one moment more, his expression searching, before relaxing back into a good-natured grin.

"As you say." The butler turned from me and started his walk down the hall and back downstairs. "I'd be happy to make you some tea. If you're going to continue your… painting."

"Thank you, Chaput," I said wearily, feeling exhausted after the excitement of the night. "I don't think that'll be necessary. I should probably get some sleep."

"Agreed. That's my prescription for Master Vanguard too. It'd be a refreshing change to have someone in Shearhaven who'd heed me." Chaput turned his head to give a curt nod before heading out of sight. My shoulders slumped. I gave the door handle a quick turn, just in case Chaput had somehow failed to lock it. But my good fortune had run out, it seemed. I returned to bed, trying to remember as much as I could of what was inside the room. If only I'd had a little longer to look at it, or even examine it. As it was, it was mostly a jumble of impressions and nothing more. Whatever it was, it felt dangerous. And I can't say I slept any better knowing it was working away upstairs.

14

The next day at breakfast, Vanguard looked better, drinking tea, nibbling absent-mindedly on some toast and eggs, and reading the newspaper. I vacillated between relief he looked better, concern for whatever ongoing ailment vexed him, guilt over what I'd done last night, and irritation that he wasn't being truthful. Sick of running through that particular loop, I decided to find other occupations for my mind. I sipped my tea, savoring the lemony sweetness melded with the darkly herbal body of it. Vanguard assured me it was the best tea one could buy. I tried hard to enjoy it fully, as much as I did the first time I'd tasted it. It was so easy to become accustomed to these sorts of things, and some emphatic voice within me told me to never stop appreciating them. Because where did that lead, ultimately? If the best of everything became commonplace, what was there to turn to after that?

The morning had been mostly silent, as was the norm. Vanguard wasn't much of a morning person. When work or errands demanded he get up early, he preferred to be left alone with his thoughts until mid-morning at least. I'd discovered this slowly, as Vanguard was always willing to have a conversation should anyone engage him in one. Over time I noticed the man never started such conversations and derived the most pleasure from being left alone to read. I was happy to oblige once I'd figured it out. It was a change, to be sure. When I woke up at home, Dottie would start in first thing with her observations, questions, and stories. I smiled at the thought, although I also felt the sharp prick of loss when I thought of Mr. Blake. It was still hard to think he wasn't in the shop, even now, counting inventory and telling Dottie to get her behind off the counter and go sweep the floor or refill the candy jars.

"What's that little smile for?" Vanguard asked, causing me to blink in surprise. His newspaper was folded over, and he was staring at me.

"I'm not sure," I said, pushing the last crust of toast into the velvety yellow of the egg's yolk. "Thinking of old times. Thinking of last night. That sort of thing."

"It was nice to see Dottie again. And this Bellwether fellow seemed decent enough."

"I suppose so." I popped the toast in my mouth and chewed to keep from saying more. Vanguard laughed as he set the paper down next to his plate.

"Well of course, from your perspective, no one is ever going to be good enough for her."

"That's not it." I crossed my arms. "Okay, maybe there's a little of that. Mostly it's just—he was sort of boorish, wasn't he?" Vanguard shrugged.

"Many men are, in my experience. Especially when they're nervous, intimidated, or feel threatened. But he loves her. Written all over his face, the poor man."

"Why 'poor man'?"

"Because—well, Tomas, you've never explicitly told me, and I respect you keeping your friend's secrets—but it's clear Dottie would prefer other company. That's as clear to me as Bellwether's love for her is." Vanguard took a sip of his tea, but never broke eye contact with me. "Hence, 'poor man,'"

"You do take the most inopportune times to become insightful." I sat back in my chair and flashed him a devilish smile. Or, at least, the closest approximation I was capable of.

"I'm always insightful. I just don't always deem you worthy of it."

"Oh-ho! I see." I'm not sure why I'd chosen this moment to ask the question. But the tension of the previous night felt far away, at last, and I worried the more I waited the less chance I'd ever ask.

"Do you love me?" I said it, and quickly refocused my attention on my toast and eggs. They tasted suddenly too burnt and too watery as I waited for agonizingly long seconds. Vanguard gently took my chin, pointed my head up toward him, and looked at me with a cocked eyebrow.

"I'm sorry that's a question you have to ask." Vanguard kept the playful tone in his voice, although the searching look in his eyes was deadly serious.

"I didn't have to ask it. I wanted to ask it," I countered, my confidence growing now that I'd started down this path. "And that's still not an answer."

"Everything I do, every word I say to you—every word I do not say to you—that's all I'm ever trying to tell you. But if it helps to hear it put plainly then yes. Yes, I do love you. Happy?"

"Not really." This startled Vanguard, and the atmosphere of

friendly verbal sparring dissipated.

"Tomas, what's wrong."

"Love," I began, careful of my words. "Love is something in books and songs. I loved my mom and my dad. I loved Mr. Blake, and I loved Dottie. But that was different. And all of them are gone in one way or another. So, I was left with what was between us. But the sort of love we share—that I think we share, anyway—it's all new to me. As new as waking up in a house like this, with servants, and the best tea that money can import." I looked down at my tea, my confidence faltering.

"It's new to me too." Vanguard reached out his hand and enfolded mine in his. "I know that might seem strange, since I'm older. But I've wasted a lot of time and a lot of love in the wrong places. So, if I'm not good at saying it or showing it, all I can do is ask for some patience."

"And I the same." I took in a deep breath. "But to me, loving someone is sharing with them. I suppose everyone has secrets and drawing that line between acceptable secrets and unacceptable ones is probably difficult."

"What secrets do you imagine I'm keeping?"

"I'm not imagining anything, Jackson," I said, with more fury than I'd meant. "Please, don't talk to me like that."

Vanguard sighed heavily and placed his teacup down with enough force that it clattered against the saucer.

"How am I talking to you?"

"Like an errant child."

"Well, that's—If that's the way I sound then I apologize. But I'd appreciate it if you'd get to the heart of it instead of walking every which way around what you're asking."

"And I'd have appreciated you not forcing me to ask. But here we are." I looked down at my hands and was surprised to find they were balled into fists. I willed them to relax, and they slowly unfolded even though the tension coursing through me everywhere else had not abated. "How ill are you? And with what? And what is that machine in the attic for?"

"Ah." Vanguard blinked and then looked away. When he continued, he kept his tone emotionless. "Very ill, I'm afraid. My body is filling with cancerous growths. In my doctor's opinion—and that of several colleagues of his I've also consulted—there is little to be done. I might have six months or a year. Maybe more. They really can't say."

"Jackson—"

"But there are treatments that scientists in Europe are exploring. Uncommon treatments, including using electricity to destroy the growths. I've sunk a considerable amount into the equipment in the attic to see if those scientists might be onto something. So far, I can't say it's been worth the investment." As Vanguard finished, I gripped his hand and gave it a squeeze. Even though I'd suspected something along these lines, hearing it spoken aloud made it all too real.

"I'm sorry if I pushed too hard. But the wondering and not knowing were becoming too much," I said quietly. Vanguard patted my hand gently.

"No, you were right to ask. I don't know why I thought I could keep it from you. I wanted this time together, and the memories we've made, to be free of it. Free and clear. This disease has insinuated its way into my life as much as my body. So little is untouched by it now. I'm still grappling with it all. I suppose I wanted this one thing—well, *us*—to be free of it. Understand?" I nodded and resolved not to ask any more about it unless Vanguard brought it up. It would be a full three months before it came up again. And in the worst way possible.

15

Winter was breaking at Shearhaven. I painted a snow-covered pinecone in watercolor—I found I preferred it to the muckiness of working with oil—and listened to the crystalline plinking of the ice melting from the branches. An errant splotch of dark brown stopped my painting efforts in its tracks. I could fix it with a little work, but I found myself irritated rather than relaxed, so I decided to go for a stroll. I stepped out of the kitchen entrance and took in the cool misted air, a welcome change from the stuffiness inside. Vanguard had taken to having all the fireplaces going all the time to stave off the cold that had settled into his bones. It made him more comfortable, but it meant Chaput, Coghlan, and I were always struggling through sweltering heat. I was about to make my way toward the woods, perhaps to get a glimpse at the fairy story that was Mr. De Artte, when I heard a whinny I knew well come from the stable. It was Blackbriar, Vanguard's most beloved (and temperamental) horse.

"He giving you trouble again—" I began as I rounded

the corner into the stable. I was caught short when I saw the man inside. I'd expected Chaput to be there, as he'd taken up grooming duties now that Vanguard was too ill for it. "Oh, sorry. I thought you were someone else."

"I hope it wasn't too unpleasant of a surprise," said Henry, the first of the young men who had greeted me during my first trip to Shearhaven. That strange job-cum-mate selection had been almost a year and a half ago. It felt much longer. Henry's body was damp with sweat from scooping hay into the stalls. His white shirt was open, giving me a tantalizing glimpse of the sweat-dewed hair on his well-defined torso. Had he gotten more handsome somehow? Or was I just starved for intimacy?

"Not at all," I said. I watched as the man tried to hold Blackbriar still so he could comb the horse's coat. "What brings you to Shearhaven?"

"Didn't anyone tell you? Chaput hired me on to look after the horses while Mr. Vanguard is recovering."

"He didn't let me know. It must have slipped his mind." Which was probably the truth. My relationship with Chaput had grown frosty the last few months, as Vanguard's condition worsened. The butler seemed anxious and stressed and, at times, downright annoyed with my presence. Chaput took on the bulk of caring duties for Vanguard, so I didn't take it too personally. I knew it was hard work. I helped when I could, but Vanguard didn't like me seeing him at his worst.

"I was surprised to get the message, to be honest. Sad we never got that drink." Henry managed to calm Blackbriar slightly, his thick right arm straining in the effort to hold the horse still as his other arm rhythmically began to comb through the horse's silky black coat. His hair was shorter than it had been, but it suited him. I'd forgotten how icy blue the man's eyes were, as if they contained the winter chill that was now slipping away all around us. "Not that I expected you to. Not with, uh, Vanguard and all of this."

"Yes. It's been a whirlwind," I said quickly. I doubted the other man had meant anything by it, but I felt a twinge of offense with the way Henry had worded that. As if my motive for being at Shearhaven was the "all of this" part rather than simply being with "Vanguard." But I couldn't be angry at Henry. I still wasn't certain of my own motives from moment to moment. That feeling grew muddier once Vanguard revealed how sick he was. The very notion that Chaput would talk of Vanguard "recovering" was almost laughable. Except, there *was* the strange machine in the attic. Vanguard said it hadn't been working the first and last time we spoke about it all those months ago. But he'd intimated that adjustments could be made. I hadn't given up hope. Not yet. Blackbriar whinnied again and shook his head fiercely, smacking against Henry's face and sending him tumbling backward. Thankfully I was able to half-catch him, though the effort sent us both sprawling to the straw-strewn floor of the stable.

"Ouch. That's a first," Henry said, massaging his jaw. "Glad it was a soft landing." He looked up at me with those eyes—eyes that reminded me of the cold but seemed to have the opposite effect. His shirt had been thrown more open by the fall, and I saw the hard point of one nipple. I wanted nothing more than to straddle him right then and there. To encase that nipple in my mouth and lap at it with my tongue. I parted my lips to say something—even I wasn't sure what—when the air-slicing crack of a whip sounded throughout the barn. Blackbriar ceased his movements immediately.

"I'm afraid Blackbriar requires a firm hand," Vanguard said, coiling up the whip as he strode into the barn. His skin was too gray, and dark circles were etched under his eyes, but he moved with more purpose and strength than I had seen in a while. "He still has his own ideas about things. He hasn't come to accept who is *master* and who is *servant*, yet." Vanguard approached the creature, who was now eerily still except the occasional blinking of his eyelids and the slow heaving of his breath. Vanguard lifted and flattened his hand, still gripping the coiled whip with his thumb, and caressed the bridge of Blackbriar's nose gently.

"Th-thank you, Sir," Henry said, quickly getting up off the ground (and out of my arms) and dusting the dirt and straw from him. "He just took me by surprise. It won't happen again." Vanguard regarded us with cold eyes.

"Yes. See that it doesn't." He threw Henry the whip. "The sound is usually sufficient. But be prepared to follow through if you need to." Vanguard stalked out of the stables and back toward the house. I exchanged a glance with Henry—who was clearly as shocked as I was—and went after him.

"Jackson," I called out, although the other man was already halfway to the kitchen entrance. When he didn't stop, I broke out into a jog to catch up with him. "Jackson, stop, I want to—"

"You could wait until my body's cold, at least," Vanguard hissed at me. "My preference would be to wait until I'm in the ground. Perhaps a brief mourning period, even. But I don't want to ask *too much* of you."

An icy fury overtook me with such intensity I didn't trust myself to speak. I watched silently as Vanguard walked into Shearhaven. We'd gotten testy with each other before, of course. But nothing like this. It wasn't so much the venom of what he'd said, although it was an unfair and unreasonable accusation, but how dismissive Vanguard had sounded. Like I was just another servant who had to be put in his place. I slowed my breathing, and then walked calmly into the house, past the pantry, and through the kitchen. I was grateful that Cook was fully absorbed in kneading some dough, because I didn't know how well I was keeping my emotions from my face. The door to Vanguard's study was closed, as I expected. This was the room the man retreated to when he was feeling overwhelmed. This strange room that seemed so much more old-fashioned than the rest of the house.

"Jackson, it's Tomas," I said, knocking lightly on the heavy wooden door which only seemed to absorb the sound. I wrapped my knuckles against it, harder this time, and raised my voice slightly. "Jackson, you don't have to talk. I'm fine with saying what I have to say loudly in the hall. But I will say it." I heard the soft click of the lock before the door was thrown open. Vanguard immediately stalked back toward his desk. He hunched over it, looking pained.

"Do you need your medicine?" I asked, the quarrel at hand momentarily forgotten. Vanguard waved my concern away. "Okay. Well, we need to talk about the way you just spoke to me." I threw myself down into the chair across from Vanguard, and the man winced. Vanguard liked his things. Especially the things in this study.

"Very well. Talk," Vanguard said flatly before sitting down and relaxing in his own chair.

"You're being unreasonable. I know you're tired and—"

"Don't. Don't try to blame what I said on my disease." Vanguard narrowed his eyes, put his elbows on the table, and touched his fingers together. "I am sorry if I was too abrupt for you, but I have begun to realize I have less and less time for niceties."

"Henry is a friend. We met the first time I came to
Shearhaven. And, as you are well aware since I practically spend
every waking moment with you, I have not seen him since."

"Are we going to be this mundane?" Vanguard asked, pulling
a bottle of amber liquid from his desk drawer and knocking back
a sip. "Because if we are going to be this boring, I'm going to
need more to drink."

"I don't even understand what you mean." I straightened my
back, never taking my eyes off the other man.

"I want you to use your imagination, Tomas. Over and over,
I have tried to tell you that we can be different. We can be better.
We don't have to get caught up in the little dances that men
and women seemed so fond of. We don't have to indulge in lies
and half-truths. You were flirting with him. The sexual tension
was more than obvious. Admit it. If not to me, then at least to
yourself." Vanguard sat the bottle down heavily. I could see the
hand resting on the bottle was shaking ever so slightly.

"Jackson, I don't want to fight."

"This isn't a fight, Tomas. That was me trying to make
myself perfectly clear. To you, and to the new stable boy. Do you
want to feel him? Do you wonder what those muscles—sculpted
by a lifetime of hard labor—feel like? Do you want to reach
between his thighs and feel his cock? I'm sure it's tremendous.
Do you want to take him in your mouth? Taste his seed as he
releases? Or have him take you in his?"

"Jackson, don't talk like that." My cold fury was heating up
into something else now. I looked away.

"Like an adult? Like a free-thinking man? Tomas you can
do all those things. We should be able to talk about these things.
Explore these things. I don't mind. But the way you two looked
at each other and the way you talked to each other—there's

something more there. Something that, for a just a little while longer, I would like reserved for me." Vanguard's hand was shaking more now. He removed it from the bottle and stuck it below the desk where I could no longer see it.

"This disease keeps taking," he began again. "It has taken my health, my beauty, my independence. It's taken the world from me. And every day I think it's taking more of my mind. So, yes, I was angry. I probably overreacted. But I don't want to see one more thing taken from me. Something I just found. Something that's… more precious to me than even I expected."

I sat there silently, the righteous fury I'd been nurturing as I made my way to the study starting to dissipate. The truth was, of course, that there was something more there with Henry. I was foolish to think it wasn't as plain to Vanguard as it was to Henry and me. I wouldn't have acted on it, of course. I still hadn't reoriented my thinking to Vanguard's more libertine impulses. But, yes, when I saw the man in the stable my mind did wander down the path of asking what if. As in, what if this could be something once Vanguard was gone.

"It seems like you understand," Vanguard said exploratorily after I hadn't responded right away. "If that's the case, I would like some time to myself, Tomas." I nodded and got up stiffly. I was nearly to the door when I felt compelled to say something.

"I spent a long time trying to figure out what I feel for you," I said, turning back to Vanguard who kept his eyes fixed on the bottle he was still taking brief sips from.

"What a monumental waste of time, then," Vanguard said with a sigh. "Love isn't a list you tick off one by one until it's achieved. It is or it isn't. Sometimes you know it in the moment, sometimes you don't realize it until later. The best thing is to just enjoy it in the moment. For as long as you can."

"Don't you want to know where I ended up with it all? What I figured out?"

"No. I already know," Vanguard looked up finally, and smiled weakly at me. I returned it, and then closed the door. It'd been a bluff, and I was glad Vanguard hadn't called it. The truth was that I still wasn't sure. But I would have said it. To assuage my guilt, if nothing else.

My head felt fuzzy—the grogginess that comes after anger that intense, like an energy-sapping hangover. I thought about the brisk cold outside and decided to go for a walk, very pointedly exiting via the front door and arcing away from the stables. I did not walk the grounds like this often. It made me uncomfortable. To one side were the immense walls of Shearhaven with all its windows. In the day, at least, it was nearly impossible to see through the reflections. I imagined that Vanguard, Chaput, Coghlan, Gladys, or even Cook might be watching me. I hated the idea and wasn't exactly sure why. Maybe I feared someone would finally realize I didn't belong there. They'd see I walked too much like an orphaned kid who got taken in by a grocer to ever feel at home in a place like Shearhaven. No, I wasn't sure what that even meant. Sometimes fears are idiotic, I suppose.

On the other side lay the woods that surrounded the property. In the spring and summer, they were surprisingly thick and swallowed light in great gulps. Now, however, stripped of their leaves, they seemed frailer and better lit but no less ominous. The trees were older and wilder up here than any back in Gillsborough. Of course, most of the trees that dotted the land there had been cleared out to make room for that town before I was born. I thought about Vanguard's words. The implication in them that I had some growing up to do. Annoying, considering Vanguard wasn't that much older than me. In ten or twenty years the age difference would be next to meaningless. But I had to admit, in the here and now we had led two very different lives. I had certainly seen far less of the world. Vanguard always seemed too mature—older than his years. The same way Dottie felt like an older sister even though she and I were the same age. Forcing myself to not think about it too much, I arced my path away from Shearhaven and into the woods.

I enjoyed the satisfying crunch of small twigs breaking under my boots. The steady rhythm of the gentle cracking mixed with the drip-drip of melting ice and a pleasing sloshing sound calmed me as I dragged my boots through the decayed remains of the fall leaves just recently uncovered by the melting snow. As I scraped through them, they released a sweet and earthy scent. I'd become so enthralled with these subtle details, watching my boots as they slid through the leaves and welcoming the distraction from my thoughts, that I didn't notice the man in the small clearing until I was nearly upon him. When I saw the man's ratty shoes, I looked up and—already startled that anyone else was even out here—let out a cry of alarm and fear when I saw the man's face. I recoiled with such ferocity that I fell backward and landed hard on the roots of a tree at the edge of the clearing.

"Master Doyle," the man said, lumbering over me and blotting out the sun. "I've been waiting for you."

16

"Sorry if I spooked ya," the man said, holding out a meaty hand that looked like the blunt end of a club. I tried to collect myself, feeling embarrassed and guilty about having reacted so strongly to the man's appearance. Especially as, in the few seconds I'd spent on the ground, I'd realized who he must be.

"Mr. De Artte?" I asked as I grabbed the man's hand and was hauled up by him with ease.

"That's what they call me." He gave me a small nod before sitting back down on the tree stump where I'd first seen him. He picked up a branch and a long hunter's knife with a thick hilt and continued to whittle away at the wood.

"Sorry, I don't usually scream and fall about so easily." I hoped my attempt at self-deprecation might make up for the rudeness of my reaction to the man's visage. Because it was, there's no way around it, ghastly. His body, while thickly muscled and framed, was hunched. His forehead was just tall enough to look disproportionate and his skull bulged outward and at an angle in the back. His hair was long and black, hanging like a veil from the midpoint of his skull, leaving a white—almost translucent—bald pate. His fingernails were gray and rimmed with black dirt. His watery eyes were almost amber when the light caught them, which was frequent as they bulged slightly. When he talked, he exposed teeth that looked like kernels of corn that had gone bad.

"Don't think nothin' of it. People have all sorts of reactions to me. I don't take it personal. Sit a spell?" De Artte asked, hiking a finger over toward another tree stump.

"Honestly, I just didn't expect anyone else to be out here," I said, as though that were the main reason for my dramatic reaction to his appearance.

"You mean Master Vanguard or one of his little helpers didn't mention me?"

"Oh, no, they did. I just thought—you're going to think this is silly—but I started to think it was just a practical joke or a fairy story or something." The man let out a short, sharp laugh.

"Well, you've not been walking around the woods, have you? Which is a shame. She's a pretty little lot. Lots of interesting nooks and crannies and varmints to look at and explore."

"I'll have to rectify that. We've just been away a lot." I didn't add that, at any other time than in the winter, the darkness of the forest had made me too uneasy to jaunt through it.

"Right, I suppose ya have at that." The man continued to whittle in confident strokes, sending shavings of wood into the air.

"You should join us for Sunday breakfast sometime. Chaput, Ms. Coghlan, Gladys, and I like to take a meal together then. You'd be more than welcome."

"I doubt that. Mr. Vanguard isn't fond of my visage, you might say."

"Well, that's awful," I said, trying to forget I'd just screamed in terror at it as well. I knew Vanguard was an "aesthete" but to treat an employee this way seemed downright cruel. "Do you live nearby?"

"Here and yon." De Artte blew filings of wood from his carving. A moment passed, and I realized that's all he was compelled to say.

"Have you… watched over the woods for a long time now?" I tried to be careful in my phrasing. It was still unclear what Mr. De Artte did, exactly, other than hunt. I wasn't sure if he had an official title.

"Oh, yes, before the current master of Shearhaven took over." The man brought the branch up close now, and I could see that it was hollow. He'd shaped one end into a curved taper. Now he was drilling small holes into it.

"Gabriel Vanguard? Cyril's son?"

"Yes, that's the one. Though it's all the same, really, to me. The master of Shearhaven is the master of Shearhaven is the master of Shearhaven. Et cetera and onward. It's never changed my work," De Artte said.

"Right. Makes sense." I attempted to create some camaraderie with the man. The truth was I had more in common with him than I had with Vanguard, no matter how much my fortunes had lately changed. It felt important to keep a grip on that.

"Ah, there we go," the man said as he brought his newly carved recorder up to his lips and blew, his large fingers surprisingly nimble as they blocked different tone holes in a quick flurry. The sounds that came out were, it must be said, wretched. De Artte looked at the recorder as though it had betrayed him and threw it as hard as he could into the woods. "I'll get that right one day."

"I suppose I should get back inside. It'll be dark soon."

"Aye, as sure as anything," Mr. De Artte bolted his head upward and to the right, as if someone had called his name. He stared off into the distance long enough that I thought it might be best if headed back and left him to whatever had caught his interest. Then I thought of a way I might offer some small kindness to him. Something to balance my initial reaction.

"Would you like some tea? Or coffee? Or, hell, a drop or two of brandy or something? I'm sure Vanguard has plenty around for the parties."

"There's an ill-tempered wind coming, lad," the man said, seemingly ignoring my question. "And coming fast. Get yourself back to Shearhaven. I thank you for the offer, but I'll be fine. You're a good lad, aren't you?" De Artte still hadn't turn his head to look at me.

"I used to think so." I wondered why I was being so forthright with the man even as I spoke the words. "Lately, though, I'm not so sure."

"Well." De Artte slowly turned back toward me. "Knowing that's a question you should ask is a good step toward it, at least."

"I don't suppose you can tell me what the next step is?" I joked. I didn't expect the man to reply.

"Letting yourself find a true answer. And then, the real test and the last step—decide what you do with all that knowing. Now, run. That storm's a-coming." Mr. De Artte turned away and started searching through the scattered branches and twigs near the tree stump.

"I'll see you around sometime soon."

"Maybe," he said, still searching through the debris on the forest floor.

17

I had just crossed the threshold into Shearhaven when heavy sheets of cold rain started showering down, the approaching storm masked in the slow darkening of the setting sun.

"Seems like you brought the rain with you, Master Doyle," Ms. Coghlan said as she stepped forward to take my coat.

"I guess so. Just in the nick of time," I replied. Chaput walked down the stairway from the upper landing.

"Master Doyle, there you are. Master Vanguard has been terribly busy, so I'd hoped you might approve the ideas Cook and I had about what to serve at the upcoming party?"

"Of course." I rubbed my hands together to warm them. "Ms. Coghlan could you make us a pot of tea? We could discuss down here, by the fire. I feel like I've got the chills straight down in the marrow."

"Of course, Master Doyle," Ms. Coghlan said with sing-song happiness. Whenever I asked her to do something, she lit up. Something I rarely did. It still felt odd to have servants. It was a feeling I wasn't sure I liked. This seemed to enrage Ms. Coghlan in a quiet way. She never stopped smiling, but there was something in her eyes that let me know she seethed when I didn't ask for assistance when she thought I should. I thought she was going to grind her teeth to nubs the first time I drew my own bath. It was as though I was upsetting a natural balance. Why Coghlan would champion a hierarchal ladder when she was most decidedly on the lower rung was a mystery.

"I'll stoke the fire for you, Sir," Chaput said. "Too long in the cold air, *oui?*"

"Yes, I suppose so. I finally met Mr. De Artte."

"Mr. De Artte?" Ms. Coghlan asked in a choked bleat. The woman looked pale as a sheet. Chaput wasn't much better. The housekeeper cleared her throat and smiled brightly. "Sorry, I should go get that tea. I think I have a frog in my throat. Could use something warm myself."

"Of course. To answer your question, yes. Fascinating man. One of a kind, that's for sure."

"Indeed." Chaput started to turn back toward the fire. Coghlan nodded weakly and quickly skittered away to the kitchen. Then, perhaps understanding that I'd noticed their discomfort, Chaput stood up straight and addressed me more directly. "I'm sorry if we seemed taken aback. You see, neither of us has actually seen Mr. De Artte. We'd half thought him a jest on Master Vanguard's part."

"Oh, don't worry yourself." I couldn't help but smile, pleased I wasn't the only one. "I had started to think the same thing." Chaput smiled back, nodded, and then turned back to stoking the fire. I laid back in the chair by the fire and closed my eyes, relieved to be back in the warmth of Shearhaven. I was so relaxed—perhaps I'd even dozed off—that I was surprised to see Ms. Coghlan already emerging from one of the hidden doors carrying a serving tray with a pot of tea, cup, saucer, and a sandwich. Chaput was gone, no doubt having noticed I'd drifted off and deciding to save the menu approvals for later.

"Thank you, Ms. Coghlan," I said as she poured the tea. The housekeeper and I had a strange relationship. I'd never quite figured her out. She was outwardly sunny and took her job very seriously. She seemed to take great pride—one might say too much—in her job. But she seemed evasive about everything that didn't involve her job. My every attempt to get to know her better was politely and expertly swatted away or circumnavigated. I suppose I should be happy that she was so good at her job and never anything but pleasant to me, unlike the sometimes-irritable Chaput, but it was hard to feel at ease around her. I took a bite of the sandwich—which turned out to be butter and cucumber on white bread; delicious. "Oh, and if you see Chaput, please tell him I can talk about the menu now whenever he likes."

"Oh, bugger!" the housekeeper suddenly exclaimed. "I completely forgot. Master Vanguard asked we send you into him as soon as you got inside."

"Oh, no problem," I said as cheerily as I could. I was sad to have to put down the tea and sandwich. "I should go see him anyway." My stomach rumbled as I sat up, so I stuffed the rest of the sandwich in my mouth and took my cup and saucer with me. Silly to let it go cold.

As I approached Vanguard's study, the door opened. Vanguard saw me, and quickly stepped out and closed the door behind him.

"Tomas, you're back. Very good," Vanguard said sleepily. I didn't think it possible, but the dark circles under the man's eyes had gotten even worse.

"You wanted to see me?" I tried for a casual tone, hoping to let the tension of our earlier argument dissipate. It was hard to stay angry with Vanguard, especially when he looked so frail.

"Yes. Perhaps we can talk as we go? I'm afraid I'm going to have to retire to bed early tonight. I was just about to head up."

"Of course." I fell into step next to Vanguard, who was moving much slower than usual. Guilt, more than genuine regret, made me add "I'm sorry about earlier."

"*I* should apologize. That new stable boy is a handsome man. I shouldn't have been so—well, you didn't deserve my anger. One of the things this disease takes, along with my energy, is my good humor, I suppose." He sighed as we reached the stairway. I put the (mostly drained) teacup down for Coghlan or Gladys to find and tut about, and gave him my arm. Vanguard looked at it, reluctant at first, and then accepted the help. "I hate feeling old."

"You're not old, just infirm," I offered. Vanguard laughed. "Wicked boy."

"You overreacted. Sure. But you weren't wrong. I am attracted to Henry. I have been since we both met at your last party. But it's not like I'm lining up guys for after you—that's not the sort of person I am." I was pretty sure of that last point, at least. Vanguard stopped his ascent. At first, I thought he might be winded. Instead, the man patted my arm and gave me a peck on the cheek.

"I know that," he said softly. We were silent the rest of the way. I could see the strain on the man and didn't want to make his efforts more difficult by talking. We got through his bedroom door, and Vanguard was almost to the bed, when he let out a hellish cry of pain and doubled over.

"Jackson! What's wrong?" I rushed to the man's side and got

him gently onto the bed. "Is it your back?" The man's face, paler than ever, crinkled up in pain as he nodded.

"My… laudanum. I—I left it in my study… like a fool," Vanguard wheezed.

"I'll be right back." I turned.

"Wait," Vanguard hissed in a whisper. He reached into his pocket and gave me his keys. I'd need them, of course, to get into the study. I rushed back down the stairs, and around the halls and back to the study. It took me a few moments to find the right key. In addition to the supposed "master" key there were keys to both the forbidden room in the attic and the study as well, the two places in Shearhaven I wasn't given free rein. A twinge of resentment flooded through me as I searched for the correct key. I couldn't help but feel that Vanguard would be feeling less pain right now if he'd trusted me more. I pushed the thought away. There were more important things to worry about right now, and I suppose Vanguard having areas he wanted to keep private in his own home was understandable.

I was shocked by the state of the study. I hadn't seen it in months, and it was a far cry from its usual, orderly state. Piles of books sat about haphazardly, some opened with notes scribbled on them. There were three serving trays discarded in one corner, which—along with a light film of dust—suggested neither Chaput nor Coghlan had been let in here in a while, either. I looked at the skin of the Atlas Bear, half bunched up near the small fireplace. The last of his kind, reduced to decoration and then just another thing in Vanguard's way.

I brought my attention back to the task at hand, my heart racing from being in Vanguard's inner sanctum even while the pressure of getting his medicine back to him as quickly as possible weighed down on me. The man's desk was a total disaster, and I quickly opened the drawers hoping the laudanum might be in one of those. No such luck. Which meant I'd have to excavate the layers of books, papers, newspapers, and other debris that littered it. The vial of laudanum was quite small, which meant it could be anywhere. I pulled off the book that was directly on top—a scientific tome on electric currents. Underneath, I didn't find the vial of pain medicine. Instead, I found something else I recognized. I held the large piece of parchment up. It had to be the same technical diagram I'd seen before—for just a handful of moments—in the room in the attic. There were two small holes up top, as if it'd been nailed to a wall.

It was a diagram of the device. Vaguely drawn humanoid figures sat on each seat. The hands of each figure were bound to the lower benches with cable and leather cuffs. I knew I should be searching for the laudanum. But I couldn't stop myself taking in every detail. I'd wondered about this drawing since the moment I'd first caught site of it all those months ago. There were notes in ink. They were recently added, too, possibly moments before Vanguard had left the study, judging by the ink that was still drying on the slick parchment.

Power output issues. Solved by V.N.'s new cables? Vanguard had written in his distinctive, precise penmanship. Next to one of the bench posts, another note appeared. The skin at the back of my neck prickled as I read it. *Must adjust height of post B so that top reaches just under back of skull. Tomas's height is only a couple inches over mine. Maybe adjustable? Add collar to force contact with top of post and base of skull?*

My mind couldn't even begin to fathom what it all meant. I was supposed to go into the chair? Into that machine? I looked up. The door to the study was closed. I waited a moment, just to be sure I didn't hear footsteps, and read on.

Essence transfer successful at levels not currently possible. Gramme system possible solution? Essence? Essence of what? Or whom? Gramme was a name I thought I recognized. Some Belgian inventor Vanguard kept praising. But what the hell did essence mean or pertain too? I searched frantically all over the diagram for more written notes, and when there were none, I picked it up to check the back. But as I lifted the diagram up one last time to inspect it's back, I saw a note scribbled on a smaller sheet of paper.

A. certain essence of host dissipated/destroyed. But how can I be sure? Consult others. Gather hypotheses. Destroying an essence? The words just made no sense, and I found it harder to concentrate, fear spiking all through me even though I couldn't make sense of the pieces laying in front of me. I kept searching, but there were no more notes. Vanguard's handwriting was more ragged here. He might have been tired. Maybe he never finished his thought.

"Master Doyle," Ms. Coghlan screeched as she threw the door open. "What the hell are you doing? Master Vanguard is wailing in pain. I was passing by and it sounded like the wee drowned babes in the well."

"L-looking for his laudanum! I can't find it," I said. But not quickly enough. My hesitation was immediately suspect. Coghlan eyed me with that exact thought clearly in her mind.

"It's got be somewhere here," the housekeeper said, breaking away her gaze and getting down on her knees in front of the desk. "Maybe it fell? Oh, the state of this place. Disgraceful." I pretended to be shuffling papers to look for the laudanum, trying to restore the stack on the desk to some semblance of the order it had been in before. Vanguard would know I was looking through it. Still, looking for the laudanum was a decent reason. I could say I didn't even see what any of it was about because I was—as any decent person would be—only thinking of my love's pain.

"Got it!" Coghlan said with excited relief. She popped her head up above the desk and thrust the vial at me. "Now go! You're faster than I am." I swiped the vial from her hand and ran up to the bedroom where Vanguard was writhing in pain. My thoughts were clouded by the danger I was in. Because I knew I was in danger, even if I didn't quite grasp whatever form that danger was taking. I cupped the head of the man as he moaned and thrashed in excruciating pain, hoping to give him the laudanum without too much spillage. We'd been going through it too fast as it was. I looked down at the man whose forehead was covered in beads of sweat. The man I had, up until a few months ago, planned to spend the rest of my life with. A man that I loved, even if it was a messy and opaque sort of love. Tears began to form in my eyes. Even as I held Vanguard's head in my hands, brushed the hair from his forehead, and wished his pain away, I was quaking in fear. I feared for my safety. That was part of it. The other part was that I was certain that this man—this beautiful, handsome, charming man who'd swept me off my feet—meant me harm.

<h1 style="text-align:center">18</h1>

awoke to screams. My eyes shot open, I tossed off the covers, threw on my robe, and rushed from the guest bedroom to Vanguard's. I opened the door slowly, just a crack, and found him still in a deep sleep, his curtains drawn so that he was enfolded in darkness. The room smelled of sweat and bile and medicinal herbs. My empty stomach turned, and I closed the door as quickly as I could. I shook my head, closed my eyes, and rubbed the sleep away from them with my fingers. I opened my eyes, and *he* was there. Mr. Chaput, looking grim and eyeing me, some inscrutable thought whirring in his brain.

"Master Tomas," he said in a tone that was courteous but edged with irritation. "You are up early."

"Yes. I thought I—" I stopped myself. There were three possibilities. Either Vanguard had screamed, perhaps from a nightmare, and settled back into sleep. Or I had dreamt the scream. Or—the one that held my tongue—the scream had come from elsewhere. The third option weighed most heavily on me. Shearhaven was no longer the safe hideaway from the world and its judgments I had hoped. I had no idea what screaming elsewhere in the house might mean. Just the vague notion that revealing I knew anything about any of the secrets of the house might be dangerous. "I was up early. Honestly, I didn't sleep well last night. I was worried about him."

"Yes. Well, that is understandable. We've sent for the doctor, just in case. But thought it best he slept." Chaput visibly relaxed. Which made me feel more at ease on one hand. On the other hand, it did make me wonder if he was worried about what I'd heard. I made the mental note that the butler should not be trusted in any case.

"Good. That makes me feel better."

"Would you care for some breakfast? I could bring some up to you?"

"No. Not right away." I looked over at the window, diffuse morning light shining through the window, and hoped my stomach wouldn't grumble and betray me. "I think I might go for a walk. Take in some brisk air. Clear my head." The truth was, I felt the sudden need to be out of this house and away from the butler. Chaput, despite the size of the house, always seemed to be nearby.

"Yes. Yes, that sounds very refreshing." Chaput seemed overly enthusiastic about the idea. "I'll have your shoes, coat, and gloves at the ready. I'll wrap up a crust of bread for you. Just in case you get peckish on your walk."

"Excellent. I'll go change," I said, although I didn't move immediately. As I expected, the butler stood there, waiting for *me* to move. Only when I headed back to my room did he walk down the hall and toward the stairs. I gave my face a quick wash in the basin and changed out of my bed clothes, all trying to contemplate the puzzle of Mr. Chaput. Was he just playing guard dog for his master, trying to keep him safe? Did he perceive some threat from me? Thinking about it only gave me more questions, so I sat it aside, and decided to enjoy the walk.

I'd just made it out the front door when I heard a shout.

"Boy! Get back here now!"

I startled, thinking I was the one being addressed. In Gillsborough, most people still thought of me that way—as a boy. Something about being an orphan at a young age made the people around me more protective, I suppose. Sometimes to a fault. Even though I was nineteen, I had a slight frame, delicate features, and light blonde hair. Details that drew interest from girls, which I didn't particularly want, and ire from the boys. When I complained about this, Mr. Blake would just shake his head and say I had some of the old fae in me, just like my mother had. As if that somehow made anything better. Still, there were advantages to the protective cocoon the people of Gillsborough wrapped around me. Something I'd used before. Nothing serious, mind you. Just a watery eye when I was caught stealing apples from Heath's grove. Or the time I accidentally busted a crate of milk bottles and managed to convince Ma Howard not to tan my hide. Little manipulations I convinced myself were utterly justified, especially when the cocoon started to feel like it was smothering me.

A young boy ran past me.

"Get back here you unruly little sprog!" This time, I caught where the voice was coming from, and saw a leathery-skinned man with black hair in wild unkempt curls running toward me, and after him.

"Sorry to startle you, Sir. My boy's playing games with me again." the man gave the boy—who was hunched over, panting, and smiling—the stink eye.

"Not at all. You just surprised me. We don't get a lot of morning visitors."

"Oh, aye, I suppose not. Me and this little terror was just delivering some supplies for the party."

"I see." I glanced around for a cart. I must have looked perplexed or suspicious.

"We have a little boat docked down on the river. Hoofed it up from there."

"Of course." I tried my best smile. Just because my wind was filled with suspicions and doubts it didn't mean I should make the poor man feel judged.

"Ralph." The man shook my hands with too much vigor. His skin was calloused and rough. "Ralph Sanderson. That's my boy Art."

"Tomas Doyle."

Through some perfunctory pleasantries, I found out that Ralph had just delivered what he termed "specialist supplies."

"What'd you deliver? If I might ask?"

The man laughed.

"Ah, the bumbling of youth." I frowned at his condescension. "Sorry, boy, I didn't mean nothing by it. Just if there's a man from a small boat making deliveries far from the main docks. Well, better not to ask questions."

"Ah." I thought about pressing him. Pointing out that I was a member of this household. Not a servant. Shouldn't I have the right to know? But clearly the man was keeping secrets, sworn to Vanguad personally, no doubt. And right now, not asking too many questions seemed the safest thing to do. At least until I could talk to Dottie. "Well, I don't want to keep you."

"Art, quit your messing about or I'll have you over my knee

and your hide rawer than a slab at a butcher's if you don't get over here right now!" Ralph yelled it loud enough it made me wince. Perhaps sensing his father was no longer playing around at all, the boy ran up to him, shoulders hunched. Ralph turned his attention back to me.

"You seem like a good lad. Bit of advice, from an old scrounger?" Ralph was on the rough side, with a slick sheen to his personality that sent warning bells jingling in my head. I could probably guess what sort of illicit supplies he was delivering. Alcohol and drugs were in no short supply at Vanguard's parties. But it still troubled me. I can't say I'd put much stock in any advice he gave, but I shrugged all the same.

"You wear their clothes well, but I can see you've got more in common with me and Art than any of them in there. Your eyes are still wide, taking it all in." I could smell something sour on the man's breath as he leaned in. "Just keep 'em wide, is all I'm saying." I watched mutely as he walked away, Art skipping behind him. I suddenly felt too chilled for a walk.

19

I stared out from the window of my studio. Here, in the attic of the grand house, I was sheltered from the music and the hustle and bustle. The usual suspects had come for this party, as expected. I wasn't in any sort of mood for their preening banter and inside jokes. But at least Dottie and her husband said they were coming, and I was eager to tell her what I'd found in the study. She was the only person I trusted, for one thing, and I'd learned to value her insights and perspective from experience. As for the rest, I didn't feel like merry-making.

"There you are," Vanguard said as he came behind me and pulled me into his embrace. It took some effort not to flinch. It astonished me how far he was from the pain-wracked, broken man who'd been writhing in his bed, desperately crying out for laudanum. There was some color back to his face, and his eyes had a glimmer of their old spirit in them.

"Sorry, just collecting myself a moment," I said.

He shook his head. "No apologies necessary. I just missed

you. And Lady Acton was asking after you. But more importantly, Dottie and Grant are here. I thought you'd want to know."

"That's sweet of you." I patted the back of his hand that was gripping me.

"I can see why you like it up here. I doubt there's as spectacular a view of the Mississippi for miles around. It's peaceful up here, isn't it? Above everything? Watching the lights of the ships twinkle by. Or the passing lamps of the carriages. They remind me of something."

"Fireflies," I offered. When I'd first come to Shearhaven, I'd likened it to the beauty of fireflies. Something I feared would be spoiled if I tried to know it too well or keep it. Now, looking out through this window it occurred to me that I might be the firefly and Shearhaven my grand, gilded jar. I shivered. Thinking I was cold, Vanguard ran his hands quickly up and down my upper arms, and then rested his head on my shoulder. In my periphery, I saw his wry smile. The sort of thing that would have left me a melted puddle of wax, awaiting his seal, just days before.

"Hm. Not what I was thinking of. But apt. Now. Come, the party waits. And we can't be seen as terrible hosts. I won't allow it." I nodded, plastered on a smile, and followed him out of my art studio.

I was so eager to see Dottie and get her counsel, the days-long wait for the party had been torture. It turned out, now that I was in the middle of the party with its clatter of glasses and rumbling of voices and music, the truly brutal wait lay in waiting for the chance to get Dottie alone. The problem was that Vanguard's parties were too full of people who—despite their less savory aspects—were genuinely interesting. And Dottie, not realizing what a pressing topic I had to discuss, was delighting in the chatter. I found my opening when Grant Bellwether got caught up talking with an extraordinarily tall German woman who played the pan flute. Vanguard was likewise busy, chattering away with Lady Acton, who'd again made the trip from London for the party.

"Dot, want to go for a walk?" I asked as she started to drift away from a conversation that was petering out.

"Of course! Let me just see where the butler put my shawl. There's a chill in the air."

"You can borrow my jacket," I said quickly. Dottie could tell from my tone that something was amiss, so she nodded and followed me toward the front door of the house. My eyes darted round the room as we made our exit, hoping that Vanguard, Chaput, or Coghlan would be too occupied to notice. I didn't want any prying eyes or ears around for this conversation, which is why I'd suggested a walk outside in the first place. Thankfully, we slipped out. As soon as we were outside, I took off my suit jacket and draped it around Dottie's shoulders.

"Tomas, you're scaring me," Dottie said after we were a few paces away from the door.

"I know, Dot, sorry. I've just been trying to get you alone all night." I clasped my hands together to stop from fidgeting as we walked. I realized then that they were trembling.

"Why didn't you say something sooner?" Dottie pulled the jacket around her tighter.

I waved the comment away. "Dot, I need your advice. Hell, I might need your help."

"What—"

"Oh, hey there," Henry said, almost bumping into us as he came around the corner of the house from the opposite direction.

"Henry!" I said with too much cheer. "This is Dottie. This is the stable hand for Shearhaven, Henry."

"Pleased to meet you," Dottie said, extending her hand and giving a small curtsy, part of her new persona as Mrs. Bellwether. "You look vaguely familiar."

"Wow, pleased to meet you. Tomas has told me all about you," Henry said, giving Dottie's hand a firm shake.

"Everything, eh? So, I can drop the act?"

"Please do." Henry laughed.

"Thank goodness. It's very tiring." Dottie then turned away from Henry and addressed me, her eyes widening with a mischievous light. "You and Tomas talk a lot?"

"Not very much," I said quickly. "But we became friendly when we met. The first time at Shearhaven. He was one of the other servers."

"Oh, one of the other 'candidates,'" Dottie said. "That's why I remember you." Henry's cheeks reddened.

"Yeah, they brought me on to look after the horses after Master Vanguard got sick. Poor guy. He's… intense about his horses. I think it nearly kills him not being able to take care of them himself. I can tell you; he doesn't think much of my efforts."

"Well, thankfully it didn't keep him from planning this party. I shudder to think what the result would have been like if I'd done it. He's more intense about his parties than he is his horses." I looked back nervously at the house.

"Ah. Well, I suppose so." Henry looked uncomfortable, perhaps sensing the conversation was becoming a little insulting toward Vanguard. "Still, he's been a great employer. Pays well, and he really does know his horses."

"That he does, indeed." I looked from Henry to Dottie, stewing in the uncomfortable silence but hoping it might send Henry on his way.

"Well, I better get going home."

"You don't live here? I thought everyone who worked here did," Dottie probed.

"Not Cook or Henry," I said quickly. What was Dottie doing? Here I was practically being rude so Henry would leave us, and she was opening up more topics for discussion.

"I didn't want to, honestly," Henry said. "Being here, around all this luxury. Well, you can start to want things you can't have." Henry's eyes darted over toward me, just for a second, but long enough for Dottie to notice. And long enough for me to feel the heat in my cheeks battle against the cold air.

"I see. Well, we don't want to keep you. Is it far?"

"Not at all. Renting a little room in Alton. I figure there's really no way to know how long—well, not settling in just yet." Henry's attempt to dodge talking about Vanguard's impending death was clumsy, but I appreciated it.

"Safe travels, Henry."

"You too, Tomas. And to you, Dottie."

We watched Henry walk toward the path down the bluff before continuing our walk around the perimeter of the house, which was considerable. Once we thought we were clear, Dottie couldn't help herself.

"Well, he's quite a distraction," she said with a smirk. I knocked my shoulder gently into hers.

"Hush. I know you're joking but that's the kind of thing I don't want Jackson hearing."

"Is he being jealous? Is that the issue?"

"I wish. Here's a good spot." I indicated the small ledge, about five feet wide, between the back of Shearhaven and the bluff's edge. "This is one of my favorite spots for thinking. Besides my attic studio."

"Can't ask for a better view," Dottie said, looking past the narrow shore, with its dirt road and small dock to the wide stretch of gray water beyond. Even at this time of night, dark shadows of ships—many with only the wheelhouse alight— slipped through the churning waters. We pressed close together and I could feel her shivering, even with my coat draped over her shoulders. I didn't want to keep her out here long, but I was determined to tell her everything. I could tell it was hard for her to sit there and listen, and not interject, as I told her. Shock, confusion, and anger all played across her face. My coat slipped from her shoulders, and she didn't seem to notice.

"Tomas. I don't—" Dottie paused. "I don't understand this. Essence 'transfer' by some electric nightmare machine in the attic? It's like something out of a Jules Verne."

"I'm not going to be much help getting you over your incredulousness, because I'm still trying to do the same. But I'm not sure if it matters." I curled my legs up to my chest and hugged them.

"What do you mean?"

"I mean, I don't know if it matters if what it does is real or not. I don't pretend to understand all of this. The telegraph seems more like magic than anything to me. So, maybe it is possible. If they can send words through the air, why not souls?"

"I'd say there's more than a few leaps between those two things," Dottie said firmly.

"Agreed. But my point is, it doesn't matter if we believe. It matters that Vanguard does. You didn't see that thing. The electricity flying back and forth—well, let's just say I doubt it'd be good for my health in any case." I got up carefully. There was plenty of room between the ledge and the bluff's edge, but I wasn't always the best with heights. "We'd better get back before we're missed."

"You're probably right. But you said you wanted my advice about all of this, right?" Dottie accepted my hand to help her up off the cold grass. She pulled my coat around her tight as we started our sojourn back to the party.

"I do. It feels almost silly to feel so scared of something that seems, on the face of it, so ridiculous. But I keep thinking—"

"What if it's real? Yeah, I can't get that out of my head either." Dottie pulled me in close, giving me something that felt like part hug and part death grip. "Leave. Tomas, that's my advice. Just pack up and leave. You could stay at our house for a while. There's so much room. Grant is eager to fill them up with kids. You'd be giving me an excuse to avoid that for a little while longer."

"I can't do that." I gently pried myself out of her arms. "I couldn't just leave him."

"Tomas, you found a piece of paper that suggests the man is trying something which might hurt or kill you. Even if that's not his intention. I don't think you owe him any explanations."

"Maybe. But what if I have this all wrong? What if 'essence' is something shareable? What if this device just needs a little of what I have to heal him?" I thrust my hands into my pockets.

"There's a lot of questions there. Not many answers. Look, come home with us. Say you just wanted some time with me," Dottie said.

"He's dying, Dot. You haven't seen the pain he's been in. I couldn't just leave him alone—"

"He's got Chaput, Coghlan, Cook—hell, I'm sure Henry could assist him in all sorts of ways."

"Dottie, it's not—"

"That simple. I get it. You asked for advice. Advice I hope you'll take. But if you can't or won't, I understand that too.

Okay?" We stopped walking, as we were near the front of the house now. She smoothed a loose strand of my hair from my forehead and back into place.

"I'll think about it. Not tonight, though. Let me do a little more digging. Maybe I can get back up into the attic room. Give it a more thorough look." This didn't erase any of the worry on Dottie's face. She gripped both my wrists and looked me in the eyes, her own alight with determination.

"Is it the money, Tomas? You can be honest with me. If you don't want to leave all of this behind, I understand. In a way that's part of why I married Grant and became a Bellwether forever more, 'til death us do part, etcetera. Neither one of us, in our different ways, could survive all that well without it."

"That's part of it. Of course, it is. But I do really care for him, Dot. I can't shake the feeling there's more going on here than I'm understanding." Knowing she'd tried her best, Dottie relaxed and let out a small exhalation.

"Okay. But you tell me the moment you need somewhere to stay. Seriously."

"Grant would be thrilled." I allowed a smirk to work through the gloom of my racing thoughts. Dottie matched it.

"That's part of the appeal, if I'm honest." She hooked her arm around mine and we continued.

"Are you sure you aren't being unfair to him? Grant, I mean? He doesn't know you prefer the company of your own sex," I said. Dottie snorted.

"Sometimes I forget you're still a man." Dottie shook her head. "Grant Bellwether swept in almost right after Daddy died. He saw an opportunity and he took it. I think he does like me. He's good at putting up with me. I'll give him that. But it was still a transaction. A transaction he and his dad will profit from for many, many years to come. If I treated my husband the way he should be treated, he'd be grinning at the daisy roots." I laughed at this, even though I knew part of Dottie had been serious.

"Love you, Dot."

"Love you too, my ambitious little chuckaboo," she said, and gave me a kiss on the cheek.

"Now, let's head in one at a time. I don't want to draw any attention to the fact we were gone," I said. I knew Dottie was right. I should just leave. But I had to give Vanguard the chance to explain himself. I had to.

20

I could hear Lady Acton singing from the hall. She had a beautiful, technically precise voice that felt colder than the winter wind to my ear. My mom used to sing. Never on any stage, and never with an audience. But I remember how rich and warm her voice was. How much love there was in it. Still, everyone else at Vanguard's party seemed to lap it up. Hopefully Lady Acton would be enough of a distraction that I could slip into the ballroom unnoticed. I looked back down the long hallway, expecting to see Dottie there, waiting for me to enter so she could then time her entrance. I didn't, which likely meant she wasn't taking any chances and giving me a large head start. Which was probably sensible. I turned around and Vanguard was there. In front of me, as if he appeared out of nowhere.

"There's my prodigal dance partner," Vanguard said with a smile. He still looked a little haggard, but it was the highest spirits I'd seen the man in for a long while.

"Miss me?" I teased, hoping it all sounded as casual as I

hoped. I had no plan to confront Vanguard tonight. I didn't want to do it in front of this crowd, that was for sure. And, if all of this had been some gigantic misunderstanding, I'd feel bad for ruining what was likely to be Jackson Vanguard's last grand party at Shearhaven.

"Of course," he said, pulling me in close. As the man's lips parted mine, I winced. Too many questions hung between us. And his lips were cracked and dry. Not his fault, of course, and I felt callous even thinking it. But it made for a wholly unpleasant experience I tried to escape as soon as I felt I could.

"You're in a mood. Is it Acton's singing? Is she singing one of her bawdier tunes?"

"Ha! No, nothing like that. Well, at least not yet. She's just started. Have to warm the crowd up to that."

"Not this crowd."

"Very true." Vanguard took my arm and started walking—right past the ballroom door. "The thing to remember about high society is that they like to indulge in all the same vices and excesses that the 'low born' do. They just have more money to spend on the finest alcohol, drugs, and devices. The key, however, is for them to not show how much they enjoy these activities. Not at first. Like each time is their first, and they just happened into an orgy."

"Aren't we going to hear Lady Acton sing?" The tension that had formed in the back of my neck from his kiss didn't lessen. If anything, it was spreading. A high-pitched shriek sounded from behind us. I whirled, but Jackson turned me back on course.

"Was that Gladys?"

"Oh, perhaps? Maybe they've skipped the concert and gone straight to the orgy." Vanguard said, waving the notion away with his hand. "Whatever the case, I can't say I have much interest.

I've heard Bridget sing so many times. Besides, I have a surprise for you."

"A surprise? Tonight?" The route Vanguard was taking us led to the back stairs. Which led to the attic. Vanguard studied me with a confused grin and narrowed eyes.

"Of course. What's wrong? You seem almost nervous."

"I suppose I am." I stopped walking and pulled Vanguard back to me. "I wanted to talk to you about something."

"Of course, of course. But first, your surprise."

"Can it wait, Jackson?"

"But we're already here," he said with a shrug. I looked around. I didn't understand. We'd stopped in the middle of the hallway. The nearest door was eight feet away. The bend in the hallway leading to the stairs was another five or six feet. Unless the surprise was in the hallway. I looked around. Other than a framed picture of some Vanguard ancestor, there wasn't much to see. Vanguard took me closer to the wall. "This symbol in the wallpaper. You've noticed it before?"

"Yes. I asked you about it, in fact."

"Correct. And, well—I hope you won't be too upset with me—I lied. Or, more correctly, told a half-truth. This, my love, is the seal of the Vanguard family. It has some sort of alchemical symbology. But, as you've come to know, I'm a man of science. So, of course, this has little importance."

Yes, I thought, *I know you're a man of "science." That's what I'm worried about.*

"Not important to what?" I asked, realizing that Vanguard had stopped, obviously hoping for some sort of reaction.

"To your surprise. My grandfather, Cyril Vanguard, was very much intrigued by alchemy. He was raised into it, I suppose you could say. He was also a rather playful man, so when he built this house he placed this "seal" all over to protect from mysterious outside forces."

"What sort of outside forces?" I was equally intrigued and scared of what Vanguard was saying.

"Phantoms, ghosts, and goblins, I suppose. Who can say? It's all nonsense. But, being the playful sort, my grandfather was fond of words. Words, their meanings, and playing with them. You see, what is a seal but something you need to remove or break to pass through?" Vanguard put his hand up to one of the symbols on the wallpaper, and a soft metallic clunk was followed by a rattling of gears. A section of the wall moved inward, and then slid to the side.

"Another hidden door? Your grandfather seems to have been obsessed with them." I felt excitement bubbling up within me. The house had more secrets, and Vanguard was sharing them with me. The tension within me released. The attic was far away. The machine was upstairs. I didn't like the secrets Vanguard kept. But I understood his reasons for keeping his poor health from me. Had he done anything other than free me? To show me how much bigger my life could be? He was, almost literally, giving me the world. I thought of the space in Paris. A hotel would be nice there. Or maybe some sort of apartments. Whatever I wished. There hadn't been much time to get started, although I'd been thinking of ideas. All of this, he'd laid before me, and I'd given him nothing in return other than my companionship and a host of suspicions.

"Yes, he was at that. This whole house is designed with mystical intent." Vanguard grasped my hand and led me into the dark passage. He leaned right into my ear and whispered in it, as though he was sharing a lover's secret. "I don't really understand it, of course. Something about ley lines. About geometries and spaces set up certain ways to allow the flow of magickal energy."

"Where does it lead?" I asked. I didn't like how dark the
passage was. But Vanguard's warm hand and voice in my ear was
comforting. I was reminded of the alley in Paris. How intimate
it was. The two of us, in the dark. Thankfully the mélange of
scents here was much better. Earthy, and damp. But in a pleasant
way. With mossy notes and an earthen chill.

"The cellar, of course."

"I didn't even know the house had one."

"My fault, I'm afraid." Vanguard pulled me deeper into
the dark hallway. Now what light had filtered in from the still-
open entrance behind us was disappearing. I was surrounded in
utter darkness. I squeezed Vanguard's hand just a little tighter. "I
asked the others not to mention it. Not until I could arrange this
surprise for you."

"I can't even see my feet. Is the passage sloping downward?"

"Don't worry. I know the way. Chaput and Coghlan always
take a lamp. But when I sneak down here for a good bottle of my
favorite vintage, I just walk in the dark. It's calming."

"I can see how it could be," I said, trying to feel it.
Unfortunately, I found myself feeling increasingly claustrophobic.
That, and increasingly cold as the temperature dropped rapidly.
It was a great location for a wine cellar. I had vaguely wondered
where the bottles were produced from but didn't have much of a
taste for the extremely dry wines Vanguard favored so had never
sought them out myself.

"One moment," Vanguard said, putting his hand on my
chest. "We're here. Let me light the lamps down here, since you'll
need to see." I was relieved as the gas lamps flickered alive, one
by one. I wasn't sure what I'd expected, but the cellar didn't
look like much. It was a square room, perhaps thirty feet wide.

The floor was made of dirt, and large slugs inched their way across its edges, rippled bodies shimmering in the wavering light. There were racks of wine on three of the four walls of the space. The fourth wall was dominated by a heavy metal door. I looked around, wondering what the surprise might be. A certain vintage of wine? Or was it something behind the door?

"Jackson, what am I meant to be looking at?" Vanguard said nothing at first, but he motioned toward the metal door. I walked toward it slowly, reached for the handle, and pulled. But the door wouldn't open.

"Oh, it's locked," Vanguard said. "Your friend Dottie is on the other side. Chaput was able to grab her and bring her around the servant's entrance."

"What for?" I tugged on the door harder. It didn't move. Inside, I was vibrating with panic. What was this?

"Because you're going to come upstairs with me, sit in that machine, and let me escape this failing vessel, Tomas. You're going to fulfill your destiny."

21

I ran my hands along the door and pressed my ear to it. The metal was rough and pitted, as if it'd been sitting down here to decay for decades. But it was thick. I thought I could hear something on the other side. But it might have just been the pounding of my own heart.

"Dottie! Dottie are you in there," I screamed. In response, I heard a muffled scream. I slammed my fist against the door, instantly regretting it as a bolt of pain ran through it as flesh met metal. The vibrating panic threatened to overwhelm me. I had to stay calm. I had to think.

"I'm afraid we had to gag her. Mostly for the trip down here, of course. We're far down enough I doubt anyone would hear her over the sounds of the party," Vanguard said. There was no gloating or triumph in his voice, which somehow made it worse. My hands were shaking. One of them was covered in—was it particles of rust? Or blood? I knew I was in trouble. Why didn't I leave immediately after seeing the plans for the machine? Why didn't I take Dottie and run a few minutes ago? *Dottie*. Why had I let her be dragged into this? Was everyone who loved me doomed? How had it all gone so wrong so quickly? My thoughts began to spiral. Of course, I knew the answer. I was holding out hope. Hope that this life with Jackson Vanguard could continue. That there was more for me in the world than secret rendezvous. That this life of comfort could buffer me from all the cruelty the world had to offer. And now my best friend—my sister—was in danger because of it. The panic dissipated, and something new replaced it. Rage.

"Let her go. Let her go and I'll get into that damned machine. I doubt it works anyway," I spat, not turning to look the snake in the face. I was afraid to. Afraid of what I might do to him. I was overwhelmed by something I'd never felt in my life. Not with this ferocity. Like a dam had broken open with no chance to mend it.

"No. No, that won't work at all. The machine first, and then I'll let her go." I could hear him walk closer to me. The haughty confidence that had aroused some dark part of me in the past only made me hate him more. I saw him clearly now. What I'd always seen, on some level. What I'd been pushing away.

"Well, technically, you'll let her go. At least that's how it'll appear to her." What was the man saying? His words made no sense. Vanguard was close now. He brought his body right up to my back, wrapped one arm around my waist. My whole body tensed in repulsion. He spoke gently into my ear. "I'm sorry my salvation means your oblivion. I really am, Tomas. You've come to mean more to me than I—"

"Liar!" I twisted out of Vanguard's embrace. I backed away from the man, away from the metal door and back toward the entrance to the cellar. I couldn't leave Dottie down here to die, but I didn't want to die either. My mind raced for options. If Chaput had brought Dottie down here, then he was in on it. And likely lurking nearby to prevent our escape. I could agree to go up to the attic and then try to escape on the way, but that still left Dottie down here.

"Really, Tomas. The time for theatrics has passed. Now there is only the end of this long road we've been traveling." Vanguard was staring at me with sad eyes, and his tone was that of a teacher to a disobedient student. My vision flashed red and crowded with sparks of light.

"Don't talk to me like that. You don't get to talk to me like that." My eyes darted around the confines of the cellar, looking for options. Then I saw it. A glint on the floor near the wine racks. "You have so much already." I walked nearer the wine racks, pointing at them as if to highlight what I was saying. My true intention, however, was to get a closer look at the object I'd seen, trying to keep my hopes low.

"You're right. I have been given much. And I've taken even more. Maybe that it isn't fair. Yet, I find myself with the ability to do just that. How could I not take it? I'm not the sort of person who could resist," Vanguard said. His regret sounded sincere. Not that I cared at this point. The result was the same.

"That doesn't mean I'm going to give it freely," I said, lunging toward the ground, and grasping my hands around a corkscrew. It still shone silver—no doubt tossed off in some drunken state and left to rot in the cellar. Because that's what people like Vanguard did, wasn't it? They used precious things and then discarded them. I scrambled to my feet, hunched over, and wound two fingers through the loop at the end of the corkscrew so that the twisted piece of metal projected from my fist. Vanguard regarded my makeshift weapon and smirked.

"A corkscrew, Tomas? We both know that you aren't going to use it."

"Let Dottie out, and I won't have to," I growled. "I don't have a lot left, Jackson. Especially after all of this. I'm not going to let you take the last of what I do have."

"You're going to put that thing down and march up to the attic," Vanguard barked, his eyes aflame with a fearsome rage. He lunged at me. Not expecting the man to attack, I was knocked backward and fell against the wine racks, sending a few bottles flying, saved from breakage by the soft dirt of the cellar floor. Vanguard had both hands on the arm I was using to wield the corkscrew. I was surprised by how strong Vanguard was. He had always been larger and more thickly built, but I'd counted on him being weakened by his condition.

"Accept… your fate, boy," Vanguard growled through gritted teeth, pushing my arm downward so that the end of the corkscrew was near my throat. "You were made for this. To serve a higher purpose. An empty cup in need of filling."

My only response was a rumble of rage as tears filled my eyes. I was losing. I could feel it. How was the man so powerful? If I'd had a second to think, I might have wondered why Vanguard was so willing to damage the very same body he was eager to take over. Because that was what he was getting at, right? What the machine upstairs was meant to do? Destroy my "essence" and replace it with Vanguard's? But those thoughts were far away in the moment as I rallied every ounce of strength I had. I channeled all the rage and shame of a lifetime of hiding and feeling lesser than. I screamed. All I could hear or think of was the scream, my voice ragged as I pushed back against Vanguard's strong arms. And then, the look on Vanguard's face as his eyes widened. The sickening slurp as the corkscrew stabbed through Vanguard's skin and deep into his gut.

Vanguard crumpled over. Trickles of blood flowed out of the wound and coated the corkscrew and my hands. In shock, I pulled the corkscrew out, which increased the trickle of blood into a river.

"Oh, God," I stammered. "What—what did I—" For a second, silence reigned—all sound swallowed by the cold, damp darkness that surrounded us.

Then Vanguard laughed. A low, pained laugh that turned my skin to gooseflesh.

"There we go. There you are. There's… the lion," Vanguard said, his hands instinctively moving toward his wound, but not trying to stop the flow of blood.

"You're insane."

"No. I just like being right. Chaput had his doubts. Thought you were too weak. But I saw your desire. Your desperation."

"You act like you wanted this." I hated how shaky I sounded. I got off the ground and wiping the blood on my hands onto my pants, desperate for it to be gone. The red of it was lurid. I'd seen blood. The blood of the soaked-through bandages of the men who'd come back from the war. Blood from the chickens I'd helped Mom kill for supper. But here, in this strange cellar and in the flickering flame of the lantern, the blood burbling out of Vanguard's wound was too saturated. Too thick. It clung to my hands. My head swam.

"Of course, I did. Look at the ground, my love."

A faint circle had formed around us. The light was strange and unnatural. At first it looked like the ephemeral lines of sunlight through the edge of a curtain. But as I watched, it grew in brightness until it was a light source unto itself. Its light filled the room, and strange markings started to appear within the circle. Until, finally, in the center a symbol I knew all-too-well appeared. The seal of the Vanguard family.

Fear and confusion overwhelmed my senses. I had to run for the cellar door. I'd have to come back for Dottie. Maybe I could get Henry's help? Whatever was going on here, it was too far beyond me. My mind was recoiling from the unreal suddenly made terribly, horrifically real. I nearly made it to the door when I slammed into something. Hard enough I bounced off it and back to the ground. Stunned, I picked myself back up, my clothes covered in blood and dirt, and looked ahead. I reached out my hand and felt a wall where there should be none.

"What is this?" I screamed—to Vanguard, to God, or to the universe in general, I couldn't say.

"A spell. Well… a combination of them," Vanguard wheezed as blood trickled from the corner of his mouth. "Activated with my blood."

"But the machine—" I began, whirling around to look at Vanguard, who was still prone on the floor, his head lolled to the side as if it was too much effort to move it. Spell? What was this "man of science" talking about?

"A pretty distraction. An elaborate *nothing*. A false danger above, so you didn't notice the danger below," Vanguard said, his voice wet with blood now. Even though the man was dying, I could hear the note of triumph in his voice.

"For what?"

"Transfer your essence. That part was true. I thought this body would be strong and healthy for so much longer. But nature had other plans. The other spell is a field. You're bound to this spot until the transfer is done. Devised… by her. By the oldest and strongest of us." Vanguard's thoughts were drifting off into smoke. He sounded drunk. Rambling. There was a loud metallic creak as the metal door opened.

"Sorry to interrupt but my ears were burning." Lady Acton emerged from behind the door.

"You!" was all I could manage. The woman wore another crimson dress, tightly fitted with an extravagant collar. In her hand she held a small lacey handkerchief.

"How was my performance? I almost convinced Will to let me be Juliet. A woman playing a man playing a woman. What could be more subversive? But he was too busy adding in more bawdy jokes. Plus, if we're being honest—and what better time than now—I think he liked seeing the boys in dresses."

"Where's Dottie?" I managed to sputter, fearing the worst.

"Halfway home, I sus…susp…," Vanguard said, his eyes glassy.

"Why don't you let me take over, Jackson dear, while you're busy bleeding out," Lady Acton reprimanded. "Jackson convinced Grant Bellwether—reliable old boy—to take Dottie home. She was bundled into a carriage and sent away shortly after you entered the house."

"She's safe," I said, suddenly feeling strangely weak. At first, I thought it might be relief. But it felt stronger than that. Like I hadn't slept in days. I looked over at Vanguard, whose right hand twitched slightly, as if he were grasping something that wasn't there.

"Safe for now, love. But I called dibs," rang out Coghlan's voice from behind me. I turned my head, with some effort through my rising stupor, and saw her and Chaput standing at either side of the cellar entrance. Their hands were covered with blood. Dried rivulets ran from their mouths to their chin. Their eyes had an unnatural cast to them, as if they were reflecting some unseen light.

"I don't know why you're choosing her of all people," Chaput said through a blood-stained smile. "She is so *moche*. I'm quite looking forward to taking over that magnificent body of our stable hand, though. So much fun to be had."

"Well, Master said we should pick someone easy. No elaborate shenanigans like all this for us." Coghlan gestured at Vanguard and I, both half-dead in the glowing circle. She looked at her own hand, a liquid drop of blood on her fingertip. She brought it up to her mouth, and a purple tongue flicked out and lapped it up. She closed her eyes in satisfaction. When they opened again, the strange glow within them seemed more intense. Chaput noticed this and smiled.

"Dear Gladys was quite a treat, wasn't she?"

"Yes, I do enjoy the boys that Sanderson brings for our get togethers, and there's certainly fewer loose ends to tie up when it's people no one misses. But I must say I prefer white meat, as it were." Coghlan laughed at a joke I didn't understand.

"Ah, *oui*. Having someone like Gladys around to soak up all the energy here first—well, it is like a fine wine, no?" Chaput asked. Coghlan nodded sweetly.

"Her disappearance will be harder to explain. But I don't mind a little clean up."

I looked over at Acton, a look of disgust crossed her face, but only briefly. I found it difficult to speak. I watched as Vanguard's hand opened and was surprised to see my own hand opening as well, dropping the corkscrew.

"The universe, my dear Tomas, loves balance," Acton said, crouching down near me and cupping my chin in her hands. She almost looked pained. "Every time we tap into the energies of the universe to do our will, there's an opposite reaction. Destroying one person's soul so that one might inhabit their body is, shall we say, a very big swing of the pendulum."

"You know what she's going on about?" Coghlan whispered to Chaput.

"Of course," Chaput said with a harrumph, although it wasn't entirely convincing. Lady Acton looked up at them, annoyance shining through a rueful smile, before continuing.

"I don't need this sort of crude magick these days. I prefer longevity to body-hopping." She brushed a stray hair from my face. I had never noticed her skin. As smooth and hard as ivory. Her lips were full and heart-shaped yet held no supple promise. Even here, where I could smell the soured taste of wine on her breath, she was as a statue on a pedestal, removed from the petty cares of we weeping and regretful mortal men. She brought her mouth close to my ear, her breath so warm, and whispered.

"I devised this spell, long ago, in desperation. Vanguard, for all his power, isn't quite there yet." Then she pulled away from me, my face moving toward the heat of her hand. Craving one last touch. Because there was an odd sort of care in it. And I knew it was the last I would ever feel. At last, my eyes welled. At last, I understood I had no way out.

"I knew there was one very big hurdle. How to escape the consequences of such an unnatural act. Thankfully, the 'universe' is rather stupid. There's no intelligence to magick. There is simply action and reaction. So, if one could trick their victim into being the aggressor—well, you see, Tomas? *You're* the killer here.

"Jackson—or should we be completely truthful and call him Cyril, for that is truly who he is and has always been." Acton looked over at Vanguard, still on his back, his chest rising slowly. A dreamy and triumphant smile plastered on his lips. "Cyril is 'simply' repaying his murder by destroying your soul and taking your body. The universe, by the laws of magick, remains in balance." Lady Acton started giving quiet orders to Chaput and Coghlan, as a surgeon might confer with his fellows during an operation. I couldn't hear them. I was drifting. Drifting to someplace else. Darkness crowded my vision. I'd gone beyond panic now. A strange calm settled into me. But the confusion remained. Then Acton was crouched beside me again, wiping the tears from my eyes with her handkerchief. It smelled earthy and floral at the same time. I couldn't tell if I hated the smell or adored it.

"Cold comfort, I suppose. But I detest all of this. Truly. Vanguard's abuse of this spell—so many times now—sickens me. But he has something of mine. Something very precious. So. Sometimes needs must."

She stood up over me, all business once more, the brief flicker of humanity passed. She stuffed her lacey handkerchief, stained with her lipstick and my tears, into the sleeve of her dress, and walked into the dark at the edge of my vision.

My mind grasped for understanding.

"I just wanted to be home. J-just wanted to be safe." Whether I said this aloud or not, I no longer had no way of knowing. I knew, instinctively, my time to understand was almost up. With that thought, my mind was flooded with ideas and memories that were not my own. I understood that these thoughts were Vanguard's. I understood what it meant, as well. I could almost feel myself being pushed out. But with this invasion, for the brief few moments when I and Vanguard were conjoined in thought, I understood it all.

I'd been selected, and the web had been spun, the moment I was taken to the attic to clean and wrap the statue. That's when I was introduced to the secret room. The placement of my art studio was no accident either. The conversations in the night I was meant to overhear. The "chance" viewing of the machine and the drawings of it. Every diabolical piece of the puzzle was laid out before me as Vanguard's thoughts became my own. I'd been given a mystery to solve. Pushed to the brink of fear. For myself, yes. But also, for Dottie. All so I wouldn't realize the real danger. The danger in letting my fear and anger take over so that I'd lash out at Vanguard.

At the end, I thought of Dottie. Dottie, who'd loved me not because she needed to or was supposed to, but because she did. The next time she saw me, it wouldn't really be me at all. She'd sense the change. I knew she would. But what would Cyril Vanguard say to her in my body? It was this thought, more than anything else, that finally broke me. The damage Cyril and his cohorts could do to Dottie. How many times had I'd railed against the unfairness of the world? How many times had Dottie told me that the world wasn't fair and expecting fairness was just asking for disappointment? I hated that she was right. I loved her so much.

Interlude

A Fireside Chat

Tomas became himself once more very slowly. After a very long while, enough of his spirit had congealed to remember that he existed. He was a person—or had been, at least. His name was Tomas Doyle. Once he'd remembered that, he willed more of himself toward his shattered consciousness. For all the knowledge that Lady Acton, Vanguard, and the rest of their coven had, they did not know one truth. A soul cannot be destroyed. Pushed out, yes. Even scattered to the four winds. But never destroyed. It was a long time later that Tomas fully reformed within the cellar of Shearhaven. The wine racks were little more than moldering debris on the floor. The lamps were dark, but Tomas could see in the dark now. And he could see the thick coat of dust on them. The metal door was there as well, even more pitted and rusted than it had once been.

It took a very long time for him to figure out how to move in this new form. He walked up the earthen slope out of the darkness and to the secret door. He held his hand up and it passed right through it. He emerged once more into the hallway of Shearhaven and found the house changed. The wallpaper— and their damnable seal—had been removed or painted over. Tomas moved from room to room, as he walked toward the great hall. Walking wasn't the right word for it, of course. But it's what he had to imagine to move forward. Every room was empty. The elegant and strange black wood was gone from the floors in favor of odd fluffy carpeting. The molding on the walls was gone. The windows were fantastically clear and made to move up and down. The place looked utterly abandoned, which is why Tomas was so surprised that, once he did enter the front hall, there was a warm fire crackling, and he saw light again for the first time since his death. It made him want to weep, and he felt the pain, but not the cold trickle of a tear welling from his eye and down his cheek.

Stranger still was the man, whose back was turned away and toward the fireplace, sitting on a simple wooden stump. The stump emerged from the floor, roots and all.

"Mr. De Artte," Tomas said, relieved he still had a voice. Or, at least, he thought he could speak. And maybe that's all it took. The man turned around and smiled at him. It was Mr. De Artte, Tomas was sure of it. But it looked nothing like the man he'd met in the woods outside Shearhaven. This man was thickly built, with deep brown skin and warm brown eyes. He wore a white shirt with a loose V-neck collar, and black breeches with brown leather boots. He had a wide smile and pearly white teeth. He patted the space next to him on the large stump.

"It's me. Although, Mr. De Artte is just what Vanguard and his crew called me." Tomas sat down on the stump, wondering what the point of sitting was anyway.

"You won't get tired but going through the motions that the living require usually helps in the transition," De Artte said, seemingly reading his mind.

"I thought the great transition had already happened."

"They always think that," De Artte said with a chuckle. "Oh, by the way, check it out. What do you think?" He produced a small wooden recorder, carved with intricate whirls of detail, and lacquered in a deep and beautiful deep amber. He put it up to his lips and released a rich, resonant flutter of music. Short, and sweet.

"How long has it been?" Tomas asked. Mr. Reynold's eyes widened, and he laughed.

"How long did you think I needed to get this right? A hundred and forty-four years. Or something like that. And for the record I mastered making these about eighty-eight years ago. It hasn't taken the *whole* time."

"What now?"

"What do you mean?"

"What do I do now. I'm not in heaven or hell, so I guess that was all a lie," Tomas said bitterly.

"Well, slow down there. Now, you get to figure things out. Not everyone gets that luxury. Just a select few."

"Luxury? I'm doomed to wander this house—a terrible specter—and that's a good thing? I thought this was a punishment?" Tomas got up on off the stump and drifted toward the fire. He put out his hands and, as expected, felt nothing of the heat within it.

"You all think a lot of things are a punishment. And you seem to like it. To be honest, it's pretty messed up."

"You talk so strange."

"Oh. Sorry, I probably am." Mr. De Artte put his recorder back into his pocket. "That'll take some getting used to for you."

"Why do you look so different?" Tomas drifted back over to

the stump and sat down.

"Well, what you saw before was Vanguard's idea of me. This is your idea of me. Which, I have to say, I like better." De Artte turned his hands and inspected his own body.

"You look like—well, there was a man. He brought us a note, from my dad. They weren't in the same company, but they were at the same battle. Dad's last battle. I'm so confused."

"You'll catch up." Mr. De Artte patted Tomas on the knee, and then stood up. "Anyway, this time you've been given to reflect on your life, the nature of change, the change of nature, and so on—it is a gift. Or, more precisely, it can be a gift. It doesn't turn out great for everyone. But I think you'll do just fine. I can tell you one thing for certain; Vanguard won't get that luxury when his time comes."

"Then… then you haven't gotten him yet?" Tomas was unable to keep the disappointment out of his voice. All this time. All these extra years Vanguard had while Tomas's had been stolen from him. A spark—a dangerous spark—of rage and despair flared in his brain.

"Unfortunately, no."

"Then why are you here? You should be out looking for him!" Tomas shouted. Mr. De Artte came toward him and placed his hands on his shoulders. And he felt it. He felt the warmth and weight of them. Something he'd never thought he'd feel again, and it helped calm him.

"I'm sort of everywhere all at once. Kind of have to be," De Artte said. "And believe me if I knew where he was, I wouldn't let him out of my sight. But his wards have gotten better. He used to use the power of this place to keep me out. The wards and the wood and all of it. He was still in your body when he got better at the game. He moved from here to London, his newly adopted son in tow, and then to Brussels. After that, I lost him completely. He never re-emerged."

"Sorry I yelled." Tomas looked down at his hands, his anger waning as the reality of his new existence started to sink in.

"Don't worry about it. I've gotten much worse. Hell, you name it, I've seen it. Bargaining, rage, disbelief, acceptance, and welcoming—a little yelling isn't so bad."

"How long do I stay like this?"

"As long as you need. Until you're ready for the next step."

"You will get him, won't you? Vanguard, I mean?" Tomas looked at De Artte expectantly. A wrinkle formed in the other man's brow.

"There's a time I would have answered that with an emphatic yes. I might've even added an 'of course,' but Vanguard is by far the wiliest of Acton's proteges. In fact, he's one of a select group I haven't gotten to. At this point, all I can say is that there's nothing I'd like more than to do that. Not just for the grand design. But for you, and all the other men Vanguard has destroyed for his own outsized sense of importance."

"Well. If you do, and I'm still around. I'd sure love to know," Tomas said. De Artte looked at him intently.

"You might not care as much then. But I promise, you'll know. Wherever you are." And with that, Mr. De Artte was gone, taking the tree stump and the fire with him. Tomas soaked in the bird song coming from outside as the first light of dawn began peeking through the windows. He left the front hall, to the back of the house, up the stairs, and then up to the attic. So much time had passed, and Shearhaven felt like a tacky mockery of what it had once been. Tomas wondered what people were like in the here and now.

In the attic, he noted with grim amusement that the rooms

no longer had any doors. He could look into the empty room where the fake machine had once rumbled through the night. All those machinations. He thought, perhaps, he should be flattered. So much effort just to trap him. At last, he reached his studio. It was as bare as the rest, of course, but there was still a grand window there. It was larger, and octagonal versus the round one he'd known so well. He walked up to it and took his first look at the strange world he'd come back to.

Part Two

Max

1

I pushed the cart forward, relishing the rumble of the wheels as they rolled over the line of tiling near the entrance to Blake's Super Center. The scent of oranges hit me first, followed by the subtle earthiness of the potatoes. I could even smell the dampness in the air. They must have just turned off the sprinklers that kept the veggies wet. God this felt good. Five years. It'd been five years since I'd been able to do this. I'd half forgotten what it felt like, having time to do something as mundane as going grocery shopping. It almost made me feel giddy. I know how it must sound. Poor, rich bastard. Too busy and too popular and making too much money to enjoy the simple things in life. Here's the thing. I get it. I agree with you. Before I blew up, I would have thought the same thing. What's weird is, I didn't think about this stuff at all. I didn't miss it. I was too busy. But now that I'm here? It feels weirdly precious.

I loaded my cart up with way too much junk. I hadn't bothered to make a list. I'd like to blame that on being out of practice, but even when I would run to the store for my ma, I never bothered with a list. And everything looked amazing. I was looking forward to not having to be "camera ready" for the first time in my adult life. I wasn't going to pig out constantly, but I sure as hell was going to demolish some chocolate pudding cups the next couple days. I wanted one of those cheap frozen pizzas with their cracked crust and weird little pepperoni chunks. And potato chips. I wanted all the flavors of potato chips. I tried to remember all the food I'd longed for the last five years. I wanted to eat them all. This is going to sound dumb. I admit it. For the first time in a very long time, I kind of felt like an actual human and not the center of a machine designed to make money and little else.

"Welcome to Blake's," the cashier said flatly, not looking up from her phone. From the way she was punching at the screen, she was either typing something intense or playing an app game.

"Oh shit!" a male cashier from the next lane over suddenly exclaimed. "Becks, wake up, you're waiting on Maxymo Morgan!" The cashier helping me put her phone down and regarded me with sleepy eyes. Her nametag read Rebecca.

"Oh. Cool." Rebecca started to scan my items at a deliberate pace. "Sorry about the delay. My jerk boyfriend texted and he needed to be told what was what."

"No worries," I said with a quick head shake. Because it was. It was glorious. Me with my groceries. Rebecca with her boyfriend problems. No million-dollar decisions. No one waiting for the next album. No critics sharpening their knives, looking for any sign of weakness. No "friends" coming with more empty hands and empty promises. I turned to the other cashier—Ethan, according to his nametag. "And it's just Max, now."

"Ohhh, that's right. I read that article a month or so ago

in *People*. You walked away from the biz, right? Away from your channel and everything," Ethan said.

"You read *People*? What are you, fifty?" Rebecca laughed as she glided small bags of lunch meat over the price scanner one by one.

"It was a slow shift and it's right here," Ethan said.

"Yeah, left all that behind. For now. We'll see how things go. Just needed a break." I'd practiced the answer, since I knew questions like this were going to come up no matter where I went. Even here in a grocery store in Alton, Illinois. There were about twenty-five thousand people living here. At least according to Google. It's one of the reasons I came here. Not small enough to lose my mind. But small enough I might not get harangued every couple seconds. Plus, Midwest folks down this way had a way about them, in my experience. Different than Chicago that's for sure. This place, a four-and-a-half drive southwest, felt a world away. They gave you space. Some of them didn't know who I was. They weren't "in my demo" as my agent would say. But it was more than that.

Maybe that famed Midwest niceness meant they had a little respect for my space. And, maybe, that famed Midwest modesty meant they didn't want you to think too much of yourself. Because, sure, that niceness and that modesty always had little asterisks attached. They were nice to "the right kind of people" and modesty was something they weaponized against others as well as themselves. I didn't care though, to be honest. Long as it kept them at a distance.

"How long you in town, man?" Ethan asked.

"A good long time, I hope. Just bought the place up on the bluff. Shearhaven."

"You bought the old spook house?" Ethan's eyes went wide.

"I know the place has a colorful history." I shrugged. "Honestly part of the reason it interested me. There's not another place quite like it in the country."

"Colorful history? Colorful present, too." Ethan was now fully turned away from his duties to be a part of the conversation. Not that there was anyone in his line anyway.

"Don't be such a child." Rebecca sighed, not looking up as she tried to smooth down the seam flap of a package of ramen so she could scan the barcode tucked under it.

"She's only talking like that because she's never experienced it herself."

"You have?" I asked.

"Well, yeah," he said with some hesitation. "A few years ago when I was a sophomore in high school. This was before the hotel chain renovated it. It was a mess. Mostly home to meth heads and people trying to hook up."

"Wait, is that where you took Amber Horowitz? The date she won't talk about with anyone?" Rebecca stopped scanning the groceries, much to my chagrin. Not that hearing the local folklore wasn't fun. But it'd been a long drive from Chicago, and I really wanted to get my groceries and get to the new place. My stomach rumbled as I eyed the chips in Rebecca's hand.

"Yep. It's going good. We found one of the nicer rooms. I'd brought a couple sleeping bags. A candle. Half a bottle of wine."

"How could any woman resist?" Rebecca resumed her scanning, to my relief.

"She was into it! Real into it. Said I was sweet! Anyway, we're getting going when all of a sudden, it's like someone is stomping their feet above us! Just stomp, stomp, stomp. Hard enough that dust and little bits of paint or whatever was falling down on us," Ethan said, disgust crossing his face at the memory.

"So, what? Some meth heads banging around doesn't sound that scary. At least when they're on another floor," Rebecca said.

"Yeah, smartass, except we were in the attic at the very top of the house. Someone would've had to be on the roof."

"Racoons, then?"

"Those'd be some big ass raccoons," Ethan countered. At this point, I was content to be an audience member and just smiled as they continued. Thankfully, Rebecca had resumed working away at the scanner. "Besides, I was telling this story to a bunch of my friends, and Jimmy said he worked on the renovation with his dad—"

"Big Jimmy or Jimmy Zee?"

"Jimmy Zee, not that it matters." Ethan turned to me. "And let me tell you, that hotel chain saved you a lot of money. Jimmy said they hauled out two dumpsters worth of crap out of that place. It was a mess. Mold and rat sh—"

"I think he gets it," Rebecca said quickly.

"Right. Well, *I'm* telling this story and Jimmy says it's impossible anyone was up there. I tell him which room, and he says there wasn't any kind of roof access. They had to cut a hole in the roof. And there weren't any ducts or hidden spaces or anything like that."

"So, it *had* to be a ghost." Rebecca scanned the last item and told me the total. I fished out my credit card and inserted it as Ethan continued.

"Well, if it'd just been me and my story, sure, I wouldn't believe it either. But there's has to be a reason that hotel sunk millions of dollars in renovations into the place and then gave up a year later, right?"

"Didn't the parent company go belly up during the pandemic?" Rebecca was turned away from me now, more caught up in the conversation now that she'd done her job.

"Well, I better be off. See you two around," I said. I was pretty sure I was smiling like a dork, but I was ridiculously happy. I'd done my own grocery shopping for the first time in years, and even though I'd been recognized, these two hadn't peppered me with questions or fallen at my feet. Maybe this wasn't typical of the reaction I'd get, but I hoped so.

"Oh, sure, man," Ethan said. "Come back anytime. We're here to '*Help you / find the way / What you're searching for / To the break of day*'" The last part Ethan sang in a squeaky falsetto, quoting one of my songs. Not going to lie, my smile lost some of its sincerity, and Rebecca looked like she wanted to crawl under the cash register and die.

"Right!" I quickly pushed my cart to the exit. "Later." As the automated doors slid closed behind me, I heard Rebecca begin to tell Ethan what an idiot he was.

Tiny flakes of snow were drifting downward as I pushed the cart to my car. I breathed the air in deep through my nose, enjoying the briskness of it. No expectations, and—so far—no one crowding me to see what they could get out of me. Now that I was stocked with enough food to last me until the chef started next week, I was more than ready to see my new home for the first time.

"Next stop, Shearhaven," I said to no one as I slid the key into the ignition, my giddiness getting the best of me. I was so ready for this. I was ready for life on my own terms. I turned the key. The car groaned weakly, and died.

2

I really hadn't wanted my first look at Shearhaven to be like this. The winter cold seeped into my bones as I waited too long for a driver to come pick me up, staring at the app screen willing them to come get me faster. That was one clear disadvantage to a smaller town. I'd thought about waiting in the grocery store. But that felt awkward. I wondered if Rebecca and Ethan were inside, gawking at me as I sat in my useless slab of a Saab and pretended I was busy. My driver ended up being a quiet, acne-scarred kid with long hair strategically styled to hide his face. Looked like he'd just gotten his driver's license. Of course, I say "kid", but he was probably just a few years younger than I was. He nearly passed by the road that led up the bluff. I didn't blame him though, as it was easy to miss unless you knew what to look for. Thankfully, the hotel chain that had briefly taken ownership of Shearhaven had installed two old-fashioned lanterns on either side of the drive. They must have been on a timer because they weren't lit yet despite the early winter dark, but they were still enough to help me spot the entrance and point it out to the driver.

As I sat in the back seat of the tiny compact car, my grocery bags wedged beside me, I thought I should have the lamps changed to something more modern. The hotel chain had clearly been playing up Shearhaven's history with housings that looked like they were made more for oil lamps than lightbulbs. Not my style at all. I might need to put in a gate, too. I'd pissed off some of my fans when I announced I was leaving my socials. Mostly the ones who felt some kind of ownership over me. I was okay with that. The fewer boundary-less weirdos private messaging me with their bad art and cringey poetry the better. The fans who stayed were nice and patient, for the most part. Telling me to take as much time as I needed. That mental health was important. My agent reminded me that, nice as that was, I couldn't disappear forever. Or I'd return to find everyone else had moved on.

As the tiny car finally crested the bluff and crept up the smooth paved road, I thought how right the cashier at Blake's had been. I leaned closer to get a better view. As good a view as I could get from the backseat. Lampier Hotels must have sunk millions into the house. They added this newly paved road, cleaned up the landscaping, installed the lamps below, and much more inside. I'd only seen pictures so far—something everyone from my manager to my ex-boyfriend was horrified by—but Shearhaven already felt like somewhere I could call home. It's hard to explain, but as soon as I saw the pictures it felt like the sort of place I needed. That, and it was practically a steal. There weren't a lot of buyers locally with the money to not only buy it, but maintain it, and pay the taxes on it. Plus, the bank selling the property had grown increasingly eager to offload it.

Now I found that none of the pictures adequately

communicated the scale of it. I gasped as the car emerged from the thick trunks and branches of the oaks that surrounded the house. The east and west wings of the house hadn't been opened yet. But the central house was gloriously lit up for my arrival. Construction crews would be coming in a couple weeks to break up part of the parking lot the hotel had installed. I was hoping to plant a garden in the space instead. I wasn't a gardener, but I thought I could be one. The thought of letting my mind drift while I planted seeds or weeded or watered appealed to me.

"Whoa, they really cleaned this place up," my driver said as he parked the car in the circle drive in front of the house. I was surprised to hear him speak, as he'd mostly communicated by nods up until that point.

"Yeah, still some work to be done, but it's… well, it's big." I was still trying to take in the fact that I owned this behemoth. The thought of that had filled me with excitement throughout the buying process. Spurred on by the pictures Felicity, my assistant, would send me of the progress. But now I realize I'd been looking at puzzle pieces. Never realizing how vast the whole puzzle might be. It felt like the sort of place that could swallow you whole. "You've been here before?"

"Oh. Yeah, a while back." He hunched his shoulders sheepishly. "It was pretty banged up then. Broken windows and plywood on all the doors. Not that it stopped anyone."

"I'd heard a little about that," I said casually, hoping he understood I didn't care about whatever teenage shenanigans he'd gotten up to in the house.

"Yeah." He twisted his hands on the steering wheel.

"There's something else," I ventured. Because it was plain to see he was practically exploding with desire to tell me.

"There is. I just—I know who you are. Just don't, like, write

     Jon Wesley Huff

a song named 'Weirdo Driver Boy' or something if I tell you, okay?" I couldn't help the short laugh from escaping. What was this guy so afraid of?

"That's not really my style."

"I know. I know that." He blew out a stream of air and relaxed back in the driver's seat. His eyes flicked to the rearview mirror, catching my own. They were wide, and haunted, and the bemused smile faded from my face. "I went up here with my buddies when I was twelve. Just stupid kid stuff. Smashing bottles the older kids left behind. Scratching our names and dumb jokes about our enemies in the old wood. That sort of thing."

"Yeah, I get you." Except, I didn't. My mom, deathly afraid of the city she lived in, kept me close and indoors until I was eleven. And then after that there wasn't any time for a childhood.

"Well, my friend Freddie had some matches. Thought we should start a fire in one of the fireplaces in the big front room. Which was a damned stupid idea. But I didn't know anything about fireplaces. About having to clean them and opening flues and all that. So, we get a decent fire going using some pieces of the old wood molding and whatever else we could find. Instantly I know something's wrong. There's smoke everywhere. It smelled weird too, like copper. Freddie and I freak out."

"I don't blame you."

"The rest of our buddies hear us yelling, come downstairs, and freak out too. Everyone's yelling different ideas about what to do, and I'm trying to decide whether to run or call the fire department. Then there's this ratty old sleeping bag in front of the fire. I'd seen it before and thought about using it as kindling. But it was kind of gross. Damp and moldy. But it just flies up off the ground and onto the fire. Smothers it in seconds."

"Flew up?" Suddenly I felt very cold and tired. I'd sat in the car while it idled feet away from my new house for this?

"I know how it sounds. Freddie thought he was real smart. He was so freaked out, he fessed up to his dad and told him what happened. Freddie's dad said it had to do with changing pressure in the chimney from the heat or something. Dumb ass."

"You didn't agree?" I was a little more intrigued now. It seemed like it'd take a lot for a boy to admit to his dad he was lighting fires in dangerous old houses.

"No. Because I saw *it*. Or saw where it would have been if you could see it. The smoke kind of revealed it. Like it'd flow around where the thing was. It looked like a man. It lifted that sleeping bag and threw it at the fire." The driver looked at me with determination, almost as if he was daring me to disbelieve him. I was saved by a rapid knock on my window.

3

"**M**r. Morgan, welcome home." Felicity Capshaw smiled at me through the foggy car window, clad in a winter coat with a wide collar of faux-fur and a knit cap. Felicity had been my personal assistant for years, which is why the formality of the greeting had a playfully mocking undertone. There'd been no question in her mind whether she'd join me at Shearhaven. Even though I was taking some time away from it all, I still needed someone to manage the business of Maxymo, LLC and to coordinate with me when there were big questions to answer. Plus, I needed someone who could manage the everyday needs of the house.

"Heya, Felicity," I said as I got out of the car, grateful for her consistently perfect timing. "Stopped by and got a few groceries. Can you help me carry them in?"

"Of course," she said. "But I wish you'd told me. I could have gotten a delivery of whatever you needed. And saved yourself a towing charge."

"Eh, I know. But I wanted to see a little more of the town. And I wasn't sure what I wanted," I said. Felicity appraised the bags of groceries as she twisted the plastic handles into her fingers for a better grip.

"Apparently what you wanted was an extra thirty pounds," she said, her eyes wide.

"Don't you start."

"Hey, *you* can eat whatever you want. But I'm sure as hell going to get some more cottage cheese and fruit delivered here for me. Not all of us can be musical boy genius hermits." With both our hands laden with bags, I turned to the driver.

"Thanks for the ride. And, uh, the warning," I said. The driver said nothing in return but nodded. Clearly, he didn't think I believed him. Which, of course, I did not. He sped away with such speed the car fishtailed a little as it rounded the circle drive.

"Warning?" Felicity asked.

"Later. Right now, I want two things: To see my ridiculous house. And to get warm." I followed Felicity up the steps to the grand porch. It felt a little cold and uninviting. I thought about getting some potted pines or something for the front, though I wondered if everything would just be dwarfed by the immensity of it.

"Right this way Mister—actually, should it be Master Morgan?"

"How did I end up letting you move in here?"

"I seem to remember it being less 'letting' and more 'begging.'" Felicity pushed the door open with her hip, and took a step back so I could enter and take it in.

"Fuck me," was all I could manage. Not the most eloquent words to greet my new home with, I know. But it's all I could think of.

"It's something else, right? Most people settle for a cabin in the woods or something for a creative retreat. You buy an estate."

"It is a lot, isn't it?" I could feel the heat from the twin fireplaces, newly clad in gleaming black brick, as they blazed. I'd worked for hours and hours with my favorite interior designer, flying him in from Italy to Illinois to oversee the renovations. At first, I'd been too busy to visit the property as I wrapped up my last commitments to the label, my clothing brand, and the other various arms of the company. Then, it became something akin to waiting for Christmas to open a present. I liked the idea of waiting until the renovations were done.

"You want to go through the secret door? Well, one of them." Felicity gave me a mischievous wink. She'd spent a week in the house, getting it as prepared as possible while I was in Greece filming my "goodbye" music video. I had every intention of getting back into the thick of things again. I just needed a long recharge. But everyone from my agent to my public relations people to Felicity thought I shouldn't say that. Make it a clean break. For most of those people, it was a marketing move. For Felicity, I was pretty sure she hoped the break would be permanent. She, more than anyone, knew the toll my old life was taking on me.

"You know I do. Damn, that Italian marble looks even better than I thought it would." I stared at the white slabs that served as mantles for both fireplaces. I took in the details, delighting in seeing all my planning and curation made manifest in the house as we slipped through the hidden door and into a long hallway that led back to the kitchen.

"I've got a couple local candidates for your personal trainer. Chef Ambrose will start next Monday. He's making the drive up from St. Louis twice a week." Felicity proceeded to rattle off the other services she'd procured for the regular maintenance of the property, as well as when they started. I was only half-listening. Shearhaven had lived in my head for so long. I'd tried to imagine it in my head during the renovation process. Now that imagined thing was solidifying into the very real, very large thing all around me. We'd packed away the groceries into the kitchen's pantry by the time she paused. "Oh, and the stove we ordered didn't end up fitting. It was, like, a millimeter off. But I'm going to—"

"Felicity, you're doing it again," I said, shoving a box of cereal onto a shelf. The woman's delicate pale skin blossomed red splotches.

"Oh, sorry. I am trying to get better about that. I just want to make sure you're up to speed," Felicity said, grabbing at the ponytail she usually kept her mane of curly red hair in, pulling it to the left of her head, and smoothing it downward. A nervous tick she'd also not been able to train herself out of. I shook my head.

"And I appreciate it. But I am kind of tired. I don't know if it was the driving, the anticipation of seeing the house, the grocery store, the car breaking down, or the driver's ghost stories—but I'm kind of exhausted. I wouldn't mind a little alone time to let it all sink in."

"Of course," Felicity said quickly. There was a hint of something—maybe even hurt—in her eyes, but she was too professional to show it. "I was going to head into town and grab dinner. Get away for a while. Do you want me to bring anything back?"

"Nah, I'm good. I stopped through a drive-thru on the way down. And I've got plenty of snacks if I get hungry later," I said.

I saw Felicity to the door, feeling a little bad about practically shooing her away. But I was feeling drained. Maybe it was the wave of heat from the fireplaces after being out in the cold. Or maybe it had just been an eventful day. Felicity walked out the door and down the steps before swiveling around.

"Did you say ghost stories?"

"Later. I promise." I waved goodbye as she got into her tiny coupe. I hoped she wouldn't ask me about the driver's tale. I really didn't want to think about it anymore myself. I felt idiotic even worrying about it, but my mental defenses felt brittle. They were currently trying hard to stave off the panic attack that had been creeping up in my chest. I closed the front door and turned around. The great hall of Shearhaven greeted me. I still needed to find some art for the walls. There was a ridiculous amount of wall, though, here. Two stories worth, in fact. The walls had all been painted from an overbearing green to something lighter and more neutral. My designer preferred to let the art do the talking, and let the wall remain neutral. The furniture was all aggressively modern. Metal, wood, and glass all combining with different textures to bring the aged estate into the twenty-first century. There wasn't a decision I hadn't been involved with. But every individual piece I'd approved, now that it was collected all at once here, well—

"What the fuck have I done?" I wondered aloud. I heard a soft clatter to my left. I saw a small wooden owl—carved by an artisan in India if I remembered correctly—had fallen off a skinny table near the entrance.

"Now how did you get there?" In the cavernous hall, the question returned to me in a muffled echo.

4

brought a gust of winter chill in with me as I entered the café. This was quickly rebuffed by the warmth of the café itself, awash in the scent of ground coffee beans and the low chatter of its patrons.

"Welcome to Brews & Clues," said the man behind the counter, looking up momentarily from his milk steaming to flash me a bright smile. "I'll be with you in one sec." The man was tall with rich tawny skin. His wide shoulders sloped slightly to a barrel-shaped middle with a pleasingly round belly. The white shirt below his black apron (embroidered with the café's logo and the man's name, "Ty") had the first two buttons undone, letting an enticing patch of curly black hair poke out. I tore my eyes away and looked at the menu. Alton had no shortage of coffee shops, but I still hadn't found one that made my favorite drink as well as my favorite café back in Chicago.

"What can I get for you?" Ty asked.

"Well, I'm hoping I found the right place," I said, flashing my green eyes with a quick, subtle intensity designed to test the waters. Ty noticed, the corner of his mouth bending into a quick smile before he forced it back into submission. "I'd like a large latte with three shots of espresso and oat milk. I've tried three different places in town, but the woman at the bookshop said this was the place to go. So here I am."

"You must mean Jess," Ty punched my order into the computer. "She's one of my best customers. And one of my best ambassadors!" I pretended to peruse the pastries, although I knew exactly what I wanted. I wanted to give Ty enough time to look at me. I glanced up, and he was doing just that. I smiled and pointed to a large cinnamon roll with a flakey-looking golden crust and a thick creamy glaze.

"Good choice."

"That implies there are bad choices."

"Or nothing but good choices. One of which you chose."

"Good point."

"It's elementary, dear Watson," Ty said, mimicking the pose of Basil Rathbone as Sherlock Holmes in a large, framed movie poster of *The Adventures of Sherlock Holmes* that was on the wall behind him.

"You're very committed to your theme," I said, taking a good look around as Ty finished making my drink. The place had a rustic coziness about it. If I had to guess, I'd say it used to be some sort of western-themed bar or restaurant. It'd been made over with a mystery and detective theme, with old boxes of games like *Clue, Whodunit, Alfred Hitchcock's Why?, Intrigue,* and *Mr. Ree* lining shelves, along with vintage Hardy Boys and Nancy Drew hardcovers, a deerstalker cap, magnifying glasses, movie posters, and other mystery-related paraphernalia.

"Ah, yeah, the mystery theme," Ty said. "Used to be a bigger deal. When I first opened the place, we had a murder mystery night, book clubs, that sort of thing. I take it you're new in town?"

"Yeah, moved in a couple weeks ago. Still trying to get a lay of the land."

"It's a nice little town. I mean, it must be a big change from Chicago. But it's got its charms." An undercurrent of red blossomed underneath his brown skin, and he quickly added "And, yeah, I know who you are. I was trying to play it cool."

"Ha! I appreciate it. But, yeah, there's been some culture shock. Not gonna lie. I knew there would be. But honestly everyone's been chill. It's refreshing." I watched the muscles in the man's arms bulge a bit as he worked a metal jug under the milk steamer. "You kind of get stuck in this bubble, you know? When you're—ugh, I don't know what to call it. 'Famous' sounds pretentious. But you know what I mean. You kind of forget most people are just living their lives and you're not the center of the universe. You know?"

"Not really, but I can imagine." Ty handed me the large steaming mug.

"Sorry. I'm babbling like an asshole. I do that sometimes when I'm nervous."

"Something got you nervous?"

"Maybe," I said. "Hoping I like this latte because I'd like to come back."

"You will. I've got another barista coming in soon. I could take a break. If you want to chat? I've lived here my whole life. Maybe you could pick my brain a little if you've got any burning questions about the area."

"That sounds great." I nodded and turned to find a good spot to sit. I'd forgotten to order my coffee to go. I had a meeting in a half hour with the record company. But I figured that could wait. I texted Felicity asking her to rearrange the meeting and settled into a corner booth. Ty walked up, taking his apron off.

"That was quick," I said.

"Oh yeah, my barista showed up early." Ty nodded his head at the young woman taking an order behind the counter.

"So, you were telling me about murder mystery parties? But in the past? You don't have those things anymore?"

"Not really. We stopped all that during the pandemic, and honestly, I just haven't had the energy to start it up again."

"Well, you're still carrying on the theme well," I said. "You ever miss it? The other stuff?"

"Yes, and no," Ty took a sip of his drink and sat back thoughtfully. "It was a lot of extra work. But we did build up a nice sense of community around it. I figure I'll get back to it eventually. Eventually just hasn't gotten here yet."

"You like a good mystery, then?"

"Definitely. For instance, why does a mega-successful social media-star-turned-bona-fide-pop-star-slash-entrepreneur end up in Alton, Illinois of all places?" Ty cocked an eyebrow as he regarded me from over the top of the rim of his mug.

"Fair. I guess you'll just have to dig for clues, detective." I took a sip of my drink. It was good. It was very good. "What made you open a mystery-themed café in Alton, Illinois?"

"Well, that's easy. My family's lived here for generations. I thought about moving to St. Louis or Chicago or Indy. I was close to going to Purdue. That didn't work out. I took the money my folks had saved up for college and opened this place instead."

"How did your parents feel about that?"

"Oh, the first year they were freaked out." Ty's eyes went wide with the memory. "But then I managed to keep it open through the pandemic. And now it's doing real well. I mean it when I say people like Jess are ambassadors. Word of mouth means a lot in a place like this. Alton's decent sized, but just small enough that your reputation can make or break you."

"I wonder how mine is holding up here, so far," I said, and then kicked myself because I'd somehow brought the conversation back to me again.

"Oh, everyone's excited. Not sure buying Shearhaven won you a lot of good will from some folks, but I don't know if it matters to most people anymore."

"I'm surprised people have strong feelings about it one way or another." I was instantly intrigued by what Ty might mean, but he looked like he wished he hadn't brought it up.

"Eh, towns like this can have long memories. Especially when you've got historical haunted tours and all that. Alton takes pride in its history, even the rougher parts."

"What problem do people have with Shearhaven? I mean, as its current owner it'd be nice to know." I felt bad for trying to push Ty further on the topic when he seemed so hesitant. I wouldn't have mentioned it, but my curiosity was growing. Ty nodded and sighed.

"I get that. It's just that it's a lot of old—well, I don't want to dismiss people's anger or hurt. Even if it feels kind of pointless these days. But a building is just a building in the end. No matter what sort of things happened in it."

"What sort of things? I know it's supposed to be haunted."

"Yeah, definitely there's a lot of talk about that."

"I'm not really into that kind of thing. And so far, I haven't run into any ghosts." *Mysterious falling objects, sure,* I thought to myself. There'd been a couple more since the little owl decoration. But those were all small, silly things. Changes in air pressure from opening doors or vibrations from walking by on old floors.

"The family that built it—the Vanguards—were always considered odd ducks. Most of the stuff, stories about curses and infertility, you could just chalk up to small-town gossip and equally small-mindedness. There were rumors the third Vanguard to own the property was—prepare yourself—a *homosexual*," Ty said, mouthing the last part dramatically.

"Oh no! Well, that's the worst."

"Well, except he *was* kind of the worst," Ty said, his mood sobering a little. "Not because he was *maybe* gay. Obviously, I have no problem with that. But my great grandad used to tell stories that got passed down. They were so over the top, I sometimes wondered if they were true. But the way my parents and aunts and uncles talked about them—whispers around bonfires or late night at drunken family get-togethers—I think they're true." Ty took a sip of his coffee.

"Well," I urged. "You can't leave me hanging with that!"

"Ty, can you help me?" the woman at the counter asked, with a hint of fear, from across the café as a bus load of teenagers started filtering into the place. Ty sighed and got up quickly, turning just long enough to regard me with those enormous golden-brown eyes.

"Guess you'll just have to come back for the rest of the story. Assuming the latte was to your satisfaction?"

"Best I've had so far," I said, which was true. I couldn't help but note the man's tight pants as he ran back behind the counter to assist with the flood of customers. The last thing I needed was a relationship. But the universe had sent me a beautifully thick man with curly hair, adorable eyes, and a beautiful behind. Who was I to argue with that? Besides, I'd only been in Shearhaven a few days, and I was already starting to get lonely. Felicity was great, and we were close. But at the core of it all, I was still her boss. It might be nice to have a distraction. Plus, the history of Shearhaven was kind of exciting. I wondered if I could even theme my next album around the house and its stories. That might be kind of fun.

The whir of the coffee grinder pulled my attention back to the counter, and I saw Ty staring at me again. Just a moment, before he looked away. I felt almost giddy. This is what I wanted. A life full of unscheduled possibility. I wished I'd taken in that feeling more. Lived with it a little longer. But you never know when life is going to twist on you. You never know when you've got a visitor waiting for you at home that's going to turn everything upside down.

5

The snow pelted my car in thick chunks as I maneuvered up
to Shearhaven. Thankfully I'd had my wipers changed when they
replaced the battery in the Saab, but I still had to concentrate,
white-knuckled, as I went up. The roads were slippery, and I
hadn't driven myself anywhere in four or five years, let alone
in the snow. But my thoughts kept drifting back to Ty. God his
arms were amazing. And that smile. I pushed the thoughts away
and concentrated on the drive. I was surprised, then, to see
another car in the drive beside Felicity's compact: a sleek, shiny
red coupe. Felicity was on the front porch of the estate, hugging
herself against the cold. There was a woman next to her, wearing
a short red dress with a white outer jacket, and a red hat with a
wide brim. The two women turned as they heard my car sloshing
through the wet snow. Closer, I could see the annoyance on
Felicity's face.

"Heya," I said as I stepped out of the car.

"Max, this is—" Felicity began, but the other woman cut

her off, striding up to me with her hand outstretched. She moved with purpose, despite wearing high heels.

"Brianna Acton. Bree for short. I'm a solicitor from London," the woman said as my hand gripped hers.

"I was trying to tell her we don't accept solicitations," Felicity said through gritted teeth.

"*I* was explaining that's just what we call lawyers in England, dear." Acton glanced back at Felicity through a tight smile.

"It was a little joke."

"Yes. Positively microscopic."

"We don't accept lawyers, either." Felicity muttered as she crossed her arms. I don't particularly love tense situations. I wanted nothing more than to jump back in the car and flirt with Ty some more at Brews & Clues.

"I represent Mr. Ernest Nestor, late of Lampier Hotels." Acton focused all her attention on me. She leaned in, as if we were the only two people in the world. "A personal item of his was regrettably left behind here, and he's eager to get it back."

"Really? This whole house has been scraped and painted and waxed and redecorated and no one mentioned anything. What was it?"

"Well, it's a book. Perhaps we could go inside and discuss it?" Acton motioned back toward Shearhaven, a dainty crook in her hand. Felicity walked up and physically wedged herself between us.

"I'm afraid Mr. Morgan has an important, pressing call that he's already postponed once today." This is why I pay her so well. I would have smirked if it hadn't felt so rude.

"That'll give me time to check with the crew who did the remodel. See if they saw anything," I said, hoping to smooth the situation a little. Acton let out a girlish giggle and smiled breezily.

"Of course! I certainly don't want to keep you from your business. I'll be in town a few days at a local hotel. It really is very important." Acton withdrew a card from an inner pocket in her jacket and handed it to Felicity.

"Yeah, uh—I'll get in touch soon," I said, giving the woman a weak wave. Felicity glared at her as she gracefully slid into her car, turned, and headed into Shearhaven, with me on her heels. After closing the door, Felicity sighed and threw the business card into a small bowl near the entrance.

"Fucking rich people." Felicity marched over to the mini bar we'd installed next to the left fireplace in the great hall.

"Agree. Although, well, I *am* one of them." Felicity waved a tumbler at me.

"Yeah, but you're… you." She poured a generous amount of whiskey. "You're not some entitled ass hat."

"I got close," I said quietly. Felicity took a drink, closing her eyes as the liquid burned down her throat, and then looked at me. The anger had drained from her.

"And you pulled yourself back." She walked over to me and put her hands on my shoulder. "Before you did any damage."

"There was a little damage."

"Okay. Yes. A little damage. But you never spoke to me like that. Like I was… *nothing*. Possibly because you knew I'd knee you in the balls."

"That might have had something to do with it. Oh, by the way, I might have met a guy? Maybe?" I poured myself a whiskey, plopped in a stone, and cursed when I dribbled some on my hand and the side of the cup. Felicity snapped it away and downed it.

"Hey!"

"After the call with the label. Also, I needed another if you're getting back in the dating pool."

"He's nice. He's normal," I countered.

"Historically you're not the best judge of that." Felicity's eyes narrowed, challenging me to disagree. Since I couldn't, I decided to change topics.

"You want to ask the renovation crews about this book of Acton's? Did they keep an inventory of what was in here when they started work?"

"I didn't see anything like a book. It was all furniture. Some art. We donated everything to a local charity." Felicity sighed, setting her glass down with a clunk and massaging her temples. "But I can double-check and help the horrid British lady out."

"Hey, the sooner we check, the sooner we get rid of her. Besides, maybe she's nice once you get to know her," I offered. Felicity was about to respond, and it was clear from her expression she wasn't going to agree, when a bright shattering crash sounded behind her. She turned and took a step back. On the ground were the shattered remains of the whiskey tumbler.

"Sorry, Max. I guess that was my fault. I hope that wasn't expensive. Let me go grab a broom."

"It's fine. Just leave it for the cleaning crew. They're coming tomorrow, right?"

"Well, yes, but I don't want broken glass all over," Felicity said with a head shake. "I'm going to get the broom. Refrain from dancing around that area until then." I waited for Felicity to leave, and then dropped the smile I was faking. I tiptoed over to the minibar. I'd seen Felicity set the whiskey down. She hadn't set it anywhere near the edge. I looked down, and sure enough there was a small ring of liquid where she'd sat it down from the whiskey that had spilled onto the side as I poured it. The ring was smeared on the right side, exactly as it would be if someone had swatted the tumbler off the minibar. I stared at the smeared ring, wondering what it could mean, and reminded myself I didn't believe in ghosts.

219

6

Days passed before I got back to the café. I'd wanted to get back earlier, because I was genuinely intrigued by what Ty had to say. Also, of course, I was intrigued by Ty himself. But I'd gotten caught up in recording a new song.

"Mr. Morgan, good to see you," Ty said as I entered Brews & Clues and he finished wiping a counter.

"Call me Max," I said. "And I'll take my usual."

"Does ordering something once make it 'usual?'"

"Well, it's going to become my usual. I don't suppose you could take another break? Give me the resolution of the little mystery you put in my head the other day?" I attempted to ooze every ounce of charm I had. The same charm that had gotten me millions of followers and a record contract. Plus, a few stalkers and a bad drug habit. Though my family certainly assisted with that last part. All things you do not say to the gorgeous man you just met. Ty nodded.

"Why don't you go sit at your 'usual' table over there and I'll be over. Sal's out back taking the trash out. Hopefully a busload of drama students on a field trip won't interrupt us this time."

When Ty joined me, we started talking about everything other than the topic at hand. We made small talk about my move and settling in, compared the cuisines of Alton versus Chicago (Alton fared poorly, but it was hardly a fair fight,) and Ty told me about the last murder mystery he'd devised, before he'd stopped doing them. Which sounded intimidatingly complex and clever and honestly made Ty just a tiny bit sexier in my mind. A half hour passed before I eased into the subject.

"So, about that secret family knowledge about Shearhaven," I said, sipping the last of my (now cold) latte. Ty glanced at the time on his cell, and his eyes went wide.

"Oh, crap! I've left Sal on her own for a half hour. Let me just go check in on her. I'm sure she's fine or she'd have yelled at me way earlier. But I'd be a bad owner if I didn't check. Plus, I've got something to show you."

"You're just trying to be a master of suspense, aren't you? This secret better be worth all this waiting."

"It isn't. I mean, I'm not trying to create suspense. I just need to check on Sal, honest!" Ty put his hands up in assurance. Less than six minutes later, Ty was walking back to the table with a small frame in his hand.

"I thought you might find this interesting," Ty said as he handed me the frame. In it was a small document, only slightly larger than a postcard, with a creased and yellowed bit of paper. The bottom was charred and flaking. "That's the last remaining evidence of my great-great-grandfather's business."

"Sanderson & Sons' Shipping," I read as I scanned the document. It was the top half of some sort of letter.

"His name was Ralph. He had two sons—Art and Rich."

Ty settled into his chair, put his elbows on the table, and watched me as I studied the document. "Rich died on the river. Not sure how. The family history is fuzzy about that. But they suspect he got caught up in one of Ralph's schemes. Art is my great-grandfather. Worked with his dad until he was about fifteen, until he'd had enough."

"Wasn't a fan of the shipping business?" I scanned the rest of the letter, but it seemed to be nothing more than a typical business communication with a client about pick-up times and locations. Ty shook his head.

"Shipping was a euphemism. I mean, yeah, that's what they did. But it was *what* they shipped that really mattered. They didn't bother with cotton or grain."

"Were they rum runners or something?"

"Well, prohibition wasn't until about fifty years later. But they did transport the occasional 'off the books' alcohol now and again. Usually imported stuff. That wasn't their bread and butter, though. That was in more illicit substances." Ty sat his mug down, and a troubled expression washed over his face. "The thing is, if it was a little alcohol and drugs, then it'd be a fun family story. You know, a little dark branch of the family tree. Nothing too serious. But I'm afraid it wasn't just that."

"What is it?" I barely knew Ty. But I didn't like seeing him like this. The joyful essence at the center of the man seemed dimmed. Ty just exuded joy in a way that I forgot was possible, if I'd ever even known it. To see that joy diminished was painful.

"Sorry. This topic is just—well, I've thought about it a lot. When my dad first told my mom, she was angry for a week. Not at Dad. Just at the world, I think. Anyway, the thing is—and this is where Shearhaven comes in—my great-great-grandfather shipped, uh, people too. For all kinds of reasons. Especially brown people. Mostly brown people. Which, as you can imagine, was a weird thing for me and my mom to find out."

"Shit," was all I could manage.

"Yeah. I know. That's some heavy stuff to lay out there," Ty said. "But, hey, you wanted to know."

"Vanguard had slaves? Wait, was this before or after the Civil War? My history isn't the greatest." I suddenly felt very uncomfortable, as if I shouldn't even be asking these sorts of questions. Something about it all seemed very raw for Ty. But he shook his head.

"No, this was after the war. Not that people didn't have slaves still. But I never heard about the Vanguards having slaves or anything. From what I understood, Jackson Vanguard—the third Vanguard to live in Shearhaven—used to have these wild parties with his coven that broke out in orgies of drug-fueled sex and violence after midnight."

"Covens and orgies?" I said, too loud, drawing a look from Ty. I matched his hushed tone. "Sorry. Got it. Public space. Please go on."

"Thanks. It's not the sort of thing I want connected to my family. The main event for these parties was always a sacrifice to whatever dark gods they'd pledged allegiance to. Art was haunted by helping deliver boys and girls—some his age—to Vanguard. His dad beat him, called him weak. He ran away when was fifteen. Didn't come back until after his dad died."

"I didn't mean to make you drudge all of this up. When you said Shearhaven had a history, I thought I was going to get some ghost story about your ancestor seeing a woman in gray that walked the shores of the Mississippi at night or something."

"I'm probably being too uptight. I don't know how much of this has been shared outside the family. I've got a lot of aunts and uncles and they're all loudmouthed bullshitters." Ty turned and looked out the window. Shearhaven was miles away from the café, but I was sure he was picturing it. "So, hell, maybe half the town knows. Plus, trouble has always followed that place. In the seventies a tribe out of Oregon, the last remnants of the natives who used to live around these parts—tried to get the land back and tear down the house. This was back when it was a rotting dump, too. Most of the people in town would've been happy to see it go."

"Why didn't it? I mean, why wasn't it torn down?"

"Some bigshot lawyers from London swooped in and produced the original agreement Cyril Vanguard signed with the tribes in the area when he built the house. I mean, who would have thought? No one's even sure who the lawyers worked for, but everyone figured Vanguard still had relatives over there.

"History lost track of the last man named Vanguard who'd lived at Shearhaven. Tomas Vanguard was his name. Jackson Vanguard's supposed adopted son, although most think that was just a cover for a romantic relationship. A way for Jackson to pass Shearhaven to Tomas. By this time the community was souring on the Vanguards. From what I heard Tomas was forced to flee Shearhaven under the cover of darkness. Never did return."

"Jesus," I said, staring at my empty mug. "I might need something stronger. You're basically saying that I didn't just buy a spook house, but a spook house owned by a family of racist murdering witches?"

"Pretty much. So, want to go on a proper date?" Ty asked, turning the conversation a couple hundred degrees from where it'd been heading. "I wouldn't usually be so bold, but I do have to give Sal her break soon. And, you know, you being famous does have its perks. Like no guessing games on my part about which way you swing."

"You read the *People* article, didn't you?"

"'Maxymo: Outgoing and Out Gay' by Margaret Bonvillain," Ty said, hiding his smile behind his mug. I groaned.

"The editor who handled that piece was fired," I said with some satisfaction. "And it wasn't even me who raised the ruckus. They changed Marge's headline. You don't want to cross Marge."

"Noted. If I ever become famous enough to interview."

"As for that date… how about Thursday? You pick the place. I like pretty much everything except stuffed crust pizza. That cheese is nasty." I screwed up my face in disgust. Ty laughed and got up out of his chair, downing the last of his drink.

"Sounds perfect. You want me to pick you up?".

"Nah, that's silly since we'd just be coming back to Alton. I'll pick you up or I can just meet you there. Either way." I got up out of my chair, and there were a few odd moments where we weren't quite sure how to say goodbye to each other. It felt like we'd crossed over the line far enough that a handshake would feel facile, but a goodbye kiss seemed to hold too much meaning, as well. We settled on a quick, if fervent, hug.

I was distracted when I got home, thinking about Ty mostly, but also thinking about the dark history around Shearhaven. If there was ever anyplace that could be genuinely haunted—if the Sanderson oral history of the place was accurate—this would be it. I thought about the seemingly innocuous events I'd written off since I'd moved in. Mysteriously falling objects, the sound of footsteps, the rustle of drapes in a closed room. I'd had every reason to write them off before. As I entered the house this time, however, stepping through the large oak double doors, I seriously entertained the idea that I might not be alone in it. I jumped when Felicity entered the front hall and said my name.

"Jesus, Felicity, can you not just pop up like that?" I asked.

"Okay," Felicity said with controlled calm. "I'll try to enter through the secret door more loudly in the future. Your dad called. By the way, still so happy you gave him my phone number instead of yours."

"You are a lifesaver." I clasped my hands on her shoulders "Also, that's why I gave you that big raise last year, remember? To run interference."

"I'm starting to think it wasn't enough."

"Probably not." I let out a long sigh.

"You did pay for my top surgery. So that bought you a little more leeway, I guess. *A little.*"

"I should probably call him back. After I eat."

"Guess I'm making two grilled cheese sandwiches then. I thought part of the reason you went to town was for food?"

"Technically, yes. But I stopped by the café, and I got caught up in a conversation with the owner," I said, throwing the sentence away as if it meant nothing.

"Ah, yes. This Ty person. Distracting enough you forgot to eat, huh?" Felicity stopped at the door to the back of the house and smirked at me.

"Don't start. And remember to use the cheese slices on mine. Not the cheddar, please."

"My boss. A man of refinement," Felicity said with a nod. "By the way, I checked with the renovation crew. No one saw a book of any kind."

"Shit. I forgot about the London lawyer. I should probably give her a call. See if I can't send her on her way." It wasn't that I'd forgotten about Brianna Acton, exactly. But her presence seemed almost absurd. I got that she was only doing her job, but what kind of book could be worth all this fuss?

7

"How's the day been?" I opened the prepped containers of food Chef Ambrose had prepared for me the day before.

"Not bad, the rain is driving customers into our loving arms," Ty said.

"Lucky customers."

"Too bad you couldn't make it for lunch today."

"You know I'd rather be there with you instead of entertaining a lawyer. I looked her up online. She's one of the main partners in this firm. And she's flying here to track down a book for a client? It makes no sense. I'm intrigued." I scraped zoodles onto a plate and covered them with a chicken breast and some creamy sauce.

"I thought I was supposed to be the lover of mysteries in this relationship." Ty said.

"I mean, they're not a small outfit either. They've got to have an army of people who could do it. Hold on. Did you just use the 'r' word?" I asked, closing the door to the microwave, but not hitting the start button, because I wanted to hear Ty's reaction. There was a pause on the other end.

"Well. Maybe. That a problem?" Ty was being hesitant. I felt instantly guilty.

"No. I love it. I was just teasing."

"Mm hm. I'm going to get you back for that one," Ty said.

"I look forward to it."

"I bet you do—what the hell are you doing by the way? I'm hearing all kinds of racket in the background."

"Sorry. I'm just getting lunch zapped. Ms. Acton is supposed to be here any minute."

"Rich boy microwaving his own food? For shame. Where's your PA?"

"Felicity's back in Chicago for the next few days. A few legal things to work out up there on my behalf. So, I'm reduced to microwaving my own meals, it's true."

"The meals your personal chef made for you," Ty reminded.

"Yeah, yeah. Want to do dinner sometime this week? You still haven't been to see the place."

"I wish I could, Max. With my night guy out, I'm having to work open to close all week. I'm usually wiped by the end of the day. Next week? I want to see this old mega-mansion that brought you into my life. I probably should thank it."

"Be careful, this house might say 'you're welcome' back."

"Starting to believe in ghosts?" Ty tried to say it like a joke, but I could detect the note of sincere concern in his voice. I wasn't sure if I'd meant what I'd said as a joke or not either.

"I don't know what to—" The doorbell let out a soft bong. Brianna Acton was right on time. "Gotta let you go. Talk soon."

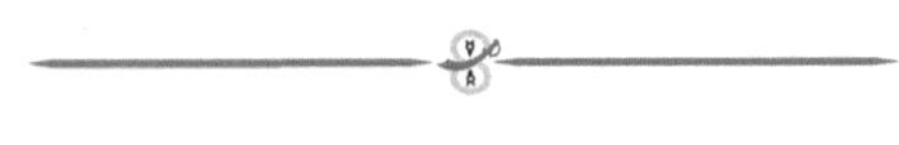

"This is really delicious," Acton said, as she took another mouthful of the chicken.

"Chef Ambrose is one of the best in the area. I was lucky to nab him," I said. Acton had all the bearing of someone used to formal dining. Her back was straight, and she ate delicately and slowly. She was dressed in a smart business suit draped by a finely knit shawl. There was a precision to her that I found fascinating and unnerving. It was hard to imagine her wearing anything but the chicest clothes, enunciating each word with clarity, and approaching the world head-on with poise.

I remembered when I was first starting out in the music biz and I was just some suburban kid who blew up on social media. No real music experience or knowledge. I didn't know how to read or write music or play an instrument. I'd go into rooms of people just like Acton—assured and put together—and feel instantly out of place. More than a few of those people made sure to remind me that I was. Now, after everything I've been through, I knew this was a form of manipulation. Maybe not even one those important, poised people were aware they were perpetrating. But it always kept me just low enough—making me doubt myself and my abilities—that they kept me under their thumbs for years. I pushed the thoughts away as best I could. It was unfair to saddle new people with one's old baggage.

"How long are you in the States?" I asked, hoping to break through the silence.

"Not much longer. I'll be on a flight back tomorrow if I can be." Acton let the rest of the sentence—*if I get what I came for*—go unsaid. "This was unnecessary, Mr. Morgan. Though I do appreciate it. I didn't mean to take so much of your time."

"I must confess. I suggested lunch here because I wanted to take more of *your* time," I took a sip of the wine Ambrose paired with the meal. I still wasn't a huge fan of wine. When I had it, I liked it as sweet as possible. I ended up taking polite sips of the bitter, dry red more to wash down my food than for any pleasure.

"Oh?" There was a note of suspicion in the woman's voice, and I realized that she might have taken what I said the wrong way. I forgot that not everyone was familiar with me. A bad habit. Also, a little egomaniacal. This woman might not realize she wasn't my type, and I wasn't hitting on her.

"I did a little homework. To be blunt, I wanted to know more about this book you wanted. Why you personally came all this way to retrieve it."

"Ah, of course. I imagine you are wondering about its value. I realize that, strictly speaking, you own everything in this house free and clear. We'll be more than happy to reimburse you for the item." Acton carefully sliced a sliver from the chicken and ate it delicately, never taking her eyes off me. The truth was this woman made me nervous. And my nerves weren't doing my communication skills any favors.

"Sorry, I'm not making myself very clear. If there's a book that belonged to your client, he's free to have it. I don't need more money. I guess I—well, I'm a slightly bored shut-in who should be spending more time on his music. I was just intrigued."

"Oh, I see," the woman said, her good humor returned. "Well, I hope I'm not too much of a disappointment in that regard. I'm afraid I know precious little about the book myself. It's apparently of more personal value than monetary. I don't know if it's a photo album, a family bible, or a book of recipes, to be honest."

"Ah." I hoped my disappointment wasn't too obvious. "This Mr. Nestor you spoke of, I take it he's an important client?"

"He used to be," Acton said ruefully. "Until his son used

his hotel chain for a system of high-class brothels and sex trafficking."

"Fucking hell," I spat. I winced in irritation at myself. I can't imagine I was coming off particularly refined. And I was irritated I cared that I wasn't. I started to take larger gulps of wine as we talked. Who was this woman to me? No one. And yet, I was falling back into the old pattern. All the album sales and awards and I was still trying to prove myself. With some effort, I pulled my thoughts away from the cliff and back to the conversation at hand. "I hadn't heard about that."

"That was by design. We're very good at our jobs. Not that the lack of publicity really made any difference in the end. It wasn't the elder Nestor's fault. Poor dear. I'm really here as a personal favor to him. Before he lost everything, he was one of our best clients."

"I wish I could be of more help. But between all the redecoration and getting everything updated to run as part of the home management system here, I doubt there's a nook or cranny left for a book to be found in," I said, my nose feeling the first tingles of the alcohol. I'd forgotten I hadn't had breakfast this morning. Acton smiled at me mischievously.

"Well, there is one place where I'm guessing your people didn't even know to look. A secret passage, as it were." The woman drank the wine deeply and smiled.

"Okay, now you definitely have me intrigued."

Both Acton and I were eager to finish our lunch, so we decided to skip the dessert, and proceed to the secret passage. I was astounded when part of the hallway wall opened, and an earthy smell wafted up from the darkness beyond it. We turned on the flashlights on our phones.

"I feel like I'm in a video game." I immediately felt silly for how excited I was by all of this. But it was certainly helping to break up the monotony of the week. Plus, the pixie-like glee that Acton had in being able to show me the passage went a long way to warming me up to her. Maybe there was some life in there.

"It is all rather exciting, isn't it? When Mr. Nestor gave me the instructions for how to open the passage and where it'd be, I honestly wasn't sure if he was being serious at first," Acton said. "The walls are rock. The floor too. Watch your step. It's slippery."

I decided to take the lead. It was my house, after all. I didn't want the lawyer bumbling into something dangerous. I wish I could say my thoughts were entirely toward chivalry, but I did consider she was probably the last person I'd want launching a lawsuit against me.

"Do you think they carved all of this back when the house was built?"

"I'm not sure," Acton said. "I hated the one geology course I took. I suppose it could all be natural. Something fortuitous they took advantage of. My client didn't really talk about any of that. Although I do suddenly wish I'd brought a parka and a sensible pair of boots."

"I know what you mean. My Freestyles are probably a lost cause." I slid a little in my far-too-expensive sneakers. The rock below me was wet, probably from the torrents of rain pouring above ground and trickling through the soil.

"Oh!" Acton yelled, her high heels losing all traction. She slid right into my back. Thankfully I'd had just enough time to brace myself thanks to her exclamation. Acton took off her heels and went barefoot, the bottoms of her pantyhose instantly soaked. "I hate this day."

"Looks like there's a larger chamber ahead."

"That's our destination. Apparently, they used this as a wine

cellar. There should be a vault door. The book was kept within."
Acton worked her way past me then, her excitement getting the
best of her. The wooden racks that once lined the chamber had
decayed and moldered to nearly nothing, with thick layers of
spider webs draped all around.

"I'm going to pay someone to spray the hell out of this
palce," I said, a shiver running up my spine as a replay of a video
I'd seen online played in my head. A spider egg sac that had
exploded into a stream of baby spiders.

"There. There's the vault door." Acton shone her flashlight
on an aged metal door tinged with rust. She ran to the door,
paying no heed to the webs or the squelch of mud as her bare
feet raced across the dirt floor of the cellar. I followed more
cautiously behind her. There was a change in the woman. The
carefully composed demeanor hadn't fallen away, exactly, but it
had slipped. There was a desperation to her quick movements.
A sudden flare of blue light, shielded by Acton's shadowed form
before me, illuminated the room.

"What was that?"

"Sorry, just my phone's flashlight. I was trying to make
it brighter." Acton gripped the handle of the rusted door and
pulled. It creaked slightly, but stayed shut.

"What the hell sort of phone do you have?" A fading blaze
of white light still seared my eyes. I moved more quickly to catch
up with her. I'd need a very long shower to not to feel the spider
webs on my skin and in my hair. Acton ignored the question and
kept pulling on the handle.

"I have no traction in this mud. Maybe you and your
thousand-dollar sneakers will have better luck. My firm will be
happy to cover their replacement, by the way."

"No big deal." I gripped the handle and pulled with all my

strength. The door didn't move an inch, no matter how hard I pulled. "It must have rusted shut."

There was another flash of blue light from behind me—so brilliant it bounced off the parts of the door that were still reflective and seared my eyes again. I was just about to shout at Acton and tell her to turn her damned flashlight off when the door flung open. I lost my balance and fell backward toward the muddy ground. Thankfully Acton was there, stopping my fall just in time. She made sure I'd found my footing again before bolting inside the vault. I couldn't help but wonder at the woman's dedication to her task.

"God damn it!" Acton yelled with surprising ferocity. I shone my flashlight into the room. It was small, not much bigger than a changing room. In the center of the room was a dais, atop which stood a rust-streaked metal book stand. An *empty* metal book stand. At the edge of the glow of my flashlight, I saw Acton. She was bent over slightly, holding her palm against the rocky wall. Her back rising and falling as she tried to calm herself. I was unsure of what to do. My sympathy for her was tempered by distrust. The intensity of her rage made no sense for a disinterested third party recovering an item for a client. Any thought of whether I should comfort her or not was lost the next moment. I took another step and felt my leg brush against something. I looked down, and saw the bodies, half buried in the mud. This time, I was the one screaming.

8

"I should—should I call the police?" I asked as Acton and I emerged from the tunnel and back into Shearhaven. Spiderwebs coated the light hairs on my arms, tangled in my hair, and even clung to my lips. I wanted a shower. But I kept seeing them. Two bodies, right by the door to the inner vault. Skeletal frames with flaking, dried skin giving a slight impression of the humans they might have been.

"No. You should not," Acton said flatly. She had a weary, faraway look in her eyes.

"But what if they've been missing—"

"Mr. Morgan." The woman said my name too sharply. With too much annoyance. She drew in a quick breath and released it slowly. "I'm not a forensic scientist. But that looked like an old-style butler uniform and a housekeeper's dress. And based on the condition of the bodies—well, I believe if anyone had ever reported those two missing it'd be a very cold case indeed."

"I suppose but—"

"And look, I'm not your lawyer. But you're new in town. You're trying to get away from it all, right? Why else would someone like you be living in place like this?" Acton's eyes locked hard on mine. All artifice had been dropped now. But I could tell there was more to tell than she was sharing with me. "Reporting two long-dead corpses in your house is not a good way to lie low. Even less so than buying a ridiculously huge estate. Even if it was in Nowhere, Midwest, USA." My irritation at her rudeness was somewhat lessened by the fact that her advice was sound.

"What am I supposed to do? Lock the vault with the skeletons in it away, and ignore the creepy secret underground passageway forever?"

"Not secret enough, apparently," Acton said bitterly. She shook her head. "I'm sorry. I'm being a complete and utter tosser." She pinched the bridge of her nose, straightened herself up, and regained some of her former composure.

"It's okay. Although I get the impression this book is more important to you than you've been letting on." She sighed deeply and then threw me a sheepish smile.

"I haven't been completely truthful, no. The book is quite valuable, and my job might be on the line if I don't find it," she said. I nodded. It was a reasonable explanation. I sensed, however, that it was another lie. I suddenly felt as though I needed this woman out of my house as soon as possible. I wasn't sure what her game might be, but it certainly felt like one.

Then it appeared to me. The yawning hole in her story. I'd have noticed it instantly, if I'd not been so shocked by the fact that human remains were entombed below my house. If Mr. Nestor stored his beloved book down here, why had he allowed the room down there to remain such a disused wreck? If those bodies were so old, how had Nestor not seen them? In short,

Acton's story made no sense at all. I watched as Acton flexed her jaw, deep in thought. Who was this woman? I decided my best course of action was to play along, and to play it cool. The sooner I could get rid of her, the better.

"Who would have taken the book? Who could have known about it?"

"An excellent question. I'll have to consult with my client and figure out how to proceed. But thank you for your hospitality and—" Acton looked away from me and down the hall. She paused, as if she'd just remembered something. "Do you mind if I freshen up a bit before heading out?"

"Just down the hall and to the right."

"Thank you." Acton nodded abruptly and strode down the hall with some urgency. Her behavior so far could have been described as overbearing or focused. But it hadn't been this erratic. I waited until she rounded the corner before I crept down the hall to just the edge of the corner. Of all the things I'd expected to see or overhear as I decided to follow her, I hadn't expected a conversation. Both sides whispered fiercely.

"I see you little ghost," Acton whispered. I'd planned to peek around the corner, but the voices seemed frightening close. I was too scared to give it a try, certain that they were just feet from me. I know it must seem strange. Shearhaven is my home. But the way Brianna Acton moved through the house, it was almost as if she were its owner, and I the eavesdropping interloper.

"How?" asked the other voice. A male voice. It sounded youthful, but strange. As if it'd had too much reverb applied to it. A chill darted through me, tickling the hairs on the back of my neck. Who did this voice belong to? Who was in my home?

"At this point I'd say I'm as close to death as I am life."

I was trying to ponder what this might mean when my

phone buzzed to life. I was shaken, but I impressed myself with how smoothly I recovered. I took an improv class once. It didn't go well. I guess I just needed the right motivation. I didn't wait a second before answering the phone and talking loudly into it, right before I turned the corner.

"Hey, Dad! It's good to hear from you," I lied. "Sorry about not calling you back the other day. It'd been a long one. One second, Dad." Acton was pretending to inspect a painting, smoothing the side of her hair. She gave me a casual smile I tried to return. "What do you think?"

"This modern stuff all blurs together to me. There's so much restraint, it leaves me cold." She did have her phone in her hand. Assuming she'd been talking on the phone made the most sense. But try as I might, I couldn't go along with the idea that the male voice I'd heard was on the phone. It sounded echoey, true, but it also sounded very "present" in the room. If there's one thing I had, it was a good ear. But if I didn't follow Occam's razor and assume the simplest answer, what did that leave me with? The ghost story that'd been slowly building over my time in this house, I suppose. But my mind wasn't willing to cross that final gap. Not yet.

"I've got to take this call from my dad," I said.

"Of course. Thank you for your time. I'm sure your research has been thorough. But I might stay a few extra days. Just to do some more of my own. To make myself feel more confident that I did my best if nothing else." She held her dainty hand out. I took it and was surprised at how strong the grip was. An urge burst forward from me as I found myself asking:

"Would you want to grab dinner? If you're in town a few more days?"

"Only if you let me treat. My way of making up for your

shoes, the mess, and the inconvenience.”

“Sure. That sounds fun. Do you like Thai food? There’s a great little place downtown,” I said. The woman intrigued me, and Ty couldn’t do dinner the rest of the week. This would give me some time to do a little more digging. If I had any inkling she was actually dangerous on top of being a practiced liar, I could always cancel. I had the vague notion that maybe I could look around the place more and find the book. There was too much about this woman I didn’t know or understand. She was a mystery. And, I thought, Ty would get a kick out of all this stuff. I blushed at the thought. Had the café owner already gotten so far under my skin? I’d taken a year off the dating scene after my recovery, and then seemingly forgot how to do it. Ty was the first person I’d felt any sparks with for a long time.

“I look forward to it. I’m sure I can find my own way out. Good day, Mr. Morgan.” Acton was fully herself again. Confident, and already striding toward the front of the house. Again, I had the sneaking suspicion she’d have no trouble finding her way to the front door or anywhere in the house.

“Max, please. Call me Max.” With that, I closed the door, and returned my attention to my dad on the phone.

“Who was that? Sexy accent,” Dad said.

I snorted and rolled my eyes. “Too young for you. And too female for me. You at Faraday?”

“I am, but I’m just sitting in the club, eating a mediocre turkey on rye sandwich, and watching a metric ton of rain blast the course. So, I’ll probably just be getting back home after I choke this down.” My dad’s voice was rough from a lifetime of smoking. When I was a kid, I saw Harvey Fierstein on some late-night show, and I mentioned how he sounded a lot like dad. This was a comparison my father was not pleased with.

"Tragic."

"And have you tried it?"

"Tried what?"

"The female."

"Jesus. You sound like an alien. But yes, I have. Just wasn't my thing."

"Eh, figured it was worth one last shot." I heard the wet crunching of a salad being consumed.

"So, you called?"

"Oh. Yeah. Well, I went and saw your mom." And there it was. The hidden explosive ticking away in the background of our conversation. I knew it was there, and likely to soon detonate. My dad didn't disappoint.

"Dad, please do not do this. I have—" How should I finish that sentence? I have ghosts, maybe, and a London lawyer talking to echo voices. Oh, and maybe a new boyfriend? Or at least someone I'm hopeful could turn into a boyfriend? Oh, and I bought this massive house that's feeling a little overwhelming? The point was I had a lot going on already. I realized, then, that I didn't need a reason. It should be enough that I asked him to stop. "I just don't want or need to hear it. Again."

"Maxy, the doctors don't think she has much longer," Dad said softly. And there it was. The other bomb that had been ticking away in my life for far too long. The weight of the thought tore through my insides and landed with a thud in some dark recess, to be dealt with some other day.

"I'm sorry to hear that." I could feel myself shutting down. A metric ton of conflicting emotions collided and cancelled each other out.

"I just think you need to see her again, son. One more time. She'd love to see you."

"No, she would not!" I calmed myself a fraction and continued. "And that's the problem. I know you don't want it to be real. I know you don't understand it any better than I do. But I am the last thing my mother wants to see. I am a wrongness in whatever scary little universe in her head she's living in."

"Max!" He was angry. My words weren't particularly kind or thoughtful, I admit. But that didn't make them lies. I had my heart ripped out too many times trying to appease her. I had no idea why she flinched when she hugged me. Not until the day I figured out I was gay. Then I understood my wrongness in her eyes. This understanding might have been the knife that finally cleaved me in two, except I'd gotten so angry I wanted to live a full life just to spite her.

"Dad, I don't want to upset you and I don't want to let down Mom. If I thought it'd help her or if she wanted it for even one second, I'd do it. But I feel like the kindest thing I can do is not be there because —" And then it hit me. My grief sprung back up as tears filled my eyes and my mouth began to quiver. My mother was going to be gone soon. And with her, that last little sprig of hope I'd kept nurturing, even after all we'd been through together, that she and I might connect. My dad let me weep for a long while, just sitting and listening.

"You're a good man, son." And with that, he disconnected. But I understood. He freed me from his hope that I'd visit my mother. This was no small thing, and I reminded myself how lucky I was that I at least one parent whose love was uncomplicated and freely given. Not that he was completely off the hook. My parents, both academics, hadn't really understood the danger of sending their precocious teen son into the arms of the entertainment industry.

If I hadn't met Felicity, I'm not sure where I'd be today.

When she was younger, and before she'd transitioned, she'd gone to California to pursue her dreams of becoming an actor and ended up on the wrong side of a big producer's affections. The sort of producer where *any* side of his affection was the wrong side. She hadn't been able to shield me from everything. But she'd tried her best.

I made my way back to the hallway and pressed the hidden button. I stared down at my mud-covered Freestyles, and then back at the door. I could feel the breath of the cavern, misty cold on my grief-heated face. I stared at the door, considered going back down to have a second look, and then remembered the thicket of spider webs that waited down there. I took the shoes to the kitchen and dumped them in the large trash cannister there. Then I took out my phone and rang Felicity but got her voicemail.

"Hey there. No emergency or anything, but can you schedule an exterminator to come around in the next few days? Oh, and go on eBay and see if you can get me a pair of Freestyles. Mine got ruined. Talk to you later. Let me know how the contract stuff went. And, thanks. Thanks for a lot of things." I passed once more by the secret entrance. I paused, my hand running over the expertly hidden seam. I had a strange sensation, a pull from beyond the door. I would have chalked it up to my interest in the adventure of it all. But there was something more to it. The thought of going back into the chamber was more like a melody I couldn't shake. Egg sacs flashed in my head. Spiders emerging from them. So many spiders. I tore myself away from the thought of going back down there. It wasn't going anywhere. I could wait until the spiders were cleared out.

9

"That is wild," Ty said as he scooped tuna salad onto a cracker. "I just can't wrap my head around it. That's some video game shit right there."

"Ha! That's exactly what I thought." I leaned back in my chair. Since Ty couldn't do dinner this week, we decided on a lunch date at the little bakery across from Brews & Clues. The day was warm enough that we were able to sit outside. "If you do find that book, I'd get it appraised before you hand it over."

"Eh. I don't want to make a big deal out of that."

"I know, I know. Money is just so passé for you. But I'm not talking about that. I mean, I wouldn't just take the word of this mysterious London lawyer, you know? Have it checked out first. She might be scamming you. Who even knows if this Nestor guy is the owner of the book?"

"That'd be a pretty specific scam," I said, although Ty did have a point. I hadn't even considered that.

"Sure. But maybe she—or this Nestor guy—found out

about it from someone else. I don't know. Just seems strange. The
whole thing. Of course, it's not like having a secret cave in your
mansion is a normal thing. Unless you're Batman. You're not
Batman, are you?"

"No, but I could wear the outfit sometime if you're into that
sort of thing." I flashed him what my ex-manager liked to call my
"DTF smile." The same smile I had on the cover of my debut
album, which that same manager insisted was half the reason
people bought it. I was sixteen. Which was also the reason he was
now my ex-manager. The grin on Ty's face seemed to say he'd at
least consider it.

"How about I dress up as Batman and you can be Robin."

"I'm the sidekick now, huh?"

"Or, even better, I'll dress up as Black Panther and you can
be that white guy in the suit who bumbles around and helps
him." Ty barely suppressed his laughter.

"Yeah, yeah, you should give up on the coffee and become a
comedian. Hilarious." I shifted in my seat. Ty watched me. The
way he looked at me thrilled and worried me in equal measure.
He had a way of making me feel like I was at the center of the
universe, as if he was studying every move, every expression, and
every word to make sure he didn't miss anything. There was a
little of the "fan stare" to the way he regarded me. He'd admitted
he was a fan of mine before we met. He was low-key about it,
but it was still there, like background fuzz. It worried me. Ty
had never given me any reason to think that he was anything
other than sincere about his interest in me—as a person, not as a
"famous" person—but I still worried about it.

I'd been worrying about it since I was a kid. The only time
I hadn't had to question a date's motives were the awkward
(engineered) dates with Jessa Franklin early in my career. She

was a mid-level Christian singer. I was a fresh-faced internet singer. Way before the shaved head and the sleeve tattoos. My management and her management thought it was a match made in (literally, for her team) heaven. I shook the memory away and focused on Ty and his stare. Maybe he was just emulating his detective idols. Except, the mystery he was trying to unravel was me. Sometimes that's all it took. Believing the best in someone, instead of the worst, and hoping you weren't being an idiot.

"All right, Mr. Morgan. Spill it. Something's eating at you."

"You? Later?"

"I'm serious."

"Yeah. I suppose there is." I gave up trying to use my charm to deflect. It was irritatingly ineffective on Ty. "It's just a little… I don't know… woo woo." I wiggled my fingers in the air to accentuate my point.

"Woo woo, huh? Is that the technical term?"

"You know what I mean."

"Do I ever. You wanna talk 'woo woo,' I grew up with plenty of it."

"Really?" I said, forgetting my sandwich and leaning in.

"Oh yeah. You tell me yours and I'll tell you mine."

"That's fair. Well, I grew up with the exact opposite of it. My mom and dad were both professors. Rationality, scientific thought—those were what they believed in. Not that they'd call it belief, exactly, when it comes to science. Anyway, all this stuff with the house—I don't know, it's got me thinking, I guess? Or got me in a mood? The other day, after Brianna left, it was like I could feel something."

"Like a ghost or something?"

"Not a 'presence' or anything. Not a person. I don't think. It's hard to explain. Have you ever been to a new place and had a feeling about it? Like a place 'feels' good or bad or empty somehow? Am I making any sense?"

"Yeah, I think so. Keep going." Now Ty had abandoned his food, and had both elbows planted on the table.

"Well, I always felt something from Shearhaven. I suppose that's part of why I've been so interested in the history of it. The way I was raised—I don't know, entertaining the idea of all this supernatural stuff wasn't something I'd have done at first. But the more time I spend there, the more aware of the feeling I am."

"So, is what you're feeling good, bad, or something else?"

"That's just it. I'm not sure. But the other day, what had felt like background static changed. Like I'd been tuning around on a radio and suddenly hit a station."

"Can I get you a refill?" our waitress asked, breaking the intimacy of our conversation just a beat before realizing she probably shouldn't have. "Sorry, I can come back?"

"No, that's fine. Thank you," Ty said. "I could use another." I nodded in agreement.

"Honestly, I'm kind of creeping myself out." I thought back to the strange yearning I'd felt the night before to go back into the secret passage. "Maybe you should take your turn."

"Well, I don't know if what I have to say is going to make you feel any better."

"It probably won't. But at this point I'd rather feel like I wasn't alone in my madness as far as this stuff goes."

"Okay. Well, my family on my dad's side—the Sanderson side—have a history with all that stuff. Unfortunately."

"Unfortunately?"

"It's considered something of a family curse." Ty waited a beat to see if I'd laugh in his face. I was silent. "It started with Ralph Sanderson. Before my great-grandfather Art ran away,

Ralph was plagued by—"

The waitress brought our drinks. I smiled stiffly at her. It wasn't her fault she was being irritatingly interruptive. But the results were the same.

"You were saying," I pushed. Ty had been so forthcoming about so many things. But he was frustratingly cagey about Shearhaven, as if he were sharing secrets he shouldn't.

"Just don't think—I just don't want my family history to change the way you think about me." Ty didn't wait for an answer, though, and instead just plowed forward. "Ralph said he was plagued by visions. He started claiming he could hear other people's thoughts. That sort of thing,"

"Full woo woo then."

"Exactly. Well, it got bad enough that a few years later he put a gun in his mouth. I mean, that's the family lore. Who knows what else was going on with him."

"That's intense. Look, I don't want to make you feel like—"

"It's all good, Max. Really. In some ways it feels helpful, somehow. To talk about it. My family always liked to whisper their secrets to each other. At some point it becomes a chamber of echoes, you know? You just want to shout it out to the world to see if it still makes any sense." The chime above the door sounded as a group of teenage girls invaded the café on their lunch break from the nearby high school. They carried with them a cloud of chatter and laughter as they decided on their orders in between reciting school gossip in scandalized tones that didn't match the joy and hunger in their eyes. It was the most ordinary thing in the world, and a stark contrast to the conversation I was having. Finally, one of the girls spotted me and a murmur went through the group that silenced them somewhat. Ty, thoroughly interrupted by the scene, smiled behind his coffee cup. I grimaced

at him, but plastered on my best smile as I turned to them and
gave them a quick wave. A peal of delight, and more fervent
murmuring followed. I turned my attention back to Ty and
purposefully shut the girls out.

"Sorry. Please continue," I said quickly. But Ty wasn't going
to let go that easily.

"Your target demo. Go greet your public," he teased.

"They probably just remember my poster hanging up in
their sister's rooms."

"Oh yeah. That one where you're stretched out on the hood
of that old car, your shirt strategically drifted up just enough to
show a couple abs."

"Sounds like you've studied it in great detail." I'd just been
trying to give back what he was giving but felt a little bad when
Ty's cheeks blushed. I tried to steer us back on topic. "You were
revealing your family secrets."

"Yes. Yes, I was. Well, the same stuff starts happening to
Art. He goes and sees a *brujo*. He was living in Cuba at the time,
trying to get as far away from his father as possible," Ty said.

"*Brujo*? That's some kind of Mexican witch, right?"

"Well, warlock. A *bruja* is a female. But, yeah, kinda. And it's
not just in Mexico. He goes to see this guy. And the thing about
Brujería is that you never know what you'll get, exactly. There isn't
a big organization or set of rules. Usually, the tradition is passed
down and forged by the family generation to generation. One
consistent thing, though, is that they're good with spirits. And
this guy takes one look at Art and starts shaking. He says there's
a whole mess of spirits flying around him—good, bad, and in-
between. He's never seen anything like it."

"You're right, this isn't making me feel any better," I said,
right before stuffing a fluffy and porous hunk of rye from the

complimentary breadbasket into my mouth.

"Obviously, Art wasn't too happy about this. The *brujo* suggested he was carrying his father's burden. That the spirits around him might have been the victims he'd helped deliver to Vanguard. He tried every trick he knew, which was a lot, to get the spirits to go away. Finally, something worked. It's always been a mystery to the family, how Art got rid of them. A secret he took to the grave. But the spirits were gone."

"Damn. The only lore my family had was about my grandfather meeting Frankie Valli once." I swallowed down the last of the rye.

"Oh, that's not the end of it. Unfortunately for me. The spirits were gone. But everyone on that side of the family—well, they see and hear stuff they shouldn't. Feel stuff they shouldn't."

"You included?"

"Yeah. Me included." Ty was no longer relishing his tale. Now he was positively sheepish.

"Wait, is that why you haven't been to Shearhaven yet? Are you dodging it?"

"No! No, I've really been wiped this week. But, well, I'd be lying if I said a part of me isn't a little nervous about stepping into that place. With its history and my family's history being all entwined. I'm not sure if I even believe all this stuff. I mean, I've seen some weird shit. Had odd feelings about things. But nothing so in your face it felt like proof." Ty took a large gulp of his beer.

"Well, look," I said, selecting my words carefully. "I'd never want you to do anything you felt weird about. But it'd help settle my mind if you could come and feel the place out. Make me feel less like a complete weirdo." Ty crossed his arms and looked off to the side, contemplating how to respond.

"Yeah. Why not. I mean, I can't avoid your house forever.

Not if we keep—well, I should just get it out of the way. How about Sunday night? Dinner at your place?" Ty asked.

"Sounds good. The exterminator is supposed to spray tomorrow. I'd love to take you down to the passage just to scope it out. Oh, and uh… bring some old shoes. Even though the rain's stopped, I have no clue how long it'll take for it to dry out down there."

Ty smiled and swirled the last of his beer in his glass before swallowing it down. His smile didn't falter, exactly, but there was a moment where I saw a thought flash across his face, probably wondering what he'd gotten himself into.

10

"No problem, Felicity," I said as I swiped a fob over the newly installed reader on the front door of Shearhaven. Little by little, I was going to bring the old building into the twenty-first century. "Take all the time you need. And tell your sister I said hi. And buy the baby something and charge my card." I put my phone and keys down, suddenly feeling very tired. I'd been away from Shearhaven for two days, staying at a nearby hotel, and hadn't gotten a lot of sleep. I'd found myself itching to get back to the old house, but the exterminators had a big job, and I was lucky to find a service that could get it done in two days. I walked over to the couch by the dark fireplace and laid back.

I told myself the eagerness to get back to Shearhaven was all about getting back to my home studio and back to the album I'd been slowly chipping away at. But that wasn't necessarily true. I couldn't record new stuff, sure, but I had plenty I could do at the hotel as far as trying out different mixes for the songs I'd already recorded. The truth was, I wanted to get back to the house itself.

I just wasn't sure about why, exactly.

The conversation with Ty was certainly part of it. There was a distinct thrill to the possibility that my mom and dad, in all their academic certitude, had been wrong about some of the most basic parts of life. I'd suffered a lot as a kid because of their attitudes. Some in small ways. Books I wasn't allowed to read because they'd fill my head with "nonsense." Or not being able to play Dungeons & Dragons, and eventually falling out with my friend group that did. Leaving me friendless and in front of a camera, singing songs on social media. I'd suffered in larger ways, too. Ways that I was still trying to cope with and would be my whole life. This thrill, however, was balanced out by how frightening this world of spirits and magic could be.

My phone rang on the table next to the door, and I let it. I needed some sleep. Ty was coming over the next day. I was excited to show him the place, especially the passage to the cavern under the house. I supposed Ty might be the one calling, but it was more likely Bree Acton. She'd called me three times in the last two days. I felt bad, as I had agreed to catch dinner with her, but I couldn't help but feel that something was off about her and her story. I'd asked Felicity to investigate it, but then her sister had her baby early. The baby was going to be fine, thankfully, but I didn't want to remind Felicity about her task just yet. It could wait for her return. Acton could wait, too. I was doing her an extraordinary favor anyway. I rubbed my temples as my head grew fuzzier by the second. All I could think of was laying down in my bed, my pillow surrounding my head, and drifting off. Which is why it was so strange that I didn't turn toward my bedroom at all.

Instead, I walked toward the door that led to the East wing of the house. *I should probably double-check that the exterminators didn't leave anything behind*, I thought. This made a vague sort of sense, but why would I do that now? Why even do it myself? I could have the cleaning crew investigate it next week. The thought drifted away like vapor, and I trudged through the door and down the wing's main hall. I had the vague notion I might smell the last remnants of the toxins the exterminators used. What I didn't expect was the smell of leather and earth. I moved toward it, even as I realized the "smell" wasn't exactly a scent. It was too full and strong. It was more like the memory of a scent and not the scent itself.

"What the hell is wrong with me?" I asked no one, stopping myself—with some effort— from walking any further, and leaning against the wall of the empty hall. The "scent" was stronger now. Was it a scent? Or was it a noise? The "static" I'd told Ty about? Whatever it was, there was a sense in my head that I should move toward it. That I needed to move toward it. As I neared it, I walked faster, until I was nearly at a jog by the time I reached the closed door to one of the disused rooms. Fear rushed through me. It felt like I was having a panic attack in reverse. Instead of feeling like everything inside me was closing down, which was how I usually experienced panic attacks, it felt like everything inside me was opening up. I was a hall of endless doors—too many doors—being flung open one by one.

I opened the actual door in front of me and fell to my knees. My mind was ablaze and buzzing. The room dipped and swayed, as if I were on a ship at sea. There, on the floor, was a book—*the* book, no doubt. It was open, and one of its pages was standing straight up, as if held by some invisible hand. This only lasted a second, though, as the page drifted downward almost immediately after I opened the door.

"Air pressure. Currents," I huffed through strangled breaths.

The words sounded as hollow on my tongue as they did in my head. Almost funny, really. I was too tired to think or laugh about it. The twin scents of leather and earth filled my senses now. I wasn't just smelling them. They tasted bitter and briny and coppery. They sounded like the thrum of deep drums. I inched closer to the book, as though touching it might make the cacophony stop. I did like those drums, though. I told myself to remember those drums. I could put them in a track. *Stupid! Idiot!* A part of me yelled. A part that felt small and tiny—that thought all of this was ridiculous. I felt foolish crawling along the floor of this empty room in a cavernous house toward a book. But it was all that made sense.

"What is this?" I wondered aloud. I made my way to the book, my eyes heavier than ever. I leafed through the pages. This was no family photo album or cookbook, that was for sure. The book was full of words in a language I didn't understand and didn't look like anything I'd ever seen before. All ragged curves, spikes, and diamonds. There were diagrams and pictures, as well. Strange diagrams of symbols and weird geometries. A diagram of the human form, calling out different parts of the body. The diagrams were too detailed, as if I could smell blood and bile just looking at them. My head swayed, as darkness threatened to overcome me completely. Was I dying? After all the drugs and idiot nights in fast cars trying to be something I wasn't. All the risky hookups with headless torsos on apps I'd survived. Was I going to die here, on the floor of an empty room in front of a strange book? I thought of my mom, trapped by her own mind. She'd always hated me, and that hurt. But should I have seen her one more time? And Ty. Poor, sweet Ty. Who already meant enough to me that it scared me. The thoughts were too much. Every sense burned. Then the book moved.

I thought it was my imagination, at first—a symptom of being halfway between waking and dreaming or life and death. But it was real. The book slid from my hands and across the floor. And then I heard it, a barely audible voice that seemed to come from everywhere and nowhere at once. Tremulous, echoing, and familiar.

"—dangerous!" the voice said. It was strangely clipped, as if I was hearing a small section of a longer sentence. I looked helplessly as the book slid further from me across the ground, and then into the air. Anger welled within me. Anger I didn't understand. I roared in fury, rallying my energy, and ripped the book from the air. There was resistance, as if someone was trying to keep it away from me, but in my ferocity, I managed to wrest it free. With energy that would have seemed impossible moments before, I dragged myself to my feet and ran from the room.

I ran down the hallway, heart pounding in my ears, joining the pandemonium in my head, and back to the central heart of Shearhaven. I ran to my room, opened the safe, and shoved the book inside. I saw my hands covered in dirt, transferred from the book, and then collapsed backward to the ground. Whatever fury had gripped me let me go. The darkness called to me with its alluring offer of rest. As my eyes fluttered closed, I saw two men in the doorway to the bedroom. Looks of concern on their face. Strange, old-fashioned clothing. A blonde twink with pouty lips and a lantern-jawed daddy with graying temples and brilliant blue eyes. I wanted to make a joke about an orgy. But the depth of my exhaustion stole the words away. I wanted to tell them it was all right. The book was safe. There wasn't really anyone there. They were phantoms. I closed my eyes and let the darkness overtake me.

Interlude

Chicago. August of 2001.

Cyril Vanguard ran for his life, blood blurring his vison. The bullet had only grazed his temple, thankfully. He ducked down an alley, wading through the pungent remnants of a torn open trash bag, its contents left to scatter on the wind. He tried a quick illusory spell, hoping he could project the image of a wall or something behind him. But the pain was too intense, and the men following him had already entered the alley. Another bullet flew through the air. A brick shattered near him. He emerged from the alley with a dull clatter as he sent a plastic garbage bin spilling to the floor. A young woman listening to a portable CD player yelled out in alarm as he careened into her, letting out a string of expletives as he dashed down the street. He chanced one look back. The men were still pursuing him, but they'd holstered their guns. Apparently, they didn't want this to become too public. An ambulance sped by him, sirens blaring, and Vanguard realized it was headed to a large hospital just a block ahead.

With renewed hope and energy, Vanguard surged forward.

Thankfully his latest body, Vic, had been a former high school football player turned career criminal. The man had been strong when Vanguard took over his body, and he'd worked hard to maintain his level of fitness. Vanguard had been on the run for a long time now—too many close calls with too many powerful people—and wasn't able to be that choosey. He decided to avoid the main entrance. There'd be forms and too many answers to questions he didn't want to answer, thanks to his wound. But if Dog Boy's goons didn't want to make this too public, he could use that to his advantage.

He ducked down the alley at the side of the hospital. To his relief, he saw a young doctor on a smoke break next to a bright red door. The man had a long beard and turban, possibly a Sikh. His eyes narrowed, then widened, as he saw Vanguard's wound. He threw his cigarette down and stamped it out, moving toward Vanguard to help. *Thank you, Hippocratic oath*, he thought.

"*Niālu amāru*," Vanguard intoned, his fingers splayed and wrists rotating in gentle arcs, just as Acton had taught him so long ago. The other man's eyes rolled back in his head, and he crumpled to the pavement. Vanguard removed the man's white coat and turban, shoving his sleeping form against the wall behind a nearby dumpster.

"End of the road, Vic!" yelled a voice down the alleyway, just as a new volley of bullets shot toward him. Vanguard scrambled up the stairs, its metal railings deflecting two of the bullets, leaving the third to sink into the side of his left thigh. Vanguard fought through the pain and closed the red door behind him. The door led to a stairwell, thankfully empty. He hobbled up the stairs as he put on the coat and turban. He used his own jacket to wipe the blood from his face as best he could. He didn't make a very convincing Sikh, but he didn't need to maintain the disguise long. His leg screamed at him with every step. He wasn't going to make it far up these stairs. He stopped at the first door he came to, looked through the small square window to see if the coast was clear, and then threw his jacket further up the stairs, hoping he'd convince the men following him that he'd gone further up.

He emerged into a quiet hall of the hospital, a collection of neutral tone walls, blonde wood, and chairs upholstered in pastel purple and teal. He slowed his pace, trying to slow his heart rate as well. He was very aware of the sweat pouring from his armpits. He looked down at his left leg and saw a bloom of blood there. Thankfully he'd been wearing dark pants, but that wouldn't hide his wound from someone paying attention. He walked on the left side of the hall, keeping the wound to the wall. He grabbed a chart from a cubby attached to a nearby door and pretended to study it as a nurse rounded the corner. Thankfully, she seemed preoccupied and was walking quickly, regarding him with a quick nod and nothing more. Vanguard's pulse calmed the more time that passed without a new round of shouts and bullets. He smiled as he saw the double doors before him, marked as the entrance to the maternity ward. Hopefully Dog Boy's men were bound up enough in petty mortal morality they wouldn't dare shoot at him there.

He thought of his next move. If he could get to the Amtrak station, he could head South to Alton. He hadn't risked going back there in decades, although he never liked to be far from the book. He was linked to the book, now. It had soaked up so much energy, he was able to tap into it even across the ocean in Europe. Here, just hours away, he could accomplish wonders, when his mind was clear enough. He stopped in front of a large window that provided a view of one of the nurseries in the ward. It was a full house, with more than a dozen babies cooing and gurgling, occasionally moving their pudgy appendages.

"Lucky assholes. Not a care in the world." Vanguard looked at his own face. The dark circles of sleepless nights on the run. He looked haggard. Changing faces never got easier. He'd had so many, now, none of them felt like they belonged to him. Even his real face—that ghoulish, thin-skinned, inbred-European visage that his mind called home—was too distant to recall with much detail.

"Hello, Doctor, I've been looking for you," said a voice behind him, in an easy Southern drawl. Vanguard spun around, expecting to see one of the men who'd been tailing him. But this man, he didn't recognize. He wore an expensive, tailored blue suit which contrasted with his spiky red hair, frosted at the tips.

"I'm afraid you've mistaken me for another."

"Oh, I don't think so 'Doctor' Vanguard," the man said, a glint of mischief in his golden-green eyes.

"And who the hell are you?"

"Arlington Shadowsmith," the man said. "I doubt you've heard of me, though. Sort of an up-and-comer in our world."

"And which 'world' is that?" Vanguard looked around him. The man before him was young. A magick user, clearly, but young. No more than twenty, at a guess.

"Aw, don't be like that. When you've got got, you've got got, you know?"

"I'm sure I *don't* know." There was one way, Vanguard realized. Tricky. Something he'd never tried before. There would be consequences, of course. There was a reason Acton had never attempted something like this. She was always a worrier, and too careful. Too afraid of upsetting the balance. It's how she'd lost the book in the first place, after all. He reached out with his whole being. He reached out for the book. The *Eṣāru Bēt Tuppāti*. The Archive of The New Magick, still sealed away in the vault at Shearhaven. His treasure. And it answered, open and willing and so full of power. He began to chant the old words. The words he knew so well by now.

"You're not going to just come with me, are you Vanguard?" Shadowsmith sighed. "You've made a lot of important people very mad; you know that don't you? I thought about giving the gun-toting gentlemen following you a little psychic nudge. Let them get their hands dirty."

Vanguard wasn't listening. Instead, he let his consciousness slip from him body, and filter out. Probing the edges of the young minds before him. There was no resistance, they weren't developed enough for that.

"But then I thought, what if that wasn't enough for my employers? They might feel like I didn't deserve to get paid. And you came in here. Which, you know, is cowardly and gross but I get it. Those guys probably wouldn't fire a gun in here, right? All these precious little lives?" Shadowsmith raised his hand, forming them into a finger gun. "The great thing about me, though, Vanguard, is that I don't need guns. *Pow*."

Vic's head exploded, coating the window of the maternity ward with a red spray. A chorus of crying erupted from the nursery. The infants couldn't comprehend what had happened, of course. But the sound was loud and horrific, and that was enough for them to react.

"Cleanup in the maternity ward," Shadowsmith said. "Good riddance." The man stepped back into the shadow at the corner of the room and disappeared. But there was one infant who was not crying. In the second row, third from the left, a baby boy slept peacefully in his bassinet. On the bassinet was a label, applied just hours before, that read "M. Morgan."

Part Three

Ty

1

I rang the doorbell again. Ba-dong-ding-ding it chimed for the third time, each with long pauses in between. I missed old-fashioned door chimes. Nice simple things without complex trills for bells and without cameras integrated into them. I straightened up and smoothed my shirt, suddenly remembering that Max might check the camera. It was a big house. It was possible Max was in some faraway room, and it was just taking him a while to get to the door. His car was here, so he had to be home. Besides, we'd made plans. I shifted the weight of the picnic I'd packed from one arm to the other. Even the bright and breezy Sunday morning couldn't dispel the cold shiver running up my spine. I officially did not like this place.

I wasn't sure if it was the special "instinct" that ran in my family, or simply knowing brown boys and girls like me had been taken to this house and never came out alive. Unlike the rest of my family, I'd never really tried to develop my abilities. I didn't push them away, exactly, because they'd saved me in a tricky situation or two. But I didn't actively engage with them either. I'd seen the damage it'd done to those in the family brave or foolish enough to try walking in the hidden world. Aunt Bette got lost to it for a while and came back whispering about the hidden things of the world that chattered at the edges of our perception. When she tried to carve an image of one of them into her arm, they doped her up enough she stopped whispering. For a long time I'd assumed these visions were just a strain of mental illness. Believing in the abilities my family had was easy, since I felt it too. But the rest of it? Ghosts and demons and whatever else my Aunt was seeing? It just felt like a bridge too far. My uncle used to scowl at me, and say I was too worried about what others thought. That one day I'd wake up and not have done anything with my life. He wasn't my favorite family member.

Okay, enough of that. I was nervous enough as it was. I wondered if Max might be in the passageway he'd described under the house. I doubted the doorbell carried all the way down there. I tried to call him, but I could hear a phone ringing just on the other side of the door. Which meant Max must not have it on him, unless he was standing on the other side and this was just some sort of cruel joke. But I didn't think that was it. Not really. I wouldn't say that I knew Max well. Not yet. But he'd never been plain cruel. I was just about to climb back into my Jeep and try again later when the door creaked opened.

"Hello?" Max said, blinking into the bright light. He looked like hell. A crust of dried drool was stuck to the side of his chin. Suddenly, the shock of recognition seemed to hit him. "Oh, shit. Ty! We had a—you were coming over. Come on in." Max stumbled from the doorway, grabbing his phone from the side table as he did so.

"Is now a good time?" I asked, trying not to be boggled by

the immensity of the house, and the overwhelming luxury of its furnishings. I knew Max was rich. It was practically part of his brand—boy music genius turned young billionaire—but I wasn't prepared for its manifestation. Even though I was aware of how immense Shearhaven was from the road, seeing it up close was a different experience. Max's disheveled look was enough to keep me focused on that instead of the feeling that I didn't belong in this world at all.

"What? Oh, yeah. No, sorry. I'm fine. I've just been sleeping too long." Max waved me on. "Come with me to the kitchen. I'll make some coffee. Then maybe I can take a quick shower? Sorry again about this."

"Works for me." I wasn't sure what to do with the picnic basket, so I decided just to bring it with me. Then I felt dumb for carting it around. "I packed us a picnic. Thought maybe there was a nice spot in the woods up here or—"

"No," Max said quickly. "Sorry—the woods are—they're sort of spooky. But we'll find a place. I know a few spots."

"Spookier than this house?" I'd asked it as a joke, but a strange look came across Max's face in response, trapped somewhere between annoyance and fear. I cursed myself. Always making jokes. Not everyone likes jokes. "No offense. I know this is your home."

Max soothed my worries with his cute little smile as he took me through the great room (via an actual-honest-to-God hidden door) to the hallway beyond and to the kitchen.

"No, you're fine. Sorry. I'm not all here yet. I—"

"Slept too long. Yeah, you said." I'd never asked Max if he was into drugs, or which kinds. That'd been a mistake. I was overlooking a lot of red flags, to be honest, because of who Max was. We were about the same age. He might be a year younger?

But I'd followed his career since the early days when it was just him singing into a camera and playing his tiny electronic keyboard. I'd had the hugest crush on him. I couldn't imagine getting in front of all those people and singing like that. And his stuff was really good. Even back then. I used to play "Mad Honey" over and over. It wasn't poetry, exactly, but it was fun to sing along to. Maybe I'd been making too many compromises for him, though.

I know I'd seen too many *E! True Hollywood Stories* growing up, but the last thing I wanted to get mixed up with was a drug addict. I'd heard the rumors same as anyone else. There'd been a cancelled tour, and Max disappeared for a full year. He came back with his best album, though. And explanations that he'd had a bout of depression. That seemed to make sense at the time, so despite the rumors I'd chosen to believe it. But now? I felt the old walls starting to go up. Cold steel bulkheads sliding into place. I fought them back, though. I hadn't dated anyone in a very long time. Not since Mom had been sick and my ex bailed on me just as things were going south. I willed myself to stay open. I was over-reacting to Max being sleepy. That was all. The house wasn't helping either though. The fuzzy prickling was already in my head, a thorny little thing rumbling at the base of my forehead, just above my eyebrows.

We entered the kitchen, a gleaming wonder of stainless steel and beautiful gray marble. On the center aisle was the large black square of an induction cooktop. I sat the picnic basket down on the counter, happy to be relieved of its weight. I watched Max fiddle through the cabinetry for a moment.

"You know, I'm not sure I remember how to make coffee? It's been a while," Max said finally. I chuckled and relaxed a little, even if the house was setting off alarm bells in my head.

"Okay, Rip Van Winkle, how about you let the professional take care of the coffee and you go take a quick shower." Max grinned at me—a strange lopsided grin I'd never seen before, but that I decided was charming—and gave me a hug.

"That sounds wonderful, you're a peach." Max gave me a peck on the cheek. My nose bunched up instinctively, not loving the sour scent of the other man. But I patted his back with awkward affection. At least he didn't reek of alcohol.

"Don't worry about rushing. Take your time, the coffee will keep," I said, quickly finding the French press, beans, and a grinder. I watched as Max exited the kitchen and then got to work, happy for the distraction of something easy, normal, and familiar. This was not how I'd imagined the day going at all. But a rough start didn't mean anything. Maybe Max had just been up late recording. I had no clue how the man lived his life or spent his days. That was part of why I was here, wasn't it? To learn more? I reminded myself not to jump to any conclusions as the grinder got to work on the beans. I let my mind drift into the familiar ritual of it.

It wasn't long before I poured the coffee into two matching mugs. I wanted to put the awkwardness of my arrival behind us, and thought I had a good solution. A devilish inspiration, you might say. My mom used to see the look cross my face and throw her hands up in the air.

"Ty honey, whatever you got cooking, turn off the burner," she'd say. We'd both laugh. But it never stopped me. I grabbed the mugs and set off in the direction I'd last seen Max heading. As I went, I poked my head into different rooms hoping I might hear or see Max. Finally, I heard a shower running, and Max singing, from somewhere just ahead. I was about to call out to him—I'd been mentally composing something sexy (but playful!) about joining him in the shower or wanting a peek—but was stopped short as I rounded the corner. Next to the door to the bathroom were two men, dressed like extras in a period movie.

"Sorry, I didn't realize anyone else was here," I said, suddenly thankful I hadn't tested my sexy come-on yet. I was equally confused about who the hell these people were.

"Ty? Is that you?" Max said from the shower, his singing abruptly halted.

"You can see us?" one of the men—a young blonde with, it must be said, beautifully shaped lips—whispered.

"Uh, yes," I said awkwardly, trying to answer both questions at once.

"Well, pretend you didn't!" hissed the other man before me, square-jawed with brilliant blue eyes. He grabbed the younger man by the shoulders, and the pair of them stepped backward, through the wall, and out of sight. I opened my mouth—to cry out in alarm or scream I can't say—and found myself unable to form any words. Instead, I gripped the mugs so tightly my hands almost hurt.

Max emerged from the bathroom amid a cloud of steam. He gazed at me appreciatively, that same new lopsided smile on his lips. He was clad in nothing but a towel, his body was still ridiculously ripped even after a few weeks of taking a break from his regular fitness routine. Beads of water trickled down his taut torso, collecting for a moment at his hard brown nipples before continuing downward toward his abs. I watched the man's bicep flex as he reached out for one of the mugs, his tattoos warping their shape with every veined ripple.

"Like what you see? Not bad, eh?" Max said. I was caught between fear, confusion, and lust. I'd just seen my first ghosts. Standing there, casual as hell. I ran through the options. The last thing I wanted to do was scare Max. My entire life, I'd been told they existed. I'd even felt them a time or two. But seeing them. That was something else. But it'd have to wait. I reminded myself I was trying to make things *less* awkward between us. Somehow, I was going to have to push the shock down and act as normal as I could. Besides, the man did look damn good.

"Not bad at all. Not going to lie, I've been looking forward to seeing what was under all those sleeveless hoodies," I said, taking a sip of my coffee to prove just how utterly normal all of this was. I was normal. This house was normal. Max was normal. I winced, the bitter brew was too harsh and flat. It tasted more like burning than coffee. "This coffee isn't that great. I can source you some better beans."

"Oh, I'm certain you can," Max said. I looked at the wall where the two men had just disappeared.

"Do you wanna go back to the kitchen?" I asked, desperately wanting to be anywhere else.

"We could do that." Max said nodding his head. "Or…" he flexed his torso and the towel dropped to the floor. It was nearly comical. Except, I liked what I saw. Max looked at me with a hunger I'd never seen before. It was raw, wanting, and a little scary if I'm honest. All of which sent pulses of pleasure straight to my dick. I was irritated with myself at how easily a hard body could thrill me and throw me off balance. It wasn't fair, to give this much power to someone just because they kept their body looking like a sculpture. Then again, this was Maxymo Morgan. I realized, then, I was utterly lost to him.

"The coffee will get cold," I said, my voice husky.

"Let it." Max took my mug and set it on the bathroom counter. He reached toward me and kissed me. The kiss was different than the ones we'd shared before. Max was forceful, searching, and hungry. His tongue caressed mine before plunging further in. I'm not usually much for that sort of thing, but something in his deep kisses called to something in me. The sourness was gone, and he tasted like spearmint. As we parted, he raked his teeth over my lower lip, with just the slightest pressure, and my body arced toward his. *This was new,* some far away part of me thought. *I like it.*

"You are in a mood." I let myself be led to a staircase, and then up it, watching the delicious dimpling of Max's behind as he walked before me.

"I suppose I am. But I've missed this."

"Been a while?" I asked.

"Oh yes," Max said, turning his head and looking at me with a dark intensity. "It feels like it's been a lifetime."

2

I pulled up my Jeep and sighed, as I could hear the TV blaring inside the trailer. I'd started renting it a couple years before, after the twin pressures of running a small business in the middle of a pandemic and trying to pay the rent on my downtown apartment became too much. It was a nice trailer. It was about ten years old, and I made sure it was kept in good condition. I'd put window boxes with flowers on the windows and maintained a little garden next to the wooden steps that led up to the door. Trying to make it feel a little homier and a little less bleak. Why the original owner thought light gray siding with gray shutters was a good look, I'd never know. I shuffled up the steps, not wanting to have the argument I knew was about to happen. Cigarette butts littered the tiny deck by the door. Which didn't help my souring mood.

"Pops, you gotta turn that TV down," I yelled, competing with an episode of *Alf*.

"Hey to you too," Dad said, not even turning from the

television. Aldo Sanderson moved in with me the year before. He'd spent five months in the ICU, lost his job at the local repair shop, and now faced a sea of mounting medical bills that social security and Medicaid had no chance of keeping up with.

"Sorry. Hey. But it's so freaking loud. You're going to ruin your hearing." I grabbed the remote from the end table—knocking over several of the plastic red cups that covered nearly every square inch of it—and held my finger down on the volume button until the television was near an acceptable level.

"Why do you think I have it turned up? Spend a lifetime working in a car shop and see what you can hear." Aldo adjusted his position on the couch, sending an avalanche of potato chip debris cascading to the floor. He'd ballooned in weight the last few months, and I was getting increasingly worried. It was clear Dad had fallen into a deep depression. But he also seemed unwilling to do anything about it. Which I understood. It ran in the family. It didn't make it less frustrating day to day.

"Dad, you need to wear your compression socks." The pair he had on had been rolled down to just the tips of his feet.

"They're uncomfortable." Dad looked down at his toes and wiggled them in irritation. I hated this. I hated the tone of my voice, like a nagging parent. I hated Dad's defeated, juvenile whine. I could feel the tears well in my eyes, and turned away, ruffling through the kitchen to see if there was something breakfast-like to eat in the house. The strange, passionate night I'd spent with Max Morgan in Shearhaven already felt like a fever dream or a peek at some half-remembered life in a different universe. Now I was back to the cold shock of reality.

"Then we'll order you some larger ones."

"Already talked to the medical supply. That's a special order. They said the insurance might not—"

"Then I'll cover it! Fuck!" I regretted the outburst as soon
as I said it. Dad went quiet. I knew Dad hated being here and
relying on me. He'd always been prideful to a fault. But the loss
of Mom a few years back, and then everything else the world had
thrown at him had been too much. I dug deep within me for the
patience and love I knew my dad deserved. Both of which felt
in short supply lately. I closed the refrigerator, giving up on my
search for breakfast. I needed to get to Blake's soon and restock.
I drew in a long breath and turned toward Dad again. He stared
at the TV as the unseen studio audience of the sitcom suddenly
burst to life in strained laughter. "I'm sorry, Dad. You're fine. I
just worry."

"It's okay, son," he said softly, scooting over so I could join
him on the couch. I complied, sitting down heavily as I let my full
weight sink into the couch beside him. Followed immediately by a
loud crackle and what seemed like a hundred tiny crunches.

"Did I just sit on a bag of tortilla chips?"

"Yeah. Probably," Dad replied, not hiding his amusement.

"Guess we're having taco salad tonight." I lifted my butt and
pulled the remains of the bag out from under me and placed it
on the table.

"I am not sprinkling chips you smashed with your ass on my
taco salad. No offense."

"No offense taken, when you put it like that." I smiled
and laid my head on Dad's shoulder. I liked seeing him smile.
It reminded me of the man he used to be, so full of piss and
vinegar. Playing jokes on Mom and me.

"Can't we turn it up a little?" he whispered.

"It's *Alf*, Dad. Alf did something stupid, probably tried to eat
a cat. The kids are trying to fix it before Willy Tanner finds out.
The end."

Jon Wesley Huff

"You used to love the reruns of *Alf* as a kid."

"Okay, fine, we can turn up *Alf*!" I grabbed the remote again and turned the television up. We got to the next commercial break before either of us spoke again.

"How was the night? I mean, I'm guessing good since you just got back," Dad said.

"It was good. A little weird. But good," I replied.

"Who's the new guy? You were kinda being mysterious about it yesterday when you headed out with that picnic basket." Dad reached for the beer on the end table by his side of the couch. He misjudged the distance and sent the beer toppling over instead. "Oh, shit." Before he could get up, I motioned for him to stay seated.

"I'll get it. I need to load up the dishwasher anyway." I was relieved for the distraction from Dad's question. Unfortunately, he wasn't going to leave it alone.

"Uh-huh. Sounds good. Now about this guy you're seeing… why are you being so weird about him? Is he a Republican or something? Or, fuck, a Notre Dame fan?"

"No, Dad. I don't think. It's not so much who he is, but where he lives," I bent over the dishwasher, making a little clatter as I filled it. Hoping to Melmac that *Alf* would come back on the television and distract Dad. But I'd taken about as long as a human could reloading the dishwasher, and the show still wasn't back on. When I poked my head back up, I saw Dad had his head cocked to the side and was eyeing me, as if I were a riddle that needed solving. I knew the look well. Dad was the one who got me turned onto mysteries. Like *Alf*, it was something from his own childhood he liked sharing with me. He loved riddles and puzzles. He and Mom had been some of the best customers for my mystery parties. There would always be a point, when Dad had clearly worked everything out, that he'd wink at me. But he'd never say anything. Usually, it was way too early in the evening, for one thing. But he also wanted to let the other people figure it out, or at least get a chance to do it. I felt a familiar ache, much smaller than it had been a few years ago, but still there. I'd never told anyone, although I was sure Dad understood, that the reason I didn't have mystery parties anymore was that Mom wouldn't be there for them.

I took the mugs and cups from the end tables and loaded them in the top drawer of the dishwasher. On the windowsill of the trailer's tiny kitchen was a family picture. It was taken at some place in the mall, complete with an embarrassing blue background filled with fake puffy clouds. Dad was strong and thickly muscled then, his grin wide under the shadow of that terrible farmer's cap he'd never throw away. Mom, her long black hair braided with brightly colored beads, held baby me in her arms. Her rich brown skin enveloped my tawny tones. I remembered the earthy scent of the patchouli oil she wore as perfume.

"All right, spill the beans then. I can't stand the suspense," Dad said.

"The guy's name is Max Morgan, he—"

"Wait, Maxymo? The singer? I heard he was in town but—oh, *shit*, Ty. He lives up in Shearhaven. You were in that godforsaken place? *All night?*" Dad was animated now, bolting up from the couch, his face twisted in concern and anger.

"Dad, it's okay," I said, holding my hands up. "I had fun. It was a good night. We had a nice picnic. He showed me around the house. He didn't sacrifice me on an altar. I'd say it was a win all around."

"I'm sure he's a nice guy, Ty. You've got good instincts for people. But that place—"

"Is a place. A building. It's not good or bad, no matter how much bad was done in it."

"Now, you and I both know that ain't true." Dad set his hands down gently on my shoulders. "I wish it were. I know you've spent most of your life trying to deny who you are. What we are. This—whatever we got in us. It's tied directly to that place. You're telling me you didn't feel anything up there? I get the heebie-jeebies just passing by it. You'd never catch me up on that bluff, let alone in that house."

"Dad, it was fine. Nothing weird," I lied, omitting the part about the ghosts. A detail that, frankly, I was having a hard time keeping in my head. The unreality of it made the memory slippery. "Honestly. It's a really nice place. Max is a great guy. I mean, he's rich. So sometimes it feels like he's from another planet. But he's down to earth, for the most part."

"Except for having a house that could fit about thirty of these trailers in it," Dad said, making his skepticism clear. "Real salt of the Earth, I bet. But, fine. I'm happy it's not setting your radar off, at least."

I didn't answer, filling the dishwasher reservoir up with detergent and closing the door with a click.

"Tell you what, I know I've been a big lump. Let me make you dinner, tonight. What do you say? Anything you want. You just, uh, have to buy the ingredients."

"I have been dying for some five-bean chili," I said, relieved that the conversation was moving on.

"Done. I'll make you a grocery list. And, uh, I'll go ahead and open the windows. You know, in anticipation."

"You are so gross." I shook my head and chuckled. The place needed a good vacuuming too. Then I'd need a nap since

Max had kept me up most of the night. The rest of the night I'd been up thinking about the two ghosts. I hadn't seen them again last evening or this morning. I'd always wondered how a ghost might look. I hadn't expected them to just look like people, standing there. No blue glow. No translucency. No misty forms. Just people. Well, people who could also walk through walls if they wanted. A chill ran up my spine, as I resolved to find out more about who they might be.

3

The Alton Museum of Art & History was, perhaps
surprisingly, located within the Southern Illinois University
School of Dental Medicine. I'd been there exactly once before,
during a school field trip. My favorite part of that trip was visiting
the Robert Wadlow statue, a tribute to a man dubbed "The
Gentle Giant." At his death from a foot infection at twenty-two,
he'd been nearly nine feet tall. The statue captured a gentle,
warm man with a long cane. A man so beloved the town shut
down the day he died. I often wondered—as a little brown boy in
a town where I was still very much in the minority—what the line
was between outcast and beloved celebrity. I would have hated
being called a gentle giant. But it was better than what some of
the other kids did call me.

The museum itself was heralded by an ornate white sign.
Like most of the buildings on campus, its dark red brick was
offset by grayish-white stone, and windows trimmed in white.
I hesitated as I reached the entrance. I wasn't sure what I

was looking for, and the museum looked empty. I'd hoped I could blend in with the crowd and of course there wasn't one. However, this was the closest to a historical society that Alton had. And my efforts at researching Shearhaven online hadn't turned up much, except a half-assed Wikipedia page. I was a little surprised, given Alton's penchant for cataloging everything in its history of any interest, that no one had written more about the subject. So, I soldiered on.

"Oh! Hello there," said a woman in her sixties with pink horn-rimmed glasses and silver hair dyed pink at the ends. She was sitting at a circular central desk, eating takeout from a white foam container, and watching something on her phone. "Sorry about the food. Lunch break, and there isn't anyone else to cover the desk. Can I help you?"

"I don't want to interrupt. I haven't been here since I was a kid. So, I thought I'd just browse the exhibits and look around," I said. The woman studied me for a moment as she chewed a bite of her panini. I held my breath.

"Nope." She put her sandwich down, and wiped her hands on a napkin as she got up from the desk.

"Nope?"

"Oh, I just mean—you'll have to excuse me—but I've been the director long enough here to tell when someone is 'just looking around' or killing time and when they're wanting a specific bit of info. Virginia Gallagher, at your service." The woman was well-dressed in loose-fitting, high-waisted gray pants, a pink blouse, and a short fitted gray jacket. She seemed nice enough, but this sort of one-on-one attention was exactly what I was hoping to avoid.

"Ty Sanderson," I said, stalling for time. "I guess you're right. I just—well, I'm not exactly sure what I'm looking for?"

"Of course. I assumed that's why you're here. That's the advantage of having a human being to help you versus a search engine. Give me whatever vague notions brought you in here, and I'll see if I can't help."

Well, I saw two ghosts in the huge mansion of this guy I'm seeing, and I'm wondering who they were. Obviously, that wouldn't work. Then, inspiration struck.

"I own a coffee shop. Brews & Clues? We used to host these murder mystery parties there, and I was thinking about starting them up again. I was hoping to do some research. For, you know, historical accuracy." I clasped my hands behind my back and shrugged my shoulders. A light of recognition sparked in the woman's eyes.

"That's why you looked so familiar. I used to be a semi-regular before the pandemic! For the coffee, not the mystery parties. They always sounded fun. I just never got around to it." The woman extended her hand, and I shook it.

"Sorry, I didn't recognize you."

"Oh, don't be. That's been a few years. And I looked different. I was basically stuck in the house for two years, so I took the opportunity for a 'glow up' as the kids say. Do they still say that? Lost a hundred pounds. Learned how to cut my own hair. Watched some fashion videos on online. That sort of thing." There *was* something vaguely familiar about the woman. I looked at her again with this new info.

"Wait. Medium London Fog. Skim milk. Extra lavender garnish. For Gina!" I said, the memory flooding back to me. The woman looked impressed. I was a little impressed myself, except the reason I remembered her so clearly was the lavender. She went on and on about it. Which made me a little proud.

"That's it! Gina is what most people call me. I only use my

full name for professional reasons." A dreamy look came over
her. "Oh, I do miss that London Fog. The lavender. That was the
extra special touch. I started making it myself at home and used
the saved money for clothes. But it was never quite the same.
Now, back to business. What sort of history are you wanting
to draw from? The prison fire? The underground railroad?
Although, come to think of it, some of that might be considered
a little tasteless."

"Shearhaven," I said quickly, feeling more comfortable.

"Interesting," Gina said quietly. "Funny you bring it up. I
had a woman in here the other day asking about Shearhaven
too. Pretty British gal. Maybe it's in the air, with that famous guy
moving in?"

"You got me. I kind of half forgot it was up there before
that, to be honest."

"Well, follow me! We don't have any exhibits currently about
Shearhaven, but we have some goodies in the basement archive.
I'll show you." Gina motioned for me to follow her.

"Is that okay? What if someone comes in?"

"Oh, honey. It's Monday. And there aren't any school groups
scheduled. My day was going to be games on my phone and
some dusting. Come on. Thankfully, since the British woman
came in the other day, I know exactly where the Shearhaven
material is. There's not a lot, but maybe there will be something
to spark your imagination."

"I appreciate it." I followed Gina to a wooden door that
led to a concrete staircase and a cold basement comprised of
gray stone. Rows of metal industrial shelving filled the space, all
stuffed with cardboard boxes of various shapes and sizes. The
British woman had to be Acton, the lawyer that Max mentioned.
It was too much of a coincidence otherwise. Gina led me past the

shelves to a row of filing cabinets.

"My predecessor, Mr. Michaels, was very into Shearhaven. It's funny how you mentioned sort of forgetting it was there. I did the same. I don't know why we never put a display up about it. I certainly think Mr. Michaels was planning on one before he left, anyway." The woman fingered through the file folders, until finding the correct one. "The archives are a little bit of a mess. Mr. Michaels was great in a lot of ways. Organization wasn't one of them. I keep thinking about coming down here to sort it all out but frankly it seems overwhelming"

Gina put the folder on an old school desk next to the cabinets, clicking on a small desk lamp. She opened the folder and began to carefully leaf through the contents.

"I was surprised there wasn't much about Shearhaven online. Especially with how much Alton loves its history," I said.

"Ha! I should take you to the next meeting about funding this museum and then see if you can say that again with a straight face," the woman said. She turned to me, and seeing my apologetic expression, shook her head. "Sorry. I've gotten a little bitter. Alton does value its history in some ways. Especially when it comes to tourism. Maybe that's why it doesn't make a big deal about Shearhaven. It's far enough away out of town. And it's private property. It sat empty for so long."

"I'd heard someone had paid for its upkeep for a long time. Before it was bought up by the hotel chain?"

"Yes. In fact, here's a little clue about that. A bit of ephemera Mr. Michaels scooped up when they were tearing down an old building downtown in the eighties." Gina handed me a thin piece of paper. It was yellow and brittle, and the ink was fading. But it was easy enough to read. A receipt from a local landscaping company.

"This is for the maintenance of the grounds around Shearhaven. And it was paid by a bank in Paris?" I asked.

"Indeed. Here's a relatively more recent one. From the last company to work on the grounds before they stopped getting paid. This one is a smaller credit union from out of Chicago." Gina handed me the document.

"No names, though. Not even businesses. Just banks. Seems like there's a mystery right here already," I said, wondering what it could all mean. Gina nodded.

"Wait! What am I doing?" Gina cried out, making me jump. She patted my arm. "Sorry. I just realized I'm being the worst historian in the world. We need gloves. Let me go run and get some from upstairs." I put the receipt I'd been holding down like a hot potato. The older one, especially, did feel like it could fall apart with a wrong look.

"While I'm up there, do me a favor and take down those four paintings from that shelf over there. The ones sticking out on the very top. I couldn't reach those without a stepladder, but you should be able to," Gina said, cocking her head to the shelf nearest the cabinets. "Michaels managed to grab those from Shearhaven before they renovated it." I nodded, and the museum's director headed up the stairs. I grabbed the paintings one by one, as they were different sizes, and all had different frames. Suddenly aware I was handling precious historical objects; I gently placed them against the cabinets in a line. For a moment, I was distracted by the slightly ghoulish visage of the oldest of the four. Then I looked at the rest, and a chill ran down my spine. The basement felt colder than it had moments before as I realized I recognized two of them.

"Gina. These paintings. Who are they?" I asked, finding my voice unable to rise above a whisper. The woman looked at me in concern, not even bothering to hand me the set of gloves she'd retrieved for me, and stared at the paintings.

"The older one in the ornate frame—the one with the mean-looking eyes—that's Cyril Vanguard. He's the one who built Shearhaven. Next one's his son Gabriel Vanguard. Not much we know about him. Seemed to keep to himself."

"Gabriel Vanguard," I repeated, recognizing one of the ghosts I'd seen. The one who'd told me to forget seeing them.

"Uhm. Yes," Gina said, at this point clearly a little weirded out by my behavior. I willed myself to act more normal, if possible. "Next up is Jackson Vanguard. He's where the history of Shearhaven really starts to get, well, colorful."

"Wild parties, orgies, Satan worship—that sort of thing," I muttered, still trying to wrap my head around all of this. I stared at the boy in the painting. "But he's just a child."

"You do know a bit about Shearhaven, then? But, yes, that's the scuttlebutt. Jackson Vanguard died young—in his late twenties—from some sort of cancer. He never had a new portrait made before his death. Also, with all of this you must remember, the Vanguards didn't leave any of their own history behind. Except these paintings, strangely. All the history is from the townsfolk here in Alton. I imagine jealousy and superstition played a part. Still, might be some usable material for your mystery night."

"Right. Yeah. That's true," I said it too hastily, having momentarily forgotten about my cover story. Something that the keen-eyed woman noticed immediately. Still, she continued.

"Although, the part about the big parties full of out-of-towners is at least true. There are some accounts from men and women who were hired to work at some of their parties." Gina, her hands now gloved, picked up a file folder and leafed through photocopies of old newspapers. "The parties were the only times the Vanguards lifted the cloak of mystery that surrounded Shearhaven to people nearby. One party in particular—one of Jackson's last—seems to be the moment when the fortunes of the Vanguards in Alton really started to turn. Letters to the Editor in the Alton Telegraph, that sort of thing."

"What was so special about that one?"

"The accounts of the men who came forward mentioned that only men were hired as part of the staff that night. And they were told they were selected for their looks. Now, one of the dangers and fascinations with history is that one can read between the lines. A bad habit, as it can lead you astray." The woman took off her glasses and bit at the rubbery end of one of its temple arms thoughtfully. "In this case, I don't think it's a bridge too far to assume some of the men were uncomfortable with that. The first person to come forward was the father of one of the young men. The rest came after. Perhaps fearing guilt by association if they didn't come out against Vanguard and his strange friends."

"Did the men's accounts verify any of the wilder claims?"

"No Satan worship or anything like that. Just general decadence. But that was enough, frankly. Which leads us to the worst of the worst. The most notorious of the Vanguards. Tomas Vanguard né Doyle."

"Looks like he could be a model," I said. This was the other man I'd seen at Shearhaven. But the portrait looked different to the man I'd seen. There was a harder edge to the countenance. A crueler look in this person's eyes. I hadn't seen the ghostly figure of Tomas Vanguard very long. And perhaps the painter of this portrait wasn't good at their job. Still, the thought lingered.

"A local poet wrote about him in the 1880s, just before he

moved away from Shearhaven to parts unknown. I don't think we have a copy, but I remember the title. 'The Cruel Beauty.' He was Jackson Vanguard's adopted son. Although he was in his twenties as well. Michaels believed, and I share it, that Jackson and Tomas were lovers. That their marriage was a way of ensuring Tomas could smoothly take over the estate after he passed. Vanguard's passing was cloaked in mystery, though. Tomas's adoption completed only days before the man's death. There were plenty of suspicions, but the staff at Shearhaven backed up Tomas's account.

In any case, Tomas might be an early figure of note for historians of gay culture to grab ahold of. Except, well, the parties seemed to get wilder when he took over. Whispers of drugs, sacrifices, and more started spreading."

The prickling cold feeling that had been tingling around the base of my neck seeped throughout my body. I needed to get back to Shearhaven.

"Well, tell you what, Gina. Come over anytime and I'll give you a London Fog on the house," I said, trying to push away the dread I was feeling with a little normalcy, and to hasten my exit. I didn't even hear the woman's response. I stared at the young blond man in the painting. Max didn't just have a ghost in his house. He had the ghost of a monster in it. I had to tell Max. The sooner the better.

4

I looked down and saw I'd torn the paper napkin ring to shreds. I balled them up and put them in my pocket. I was trying hard not to look nervous. Finally, Max entered Mama's Casa, smiled, and waved at me. I managed my best smile and waved back.

"You're looking dapper," I said. Max was dressed in an elegant and well-fitted blue suit with golden pinstripes. It accentuated his tapered torso, and my desire for him manifested as a tightness in my pants. Which was annoying because what I had to tell him was sure to be a mood killer.

"Yes. I thought so. Found this in the closet and felt like a change. Now are you going to tell me what's so urgent, or are you going to make me wait until the third course?" Max sat down, broke the paper ring around his napkin, and then placed the napkin on his knee. Before I could answer, Max flagged down a passing waiter. "I'd like a glass of red wine, please. Dry as you have."

"Of course, sir," the waiter said, not letting a hint of annoyance at being stopped mid-stride show through. I smiled apologetically at the waiter. I knew how it was at the café when you were already helping one customer. On the good nights, another customer hailing you down wasn't a big deal. On the bad nights, though, it was a pain. Another thing to remember. I couldn't get a sense of what sort of night the waiter was having as he hurried to the kitchen, which was to his credit. I doubt I ever looked that unflustered when things were hectic.

"I suppose I should just get to it," I said. Max looked at me, cocked an eyebrow, and leaned in. He was acting strange. As if, in his head, he was laughing at some joke he didn't feel the need to share. Was he drunk? Or is this what he was like in public? Feeling like he owned the room? I can't say the display really eased my mind about what I had to say. I knew Max had become more open minded to the supernatural lately, having lived at Shearhaven. But I realized a major suspension of disbelief would be necessary here. It was the first major stress I'd put on the bond we'd developed since meeting. I didn't relish it.

"Well? Go on. The suspense is killing me."

"Oh, actually, I see some friends of mine. I'll just join them," a voice called out from across the restaurant in a distinctive British accent. My eyes bulged as a woman walked up to our table, wearing a slender red dress and matching cape. Max, I noticed, eyed her suspiciously. *And, with good reason*, I thought. This had to be the lawyer, Brianna Acton. A waitress brought an extra chair to the table for her, just as our waiter brought Max his wine.

"What a fortuitous meeting. Would you be a dear and bring me your best, sweetest white?" Acton asked the waiter as she sat, before addressing us. "I've been trying to get ahold of you for ages now, Max. About the book? You must be Ty. I've heard so much about you."

"Who from?" I asked. From what I'd heard, she and Max had barely exchanged a few sentences. Acton ignored the question.

"Their website says they have the best lasagna in Southern Illinois. Which, admittedly, might not be the boast they think it is. But I was intrigued."

"This is quite a surprise, Bridget," Max said. "But I think—"

"Brianna, dear. That's my name. Bree for short," Acton said through a forced smile.

"Ah, yes. Of course. Time marches on."

"For some. Did you see the spinning dessert rack? I've missed those. You just don't see that anymore. The chocolate pie looked divine. It must have been," Acton began, forming the thumbs and pointer fingers of both hands into a roughly triangular shape, "this big? No, that's too small. More like this." Acton expanded the imaginary triangle, bumping into Max's glass of red wine, sending its contents spilling onto him.

"Of all the stupid, idiotic—" Max began, pure rage flashing into his eyes. I'd never seen him act like that. He must have seen it in my eyes because he quickly calmed himself. "Well. I'd better go try to save this as best I can."

"Terribly sorry," Acton called out with little sincerity as Max rushed off to the bathroom.

"What's your game, Acton?" I wasted no time, barely waiting until Max was out of earshot. "Badgering Max. Visiting the museum looking for info about Shearhaven. Now this." I'd hoped to catch her off guard with how much I knew. She was unfazed.

"I might ask the same. I might ask why you, Mr. Sanderson, visited the museum yourself. Except I know."

"How did you know I—"

"I paid the very nice woman who worked there—Gina, I believe—to let me know if anyone else inquired about the history of Shearhaven. It seems she provided you the same service for free. Now, we don't have much time before he returns. I know that you—correctly—identified the two specters you saw at Shearhaven as Gabriel and Tomas Vanguard."

"Who are you?" It was all I could manage to ask. How did she know so much? How did she know Max and I were eating here tonight?

"Someone who knows a thing or two about magick. You could say I wrote the book on it, as it were. I can sense in you one of the strongest natural affinities toward it I've ever felt, Mr. Sanderson. Magick can be very instinctual. When you saw Tomas and Gabriel's ghosts, you didn't tell Max right away, did you? Why was that?"

"I just didn't think it was the right time. I didn't want to freak him out." I tried to ignore the prickling sensations erupting across my neck and back. It was more than that, I knew. In the strange misty cloud that sometimes formed in the back of my mind, I felt there was some sort of danger. I'd assumed it was the ghosts, in some way. And certainly, the trip to the museum seemed to confirm that.

"It was your first, instinctual response. Now, I'm here to tell you that you mustn't tell him about those ghosts." Acton gripped my wrist, all traces of her light and casual affectation obliterated. "It could be very dangerous if you do."

"Are you threatening me?" I tried to pull and twist my wrist from her grip, but she was far stronger than she looked.

"A warning. For all of us."

"Okay. I'm at my limit. This is all too ridiculous." Except,

I knew it wasn't. Her words seemed to chorus with the vibrating dread I'd been trying to ignore in a way that made me think she was telling the truth. But why would it be dangerous?

"I'm not asking you to trust me, Mr. Sanderson. You have no reason to. If you knew more about me, you'd probably have even less reason. But I'm asking you to trust yourself. Trust your first instinct. Now, I'm going to do something to you. Nothing harmful. A simple spell. It requires touch. It won't last long. Just think of it as a temporary boost to your natural abilities." She gripped my wrist tighter, which I wouldn't have thought possible, until the pressure began to hurt. She muttered indecipherable words under her breath.

"What did you—" the question died on my tongue as the spell kicked in. She removed her hand from my wrist, though it still felt warm. What left me speechless was the horror I could see now before me. Like a secondary image on top of Lady Acton's beautiful visage. It was a woman with olive-brown skin. From the right side of her face, I could tell she had once been beautiful. A beauty to rival Acton's, to be sure. Amber eyes shone in a spectral light as she regarded me, her long black hair held back with a copper circlet. Her beauty faded to ruin on her left side. Her mouth was slack on this side. Her skin was papery, stretched over a skeletal structure too close to the skin. Her left eye was clouded, and deep lines cut through her forehead, at the corners of her eyes, and around her lips.

"Now, you must do something difficult. You must look at me as though you don't see my true self—my first self. The woman I was. And you must do the same for Max," Acton said. The image of the desiccated beauty overlaid on top of her mouthed the same words. I felt my stomach churn.

"Well, I think I blotted and dabbed the worst of it away,"

Max said bitterly as he returned to the table. I shivered as he sat beside me. With Acton, the vision of her true self was at least recognizably human. For Max, it was a different story. The creature within him was by turns bloated and pustulous or shriveled and mummified. Its skin was too clear, showing blue blood flowing in scattered bursts of movement through its veins. Its right eye was bulged and rheumy. Its left eye shriveled like a rotten grape. Acton touched my shoulder lightly, a gentle reminder of her warning, perhaps.

"Yes. Well, Mr. Sanderson has made it perfectly clear that I'm an unwanted presence," Acton got up from the table, taking the glass of white wine from the just-returned waiter, and downing it. "Please put that on Mr. Morgan's tab." She stalked away, doing her best to act put out and offended as she went. I watched her go, my mind boggling, like a tornado victim left to rummage through the wreckage. I had the distinct feeling that whatever precipice I'd been tiptoeing on had just given way and plunged me into the deep end.

"Thanks for getting rid of her," Max said, his mood lightening considerably. "And they call Americans pushy."

"That's, uh, no problem," I said, fighting the gorge rising within me. I wasn't sure how to proceed. I could barely look at Max. Not knowing that thing was within him. The strange behavior as of late started to make sense. Was he possessed? I felt tired and overloaded. I wanted a nap. I wanted a drink. I wanted to move as far away from Shearhaven and all this insanity as quickly as possible. I forced myself to look at Max. If I didn't, he'd get suspicious. Thankfully, the foul vision of the man inside of him faded. But I'd seen enough. Even as distorted as he was, there was enough there to recognize him from his portrait. It was Cyril Vanguard, the man who'd built Shearhaven.

"Now, you were about to reveal to me this incredibly urgent news you had for me?"

"Right." I tried to sound casual, even as my thoughts were racing. There was too much to consider. I wasn't sure if I was more disturbed by the things I didn't understand or the things I thought I shouldn't understand. I felt my world getting too wide too quickly. As if I was shrinking and falling at the same time. I resisted the thought and decided to fall back on a trick that had worked earlier that same day. "You might think it's silly. I just got excited. I was wondering if you'd be open to me hosting a murder mystery at Shearhaven?"

5

"Hey, Max," I said as I tapped my earbuds to answer the phone. I slowed my egg-whisking, so it didn't make quite as much noise. Dad, who was sitting in his usual spot on the couch, turned his head at the mention of the name and scowled. I turned away from him. "No, it's not too soon to call. We're not teenagers."

"Well, sure, but I still don't want to seem desperate. I've got a rockstar rep to maintain, after all," Max said over what sounded like an industrial fan.

"Where are you? I can barely hear you."

"One sec. Let me roll the window up. I'm on my way up to Chicago. My agent set up interviews with some writers up there to help with my memoir. We were going to do them over the computer but, I don't know. Something like this, it seemed important to meet them face to face. Sorry about the sudden trip. I should only be out of a town until Friday."

"No problem. It's going to be a busy few days for me anyway," I said, trying to keep my voice light. I'd ended our dinner date at Mama's Casa as quickly as I could. Making up some weak excuse about my stomach feeling bad before Max could order dessert. Every time he touched my hand, all I could see was the grotesque husk of the thing inhabiting his body, and it made my skin crawl. Part of me still felt guilty, though. Because I didn't want to believe Acton was right. I wanted to think she was tricking me, despite what my own instincts were telling me. Of course, when I announced I needed to leave, "Max" said that was too bad, and proceeded to order himself dessert without even escorting me out. Something *Max* never would have done.

"I have to confess, I do have an ulterior motive for calling," Max said.

"Okay, I'm intrigued," I said, giving the eggs in the hot pan a quick stir. Dad didn't like his scrambled eggs wet. I was very much aware of my father's presence in the room. I knew the man would be listening closely because I was on the phone with the new owner of Shearhaven. I was also worried Max might try to initiate some sexy conversation. Which was the last thing, on many levels, I wanted right now.

"I was hoping you might house sit for me?" Max asked. *Well, not sexy at least,* I thought, before Max continued. "Felicity is still up in Chicago with her sister. And with that British lawyer still around… I don't know, even with the basic security system in place, I'd just feel better having someone there. The full camera suite is getting installed next week. Which is a pain in the ass. You'd think these people would want the money! But trying to get someone to call me back has been near impossible. Felicity is so much better at this shit. Anyway, I figured it'd give you a chance to explore the place, seeing how you might want to set up your murder mystery."

"That's a great idea." I screamed at myself for coming up

with that cover story. Because more and more it seemed like I was
going to have to actually put it on. Creating the events used to be
fun. That was before the coffee shop was perpetually on thin ice
thanks to the pandemic, before I'd had to move into the trailer,
and before we'd lost Mom.

"So, you're up for it? I can text you the key code for the
security system."

"I'm in," I said. "I better get my dad's breakfast finished
before I burn his eggs. Talk to you soon?"

"What was all that about?" Dad asked. I decided, since I was
already deep into one lie, another one wouldn't hurt. Especially
one that would spare me a lot more grief from one Mr. Aldo
Sanderson. The last thing Dad would ever want me doing is
housesitting at Shearhaven.

"Just Max asking if I wanted to see a movie later." I dolloped
some salsa onto the scrambled eggs and set it in front of Dad
with some black coffee.

"Couldn't just put one slice of American cheese on it?"

I ignored the question, partly because Dad knew that wasn't
a part of his doctor-approved meal plan. And, partly, because I
had other things on my mind. I'd been trying to figure out my
next move. Mom passed, Dad got sick, and the whole world
shut down. The last five years had been one nightmare after
the other and without a doubt the most difficult time of my life.
But all of them had been ones I'd understood. I'd been able to
keep it together because my dad needed me, and my employees
at Brews & Clues needed me. During the pandemic, something
most of us really didn't see coming, despite all the warnings, I
could commiserate with others. Even when the civilized masks
of neighbors and friends came off, and you saw the ugliness
underneath, I could understand the fear and pain underlying it.

This, though. This was a nightmare with dimensions that felt too big to really grasp. Forget about masks coming off, this felt like the façade of the entire world came crumbling down. I desperately wanted to talk to Acton but had no way of contacting her. I did try phoning up a few hotels, but it turns out they get cagey quick when you start asking about whether so-and-so is staying at their hotel.

"Dad, can I ask you a question?" Dad put the remote down, a second before he was going to turn the television back on.

"Always."

"When it comes to our… well, you know. How much do you rely on it?"

"Go with your gut, son. Every time. Well, unless someone else is in danger," he said, taking a forkful of eggs and chomping on them. "Or if you're in danger. Those times, I'd say do a little more thinking. That help at all?"

"I think so," I said, with more certainty than I felt. "I'll leave you to your eggs and the morning news. I better get to the café." Dad looked at me, a million questions in his eyes. His lips parted, and I feared having to tell him more lies. Instead, his voice was a tremulous whisper full of unasked questions.

"You be safe out there, Ty, okay?" He knew something was up. Of course, he knew. He was afraid for me but respected me enough to handle things on my own. That I'd ask for his help if I needed it. I willed the tears to stop before they came.

"You know I will," I said with a breeziness that neither one of us believed. "See you later. I'll come around before I head out." I opened the door, but before I left, I looked back at the man who raised me. Dad dutifully ate his eggs as he popped the television back on. Life hadn't been kind to Dad in a lot of ways. A life of hard work hadn't gotten him much of anything, other than the heartache of losing his wife too soon, and then his job, and then his home.

I walked to the back of the couch, crouched, and wrapped my arm around his neck. "Love you." A few seconds passed. I could feel a tremor within Dad, sobs that he wouldn't let escape. Instead, he reached up and patted my hand gently.

"I'm the luckiest bastard in the world," Dad said. I gave him one more squeeze, and then bolted for the door as the tears began to well in my eyes.

I got into my Jeep and started the engine. But I didn't shift into reverse just yet. I stared at my phone. I'd always tried to stay safe. It was practically the defining feature of my life. I didn't skateboard. I didn't do tricks on my bike. I didn't go more than five miles over the speed limit. There was a girl, Hannah Bracewell, who used to pick on me all the time in middle school for being a dull stick in the mud. The thing I'd never been able to explain to her, or anyone, really, was that those constraints were a kind of armor. I had too much to hide.

I'd always tried to be a good son to Mom and Dad, and to treat people with respect. Some of that was my personality, sure. But some of it was the knowledge instilled in me by my mom during some of our late-night chats. I had a lot of issues with my stomach growing up. I'd have to get up in the middle of the night and take something to settle it. My mom, her brain flooding her body with nervous energy and anxiety, would usually be sipping coffee and chain-smoking at our tiny little kitchen table.

"Rough time, kiddo?" she asked. I'd nod my head, and she'd get me an antacid. Or maybe some peppermint tea. Or warm me up some milk. Sometimes we sat there in companionable silence as I finished my drink, and she did the crossword. And, sometimes, she'd sigh and look up at me with tired eyes. And she'd tell me truths she probably wouldn't have if she'd been well-rested and not lost in the chaotic swirl of her own thoughts. One of those times was imprinted on my brain like a tattoo.

"You're gonna have a hard time of it, sweetie. I'm sorry," she said, shaking her head and blowing out a stream of smoke. "It's just the hand you were dealt. You got the parents you got. Lord knows me and Aldo try, but—well, anyway. It is what it is. And you got the color of skin you got. That you wear with pride. Fuck any of those who say you shouldn't."

I giggled at that, and a tinge of amusement colored her haunted eyes.

"And you're—well, I suspect you'll understand all the ways you're special the older you get." Her hands were flat, palm-down on the table. She laid her head on top of them with her head cocked to one side. She smiled up at me, eyes trapped between wonder and fear. "You're the best thing I ever did. And it worries me every day." She didn't mean to do it. She didn't mean to connect my life with her worries. But she did. And from that day on, I tried to never give her a reason to worry for me.

She'd tell me that I had to be a little more careful than the other kids. That the consequences for me might be worse than those of my friends. I made every effort to make myself smaller and less conspicuous. I've done a lot of work to get back from the place this took me. From someone who diminished themselves so much they barely existed. But all of this? From the moment I'd flirted with Max Morgan, I'd felt like I was walking a tightrope. I tried desperately to be someone he'd find interesting. Someone more forward and adventurous. And I'd gone and lost my heart to him, as much as I didn't want to admit it. As foolish as I felt falling so far so fast.

I couldn't name it, but I knew—in my gut, the one Dad

told me to trust—that this was not safe. My dad wouldn't survive
losing someone else. I had to be careful. But, like my father, I
couldn't let a good mystery go. The thing that really cinched it
for me, though, was the thought I might lose Max. That Cyril
Vanguard, whatever inconceivable magick he used, might take
him away from me.

I turned the key, and the engine of the old Jeep coughed to
life. I drove in silence to the Mississippi, and then up the tree-
capped bluff where Shearhaven watched over the river's mighty
churning waters. The house was dark, with just a few windows
illuminated in the great hall. More than ever, the east and west
wings that jutted outward and encircled the main drive and
roundabout felt like two coal-black arms reaching out to pull me
in. I stood on the porch, just under the overhang of the upper
stories that cast most of it in shadow.

I turned from the front doors of Shearhaven, and looked out
into the overwhelming dark of the trees that circled the house. I
was surprised to see thick clusters of yellow-green lights moving
through them. Fireflies—more than I'd ever seen in my life in one
place. They floated and whirled and danced in amongst the dark
branches. I don't know why, but I sat down on the porch, then,
and watched them. It was like sitting down to an old movie you'd
loved as a kid but somehow forgot about in the intervening years.
I thought of the camping trips we used to take. Mom trying to
catch fish with hot dogs. Trying not to laugh as dad tried (and
failed) to start a fire the old-fashioned way by rubbing sticks,
and then giving up and using some lighter fluid and his cheap
plastic gas station lighter. The confused look on my dad's face
when I refused to catch the fireflies in the jar he'd given me. The
absolute certainty in my little boy brain that they were meant to
be free. The memories, and the display in front of me, filled me

with a strange sort of courage I can't really explain.

I punched in the key code Max had texted and opened the door. Next to the door was a small table with a silver bowl in it, where Max and Felicity threw all the business cards of anyone who came to call. It didn't take me long to find the one I needed.

"Ms. Acton," I said, a twisting worry knotting my stomach. "Yes, this is Ty Sanderson. Can you meet me? At Shearhaven? No, that's not a problem. Max is out of town for a few days. I think it's time we had a conversation."

6

I put my phone back in my pocket and dropped the business card back into its silver bowl. I stared at the immensity of the great hall. Its twin fireplaces, two great hollow eyes, disturbed me enough I decided to light fires in them. Figuring out where the firewood was stored (just inside the kitchen entrance,) where the lighters or matches might be (in the kitchen, in the second drawer down to the left of the stove,) and getting the logs arranged and the fire started kept me busy as I psyched myself up for the next step. Part of me had hoped Tomas and Gabriel would just show up. Part of me was glad that hadn't happened. Once the fires were roaring, I stood in the center of the great hall again, watching the firelight flicker across Max's tasteful, modern décor. Reflections of flames licking chromed legs and glass tables. Despite the two massive fires, I still felt chilled.

"Tomas. Gabriel," I said, my voice cracking. I cleared it with a cough, and began again, this time louder. I forced aside how silly I felt. After all, I knew these two were here. "Tomas! Gabriel!

Please come out. I know you're there. You're near, even. I can feel it. There's a tingling little spark at the back of my neck. I get it every time."

"I'm here," said a voice. It sounded doubled at first, as if the sound were emanating from two different places at once—one near, and one far. I looked up, and saw Tomas at the top of the stairs, on the landing. He looked apprehensive, as if he was more scared of me than I should be of him. There was a haziness to him at first, but as he walked down the stairs, both his image and his voice became more distinct until finally he was as solid as if he were still living. "Gabriel thinks this is foolish. He refuses to show himself. I'm not sure what he imagines you might do. We're already dead after all. But there it is."

"I guess there might be worse things than death," I said, willing my body to walk up the stairs and meet the ghost halfway up the stairs. Moving felt better than standing. That being said, my own words surprised me. I didn't know where they came from, but as soon as they passed my lips they felt true. Tomas shivered in response. A strange thing for a ghost to do, I thought, but it was probably some automatic response learned from a body that was now long decayed.

"That's true enough. There are… creatures here with us. Shapeless shadows that huddle in the corners, gibbering away." The specter stopped on a stair about midway in the climb. Despite the fact the chill tingling in my spine had now flooded my entire body, I walked the last few steps to join him. My eyes darted to the shadowed corners caused by the firelight.

"Are they ghosts? Humans?" My voice was softer than I intended, as if these shadows might hear me.

"We're not sure. Sometimes they almost seem human. Gabriel thinks they're very old. Maybe ancient. That they tarried too long in this world between places and have lost the essence of whatever they once were. Barely shadows themselves."

"What do you think?"

"Well, Gabriel's had over a hundred years to think it over. I've only been here a short time. I suppose he could be right. But who's to say? I never imagined any of this might be real. The world is wilder and stranger than my worldview ever allowed." A flicker of a smile appeared on the man's face. It disappeared quickly, as he reached up to brush the blond hair from his forehead and eyes. His skin was pale, but luminous. His lips, in a perpetual state of parting, were full. There was none of the hardness or cruelty that his portrait held.

"Vanguard. He took you over, too, didn't he," I said, the pieces falling into place. "Lady Acton showed me. Cyril Vanguard—or a terrifying creature that used to be him—had taken Max over."

"He stole my life." Tomas's eyes narrowed and he sneered. "Pushed me out of my body and took it over."

"And he wasn't the first," came another voice. Gabriel floated up through the stairs, causing me to jump back a little. He stared at me with his ocean-blue eyes, his lantern jaw set hard in disapproval. I got the impression he enjoyed my reaction. "I enjoy that distinction."

"Gabriel. You decided to join us," Tomas said.

"I suddenly got worried Mr. Sanderson here would get your dewy-eyed view of everything and not understand the gravity of the situation." Gabriel floated near me, as if daring me to recoil. I stood my ground.

Tomas sighed. "Forgive Gabriel. I'm not sure if he was always terse or the decades stuck in this house have made him that way."

"I can assure you he was always that way," Bree Acton said. I turned to see her close the front door behind her, take off her jacket, and throw it on a nearby chair. Gabriel narrowed his eyes at her. I watched Tomas as he descended the stairs toward Acton, and then followed him. It was such a strange feeling. The man looked like any other man might now, other than his outdated clothing. Only the barest hit of blur around his edges indicated he was no longer among the living. Gabriel followed us, no longer floating, and I noted that he seemed slightly less substantial than Tomas. It made me wonder if his theory could be true. Perhaps the longer spirits lingered, the less distinctly human in form and thought they became. This thought scared me more than the mere existence of ghosts ever had.

"I realize—we all realize that this must be a lot for you to take in," Tomas said, perhaps sensing this new dread blooming within me. I nodded, and then reached out toward him. As I expected, my hand passed through it as if there was nothing there. The effect was no less disconcerting.

"I think he's still stuck at the 'Ghosts are real?' stage of things," Gabriel mused.

"To be honest? Yeah, I am. But I'm hoping the more I know, the less frightened I'll be," I said. Acton sat in a large chair next to the unlit fireplace.

"I hope that's the case after you hear what we're about to tell you." With a burst of flame and a quickly dissipating puff of smoke, the fire in the hearth roared to life.

"And I can fill in the details that none of you have," a deep voice intoned. There was a man sitting on the couch, where only seconds before there was no one. He was a short black man, with a balding head and a full white beard. He was dressed in a suit with a shiny red velvet handkerchief stuffed into his front pocket.

"Mr. De Artte, I didn't expect you here," Tomas said. "Thank you for coming."

"I shouldn't be here," the man said. "But I'm bending the rules. My patience with Vanguard is thinning by the second. I can't do anything. But information? I can give you that. As long as it's about past events, at least." I didn't have the reserves to ask who this man was, how he came to be here, or how he knew what he knew. I just nodded and sat in the chair opposite Acton.

"Well, let's get to it," I said, "How do we get rid of this 'Cyril Vanguard?' How do I get the real Max back?" Acton's eyes widened. She looked from Tomas to Gabriel and then to the stranger, Mr. De Artte. She sighed, realizing the job fell to her, and her jaunty affectation fell away. In its place, something old and very sad took its place. She stood up, walked over to me, and crouched beside my chair. She placed her hand on mine, and my stomach clenched.

"I'm so sorry, Ty. I thought you—that is to say, I didn't explain it well. I assumed you understood. Your Max is gone."

"No," I said lamely. My mind rebelled against the truth, as plain as it was. Who was this lady anyway? How could I trust a word she said?

"In some ways, he never really existed," Acton said softly, giving my hand one more tight squeeze before returning to her chair. "If my theory is correct." She looked to Mr. De Artte, who nodded his head.

"I've an acquaintance who was sure he'd ended Vanguard," the older man said, his eyes shining in the firelight. "But he jumped into the mind of an infant. Whoever Max Morgan might have been was pushed out."

"Except, magick is all balance," Acton continued, giving me a look of concern. "Taking a life in this way is heinous in the extreme, and the corrective measures were swift. An infant's mind isn't developed enough to handle a mind as old as Vanguard's. Most of his mind was locked away in a realm outside the physical world, with just a shadow inhabiting the infant. As that infant grew, so did this shadow self."

"Until he touched the book. Once that happened, his connection to the book drew the real Vanguard back. And like the light of a roaring sun, it obliterated the shadow," Dr. Artte finished. I heard it all, but I'd be lying if I said I really understood it. Not this first time through. But I understood enough. I was even a little angry. Max had been more than a shadow.

"Max is gone." I slumped in my chair, suddenly feeling exhausted. Part of me wanted to just leave Shearhaven. To forget these ghosts, and the mysterious lawyer from London, and whoever the fuck this old man was, and continue my life. Not to mention Max or Cyril or whatever he was, and just go back to my life. My beautiful, small, hard little life with my sick dad and my barely floating business. At least all those things made sense.

"Perhaps we should start from the beginning," Acton said, raising her hand. "But, before we start… I don't suppose Max has some decent wine?"

7

Two hours later, I was wiped—physically and emotionally. There'd been a lot of questions along the way. There were a few moments I almost walked out, convinced this was an elaborate hoax. I knew it wasn't, but it was easier to process than the story that Acton, Gabriel, Tomas, and Mr. De Artte told me.

There were many disconcerting revelations that had made my head swim. But my brain was still stuck on one. The one that cut me the deepest. It was also the revelation I wanted to believe in the least. Give me ghosts, witches, immortals, and supernatural hitmen. Fine. But Max, gone?

I thought about the first time Max had come into my coffee shop. Carrying with him his big city vibe, not knowing how ridiculous it was in Alton. I'd always thought "Maxymo" was cute. Followed him on a few different social media accounts. Seeing him in the flesh had been as exciting as it was improbable, that first time. Maxymo Morgan in my little coffee shop. And then he flashed his beautiful eyes at me and was clearly flirting.

I could hardly believe it. In fact, I didn't believe it. Not at first. I didn't trust anything about our connection. It took a while for me to come around to the idea that Max had chosen me. The thick brown boy from nowhere. The one the lady at the thrift store called "husky" when his mom was looking for clothes for him. The tall nerd who hated basketball but loved mystery books. He'd chosen me. With his stunning good looks, all his talent, and those rock-hard abs. The thought that this "Vanguard" person had extinguished that light filled me with rage. Except, that wasn't the worst part.

Mr. De Artte smiled sadly at me, as if sensing my thoughts. Knowing more about Mr. De Artte now, I suppose it was possible he had.

"It is especially cruel that Max Morgan never really had a chance to exist. Not for more than a few hours," he said.

Acton nodded. "As Gabriel and Tomas explained, in order to maintain the magickal balance, the practitioner needs their victim to kill them. Then it's basically seen as an eye for an eye, so to speak," she said.

"That's one hell of a loophole," I said, focusing on the mystery to stave off my heartache. I'd fallen in love with someone who never really existed.

"The person you knew—the person who lived in that body—is more like an alternate version of Cyril Vanguard than anything else." Acton tried her best to break the news gently. I wondered, underneath all her bluster and superiority, if there was an actual human being in there.

"No," Tomas said. Acton looked at him, irritated to be corrected. A quick smile of bemusement and understanding crossed De Artte's wizened features. "Whatever the Max you knew was—echo or shadow—you loved him. And he loved you.

What you felt mattered. He mattered." I sniffled, fighting the forming tears.

"Thank you." I didn't realize how much I needed to hear that. I made a decision. I'd call him Max to his face. But he was Vanguard now, in my mind. And he'd murdered Max. The details were unnecessary. This was the core truth that burned within me now.

"More or less," Acton said.

"Is this 'hitman' you mentioned, Mr. De Artte—is he still around? If we let him know where Vanguard is now that could be a solution," Tomas offered. De Artte thought about it a moment, then shook his head.

"Mr. Shadowsmith and I aren't exactly what you'd call friends. Plus, his methods can be—well, let's just say he can create more problems than he solves."

"Wait a second." I nearly jumped out of my chair, the meaning of the conversation suddenly working through the fog of my new grief. "What are you all talking about here? Killing him?"

"Cyril Vanguard has been dead a very, very long time," Acton said. "What we're talking about is removing a murderer from his latest victim's body."

"Can we turn him back? Into my Max, I mean? That version? Or bring back the real Max?"

"You want them to put a baby's mind back into an adult?" Gabriel wondered.

"Well, I don't know, do I Gabriel? I don't understand any of this, really. I mean, I think I get it. But it just seems so inhuman!"

"That's what it is, exactly." Mr. De Artte regarded us as the black embers in the center of his brown eyes sparkled in the firelight. I didn't know what to think about the man. I understood what he truly was. He radiated his ancientness, even if he didn't look it. I found his presence comforting even as he terrified me in some vague, unnamable way. "Cyril Vanguard has done something utterly inhuman. He is now, himself, inhuman." The man's eyes flicked, for a second only, toward Acton. She saw the look and retreated into herself. "He's not much more than a parasite now. Feeding on other people's lives."

"A parasite you helped feed, 'Lady Acton,'" Gabriel spat, as if releasing a thought that had been building in him for a long time. The woman looked at him icily for a moment, but the expression melted away almost immediately, replaced by something more haunted.

"Yes. Thank you, Gabriel. I know—I know my own sins well enough."

"That I don't doubt. It's how you live with them I don't understand."

"Why *are* you helping us? What is your part in all of this?" I asked. I'd been too overwhelmed by everything else to address it, but the question burned within me. Acton regarded me with her piercing eyes, perhaps deciding if it was worth her time to address it. She sighed.

"Fair question," she said.

"I would think so," Gabriel said. "When my 'father' took over my body, you seemed more than happy to assist him."

"Appearances can be deceiving." Acton snarled and crossed her arms. "Although, in this case, you're not wrong. I have no excuses for how I behaved. I have been, perhaps, single-minded in my pursuits. I suppose it's easy, when you've lived as long as I have, to see life as less a precious thing and more a never-ending procession of sweaty, hairy apes fumbling in the dark."

"Oh, that's lovely," Gabriel said.

"I didn't say it was right. But I needed my book back. I still do."

"What is this book?" I asked, finally. "Why do you want it so badly?"

"Because it's mine. I wrote it," Acton said sharply, before calming herself. "I have an idea about how to stop Vanguard. But it's going to takes some trust and ingenuity from all of us. Which is why I'm going to tell you something few people know. Mr. Sanderson, I showed you the truth. You saw me, that day, when I lifted the veil from your eyes. You saw my first face." I nodded.

"I was born nearly three thousand years ago, during the reign of Nebuchadnezzar II, the last great king of Babylon. My father was a merchant, and when I was old enough, he let me wander nearby when I made it clear I wasn't going to be much help selling his wares. One day I was walking down Processional Way, running my hand over the glazed ceramic tiles of the animal reliefs that lined that street, dodging the throngs of people who were making their way through the city. I remember the day vividly. Because, although my long life has seen many division lines—moments that bisected my life between what it was and what it became—this was the first."

"Three thousand years," I said. Unable to hold back any longer. "The things you must've seen."

"Yes," Acton favored me with a hint of a smile. "If there's time in the coming days, I'd be happy to tell you what I can. But, for now, let's talk about this day. The day I saw the stranger. I'd stopped before the Ishtar Gate. The sun was low in the sky. The golden animals that adorned the gate seemed to glow of their own accord against its azure gleam. I walked toward it and could see myself in their reflection. Olive-brown skin that caught the light in warm pools. Amber eyes that more than one man had commented on for their beauty. Long black hair held back with a copper circlet my father bought me for my sixteenth birthday. My father was not amongst the wealthiest citizens of Babylon, but we were comfortable. I lived in the greatest city on Earth, walked amongst the glorious hanging gardens, and lived under the rule of a glorious warrior king who valued art and religion as much as he valued power."

"Such is the light / of the sun / reflected in my eyes / as to make my eyes eternal," De Artte said, staring into the firelight. He looked up to see us staring at him and shook his head. "A scrap of a Babylonian poem. By a bright young man whose name and work has been utterly forgotten. He wrote it shortly before I escorted him to his eternal rest."

"I knew of the tumultuous history of Babylon—a thousand years of war, destruction, and rebuilding. But in that moment— that *perfect* moment—I could not imagine it ever ending," Acton said. "I couldn't imagine its richness—and by that, I mean its richness of culture and purpose—ever being diminished. Sometimes, I still weep for what became of it all.

"In any case, in the reflection of the gate I saw a man striding forward. He wore a knee-length tunic of bright blue, a wide golden belt, and a fringed shawl the colors of sunset. Each wrist was covered in ornately wrought copper bracelets encrusted in jewels of red and amber. He would not have been terribly remarkable except there was something "off" about him. I was very interested in clothing and, well, what you'd call "fashion" today. And the dyes in his clothes were strange. The way the light played off the fabric was odd, too. The ringlets in his black hair and beard were out of style, as well."

"This does have something to do with the book, correct?" Gabriel asked. Acton pursed her lips.

"Let her finish," Tomas said. I could see the curiosity in his eyes. One I shared. Acton sat in front of the richly upholstered chair across from Mr. De Artte, who watched her with unguarded fascination.

"Do you know this tale already, Mr. De Artte? Did your all-seeing eyes see the moment I slipped away from you?" Acton asked.

"No. Though I have heard whispers. I would like to hear your story as well."

"Very well. Then let me tell it properly."

Sybella's Tale

I didn't know if it was providence or simple boredom that led me to follow him, even though I was going further away from the market and my father's stall than I was supposed to, deeper into the city and closer to the palace. I followed the man for some distance before I lost sight of him. It happened in an instant. He was there, then a woman crossed before me, running after some wayward children, and the man was gone.

"You are a curious one," the man said from behind me. I spun around, and there he was there, a bemused smile on his face and a flash of fire in his eyes.

"I could say the same of you." In truth, I was scared. But when I'm scared, I tend to get bolder. It's something that has served me well and for ill in equal measure over the course of my long life. The man seemed further amused by my comment.

"What is your name, small one?"

"Sybella."

"Indeed? That is an apt name, I think."

"How so?" I asked, but he avoided the question with one of his own.

"And what brings you to the great city of Babylon?"

"I live here. To the south, near the wall. My father is a merchant. A powerful man, with many connections." It was a silly thing to say, I suppose. I was nervous of the man. My mother had warned me that some men might not restrain themselves when met with my beauty. I didn't want him to get any ideas. But I didn't feel as if that were the man's intentions at all.

"I've no doubt."

"And what are you doing in Babylon? Where are you from? Your clothes are strange. As though someone tried to copy our style without ever having seen it." I dared to reach out and feel the fabric of his sleeve. It was, indeed, strange. It was slippery to the touch. This, it must be said, did not amuse the man. In fact, he seemed genuinely concerned, and perhaps even a little annoyed with me. But this passed from his face quickly.

"You are a clever one. I am not from Babylon. I'm from very far away, in fact. I've heard that your king favors sorcerers, enchanters, astrologers, and the like."

"He does. Although he is quick to deal with charlatans." I regarded the man. Although he was intriguing, I felt certain he was a charlatan of some sort.

"I see." The man looked up, toward the palace in the distance that overlooked the street. He looked around at the constant flow of people who streamed through the street on their way to the temples, the markets, the centers of learning, and their homes. "I wonder."

I was about to ask what him meant by that, when he held up both his hands, and touched the circlets on his wrists together. This was how I saw my first act of magick. A golden glow emitted from the bands, and all around us the world slowed and then crawled to a stop.

"You—you are no charlatan!" I stumbled backward, fearing my flippant tongue would cost me dearly.

"You've no reason to fear me, Sybella," the man said, getting down on one knee. "In fact, I have a gift for you. One I thought to give to another. But I see now that thinking was too narrow. You see, the cruelty of history is that it records only a few names of note, when you come right down to it. So many people are simply swept away in the tides of time. Being here— meeting you—has been a fascinating reminder of that." The man removed his shawl, revealing a leather sack on his back. And from it, he produced the book.

"What is this?" I said, regarding the object with suspicion and awe. You must realize, I had never seen a book. Babylon had a rich written history, but it was all cuneiform inscribed on tablets, cones, and pretty much any other shape you could form with clay.

"This is a book. The pages and its cover are made with the hides of animals. You can make marks upon it—as though you were inscribing a tablet," he said. "But it's a book that's unwritten." The man opened it, and inside was page after empty page. He handed it to me, and I grabbed it and flipped through the pages carefully, feeling their strange slipperiness, which reminded me of the man's clothes.

"How does one write in it?" My mind was alive with possibility. I thought it was all too much at once. My head felt ready to burst. Comical, really, given what came next.

"The important thing about this book—the special thing about this book—is that you can write it with nothing more than your mind."

"My mind?"

"The book is yours. My gift to you, and to all humanity," he said, sadness creeping into the edges of his smile. "Where I'm from, there is no magick. Not anymore. We forgot the wonders of the universe. We cataloged and dissected and theorized. All good things, I think, except we shut ourselves away from what the past had to teach us. We brought about our ruin, and only rediscovered our legacy after it was too late."

"I don't understand." At the time, how could I have understood? So much of what the man said was strange to me. In the years since I've thought about that day many times over. I've wondered how I would answer his next question, given what I know now.

"Do you want the book? Do you want this gift?" he asked. And I said the same thing I'd say today, if given the choice again, even knowing the consequences.

"Yes."

"Then you will write your book," the man said, whispering in my ear. He smelled of lightning and earth, and even as he faded from view as he spoke the words, I could still smell these things on the air. I opened my mouth in shock. To ask another question, no doubt. But the world around me was still frozen, so there was no one to hear it. I ran to a man near me, frozen mid-stride, and asked if he was okay. When there was no answer, I reached out my hand and tried to shake him. But he would not budge. I clutched the book to me, and it occurred to me that I might have just met some sort of demon. By accepting the book, had I made some sort of pact? I ran through the streets, and everywhere was the same. Even the columns of smoke drifting up from meats cooking on a brazier in the market were frozen in place. I ran to my father's stall, and he was there, one hand on the shoulder of the owner of the neighboring stall. His head was thrown back mid-laugh.

Just as terror was about to overtake me, a hole opened in the air before me. That's the best way I can describe it. It was wreathed in a glimmering golden light, and beyond it the wonders of creation were laid before me. I have no better description than that. I saw the cogs of all time and space. I saw the fibers that connect every living thing. I saw the flow of invisible energies that surged around and through us. I saw stardust turned to light, and light turned to metal, and metal transformed into stars.

I understood that the stranger had opened this universal well to me and gave me the means to record what I saw, in a language taught to me by the stars themselves. I have no idea how long I stood there; book opened in my hand as pure knowledge flowed through me and into the book. It was as if everything I'd ever known was simply the fleshy outside of the universe. Then and there, I was shown the skeleton of it. The blood and guts of it all. The complex mechanism of eternity.

Then the well closed and my book was full. I sat in a sand-covered ruin—to a land that had no meaning to me. Babylon was long gone, sleeping under the sand to be rediscovered once more.

I lost a thousand years in the twilight realm where I wrote the book, gazing into the well of the universe. I walked through the heat to the first sign of civilization I could find. What happened next—well, I lived my life. I guarded my book, and the knowledge it contained. I used its secrets to secure my place in the world. I was a hero, a villain, a conqueror, and—for a time—a slave. It was during this dark time that the book was taken from me. That was when I devised the spell. The spell that would let me slip from one body to the next. I took the body of my slaver, and piece by piece I destroyed everything he'd made. I searched like mad for the book, but it'd been sold off with no clues as to where it'd gone. I reveled in wealth and bounty when I had it and plotted to gain it back again when it was taken from me, or I lost it.

Since then, I've had a long time to walk this world. I've seen and been its best and its worst. The only constant was the feeling of loss that the book was no longer mine. Instead, it drifted from person to person, none of whom realized its true value. I tracked it down a couple times, once I'd regained a position of status and wealth, but the trail always went cold. Leaving behind nothing but whispers of an impossibly ancient book that defied history. Tales of a book written in a language that no one understood.

I was Lady Bridget Acton when Cyril Vanguard entered my life. I'd transferred my mind into the body of a white woman for obvious reasons long before. But London afforded me unique opportunities. Through wealth and power, I was able to maintain my presence there. I would bear a child on holiday, which was quickly sent away to school, and who would return in adulthood to take over the ancestral home. I did this three times over before anyone began to suspect it was all the same person. And even then, I'd built a network of people—highborn and low—who would eagerly take care of any problems that arose for the right fee or favor. I'm afraid the adage was true. With all that power, I became my cruelest self. That was the person Cyril Vanguard met, my book in his hands, having infiltrated one of my parties. Everything that miscreant learned, he learned from me. He was a student of the occult, and although he didn't realize the full extent of what the book was, he knew enough to know it was very powerful. He had already learned some of its magick, simply by studying some of the charts and diagrams within it.

I could have taken the book from him by force, I suppose. But I was afraid. I was afraid he'd run, and I'd lose track of it again. In my hubris, I thought to draw him into my web with promises of unlocking its secrets, secure the book once again, and be rid of him. But he was far too wily and underhanded for that sort of thing. To my chagrin, he kept dangling the carrot of the book in front of me for decades upon decades. He entertained me in his home, knowing I could feel the book calling to me and could do nothing about it. Even after Cyril fled to England in your body, Tomas—the tales of hedonistic parties and human sacrifices finally catching up with him—he held the book here, walled away from my grasp.

His sigil used to be all over this place, disguised as décor, defeating my best efforts at locating the book. Dark wood created through black magick was used as molding. Shearhaven was barely a home so much as a carefully constructed reliquary for the book. Where it could sleep, absorbing the energy of the crossing of ley lines below. I was unsure if the book was still in the house. Until the bills stopped being paid at Shearhaven. Shortly after Vanguard jumped into the newly born body of Max Morgan, it would seem. The hotel chain came in and stripped the house of its rotting wallpaper and molding. Unsuspectingly clearing away much of the protections Vanguard had placed on the property.

I came here thinking Vanguard was finally gone, disappeared from the face of the Earth. I thought to secure the *Eṣāru Bēt Tuppāti*—my long-lost tome. I broke through the wards in the secret chamber, not knowing two meddlesome ghosts were keeping the book from me.

8

"So, you're after the book so you can be back on top of the world again, hm? I might have known," Gabriel scoffed.

"That's not—look. I've actually learned a thing or two. I would never deny that I have a hard head. But give me a couple thousand years and I do figure it out. I regret my part in your death. In both of your deaths." Acton looked at both Tomas and Gabriel. "I thought getting the book back was the most important thing. It was my obsession. Let's just say, recently, my perspective changed."

"Maybe we should take a break," Tomas said. "I'm sure those of us who still need such things could use another cup of tea or coffee—"

"Or a shot of whiskey," Acton chimed in. Tomas nodded.

"Let's meet back here in fifteen minutes?"

"That's a good moment as any to take my leave," Mr. De Artte said. "What happens from here I can't be a part of."

"Mr. De Artte. A moment, if I might?" Acton asked. I tried

not to stare as she went up to the man and whispered in his ear. He listened, nodded, and then spoke softly to her. Acton watched him disappear and turned, looking grimly satisfied.

"Actually, I might make that a double." She traded barbs with Gabriel as they made their way to the kitchen. I pretended that I'd been staring at the books on the wall the whole time. In my periphery, I saw Tomas start to drift back to the ballroom. He took one more look backward at me, though, just as I was wiping tears from my eyes. I turned away more fully from him, hoping it might grant me a moment or two alone.

"Do you want some tea? Or coffee?" Tomas asked gingerly, keeping a respectful distance from me. "I might even be able to carry it to you. I've gotten a little better at carrying things."

"No, thank you." My mind seized on something, clearly wanting distraction. "You had to learn how to carry things?"

"Indeed. Not that I gave it much thought when I was alive. But my conception of a ghost was, well, not this." Tomas stretched his arms out and wiggled his fingers.

"Is it scary? I mean, being—"

"At first. Definitely. Gabriel can be a pain, but honestly, he's been great about helping me. Not sure how I'd have done if I was figuring it all out on my own."

"I wonder if Max—I mean, Vanguard—will be alone. I wonder if he'll wander these halls after?"

"You don't have to worry about that. Let's just say that Mr. De Artte will be more than happy to swiftly expedite him to his eternal rest. Whatever that may entail." The specter floated toward me, although I noticed that, unlike Gabriel, he still "walked" even though his feet never touched the ground completely.

"No one's got any solid details on that then, huh? What's

after here?" I asked. Tomas shook his head.

"Not even Mr. De Artte. Unless he's just not telling. I think it's kind of exciting. When you're dead, the number of things you can look forward to dwindle considerably."

"I'm sorry. For what he did to you." I fidgeted with the keys in my pocket, hoping that didn't sound too inane. Tomas smiled at me and sidled up next to me.

"I'd be lying if I said I didn't get angry."

"I wondered. You seem to lack the zeal for revenge that Gabriel does."

"I suppose so." Tomas stared too long into my eyes. Or, perhaps, I had stared too long into his. Either way, he looked away before he continued. His face was beautiful in profile. His eyes catching some sort of spectral light. "It's hard to understand what use I'd get out of being angry."

"Can't say I ever tied my feelings to how useful they were. They are what they are."

"Fair enough. But I've always sorted after that. You feel what you feel, but what you actually say or do after is all up to you, right?" Tomas looked up at me again, before quickly floating away from the wall of books and toward the fireplace. "That's what I always figured, anyway. What does it accomplish to be angry now? It's sort of freeing. The unknown dangers of the future don't matter. What people thought of you doesn't really matter, and you have no control how they remember you. So, I just get to be."

"Total freedom." That sounded nice. "Hell of a price."

"Oh yes," Tomas agreed. "I really miss the taste of these caramels that Ma Howard used to make around Christmas. They were so buttery and sweet and just melted in your mouth."

"That'd be the thing I'd hate the most, I think. Not being

able to taste."

"Or touch." The man said it quietly, and the desperation in his voice broke my heart. I looked at the ghost of Tomas Vanguard, and felt a familiar, giddy stir. Tomas wasn't really my usual type. Beyond the fact he was a ghost, I mean. Sometimes it felt like pouty-lipped blonde twinks were being cloned in a factory. Apparently, it'd been happening at least since the 18th Century. But there was something different about Tomas. At first, I thought it might be because the man was literally born in another time. I'm sure his sort of youthful beauty had been a boon back then as well. But underneath that there was more. Maybe it was the subtle darkness of the circles under his eyes. They were slight—a frustratingly perfect imperfection—but he had some grit about him. The hint that life had not always been so perfect.

"So, how do you find it? The present? Your future, I suppose," I stumbled, needing to change the topic.

"Well. That's a very good question," Tomas said, looking quickly toward the windows, as if he could see the world beyond them. "Obviously I haven't gotten very far. Neither Gabriel nor I can get much past the house. But I've certainly seen enough television to get an idea."

"You can't leave the house?"

"I thought it had something to do with the fact I died here. But Gabriel didn't, and he's still stuck here too. It suppose we're bound to the book, not the house."

"Makes a certain amount of sense. As much as any of this does," I said. I decided to get us back on topic. I couldn't help but feel like Tomas was avoiding the question. "You were saying?"

"Right. Well, my thoughts are complex. I don't wish to insult you, though."

"What am I, the ambassador for the twenty-first century? If I was, I'd quit. Whatever dim view you might have, I doubt my own is too far off."

"Oh, don't get me wrong!" Tomas floated toward the window now, although the only views from the front windows were of the clearing in the woods atop the bluff, and the trees beyond. "It's a world of wonders. Gabriel can tell you, I spent too much of my time after I'd pulled myself back into being boggled by it all."

"But."

"Yes. But." Tomas flashed me a quick, apologetic smile. "I suppose it feels awfully lonely? Maybe it's this house. Or my time-lost poutiness. But I thought I saw it on Max's face. And his assistant, Felicity, when she was here. It's as if everyone has all this… space. Your houses are big. Your cars are big. And then there's the worlds in your machines. All the stories on screens. All the books! And the information web. All those thoughts and lives coming at you all at once. It's like there's so much of everything. It makes me nervous just thinking about it. I didn't understand, for a long time, how you could stand it. And then one day I realized you're all just standing still, isolated even when you're together. Waiting for the great big 'everything' to come crashing in and wipe it all away."

I opened my mouth to say something. To agree, disagree, or something else I really can't say. Part of me ached at his words. Part of me wanted to scream. In any case, I never got the chance to reply.

"Okay, wine for myself, and coffee for Ty," Acton said, carrying a glass and a mug in either hand.

"And I can guarantee that she didn't splash any poison in it," Gabriel said, following close behind her. I took the mug appreciatively. It was the good stuff. The stuff I told Max he should buy. I winced. I'd really liked Max. Maybe even could have loved him. Maybe I did love him if I was honest with myself. Max wasn't perfect, by any means. But he was a good guy.

"To Max Morgan." I raised my glass and blinked away a tear. I didn't kid myself that there wouldn't be more later.

"To Max," Acton said quietly, touching her glass to my upraised mug.

"Now. Let's figure out how to send this Vanguard guy where he belongs." I took a deep gulp of the coffee, and steeled myself for what was to come.

9

"Quit fidgeting," Vanguard said. "It's almost over."

"I can't believe you're doing this to me," I said.

"Well, you're the one who's been obsessed with historical accuracy!" Vanguard finished his work and adjusted the tie he'd just knotted until it was snug with the neckline on my shirt. "There we go. Dashing."

"I hate ties."

"Anyone ever point out that's sort of ironic?" Vanguard grinned devilishly using Max's face, and I rolled my eyes in response. This new "Max" wasn't an improvement in the humor department.

"Ha ha." I turned and looked in the mirror. "Still, it does look pretty good."

"You've sure been in a mood the last couple weeks."

"Sorry." I'd never been a great actor. But I'd performed in the murder mystery parties for Brews & Clues enough that I wasn't half bad at it. Especially for an audience like Cyril

Vanguard. His ego didn't allow him to view me as any sort of threat. I turned back to him, and pretended it was still Max in there. The lonely man whose mother rejected him. Had she known, somehow? Had motherly instinct told her this wasn't the baby who'd spent all those months in her womb? I tried to pretend he was the man who became one of the biggest music stars on the planet based mostly on trying to paper over that pain. I smiled as my heart tore in two, wrapped my arms around him, pulled him in close, and rested my forehead against his. "I know I've been weird. Organizing all of this has been a bigger stressor than I expected. Even with all your help footing the bill."

"Happy to help. Plus, it's exciting, trying to capture some of that spirit of the old days. Even if just for a night or two."

"Well, if this rehearsal goes off well, then maybe we can do a couple weekends in a row. Get your money's worth." I was amazed at how good I'd gotten at lying to the man. How I could hold him, and not act repulsed. How I could kiss him, and not show my disgust. Not poor Max Morgan—killed in a hospital nursery more than twenty years before. Rather the man inside him, Cyril Vanguard, the real boogeyman of Shearhaven. I couldn't manage anything more physical than that, though—using the coffee shop and all the planning for the murder mystery dinner as excuses—which was a relief. I slipped out of the other man's embrace.

"Right. The meal's heating in the oven. Candles are lit in the dining room. I wonder if I should check the lights and the smoke machine in the ballroom?" I said, closing my eyes and checking off my mental checklist.

Vanguard shook his head. "It's all taken care of," he said. "Seriously. We've checked everything over three times at least. Besides—" Vanguard was interrupted by the chime at the doorbell. "Ah-ha! And there's our first guest. Let me go get them. You stay here and collect yourself. Remember, this is supposed to be fun. Right?"

"Yes. Fun," I agreed, after a few worrying, frozen seconds. And here I had just been thinking about how great my acting skills had gotten. Vanguard nodded, left the bedroom, and started down the hall. As soon as he left, I let out a deep sigh, letting go of a breath I didn't realize I'd been holding.

"Are you doing okay?" Tomas asked, drifting through the wall, and standing beside me. I was a little more used to this, after the last couple weeks. Tomas and I had talked on a few occasions, in the middle of the night, when I'd crept out of Vanguard's bed, too uncomfortable sleeping next to him.

"No, I'm nervous as hell," I admitted. "This plan. If everything doesn't go just so—"

"I know. But Gabriel's in position if we need him. And I will be too. You've got this, Ty." I nodded, even if I didn't feel it, and walked toward the front hall. I gripped the handle of the door that led to the great hall. I closed my eyes. We'd rehearsed it a dozen times while Vanguard was on his trip. I'd gone over it in my head a couple dozen more. My mind rebelled, wondering what the response might be from Vanguard if this didn't work. I didn't want to think about what sort of powers the man might possess. I pushed the thought away and mustered every ounce of energy and good humor I could.

"Welcome, my friends, to 'Murder at Shearhaven!'" I bellowed as I entered. Vanguard gave me a "job well done" wink. My stomach turned.

"It's so exciting!" Gina Gallagher said, gawking at the immensity of the front room. Both fireplaces were going, but only candlelight lit the rest. This meant that the upper balcony and most of the ceiling were bathed in shadow. It was a new moon, so there was little light filtering in from the great window above.

"Yeah. It's impressive." Dad said in a tone just shy of sarcasm. Then he looked at me and beamed with genuine pride. "Fancy duds. You wear'em well, son."

"That's just what I was telling him. Now, let's give you a proper look at Shearhaven," Vanguard said, leading the man and woman around the front hall and pointing out interesting features along the way. Anxiety flooded me—a light feeling in my chest—as I watched. To think, just two weeks ago, this day had seemed so far away.

"I don't like this. I don't like involving outside people," I said, interrupting Acton, Tomas, and Gabriel as they laid out the plan.

"I'm not sure it really works if we don't, does it? I mean, if we're going to use your 'murder mystery' as cover, we need people to show up who are, supposedly, going to be the 'audience' for it," Acton said. I wasn't surprised she was unbothered by the potential collateral damage. Despite her insistence that she'd learned some sort of lesson, I still wasn't sure I trusted her. But her role in the plan was key. Without her, there was no plan. I had no choice but to trust her.

"We have reduced the number of people exposed, at least," Gabriel said with ruthless practicality. "By going with the idea this is a rehearsal."

"But these two in particular—"

"Ah, the flexibility of the morally righteous," Acton said. "Would it be better if we picked two people at random? Would that feel 'right' to you, Mr. Sanderson?"

"Of course not. But we're talking about my father here. Not to mention that nice lady from the museum."

"Don't listen to her, Ty. It's to your credit that you're worried," Tomas said.

"I was just making a rhetorical point. It's better if it's them anyway. Your father has heard the stories passed down by generations of Sanderson men. The museum director knows about Shearhaven's history. That's important. They'll both act as anchor points."

"Can you translate for those of us that don't speak heathen?" Gabriel glared at Acton, although she seemed unfazed.

"Vanguard is tied to this house and to the book through magick. Magick is about belief as much as anything. It's a story we practitioners of the sacred arts tell ourselves about the world, and the world shifts to suit."

"I witch, therefore I am?" Gabriel asked.

"Yes, if you like," Acton was beginning to show some irritation now. "The point is that Vanguard has told himself that he is the master of Shearhaven, and of that book. He's told himself that every action he's ever taken was for a purpose and, in that sense, "right." All of us who will be there physically know a different story. I know I wrote the book, and that the book is mine. Gabriel, Ty, Ty's father, and Ms. Gallagher know the evil of what he's done. And you all know that Shearhaven legally belongs to Max Morgan. All of these are in opposition to Vanguard's belief and will make him less powerful than he could be."

"Can't say I love that little qualifier you added at the end," Gabriel said. "Do you know how powerful he is? What if he figures it out?"

"The truth is, I don't know. I doubt there's ever been a single human being with as much power as he wields right now. The one chance we have is that he's still new at all of this, and his ambition has always outstripped his know-how," Acton said. "In any case, this next bit is where things might be really tricky."

10

"The time is almost here," I said as I led Gina and my dad into the dining hall. Candles cast the room in a dreamy, amber glow that would have been comfortable and relaxing if my insides didn't feel like they were being ground between gears. "In a moment, our guest of honor will arrive. And at that point, our experience will begin."

"Our experience!" Dad exclaimed as he sat down at the table. "How fancy."

"Very fancy," Gina agreed, not picking up on the man's mild derision. I ignored it and pressed on.

"Max will be playing the part of Jackson Vanguard, wicked owner of Shearhaven—"

"And alleged Satanist," Gina added, taking a slice of bread from a basket in front of her and buttering it enthusiastically.

"Is that what history records?" Vanguard asked, an icy note creeping in. I couldn't help my eyes widening. The last thing I wanted was for "Max" to get angry.

"Oh, yes. Now, Satanism has been an easy scapegoat for a very long time. But I think in this case, where there's smoke, there's likely to be hellfire." The woman blinked, seemingly catching herself. "Oh. I'm sorry. I'm here to solve a mystery, not teach history."

"No offense taken. You've been most illuminating," Vanguard said.

"And I will be Vanguard's loyal but nefarious butler, Mr. Chaput," I added quickly, hoping to not get too far off track. The further we got off-plan, the more my anxiety rose.

"Who are we playing?" Dad asked, taking a swig of the wine and wincing.

"You're playing yourselves. Just, er, late nineteenth-century version of yourselves."

"Well, let's wake snakes and make this a real lally-cooler, then," Gina said, raising her wine glass high.

"Cheers to that," Vanguard said with a nod, although I didn't have a clue what the woman had meant.

"Well, uh, I believe I hear our guest of honor arriving," I said. The door to the dining room opened, and in swept an elegant figure in a long black dress featuring long sleeves cinched at the elbows and overflowing with black lace. The top of the dress was accentuated by the same lace, dotted with tiny sparkling jewels that caught and refracted the candle flame. "The birthday girl herself, Lady Bridget Acton."

"No, no, please, don't stand on my account," Acton said as she entered, although Vanguard was the only one who was about to, his old-school manners too ingrained to do otherwise. "It's just wonderful to be here, celebrating my birthday with my closest friends."

Getting Acton in on the act was possibly the trickiest part. Not because Acton wasn't willing. In fact, she seemed to relish the opportunity. It was more getting Vanguard comfortable with her being there. That's why, a week earlier, I was awkwardly standing in the short hallway that led to the bathrooms in O'Mackey's, a new "Irish pub" owned by a couple friends of mine from high school. Neither of which was Irish, but that didn't stop them from wishing they were. When they won a decent sum in a multi-state lottery, I wasn't that surprised when they opened the pub. As a business owner in the area, I did try to warn them a thousand different subtle ways to think twice about it. Not that I would have let anyone talk me out of opening Brews & Clues. Sometimes dreams are persistent, despite common sense. I was wondering how my dreams had led me to skulking in hallways and eavesdropping when I finally heard Vanguard arrive.

"You devious little bitch," Vanguard said, sitting at a small table near my barely hidden location across from Acton. I stuck my head out quickly to watch. We'd angled the chairs so that Max would be facing away from me. Just in case. Acton studied him from across the table with a cocked eyebrow. "I mean that, sincerely, as compliment."

"Yes, well, you might want to reconsider your compliments. Many women of this day and age don't appreciate that word," Acton said.

"Good that you're not a woman of this age, then. Not really. Besides, I do know that. Whatever 'Max Morgan' knew, I know."

"I think I have an inkling of how you ended up in that body with no memory—until you touched the book, presumably—but I wasn't sure how much you'd remembered."

"Well, as I say, it was clever of you to try to grab the book while I wasn't exactly myself." Vanguard took a bite of his salad, closed his eyes, and savored it. "It's amazing the variety of food they have now, isn't it? Things you had to be rich for in our day, you can get with ease at the local supermarket."

"Yes, quite." Acton shifted in her chair. "And for the record, while I was at Shearhaven for the book, I didn't know *this* was *you*, at the start. You'd disappeared from my perception. I thought you might even be dead. Securing the book seemed like the responsible thing to do."

"Oh yes, very responsible." If Vanguard's sarcasm was a physical thing, I could imagine it dripping from his words and singeing the table. "Your never-ending request to reclaim 'your' book had nothing to do with it?"

"Of course, it did, Cyril," Acton said, forking her own mac n' cheese with vicious fervor.

"Max, my dear 'Bree,'" the man joked. "Remember?"

"I'm not here to play games."

"Then why are you here? Or more specifically, why did you invite me here? I'm mostly here out of pure curiosity. I'd thought you'd be licking your wounds and hopping the pond back to merry ol' England."

"Well, believe it or not—I barely can—I'm here to apologize." Acton put her fork down. She looked down a moment, and then looked Vanguard right in the eyes.

"I'm going to choose not to believe it, then." Vanguard stuffed another forkful of salad into his mouth and waited for Acton's next move.

"Hardly unexpected." Acton drew in a breath. The secret to lying well, she'd said, was coating the lie in the truth. "But things have changed. He visited me again, Max." That got his attention, just as Acton had hoped.

"Who? Not... not the stranger? The one who gave you the

Eṣāru Bēt Tuppāti?"

"The blank book that became it, yes."

"Fascinating. After all these years," Vanguard said. He narrowed his eyes. "Why?"

It was the same question I had. I'd become pretty good at processing the impossible. I'd had to, frankly. But I didn't fail to notice, when Acton had told her tale, that she sidestepped answering what had changed. Why had she agreed to go along with this plan? Especially her part in it? A woman, on her way to the bathroom, saw me lurking in the hallway and eyed me with suspicion as she passed. I didn't blame her. But I had to be ready for my entrance. I took my phone out and pretended to look at the screen while I listened.

"I don't get why you feel bad. It's not like you lost the book. It was taken from you."

"That doesn't mean I didn't miss opportunities before that happened. History didn't just happen to me. I was too busy enjoying my power to notice it crashing down all around me." Acton pushed her plate away. "In any case, my point is this: I realized I was being greedy. You have the book. You've had it for a very long time now. I can feel it, even as we sit here. Pulsating somewhere within that house. But it doesn't call out to me. Not anymore. The book, no matter what I'd wish, is yours."

"Well, I never thought I'd hear it," I watched Vanguard's grin twist Max's face as he prepared to savor lording it over her. "Can it really be true? Have you really seen the light?"

"If you can't—or don't want to—believe any of this, it's fine. But you know me. You can believe in my practicality, if nothing else, no?" Acton asked. Vanguard nodded in answer, still chewing his latest bite. "I want to do as the stranger wished. I want to open people's eyes to magick. I want to try to usher in the world he believed could exist, in place of the nightmare we're living in right now. A nightmare, I might add, that he was convinced was only going to get worse."

"Very Kumbaya. The problem is that doesn't gel all that well with my plans, which is to wield all this power secretly and live a life of luxury and exploration—unfettered by the petty little concerns of this world."

"Except, you still have to live on this world, Vanguard." I could sense that Vanguard's paw was on the bait. Acton just had to close the trap carefully. "I'm suggesting we team up. I'm so much more powerful, even this removed from the book. Even if it no longer recognizes me as its owner. Let me share a little of its power. Not the things that would threaten you, but the magick that could save this world. That could change it for the better."

"And what, exactly, does this get me?"

"Well, a planet that's still livable, for one thing," Acton snapped, before regaining her composure. Plus, I'd give you access to the hidden pages." And, there it was. The trap shut.

"Hidden pages?"

"You've felt them, when you've read or searched through the book, haven't you? I assume you can read it now, correct?" Acton asked. Vanguard nodded. "Then you've felt it. Just after the chart explaining the cosmological connections with magick and before passages on plants and herbs."

"I thought maybe it was my imagination. Or my thirst to know more. I'd started to worry I had some sort of addiction to knowledge that'd never be satiated," Vanguard said, a smile creeping across his face as he dreamed of the possibilities. "What do these hidden pages contain?"

"The last secret. Time magick. As in the manipulation of and travel through." Acton let her words hang in the air.

"Why didn't you ever use this 'time magick' if it exists?"

"The pages, even once you can force them to reveal themselves, are blank. There's another spell on them. A sort of 'magick lock.' It took me decades with the book just to figure out what spell it was. The pages automatically reveal themselves when the book's owner reaches a certain level of magickal maturity." Acton sat back in her chair. This was working. "A maturity I know I've reached by now. And, I'm guessing, you have too. So, there you have it. All my secrets revealed."

All my secrets revealed. That was my cue. The signal that the man had taken the bait. At least as fully as he ever would.

"Oh, hey, honey," I said sheepishly as I approached them. I looked at Acton, acting concerned that the two were talking. "Everything okay, here?" Vanguard smiled wide and motioned for me to sit.

"Fabulously. Ms. Acton and I have put aside our differences, in fact. All one big happy family," he said, raising his glass in the air. Acton smiled and followed suit.

"Fantastic," she said, raising her glass as well. I raised mine, and as we clinked the glasses together, I laid the groundwork for the next step of the plan.

"Excellent." *Here we go.* Time to be struck by a sudden inspiration. I took a quick breath, and summoned every ounce of acting talent I could. "You know, I'm having trouble casting a role, and I think you might be perfect for it." Acton feigned surprise and I watched Vanguard's reaction from the corner of my eye. His eyes lost none of the greedy thirst they'd had since she'd told him about the missing pages. Hopefully this lust would blind him to the plans coming together around him, until it was too late.

11

"Hello, again," Lady Acton said as she took the chair next to Gina. The older woman's face reddened for a moment, before Acton leaned over and whispered "Don't worry, Ty knows I paid you to tell me should anyone else come inquiring after Shearhaven. No ill feelings on anyone's part."

"Oh, thank goodness, I've felt so guilty," Gina whispered back to me as, in my role as butler, I served the first course of vermicelli soup into her bowl with a silver ladle. "Although, I did get this hat with the money you gave me."

"Worth every penny." Acton winked at the older woman, and then considered her soup. A strange look crossed her face I couldn't read.

"I hope you enjoy the selections for tonight's dinner. They should be suitably… authentic," Vanguard said, his lips contorted into a wolfish smile. Acton looked up, a smile barely masking her gritted teeth.

"Yes. Master Vanguard selected the dishes himself," I said

quickly. I didn't know a lot about Acton. She had a certain charm about her, although at times her flamboyance had a tinge of desperation to it. When it came to Vanguard, though, I felt her fuse was frayed and short. The last thing we needed was some blow-up before we could enact the plan. Clearly the menu we were serving was from some past party or get-together between them. Vanguard was playing, perhaps testing this new truce to its limits. I ladled the last bowl of soup in front of my father.

"Looks good to me," Dad said, spoon in hand and ready to tuck in. "Did they, uh, I mean, do we say grace? In the 1870s, I mean? Which is, uh, now, of course." I patted my dad on the back. He wasn't as great at improvisation as he was solving mysteries, but he was trying.

"No, not in this house," Vanguard said with a wicked grin.

"Ooooh, very ominous," Gina said in approval, not realizing that the man before her required very little in the way of acting skill to play a villainous Vanguard.

"Well, godless heathen though you may be, Mr. Vanguard," Gina said between careful sips of soup, "You have a beautiful home. It brings my heart great cheer to see such a place so respected." At this, Vanguard positively beamed.

"My good woman, I thank you. I've always been very proud of this house. I—my grandfather built this place, as I'm sure you well know. Although much has changed, I'd say the soul of the house is stronger than ever before. It's nice to meet someone who appreciates it. You're a historian, are you not?"

"Yes, and I love a good mystery." Gina dipped a crust of bread into the soup and gnawed at it enthusiastically.

"Well, you're certainly in the right place," Vanguard regarded the grand dining room of Shearhaven. I had no idea how much money he'd spent, completely refurbishing it with period furniture, the centerpiece of which was the great wooden table that had replaced the driftwood and glass table that Max's interior designer had picked out. "Of course, it's not quite perfect. You see, when my grandfather built this house, he had a seal pattered into the wallpaper to protect against outside magical influences. Did you know that?"

"Well, uh, no. I must say, this is very well resear—that is, that's absolutely fascinating."

"Isn't it? I can't say I ever cared for the look of it. But needs must. I kept the den just the way I wanted it. One place in this place that was just mine."

"Really?" Gina looked from Max to me, a question in her eyes. Where had all this new information come from? Was it all true? I shrugged in a way I hoped communicated she could believe what she was hearing.

"What did—does your study look like? If I may ask?" Gina sat forward as Max began describing it in detail. I refilled everyone's water and wine glasses, beads of sweat forming on my brow. The line between playacting and reality had already blurred more than I cared for.

"Is it true there's a secret passage? Down to a cave system under the house?" Gina asked next, her curiosity about the den quenched. To her left, Acton coughed wetly in surprise.

"Sorry, a bit of vermicelli went down the wrong pipe," she said quickly, tears in her eyes from the force of the cough. "I've never heard such a thing."

"Oh, it's an obscure bit of trivia. A set of the original plans for the house was found a few years back in the home of a private collector in Wales. His great-great-grandfather or somesuch worked for the firm that drew up the plans for Cyril Vanguard, based on the man's concepts. There's a hidden passageway that was omitted from later versions of the plans. Quite intriguing!"

"Yes, well, that's one mystery I can clear up easily. There is such a passage. If you like, I can show you later. I'm afraid it isn't that exciting, though. It was used for a wine cellar," Vanguard said smoothly. "I've been meaning to get some new racks down there. Though I'd have to ask my sommelier whether the temperature is cold and consistent enough."

"I'd love to take a peek sometime! You never know what treasures you'll find in places like that."

"Well, I expect any treasures to be found in a place like this were given up long ago," Lady Acton said quickly, likely wishing we hadn't invited the historian. Not that the woman was saying anything wrong, exactly, it was just all very on the nose. She hadn't been told of the grand plan for the night, of course. To her, like my dad, this was nothing more than a fun murder mystery dinner. That didn't mean some of what she was saying didn't cut too close to the bone.

"Oh, you'd be surprised m'Lady," Vanguard said over the rim of his glass, eyes positively sparkling. To my relief, the chatter turned more mundane as the next courses were served. Dad and Gina tried their best to come up with period-appropriate small-talk, while it came naturally to Acton and Vanguard, who'd both lived through it once before. Both my father and the historian did their best to ask questions they thought might be useful for later, when the mystery part of the evening would begin. I felt another twinge of guilt that there wasn't much of a mystery here, and that the night was going to take a very strange turn at some point. I still wasn't sure how I was going to explain it all, assuming it worked.

In the kitchen, I scraped off the remains of the main course. Chef Ambrose had left instructions with me on how to reheat and serve everything. Thankfully, the chef had already booked a vacation with his family this weekend, as his presence would have been a variable that I didn't want to have to account for. I'd take any little advantage I could get. When I came out with a tray full of four fresh-from-the-oven ramekins, each bursting with a delicate chocolate souffle and served with a side of caramel sauce, I saw that most of the guests had gotten up from the dining room table and were inspecting the rest of the room.

"This is certainly intriguing," Gina said, picking up a small silver dagger with a jeweled handle and strange inscriptions on its blade from a specially constructed display stand. The dagger was well-lit, a clue in our false murder mystery. Little touches like this were meant to make it feel real to Vanguard.

"Ah, yes, an old family heirloom," Vanguard said, taking the dagger from her. "Priceless, really."

"Dessert is served, Sir," I said. Vanguard nodded and placed the dagger back on its rack.

"Well, let's dig in. I don't know about the rest of you, but I'm excited to see how the rest of the night plays out." Vanguard sat back in his chair.

The next instant, all the lights in the dining room were out. Even the candles, thanks to some Wi-Fi tech, were instantly extinguished. Lady Acton screamed, there was a sound of shuffling, and when the light came back on both Acton and Vanguard were gone.

"Look what I just got in," I said, carefully opening the package that'd arrived from Peoria. Vanguard looked up from the smoke machine he'd been fiddling with as he read its instructions.

"The leather harness you ordered for my birthday?"

"Ha! That's for Christmas, and only if you're very good."
My pulse quickened. I was still doing my best to avoid anything
that might lead to a sexual encounter. I could kiss the man
and I could lie to him. Anything more than that filled me with
revulsion. Although, I had to admit, I did miss the way his
body—Max's body—felt next to me. The possibility of that
pleasure was gone, though. Because the excitement wasn't just
the hard-muscled body, but the spark that animated it. Now
I could see "Max" as little more than muscle, fat, and organs
wrapped in a flesh sack, animated by the thing that'd killed him.
"This is from Bjorn. My prop guy? He moved to Peoria a year or
so back but still finds time to help me out."

I opened the box carefully, searching through the sea of
foam peanuts to find two objects wrapped in brown paper.

"Ah, this must be the dagger!" Vanguard said.

"Daggers, technically," I reminded him as I unwrapped the
identical daggers. Both were decorated with pictographic symbols
that would help our guests solve the mystery at hand. Bjorn had
done an immaculate job, embellishing on the design I'd come up
with and making it even better. I handed him one of them.

"'The Vanguard Blade.'" He gripped it appreciatively. "Too
bad this didn't exist. It's convincing looking. Probably fetch a
good price these days."

"Hey, be careful! That's the 'close-up' one. The one that'll be
in the dining room for the guests to inspect. This one, however, is
the one we'll hide in the ballroom," I said, taking the other knife
in my hand, and stabbing it into my arm. The blade, metallic-
painted plastic, retracted into the handle.

"Very clever."

"There's a little compartment here." I unscrewed the bottom
of the jeweled handle and revealed the inner workings of the

knife. "We'll have a blood bag in here, so the blade will push into and puncture it, leaving a grisly bloody trail."

"I can see why you enjoy all of this," Vanguard said, gripping the other dagger in his hand. "It's all very exciting. Reminds me a little of the drama of my—well, parties I used to have. Strange, they weigh about the same. I expected the fake dagger to be lighter."

"Huh," I said, taking both daggers and comparing their weights as if that wasn't exactly what I requested. "You're right. Probably just Bjorn paying attention to the details. He makes a lot of props for local movies, too. I suppose if they weren't the same weight, you could see it in the way the performer held and moved it. Especially on the big screen. But we have this to tell them apart."

I raised the two daggers and showed Max the pommels of both. On one, a ruby was set into the end of the hilt. On the other dagger, a sapphire glimmered.

"Interesting. So, which is which?"

"Ruby equals *real*—that's the real dagger. The blade isn't sharpened but the point end could still hurt someone. Sapphire equals *safe*, or the retractable one."

"Clever. It's handsome work."

"Just a shame he didn't have time to make the book. I went to the used bookstore trying to find something that looked like a spell book or something. But nothing seemed quite right," I said. Vanguard came up behind me and wrapped his arms around me.

"Oh, by the way UPS delivered one of those things—what are they called? Those things that make lines at a ballpark?"

"Oh, the line marker. I didn't expect that until tomorrow. I figured we could mark out temporary parking spaces. So, people don't park in the grass."

"You're so adorable," Vanguard whispered in my ear. I hesitated and closed my eyes. I drew in a breath, steeling myself with the thought that I only had to do this for another week. Just seconds before my pause would be too awkward, I grabbed his arms and pulled them tighter around my body.

"What brought that on?" I asked.

"I don't know. Seeing you in your element, I guess? I know you like coffee and the shop, but it feels like this is where your heart really lies. Making stories for others to experience. Working through all the details." Vanguard gave me a peck on the cheek. From anyone else, at any other time, this would have filled me with joy, and a sense of being seen. Right now, it made my skin crawl. But I couldn't pull away. Instead, I leaned my head toward Vanguard's and sighed heavily.

"I feel like the luckiest man in the world." I channeled everything I *could* be feeling to make it ring true. I imagined I was an alternate universe Ty. That Ty had finally let his guard down, and allowed himself to love someone who *hadn't* turned out to be a murderous warlock in a stolen body. "Okay, I better get back to it. The lighting set-up should be arriving tomorrow, and that'll probably take half the day."

"I suppose you're right." Vangaurd withdrew his arms slowly from around my waist. "I'll get back to my smoke machine, taskmaster!" I wondered if all this affection was an act of Vanguard's, or if the memories he retained from Max were behind it. Could memory be divorced from a person's experience of them, and all the emotions that colored them when remembered? That seemed impossible.

"Oh, don't pout," I said, trying to keep my voice playful. "This'll all be over soon enough."

12

"**W**ell," Gina said, eating her chocolate souffle and looking around the room. "I don't mean to be rude, Ty, but since this is a rehearsal, I have to say—this doesn't seem like much of a murder mystery? Two people disappeared. As soon as we find the body of one of them, we'll know the other is the murderer, right?"

"I was kinda waiting for a twist," my dad said between spoonfuls of his dessert. I smiled.

"No, you're right." I sat down in Vanguard's seat and helped myself to some dessert as well. I was starving, having little time or appetite earlier. Now, my stomach was threatening to do loop-de-loops and getting something in there seemed like a good idea. "During a real performance, there would be more people. It'd keep the question going longer. But, since this is a rehearsal, I can let you know now. This isn't a traditional murder mystery. In fact, instead of trying to solve a whodunit, you're trying to *prevent* the murder at the heart of the story."

"I see." Gina nodded, sat back in her chair, blinked, and

then shook her head. "How does that work?"

"Well, you are officially now in more of an escape room. As the faithful butler, I can hardly let you have run of the house. I've locked us in. Everything you need to figure out what is happening, who kidnapped who, and who has murderous intent—and motive—is in this room."

"Oh, thank God," Dad said. "I was afraid we were going to have to run around this entire house looking for clues."

"I was beginning to regret wearing heels." Gina took a drink of red wine, and then got up from her chair. I watched with anticipation. I had to make everything convincing for Vanguard's sake leading up to tonight. And the man had been irritatingly interested in the story and preparations. The puzzle had to be complex enough to feel real, but not so complex that the museum director and my dad couldn't figure it out.

"Well, guess I'd better see if all my *Columbo* watching paid off," Dad said, giving me a wink and getting out of his seat and inspecting the dining room. I couldn't help but smile at my old man in action. There was a glimmer in his eye I hadn't seen in years. The dining room had been completely redecorated for the night. Max Morgan's modern art, as with the furniture, had been taken away and replaced by inexpensive portraiture and paintings procured online. These were supplemented by some custom jobs that were specially printed and framed for the evening's game.

"The dagger I was looking at is missing. It was placed right next to this big candle on a stand, so I figured it had to be important." Gina picked up the stand and turned it around in her hands for clues. None of which were forthcoming. "And Vanguard didn't seem eager for me to look at it too closely."

"A missing dagger isn't going to help us too much, is it,

though?" Dad walked to the wall of portraits over the dining room's fireplace. "Well, this is a motley crew."

"I suppose not. But the dagger had some strange symbols on it. Nothing I recognized straight away, but I'd bet that was some sort of clue."

"Hold on! Look at this. This portrait of Vanguard!" Dad exclaimed. Gina scrambled over to join Dad. The portrait was a picture that I'd taken of Vanguard in period costume. Some Photoshop and a print on textured canvas was convincing enough. I brushed off a swell of pride, remembering that none of this actually mattered.

"The dagger is in the painting, and the 'artist' seems to have captured it in loving detail. Including the symbols!" Gina grabbed one of the small, singular candles from the table and held it up close to the painting. "I still don't recognize them, but they have to mean something."

"Agreed," Dad said, peering at the blade of the dagger. "Something familiar about these. I think you're right. The key to this is the dagger."

"I'll leave you two sleuths to discuss while I go to the kitchen for your digestifs. When I return, let me know if you have an answer," I said, opening the double doors of the dining room with a flourish and a dramatic spin. Only to find Dad and Gina were too busy exchanging notes on the mystery to pay much attention to me. I closed the doors, locked it, and headed toward the ballroom. Beads of sweat trickled down the sides of my face. The closer we got to the "final act" of our ruse, the more nervous I became. Although we'd wrapped up our plot in the guise of a game—and it was easy to get carried away by that— the truth was we were dealing with a sadistic killer with far too much magickal power. Any mistake could be a deadly one. As I neared the ballroom entrance, I thought of Dad and Gina in the dining room. They were out for a night of fun. I was risking their lives. That was the truth of it. And they had no clue. Whatever happened tonight was on me. I was just about to open the door to the ballroom when I heard Acton's voice ring out from behind the door. Something in her tone made me pause. Instead of walking in, I carefully turned the knob and opened it a crack. Just enough that I could hear and see in.

"My point is that you're enjoying this part a little too much," Acton said. "Besides, it'll take them a bit to work through the puzzle. The less time I spend trussed up to this thing the better." Vanguard had been only too eager to purchase "this thing" as the key prop in the finale of the murder mystery-cum-escape room. The sacrificial table was made of metal and hinged so that it could be flipped upright once the victim was manacled in. We'd found it on a magician's supply website. I said it was way too much. Vanguard insisted. The room was dark, with bright lights focused on the table at the center of the room. The fog machine belched out chalky-smelling clouds to create the appropriate eerie atmosphere.

"I suppose," Vanguard said. He retrieved a bag from a shadowed part of the room and pulled out the dagger with the retracting blade. He looked at the solid dagger, still in his hand after their hasty exit from the dining room.

"You can't tell me you're not tempted." Acton eyed the blade. "Just remember that ruby equals real."

"Ha! Yes, 'ruby equals real.'" Vanguard slid the dagger with the ruby set into its pommel into the bag. "And I'd be lying if I said it wasn't tempting. A quick end to you, my eternal friend. My eternal nemesis."

"They have a name for that now. Frenemies. Or at least

that's what it was called for a while. I have a hard time keeping up, truthfully."

"Not everything in this bright and bold future is to my tastes," Vanguard said, crinkling his nose.

"Well, one of the curses of this century can also be one of its boons. Don't like something? Wait a few months and people will be onto something else. It's quite tiring if I'm honest. But I've learned to ride the waves."

"Yes, you always were… adaptable. In any case, regarding your prospective murder, that would get very messy quickly. Too many witnesses. Plus, you have very pointedly put off telling me the secret of the lost pages in the book. Which I assume has been your safeguard all along."

"Well, I do know you well, Cyril. You're a smart man, but sometimes your in-the-moment passion can get the best of you."

"Hmm. Yes, I suppose," the man allowed. "Speaking of the book…" Vanguard reached back into the bag and pulled out the ancient tome. Relief flooded over me seeing it. I wasn't entirely convinced he'd pull through and bring it. He'd cleaned it carefully and thoroughly for tonight. Reverentially, he carried it to a wooden podium—another online find—imaginatively decorated with skulls, demon heads, flames, and screaming faces in bas relief.

"I still think it's foolish you offered it up as a 'prop.'" Acton regarded the book only out of her periphery. As if she didn't want to give Vanguard the satisfaction of her envy. But I could see it plainly in her face. I swiped the sweat from my brow. Acton was another variable in everything. Tomas, Gabriel, and I didn't have a choice but to trust her. She was the key to any of this working, after all. That didn't mean I trusted her or her motives. I was about to make my presence known. I'd lingered too long at the door as it was. I hoped Dad and Gina weren't getting antsy. But it was a chance to hear Acton and Vanguard interact without one of us around.

"Oh, come on, Acton. You of all people should know my mastery of the *Eṣāru Bēt Tuppāti* is complete. Even if, say, that old museum director decided to run off with it, it'd be back in my hands with a snap of my fingers. And it's fun, isn't it? I mean, look at this podium." Vanguard ran his hands up and down carved details of it. "The world has no idea you're to thank for all of this. All these pop-culture bastardizations and half-truths. And now the real thing will be staring them in the face, and they won't have a clue."

"I made mistakes." Acton allowed herself to walk a little closer to the book. "I thought introducing the magick in the book within contexts they could understand made sense. Only to have my book taken from me. So much nonsense sprouted up in their imaginations as they stumbled in the dark. So many ghouls in the shadows to fear."

My eyes flicked to the shadowed corners of the ballroom. Tomas had mentioned there were other presences here. Ancient things without recognizable shape. I wondered if Acton knew about them. It certainly didn't seem as though she did. I wondered if they watched our own little shadow play now. I wondered, if they had still had thoughts and minds the way we think of them, what they would think of what would play out in this room tonight.

"I was supposed to give the world a beacon," Acton continued. "A path toward something better. And all I gave them were new things to fear."

"So, do you have a better plan, this time? To bring about a brave new world of magick?"

"I have ideas, yes. But the first thing I'd really love is a cup of tea. Why don't you go get that while I change into my sacrificial robes."

"Hmmm. Yes, I can do that." Vanguard wasn't even trying to hide his suspicion. "But I think I'll take the book with me." Lady Acton sighed.

"I'm hardly going to run off with it. As you said, it'd be back to you with a thought." Acton looked at the man, whose suspicion had not waned. "Suit yourself."

"I always do. There are some chances I'm not willing to take. See you in a moment." Vanguard nodded and took the book under his arm. With a start, I realized that my time to enter had come. I took a few quick paces back away from the door so I could take long strides through it as I entered, to make it seem like I was just coming from somewhere. As it was, I nearly bumped into Vanguard at the door.

"Everything prepared in here? I doubt it'll take Gina and my dad too much longer."

"Our star here has just requested a beverage. I thought she deserved a last drink, if not a last meal," Vanguard said with a wink that forced me to repress a shiver.

"Well, I suppose there's time for that." I gave him a peck on the cheek on the way out. My heart thrummed in my chest as he exited the ballroom. I walked over to the metal table. Acton looked at me, her expression as cool and confident as ever. I admired the hell out of that, especially given what was coming next. We waited a few moments, until Vanguard was well clear, before we dared to speak. And even then, barely above a whisper.

"You should get back to the dining room. I can manage here."

"I just wanted to—"

"I know why you're here." Her smile was caught somewhere between mischievous and despairing. "You don't have to worry. I'll keep my part of the bargain."

"Sorry. I just—I can't say I fully understand why you're doing this."

"For myself. As I always do. Rest assured in my commitment to my own desires if nothing else."

"*That* I can buy. I'm just nervous."

"Yes, the copious amount of flop sweat you're producing was a clue. Come here." Acton produced a handkerchief and began wiping the sweat off my face and forehead. I closed my eyes to allow her to work more efficiently. I should have been irritated, but there was a gentleness and thoroughness to her work that I found strangely touching. When I opened my eyes, I saw she was looking at me curiously.

"Hm," she said.

"Hm?"

"You have kind eyes. I never noticed. My father had kind eyes." She studied me for a moment more, and quickly looked away. "It turns out eternity can be remarkably lonely."

The whir of the fog machine kicking on again broke the brief silence between us.

"This is going to work," I said.

Acton nodded. "It must. Or Vanguard will kill us all."

13

I was impressed with the team of Gallagher & Sanderson—I found that the museum director and my dad had made relatively short work of my escape room in my absence. Which only added to my nervousness. Vanguard and Acton needed a little more time to prepare. I'd counted on my dad holding back some, as he always did, to allow everyone else (everyone else in this case being Gina) to have some of the fun. What I'd not counted on was Gina being such a natural at it. Though, in retrospect, I should have. An eye for detail seemed like a necessity for a historian.

They realized that each symbol on the knife corresponded to a cardinal direction. On each wall of the dining room that corresponded to that direction, there was one portraiture with the symbol worked into the decoration on the frame. To the north was a painting of Winifred Blackmore Acton, a fictitious ancestor played by Acton in costume, who (according to notation on the back) was tried as a witch in England. To the East was a portrait of the equally fictitious Eustace Vanguard in a Witchfinder costume, carrying a small book in his hand.

That same book that was mixed in with some other books on a small bookshelf in the dining room. I'd taken some liberties with what would be in a dining room of this period for the sake of simplicity, but it still rankled me. I reminded myself that all of this was for show and smiled as Gina and Dad talked through the clues. I still felt guilty that I'd involved them, but I figured they were here, so at least I was giving them some fun before the finale. It helped my conscience little, however, as I used them as tools in this strange chess game with Vanguard.

"It's not a real book," Dad said, opening the Witchfinder's tome on the dining room table. "It's got a false compartment." He pulled out a scrap of parchment, and roughly carved statue.

"Looks like a depiction of Baphomet." Gina took the statue and turned it around in her hands.

"There's a poem on here," Dad said, bringing the parchment closer to the candlelight. "'Riven the heart / of the branch / of false tree / Restore the dark / lord's power / back unto me.' Spooky."

"Well, let's find the other clues at West and South. But I've got an idea or two." Gina sat the statue down next to the false book and parchment.

The clue on the western wall was the hardest to spot. The frame with the correct symbol was smaller than the others. A grainy photo of a family enjoying a picnic in Brighton near the West Pier. The mother in the photo had been photoshopped to have Acton's face.

"Something on the back," Dad said. "Looks like a census record for the Talbot family. Lawrence Talbot, his wife Esmerelda Talbot, their son Barclay Talbot, and daughter Bridget Talbot."

"And, I think, this is the final piece," Gina said, taking down

a landscape of London in the 1860s. "On the back of this there's
a family tree. Looks like it was torn out of the Talbot family bible.
And—yes, here it is. Bridget Talbot, if you trace her lineage back,
is a descendant of Winifred Blackmore Acton."

"So, Winifred obviously wasn't killed," Dad said. "Either she
somehow escaped being declared a witch or survived it."

"And the Vanguard family has been obsessed over it since.
Perhaps because of their own secret Satanic leanings." Gina
picked up the parchment and read the poem once again, it
shook in her hands as she plunged forward with her theory
excitedly. "Lady Acton is the sacrifice. If this poem is some sort
or prophecy, then it seems like Acton, as the descendant of the
witch's bloodline, has to be killed so that Vanguard can receive
the full Satanic powers that were promised him!"

"Wow. Okay, that makes sense." Dad blinked in surprise. "I'd
been heading vaguely in that direction, but you cut right to it."
There was no disguising Dad's obvious approval of Gina, and she
looked positively shy when faced with the compliment. I couldn't
help but smile, despite a stomach full of worry, as I secretly sent
a text message to Acton's phone under the table, warning her
we were about to wrap things up sooner than expected. There
were a few more clues around that would help point them in the
direction Gina had intuited, but she's jumped right to the correct
answer. I hoped Acton and Vanguard were ready.

"You've figured out the would-be murderer, and the motive,"
I said, sliding my phone back into my pocket and retrieving
a keyring with two keys on it. "Now you're ready for the next
part—finding out where Vanguard took Lady Acton. One key
will open this dining room and allow your escape. The other will
open the door to the location where Lady Acton is being held.
Good luck."

"Excellent," Gina said as she took the key ring and headed for the nearest door.

"Uh, mind if we take a quick bathroom break?" Dad asked.

"Actually, I could use one myself." Gina found the correct key and unlocked the door.

I waited in the door of the dining room, waiting for Dad and Gina to finish up their bathroom break and thanking God for small bladders. My job now was to watch. Facilitate. And try not to throw up. It didn't take long for them to find the clues as to where in the mammoth house the scoundrel Vanguard had scampered off to. A trail of fake blood led to the ballroom. The rest was up to Acton and the others. I'd been able to focus on the game while we were in the dining room, seeing Dad engaged in something that used to bring him so much joy. Something I hadn't really considered, so lost in my own grief. I thought that after all of this, I should start up the murder mysteries again. For Dad, if nothing else. That was, of course, assuming there was an "after" for any of us. Now, however, that we were out of the room and heading toward the ballroom, the warm, inescapable jangle of anxiety started to flood me again. Now, the imaginary story of witches and witchfinders and all of that was giving way to reality. And reality, or the shambles that passed for it lately, was far stranger and more dangerous.

"Here we are," Dad said, stopping in front of a large, grand door. "I wonder where this leads."

"I don't remember every detail of the plans for this place," Gina said, "but I'm pretty sure this is the ballroom."

"Something's definitely going on in there." Dad looked down and saw fine wisps of white-gray smoke escape from under the bottom of the door. Gina put the key in the lock, and it turned easily. I held my breath as the door opened.

"Help me!" Acton screamed. She was dressed in a flowing white dress, manacled to the metal table which had been pivoted upward at an eighty-degree angle.

"You are beyond help, witch!" Vanguard bellowed. A bit over the top, I thought. He wore a ghoulish copper mask sculpted to look like a horned goat man. He held the dagger in his hand, the blue sapphire set into the pommel glittering, ready to strike. The fog machine, situated behind the table, was working overtime as the track lights they'd just installed shone menacing red light onto the scene.

"Give it up, Vanguard. Put down the dagger, and you'll be saved a life in prison." Gina strode forward confidently, getting into character. Dad, on the other hand, was quiet, and stayed outside of the central red spotlight.

"What fear do I have of the laws of men? With this witch dead, all the power shall be mine," Vanguard thrust the dagger down into the woman's heart, just as scripted. Acton let out a gurgling yelp.

"Oh, that was very convincing," Gina whispered.

Vanguard waited for the next line and continued to wait— with increasing awkwardness—as the fake blood poured from the dagger's blade. I, as Chaput the butler, was supposed to say a line here. I was trembling. Unable to look away. Unable to remember what I was supposed to say. Vanguard turned to look at me. He was silent, and still, with a strange look in his eye.

"What are we supposed to do next? Did we lose?" Gina started toward Acton at the table. Acton's eyes were wide. Her expression inscrutable. Dad took the woman gently by the arm and led her back toward the outer wall. I caught his eye and understanding passed between us. I wasn't sure what my dad could see, fueled by the strange power that flowed through our family line. But it was enough that he now knew this wasn't, exactly, pretend.

"Did I say the line wro—" Vanguard began, before a wave of wooziness gripped him and he pitched forward. He caught himself from falling over, but the knife slid out of place from Acton's torso. Vanguard saw what was wrong immediately. The blade did not spring out as he pulled the dagger away. Rather, a long metal blade withdrew from a small slit in Acton's body. Blood pumped furiously from the wound. "What is this?" Vanguard dropped the dagger. I knew it was coming, and still the shock of the reality of it all had frozen me in place.

"Wrong dagger, dear," Acton said drowsily, her shock giving way to something else. Her eyes sparkled with triumph. Vanguard's eyelids drooped, his head lolling to the side as his footing became less and less sure.

"No! That was the right dagger. Why am I—why do I feel so tired?" He fell to his knees, his breath becoming heavier and slower by the second.

"The daggers were made from the same mold, Vanguard," I said. "One was solid and didn't have a retractable blade, sure. But both had ends that screwed off. The solid one didn't need it, of course. But it was still in the mold."

"Easy enough to swap the ends while you got some tea," Acton said wearily, her teeth reddening from the blood pooling in her mouth. Vanguard's eyes widened. Because it was Vanguard now. Whatever defenses had kept me from seeing his real self without Acton's help had failed as his body failed. The grotesquery I'd only glimpsed before in the restaurant was standing before me again. Hunched and rotten, pustules bulged to bursting as he spoke through the puckered and dried hole of a mouth.

"The spell? This is the spell?" Vanguard looked around frantically, expecting to see the familiar circle and glowing runes.

"You won't find the circle, Vanguard," I said. "It's outside the central part of the house. Made with that line marker that arrived last week."

"And it's a square, not a circle, to be—" Acton coughed, sending a worrying splatter of blood to the floor. "As I was saying. It's a square. An enclosed shape is all that was ever needed. The rest was all for show." Acton twirled her fingers in the air in an imitation of a stage magician. Vanguard watched the fake smoke billow around him. He looked at me, an unspoken call for pity in his eyes. He didn't realize I saw him for what he was. Whatever appeal he might have tried to make using Max's body was lost on me. In fact, it only hardened me to our purpose here. I crossed my arms and let all the disgust I'd felt since finding out the truth show. Vanguard looked at Dad and Gina, mounting concern and confusion in his eyes. And then he looked at Acton, who grew paler by the moment.

"So, you got tired of that body, you old cow? Or is this your way of getting reconnected with the book? By stealing my body? I can feel the other presence there, just at the edge of my consciousness."

"Not me, Cyril. I wasted my chance. I trust myself with that book only a smidge more than I trust you." Acton's eyes were unfocused. She blinked slowly as she said the words.

"Then who—whose mind can I feel?" Vanguard fell backward, painfully, onto his elbows, his confusion and fear making him frantic.

"Mine," said Tomas, as he floated slowly up through the floor. "Lady Acton is giving me back what she helped steal from me."

Vanguard fell backward, causing a wave of air to briefly scatter the smoke around him before coiling back onto itself. His chest began to shake. Tomas glanced at Acton in concern, but it was clear from the look on her face that she didn't know what was happening either. Then, at last, Vanguard laughed.

"Idiots," he said before mumbling something under his breath. An instant later, reality began to twist and warp. The flat wooden boards that made up the ballroom's floor burst upward and curved, sending the sacrificial table and the elegantly carved wooden podium in front of it flying. The table landed hard, wrenching Lady Acton to the side with a painful cry. Even in the chaos of light and debris, I could see the light was gone from Acton's eyes. That cry had been her last. I had more immediate concerns, however.

The podium clattered to the floor. The book that had been on it remained suspended in the air, floating. The warping effect grew out from Vanguard's position as more of the floor burst upward and curved. Finally, it reached the ballroom's wall—the front wall of the house—and the distinctive dark brick of Shearhaven separated in ragged lines, exploding into curved arcs of individual bricks as a hole appeared in the wall.

"This house and this book are mine!" Max's body floated off the ground. The shadow-thing that was Cyril Vanguard bulged around it. The pustules covering his body exploded in blood and ichor as his jaw stretched open, revealing rows and rows of sharp teeth. Beyond was a shiny black gullet. Shadow arms extended from within him, cracking bone and twisting tendons, skin tearing once it was stretched too thin. His legs followed. His ribs twisted and exploded through his stomach clawing outward and sending his insides—grimy organs of shadow and black sludge— to the floor. It was only the thing's lack of true substance that kept the little food I'd eaten down. As it was, it was still fucking hard to look at. It lumbered awkwardly at first as it stretched to its full height. I glanced at Dad, who'd huddled Gina behind him on the floor.

"No, you can't!" Tomas said, watching helplessly as Vanguard began to lumber toward the hole in the wall, out of the spell's boundary, and to freedom. He took Max's body with him, suspended and floating in the spectral nightmare Vanguard had become. I made a move toward Vanguard, but found the floor shattered and twisted up toward me the next moment, pinning me back with dangerous splintered edges. I looked over at my father, who was holding Gina back from rushing to assist Acton.

"Yes, I can. Poor, sweet, pathetic little Tomas. How long have you been here? Was it you who whispered in Ty's ear? Or Acton? Who turned him against me?" Vanguard asked, although he didn't bother to look back around. "I suppose it doesn't matter. The end for all of you will be the same once I'm out of this damned spell."

"Which is why you'll never leave, cretin," Gabriel floated up through the floor until his upper torso was visible and grabbed for Vanguard's leg.

"Gabriel, too? Hilarious," Vanguard spat between his teeth. But I could hear the strain in his voice. Unlike Tomas, Gabriel had been a ghost for a very long time.

"When Tomas first came back, he knew so little," Gabriel said, with a grunt of effort as he held onto one of Vanguard's elongated limbs. I tried to calm my breath, to keep the panic from settling in as the jagged floorboards creaked upward and closer to my neck. But Gabriel had barely slowed the thing down as it shuffled toward freedom.

"I was the one who taught Tomas to do more than hover.

And, of course, to hold objects."

"Cease your fruitless prattle. You know, of all the people I've killed over the years, I think I enjoyed ending you more than all of them."

"The biggest problem wasn't floating, of course," Gabriel clawed his way upward, finally grasping around Vanguard's waist with both arms. It was then that I realized that something like gravity was acting upon Gabriel's form. "The biggest issue is coming back down. But I taught him the trick."

"For us, movement is thought," Tomas interjected, despair turning into hope, even if it might be slim.

"And thought is reality. You just imagine you're heavier. And you sink to the ground. Or through it." Gabriel's voice was ragged from his effort. "Right now, I choose to believe I weigh a few tons." Vanguard screamed from the force and weight of Gabriel's grip as he felt himself being pushed into the floor.

"That's it," Tomas said. "Just a few moments more. His resistance to my mind is failing." Tomas's form lost shape, becoming nothing more than a vague amorphous conglomeration of light and smoke, and charged toward Vanguard. He disappeared into the creature Vanguard had become. All the rest of us could do was hope Gabriel would buy him enough time to overwhelm Vanguard and take control of Max's body. Acton had coached him on how to do it. She hadn't, however, planned on Vanguard's reckless display of power.

"You… sniveling…weasel." Vanguard pushed against Gabriel's grip. Gabriel's response was lost in the sound of more wood and brick breaking apart and twisting around us. The house itself seemed to shake with Vanguard's fury. I worried it might come down around us, but just as suddenly as it began, it stopped. In the silence I could hear Vanguard muttering. Gabriel screamed as black tendrils sprung up from the ground. Inky fluid blobs surrounded his spectral form and, much to our surprise, dug into him.

Gabriel screamed in terror as his spectral form was torn apart. Vanguard lifted his malformed head, opened his toothsome mouth wide, and howled in triumph.

"What did you do?" I screamed, finally finding my voice. I barely knew Gabriel. I wasn't sure I even liked him, to be honest. But his final scream burned itself into my memory.

"Taken to the dark space between places, forever to be denied his promised, blissful peace." Vanguard let out a laugh that, despite how inhuman it sounded, was filled with twisted glee. Vanguard turned away from us and toward his freedom. Only his lack of experience with his new form inhibited him from going faster now. And with each step, he seemed to grow in his confidence.

"We can't let that bastard go!" Dad yelled, understanding with instinct what was happening, even if he was fuzzy on the precise details.

"If we make one move, he could kill us with a thought," I yelled. With Vanguard's attention split between battling Tomas in his head and his walk toward freedom, I carefully maneuvered out from behind the bent wall of floorboard that'd pinned me in place. Free, I ran over to Dad and Gina.

"But that's—"

"Yes. It's him. It's really him. But the best thing you can do—what both of you can do— is think about what you know. Who owns Shearhaven. Who has owned Shearhaven. The things that Jackson Vanguard—that all the Vanguards—have done all these years. *Remember them.*"

"I'm in a place that's no place at all," a voice boomed. It

was Tomas, his words pitched low and slow. The walls vibrated. The windows, fractured when Vanguard first bent reality within the house, hummed as he spoke. "I'd spent so long there, before finally pulling my consciousness back together all those weeks ago."

"Damnable boy! I rue the day I saw you out that window." Vanguard slowed; his hideously distended legs wobbled.

"I never really thought about what the place was." Tomas continued, unconcerned or unhearing, wherever he was. "Even when I returned to it whenever I discorporated. And yet, here I am. I thought I was entering you. Your mind. But here I am again. Now I understand."

"Nattering, sad little boy," Vanguard spat. His hideous spectral form fell to its knees as if exhausted. He was near the hole in the wall now. Too near. A step or two more, and he'd be outside the magick square Acton and I had drawn.

"This is the house. The soul of the house."

"Nonsense! Meaningless. Drivel."

"I felt Gabriel being pulled apart and away. I'll mourn him, as irritating as he could be. He was courageous."

"You were nothing. Lost. No one and nothing wanted you. I… gave you… purpose." Vanguard clawed toward the edge of the gaping hole in Shearhaven's side with a renewed burst of energy. He was playing games with Tomas, and they were working. I gritted my teeth and rushed toward him. I heard Dad scream my name, but my course was set. My mom's loss. Dad's health. The pandemic and my business's ongoing death spiral. I hadn't lived these last five years so much as survived them. I'd stood still as the universe used me as a punching bag. I realized, as I pumped my legs toward the hateful thing, that in this moment I had a choice. It might mean my end, but at least I got to make a choice. I had a lot to hold onto. I passed my hands through the disgusting mass of Vanguard's form, and gripped onto Max. I wrapped my arms around his beautiful body. Tears streamed down my face at how cold it was. I rolled over on top of it, letting all of my weight press down into him. And, just as I'd hoped, his body was like an anchor to the shadow creature that surrounded him. Vanguard roared as his skeletal shadow claws grasped for freedom.

"I can see your mind Cyril—a searing cold light in the void. You're here with me. This house. Its soul. Your soul. The book. You're tethered here almost as much as I am." Tomas's voice rocked the house. Chandeliers swayed violently, some dropping faceted glass strands to the floor. Vanguard screamed, twisting at the spine to turn about and stare me down. He raised one claw, ready to rip into my flesh. Governed by the same rules as Tomas and Gabriel, I knew Vanguard's belief in its sharpness would be enough to kill me. But the blow never came. Instead, Vanguard raged incoherently.

"There you are." Tomas had said it, his voice booming through the house. But Max said it as well, muffled by my own body on top of him.

"You are nothing!" Vanguard flailed his monstrous arms, his body writhing to a chorus of cracking bone.

"Maybe," Tomas said, Max echoing it softly. "But finally, I can see it so plainly. You're *less* than nothing."

The shadow creature—the wretched thing Vanguard had become—screeched in terror as its body rippled outward, its boundaries blurring. And then, the next instant, it was crushed into itself. It hung in the air, a single red point glowing like a tiny ember in the air. I felt the warmth flood Max's body before I saw his eyes flutter open.

“Vanguard?” I asked.

“Gone. Gone to see Mr. De Artte.”

14

"How can we be sure? That's it's not Vanguard tricking us?" Dad said from behind me. I'd picked myself awkwardly up off Max's body. Except, it was Tomas now.

"I can feel it. Can't you? It's him," I said, helping the man off the floor.

"My gift was never that strong, Ty. But I believe you."

"This poor woman," Gina said. She was on her knees by the sacrificial table that had been overturned by the fury of Vangaurd's magick. The strange circular hole in the wall, formed by warped brick and floorboards, let the dull amber of Shearhaven's exterior lights filter into the ballroom. The cool air felt good on my face, reddened with effort and fear. Beyond, fireflies danced through the woods surrounding the house.

"Is there anything we can do for her?"

"She knew the sacrifice she was making." I didn't mean the comment to sound so cold. But I could see it in Acton's eyes earlier. She was certain of what she had to do. Prepared for it. "I think, in some ways, she even welcomed it."

"She's beyond our help anyway." Gina got up off the ground and gave us a clear view of what had once been Lady Acton. Now, only a desiccated husk, its paper-thin skin in tatters around a skeletal structure, remained. As we watched, the last few wisps of hair clinging to the thing's head fell away. Until, finally, the whole form gave way, collapsing in on itself, becoming nothing more than a pile of dust. Gina looked away, her head in her hands. She began to shake, so Dad pulled her into a hug. She allowed his arms to wrap around her.

Tomas knelt next to the pile of dust.

"Spare a few thoughts for her, Ms. Gallagher. But rest assured she had more than her share of life, just like Vanguard," he said. Tomas touched the dust, and then pulled his hand away quickly. He stared down at his hand—Max Morgan's hand—and turned it in the light.

"Looks like time caught up with her." Dad looked around the wrecked ballroom. "I don't know about the rest of you, but I could use a drink."

"Good idea. And maybe you can explain what the hell I just saw," Gina said, pulling away from Dad's hug and wiping the ash from her knees. She seemed steadied, and more than a little irritated. I didn't blame her.

"Don't look at me. That's going to be one of these two."

"I'll show you to the kitchen," Tomas said quickly, perhaps glad to be distracted from the strangeness of having a new body. "I can't wait to taste a cup of coffee again. Maybe after that we can give you both some apologies and answers."

"You all go on without me," I said.

"You okay, son?"

"I'm good. I just need a minute."

"Take your time," Tomas said with a nod. Except, it was still Max. Sexy, devilishly handsome Max with his muscled body and all his tattoos. I felt the tears start to well and was grateful the others were already through the door and on their way to the kitchen. I took ahold of the podium and righted it. Some of the delicate carved features had cracked and fallen off, but otherwise it was still intact. Looking at Tomas in Max's body was strange. I hadn't had a chance to properly mourn Max. Now here he was, walking around and making coffee, but it wasn't him. No more than Vanguard had been him. I'd need to work through that. Tomas would need help adjusting to his new circumstance, and I wanted to help. That didn't mean it wouldn't be uncomfortable being around him. That wasn't the reason I stayed behind, though.

I bent over and picked up the book. The ancient tome Acton had written so many lifetimes ago. I sat it on the podium and placed my hand on it. It was warm—almost soothing. I closed my eyes. The book called to me. Vanguard and Acton were both gone, now. I opened it, and I understood that the book was not alive, nor did it have a will of its own. But the words—the words were alive. Alive with potential. The book could not sleep, not with everything that it was. It needed a companion. It needed a reader.

I marveled as the strange symbols began to contract and pool as though the ink was still liquid. The liquid spread again and reformed into English. I flipped through the pages frantically. It had something to tell me. I could feel it. A secret between the pages. I flipped through it several times; certain I'd know the page I needed. Finally, I slowed down, and realized that two pages had stuck together. Something akin to static electricity blazed from the page to my finger as I separated the pages. This page was not hidden by accident. It took me only moments to understand what it was. For all her lies, Acton had told Vanguard the truth about the hidden pages.

"Ḫapiu edēšu," I whispered. The bricks and floorboards unbent themselves and flowed back into their rightful place as if they'd never been disturbed. The table righted itself, leaving a cloud of ashes trailing behind it. The chipped pieces of the podium returned to it and anchored themselves back in place. I closed the book quickly, my hands shaking.

15

"Well, if it isn't the famous Ms. Virginia Gallagher in the flesh," Dad said. I looked up from my milk steaming to see Gina stride into Brews & Clues, wearing a leather jacket and cream scarf. If it hadn't been for the heels and a lack of aviation goggles, I'd say she was about ready to hop into a biplane. Which seemed appropriate for a historian.

"Oh hush. I'm just here for my usual." Gina gave me a little wave and pointed at the leather satchel slung over her shoulder. "Got a free second, Ty?"

"You know I do." I knew exactly what she had for me, and I still couldn't believe it.

"Well, don't forget to come chat with the old man when you're done." Dad winked at Gina. Six months later, and their slow-motion courtship continued at its glacier pace. They were very nearly almost close to acknowledging the connection they'd had the first moment they met at Shearhaven. But at least it was something. Gina got Dad out of the house, going for walks, going shopping. He'd already lost thirty pounds and seemed even lighter in spirit.

I slid into the booth across from Gina, who gave me a conspiratorial look as she withdrew a rectangular package from her satchel. It was wrapped in stiff brown paper and tied loosely with twine.

"A friend of a friend of a friend found it for me. The price would have done me in if you weren't paying the bill." Gina handed it over. I was so tempted to open it. But it wasn't for me.

"It'll be worth every penny. Besides, using Max's money for this feels like a tiny bit of justice."

"I hope Tomas likes it."

"He'll love it. Thank you so much."

"How's your dad doing?" Gina looked over at him, and I followed her gaze. He was at the counter, bullshitting with some customers and laughing. "He certainly seems in his element."

"He's doing amazing. Sal's been a huge help getting him up to speed. He's a fast learner. I know the place is going to be in good hands. Especially with these new mystery parties you and he are cooking up."

"How about you? And Tomas? Last time I talked to him, he said you were almost all packed up."

"Almost." I looked away from Dad and was surprised to see the concern etched into the woman's face. "What's wrong?"

"Nothing. Everything seems to be going fantastically. I'm just not sure I trust this book."

"I'm sure it's perfect," I said, absent-mindedly stroking the twine of the package.

"Not that book. *The* book."

"Ah." I withdrew my hand and took a sip of my coffee. "I get the concern. But we're both clear-headed about this. It's the right move."

"I've heard London is terrible and rainy this time of year. Of course, that's every time of the year. From what I hear."

"I'm sure it'll be lovely. Quit trying to talk us out of it."

"I know, I know." The woman sighed heavily. "Your dad will miss you. Hell, I'll miss you two. I just wish I trusted that whatever's ignited this new excitement about the book wasn't from the book itself. We know so little about it. Acton and Vanguard, scoundrels though they may have been, were the only ones who really understood it."

"I know. I had those worries too. Ever since the book sort of 'taught' me how to use it that day in Shearhaven, after we'd defeated Vanguard. But the book doesn't have a mind of its own. It might have been bound to Vanguard for a long time, but there's a… purity to it. I can't explain it. But I can feel it."

What I didn't tell Gina was that Tomas had all her same fears. He'd hated the idea of taking the book with us. He hated the idea of moving, although I suspect some of that was just general fear of the strange modern world he was still learning to navigate. Especially since he was wearing the face of a celebrity. I decided to use the same tactic I had with him to win Gina over. "Just trust me, Gina. This is a good thing. The book—the book isn't good or bad. It's a tool. An incredibly powerful one, yes, but still just a tool."

"I'm not sure that makes me feel particularly good. The same thing's been said about atom bombs." My response was lost as Dad padded forward, cup in hand.

"Here you go," he said, handing the cup to Gina. "Mind if I cut in, son?"

"Not at all. I want to get this over to Tomas anyway." I got up quickly, thankful to cut the conversation with Gina short. She meant well, I knew. And her suspicion wasn't unwarranted. She just didn't have all the info I had. Before I could walk away, Gina grabbed my wrist.

"You two be safe out there, Ty."

"We'll be better than safe," I said, patting her hand gently as she released her grip.

Shearhaven was a chaotic flurry of activity. Felicity was at the center of it, helping to direct the moving guys and the charity folks about what was coming with us and what was being donated. The general answer to these questions were "not much" and "pretty much everything" respectively. She'd noticed the change in her boss. But she seemed to think it was for the better, and she'd fallen to my charms early on. She was less sure about "Max's" decision to end his music career by releasing the stuff he'd already recorded as an EP and retiring for real. The seven-figure severance she was getting probably helped smooth things over.

"Welcome to the madhouse!" Felicity was beaming.

"You love it."

"I hate to admit it, but I kind of do." Her head whipped to the side as a mover was seconds away from throwing a chair up to a fellow worker already up in a truck. "If you dare throw that Thonet I will saw off your scrotum and use its contents for Pickle Ball!" The man, eyes wide, carefully handed the chair upward. She turned to me, cheeks reddened. "Sorry. That's my little truck. Max said I could have a few of the pieces I'd helped the designer pick out."

"Ha!" I leaned in close and whispered in her ear. "I went to high school with that guy, and he was a homophobic asshat."

"Should I have him move the washers and dryers?"

"I thought those were staying with the house?"

"They are. A mistake on my part. Which I'll figure out eventually—right after they've loaded them up. And they'll have to go right back." Felicity smiled at me devilishly. I shook my head, stifling a laugh.

"Remind me not to get on your bad side."

"Ty!" Tomas practically ran into my arms and squeezed me tight. I'm not going to say it wasn't still weird sometimes. I resisted the two of us for a long time. I'm still not certain if it's going to work long term. I told my dad that, and he snorted and said *Sounds like every relationship I ever heard about then.* I hugged Tomas back. His body was softer now. Tomas thought Max's diet and workout regimen sounded like slow torture. I appreciated the change, personally. He'd grown his hair out. The more not-like-Max he became, the easier it was. Of course, I had one advantage that no one else would have had. Whenever it became too much, or I started to get weirded out, I'd tap into the bright fuzzy feeling in my skull. The seat of whatever strange gift/ curse my family had received so long ago. And I could see Tomas there, as he was in his first life.

"Miss me?" I asked after a few moments of squeezing him back. Savoring it.

"For many reasons. I'm supposed to be picking out cover art for the EP," he whispered. "They all look hideous to me. I need some 'modern' eyes."

"Oh boy. Okay, let's do it." I gave him a peck on the lips. It wasn't enough, so I pulled him in close and let our lips and tongues linger for a moment. When the kiss was over, I saw that he was staring straight at me. A strange, faraway look in his eyes. "You okay?"

"Oh. Yes. Definitely. I feel—" He looked at the movers as they loaded up the trucks. He looked to Felicity, who was busy studying her tablet. Not one sneer. Not one disapproving look. In fact, the world—at least this small little corner in this very second—seemed positively bored by us. "I feel free."

"I've got you a present." I held the brown paper-wrapped book up to him. His eyes lit up with unfettered surprise and glee. I'd never known someone like him. I was almost jealous of how unguarded he could be. "Not here. Let's open it inside."

We wandered through Shearhaven for some time, as finding a spot to be alone proved more difficult than I'd anticipated with the various movers at work. Finally, in the east wing of the house, we found a quiet little corner of an empty room.

"Have you decided what you're going to do with this place?" I asked as we settled into a corner next to each other.

"Not sure. Felicity reached out to the tribe that sued for the land back in the 70s. So that might be a possibility. Gina said the museum would love to get their hands on it but didn't think they'd be able to maintain it long term. Even if we set up a grant for it. I feel like…"

"What?"

"I feel like it deserves to be a place where good things happen. Does that sound strange? It just feels like it deserves a second chance."

"We are way past worrying about strange." I hooked my arm around his neck and pulled him into a hug. "Plus, I'm all for second chances. Now open your present! I can't stand the suspense."

Tomas untied the twine and slid his finger under one of the flaps of paper to free the tape.

"You're opening it like my Nana."

"I'm savoring it. It's the first gift you've given me."

"Yeah. I guess it is," I said. A quiet part of me loved that he cared about something like that. Finally, he gingerly unwrapped the paper, freeing a slim book. The cover was worn at the edges. It had a scratchy, slightly unpleasant, and toothy linen cover. Large letters in a gold leaf serif typeface read "Collected Works, 1895-1931" and under that in much smaller letters "Dorothy Newark." He looked up at me, clearly not understanding. I held my tongue. He flipped through the book politely, but clearly confused. It was full of beautifully captured photographs. I'm not an expert, but I thought they were very nice. All in black and white of course. One spread featured a beach scene with a lone woman walking away in the distance. The next page a mound of pomegranates on the dirt floor of a hut. The next spread was of a beautiful woman in her early 40s, topless, with her hands shielding her nipples, one hand raised to the side of her face just about to touch her cheek. In the foreground is another woman's hand, splayed outward, ready for the other woman to take it.

"There's only fifteen of those known to still exist. It was published by a small press out of San Francisco." I nudged him on. He kept flipping.

"It's lovely. I will—" He stopped at the picture of a woman in profile. The last photo in the book. She was elderly, slightly hunched in a sleek-looking chair. She wore a striped jacket with a wide white collar lying flat over the neck. Behind one could see a glimpse of an overflowing bookcase, and an open window with wispy drapes moving in a breeze. But it was the woman herself that commanded attention. Her strong jaw and proud nose. I watched as Tomas's recognition grew.

"She's so different. Except, perhaps, in the eyes." Then Tomas saw it. The object she cradled in her hand. He pulled the book closer to his face, wanting a better look. I continued to tell him all I'd learned about Dorothy Newark né Bellwether né Blake—but I'm not sure he heard it. All he could concentrate on, as tears filled his eyes, was the handsome pipe in Dottie's hand. And, most especially, the bit. It had been chewed and worn down to almost nothing.

Acknowledgements

A woman, perhaps dressed in virginal white, flees along the rocky shore, and above her, resting upon a foreboding cliff, is **the house**. Sometimes, it's a manor. Sometimes, it's a castle. But we always know there is something dark and terrible there, and the woman must escape. I've seen many variations on this picture. Perhaps, like me, you can see the scene in your head. It's played out on countless covers of gothic fiction. This book started as a simple idea. What if it was a man fleeing the house instead of a woman? And what if the dangerous relationship he was trying to escape was the clutches of another man?

Like my previous novel, *In the Dark of the Grove*, this book exists because I wanted to see more people like me in my favorite genres. It's as simple as that. Queer people have always been an integral part of horror. But we often didn't get to star in our own stories unless in some coded way. And, of course, often we'd be the villain—some perverted source of evil that had to be stopped. I like that we get to be villains. They're fun. But I also like that in this book, we're the villains, the heroes, the sidekicks—all the things we can be in real life, too.

Initially, the idea was to make a straightforward gothic horror set in the past that could slot in next to those 70s gothic paperbacks. Guillermo del Toro is an art hero of mine, and his work *Crimson Peak* was undoubtedly a massive part of why I wrote this book. I think it's one of his most beautiful movies and perhaps one of his most underrated. However, once I got to the end of Tomas's story, I wondered who Vanguard's next victim might be. The concept certainly lent itself to further exploration along those lines. So, I let the story keep going.

That's not to say it was an easy road. I've probably put more work into this novel than any other I've done, and I think the results were worth it. I hope you agree! But two people are integral to that: my faithful beta readers, who happen to be (respectively) my best friend and partner, Laura and Paul. Through their feedback, I eventually realized I had more work to do. I changed it from the third person to the first person. I re-ordered things, cut things down, and added a lot more here and there. The book you hold in your hands is much the same book they read as beta readers. But it has also significantly changed. For that, I'm so thankful.

Thanks to everyone who signed up for my website memberships, especially Skot, Dan, and Robin. Your support means so much to me.

Thanks to my mom, who has always supported my writing (along with every other creative thing I've ever done.) She got me my first electric typewriter. I thought it was a Sega Genesis when it was wrapped up for Christmas. *Eventually*, I realized what a perfect gift it was.

Thanks to the many English teachers who made a difference in my life. It's such a gay cliche. But my English teachers (and art teachers!) always made my strange too-tall queerdo self feel seen and valued.

To all the book friends I've met on BookTok. I had no clue how many amazing (and amazingly talented) authors and reviewers I'd meet on there. I was beyond skeptical. But there are lovely pockets of people on there worth getting to know.

Finally, to Chuck. I selfishly wish you were around to read this book. Thanks for being my first art and writing friend.

About The Author

Jon was born on the cusp, between Leo and Virgo, and is still trying to figure out if that means anything. But he has been told by many trusted friends that he's a total Virgo. He is a fan of so many things it's sometimes slightly overwhelming. Partly because his fandom often manifests itself in buying physical objects that celebrate said fandom. However, the connective tissue between them all is this—he loves stories. He loves learning about other people and places, real and imaginary. He loves those special moments when a story cuts through the confounding layers of humanity to reveal something beautiful, terrifying, or strange. If you ever experience a moment like that reading one of his books, he'll feel like his mission was accomplished.

He lives in Illinois with his partner and enjoys owls, turtles, watching movies, playing board games, drawing, graphic design, collecting vinyl records, photographing action figures, Thai food, biscuits and gravy, and laughing.

About The Typefaces

As with *In the Dark of the Grove*, URW Baskerville was used for most of the print. Based on Baskerville, designed by John Baskerville in 1757, it was chosen for its high readability and elegance.

The book title, author credit, section headings, chapter headings, and page numbers are all Josefin Sans. Santiago Orozco created this font at his foundry, Typemade. The font felt strong, gothic, and vintage, all qualities I wanted to be reflected in the title typeface. It proved so versatile that I used it pretty much everywhere except in the main text.

Other Works

Grace & Witherbloom (2012)

Eon Quest (2015)

In the Dark of the Grove (2021)

**For more information, or to support
the writer via site membership,
visit Jon's website at:**

www.jonwesleyhuff.com